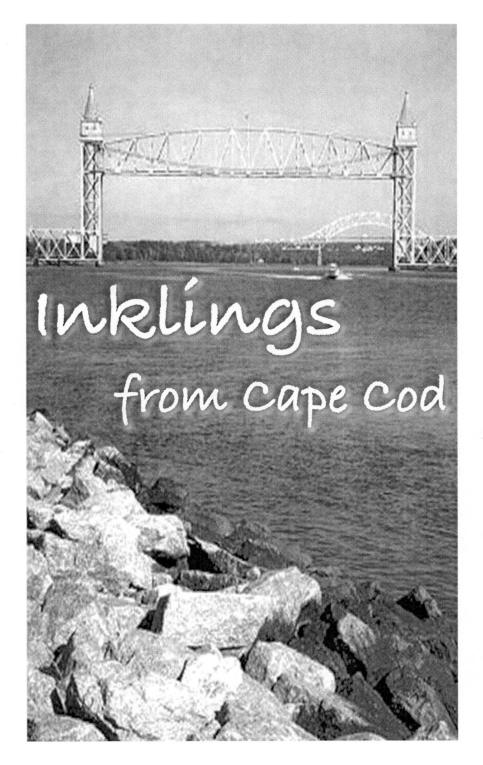

What They're Saying

"*Inklings of Cape Cod* is so much more than "inklings." It is a potpourri of great young talent that shows how much teens have to offer if given the chance. Write On, one and all!!"

—Stephanie Meyer, Sr. Editor, Teenink.com and Teen Ink Magazine

"This book is absolutely fantastic! I am very impressed with the imagery and the emotion that the student's writing invokes from the readers. My students and I cried and laughed at various stories and poems. It is unbelievable that students can come up with these feelings and still be young! It is awesome! Congratulations on a book well done!"

—Fran Sylvester, 5th grade teacher, international middle school student travel leader

"Anyone who worries about the future of American prose and poetry will be reassured after reading the collected works of young writers in this extensive anthology created by students... Filled with examples of creative writing and representative of both genres, the selections showcase a wonderful variety and range of expression. The joy of writing is clearly in evidence throughout the entire collection. In *Inklings from Cape Cod*, Stephanie Boosahda has assembled a treasury of wonderful excerpts from these young people that make it clear that the future of our literary world is in very competent hands."

—Jim Coogan, *Cape Cod Times* columnist and author of the award winning book, *Sail Away Ladies: Stories of Cape Cod Women in the Age of Sail, Cape Cod Voyage: A Journey Through Cape Cod's*

History and Lore;
I Saw A Sea Monster, Yes I Did!,
Priscilla the Amazing Pinkywink, Clarence the
Cranberry Who Couldn't Bounce, and others ...

"A class set of Inklings from Cape Cod is an invaluable resource for anyone teaching writing. Whether perusing this rich collection of student models for pleasure or instruction, readers will undoubtedly be inspired to explore the transformative power of writing."

—Diane Hartley, High School English Teacher
National Writing Project Teacher Consultant

"It takes a special kind of teacher - a non-conformist imbued with enthusiasm, faith in her students, and a passion for the art of writing - to produce a labor of love, precisely what this anthology is. Stephanie applies what most master teachers know, that we dare not ask our students to do something we dare not do ourselves. She does not ask her students to risk any more than she is willing to risk, to write and, therefore, to be exposed at some level of self.
I would recommend this volume of prose and poetry to students and teachers alike. Students will find value in the writing exercises and the published works of fellow student writers. Teachers will find the writing techniques invaluable and the writing a model for their own students. What a joy to read fresh voices!"

—Kathleen Lennox, elementary school librarian

"Every teacher needs this anthology in his or her writing toolbox. It inspires the soul of the writer, the young and accomplished alike."

—Mari Turko, retiring 5th grade language arts teacher
and regional representative to the
National Writing Project's 2010 National conference

"Having been privileged enough to spend three weeks traveling around Europe with Boosahda and some of her students, it is no surprise that the enthusiasm which she generates amongst the students is present in abundance in these students' written work. The *Inklings* stories and poetry are of such a high standard that the only disappointment was that I could not read beyond the printed excerpts. For example, the story about the Shade (main character Raiye) was incredible. I was so annoyed that it was only an excerpt.

Incredible! Well done! Fantastic writing. I am excited to see what will be produced in the future."

—Joe Eric Taylor, Classicist, University of St. Andrews, Scotland

"There's no way to tell where the attention, guidance, and enthusiasm of a dedicated teacher will stop. Stephanie Boosahda is such a teacher, and her influence on the students whose work appears in this anthology will reach beyond the week-long summer writing program they shared. If these young writers continue honing their craft, the future of American literature looks very bright, indeed."

—Elizabeth Moisan, author of *Master of the Sweet Trade*

"Ms Boosahda's enthusiasm for her students and respect for their writing is apparent in this beautiful tribute to their work. *Inklings from Cape Cod* puts a fun, diverse, and eclectic twist on bedtime or anytime pleasure reading. Snuggle up with your favorite blanket and delve into these young authors' creative writing adventures. It is very exciting to read what kids are writing for a change. Their perspectives are different from adult authors, and their works are truly sincere, totally fun, and refreshingly crisp."

—Joy Nightingale, college junior, recipient of her 3,000 students high school's senior English Award

"The variety [of writing] is very exciting; a fun, relaxing, inspiring read. It is very enjoyable; because of the set up, it is easy to put down and pick back up later without missing anything. There are sections you'll want to read over and over; they're all so different and creative. While the reading is relaxing, I found myself learning about so many different things, things the students wrote about, ideas about writing, and inspiring details about these young yet very talented students.

—Doris Scott, RN.,BSN, avid reader, mother of four, grandmother of eleven

"*Inklings* is really an interesting read, a curiously clever selection of student writing that showcases the power of young minds."

—Patrick Mont, high school student, avid analog photographer

"Thought provoking and eclectic, this collection takes the reader on a journey. It makes one ponder, and takes you to places that you will now see in a different light. Through the writers' thoughts, you will laugh, cry and wander. It will hone your sensitivities to what can happen when you and are opened up to the world of creative writing. A gem."

—Mary Anne Manley, LSW, mother of two

"Imaginative, creative, insightful ... these are just a few words that come to mind as I read Inklings. Thanks for the opportunity to take a brief look inside the hearts and minds of an exciting new generations of authors."

—Marge Frith, author of Lucky – the Autobiography of a Goldfish, a true story

"The creativity of young people never ceases to amaze me! Inklings is a wonderful collection of student work ... This book offers not only creative literary entertainment but also offers ways of encouraging creativity in all ages. Poems, short stories, quips, and even drawings and photos fill the pages for good bedtime enjoyment!

Although it's too difficult to single out any one piece, as all are unique, some activities I have used with my grandchildren with great success. For instance, I took the "terrible Twos" section and changed it to "What do you like about your little brothers?" The fear section I turned into "What character do you find fearful in the books we read together?" Then I asked my seven-year-old grandson to create a story from one of the drawings, which produced a fantastic and creative story of his own!

—Christina Gummere Laurie, author, retired pastor, workshop leader, newspaper writer, editor, and national officer in The National League of American Pen Women, Inc.

"Inklings offers uncommon youth filled perspectives. Refreshing, redemptive, a relief - print is not, in fact dead, but alive and kicking."

—Karyn McGovern, columnist Cape Cod Times

inklings
from Cape Cod

**An Anthology of Writing Lessons and
Written Pieces by the
Students of the Annual
Young Writers' Workshop**

Held at the 45th Annual
Cape Cod Writers' Center
Summer Writing Conference

Compiled and Edited by
Stephanie E. Boosahda
**Prose Instructor
Young Writers' Workshop**

iUniverse, Inc.
New York   Bloomington

Inklings from Cape Cod

iUniverse books may be ordered through booksellers or by contacting:

iUniverse
1663 Liberty Drive
Bloomington, IN 47403
www.iuniverse.com
1-800-Authors (1-800-288-4677)

Because of the dynamic nature of the Internet, any Web addresses or links contained in this book may have changed since publication and may no longer be valid. The views expressed in this work are solely those of the author and do not necessarily reflect the views of the publisher, and the publisher hereby disclaims any responsibility for them.

ISBN: 978-0-595-48677-9 (sc)
ISBN: 978-1-4502-0453-8 (dj)
ISBN: 978-0-595-60773-0 (ebk)

Printed in the United States of America

iUniverse rev. date: 4/12/10

Dedication

for my children, Nicole, Joshua, and Emily,
Algis, Rheem, and Kyle
and my grandchildren, Colin and Mitchell ...

and in memory of my grandparents,
Mathil (Dow) and Albert Swide
Nariza (Mishalanie) and Kalil Boosahda
and
John Prophet,
who was a gift to the Cape Cod writing community,
both as an inspiriting mentor and a valued friend

"You have to fall in love with hanging around words."
-John Ciardi

"Whatever we conceive well we express clearly."
Nicolas Boileau

"Books are the treasured wealth of the world ..."
Henry David Thoreau

On writing, "Make 'em laugh; make 'em cry; make 'em wait."
Charles Reade

Special Dedications

This anthology is especially dedicated to some very extraordinary people without whom our Young Writers' Workshop experience would not have been possible.

First to **Marion Vuilleumier**, the founder of the Cape Cod Writers' Center, who established "A Place in the Sun," the annual, weeklong summer writing conference sponsored by the Cape Cod Writers' Center and the Young Writers' Workshop, which is conducted during the conference. Without her dedication and pioneering work, none of this would have been possible.
It is impossible to imagine just how many individuals are published writers today because of Marion's foresight in establishing the CCWC, the annual conference, and the Young Writers' Workshop. Thank-you, Marion!

 Next, *Inklings* is dedicated to **Mary Littleford** who was, for decades - and during this conference - an active member of Cape Cod Writers' Center board of directors, and who has successfully chaired the Young Writers' Workshop Committee for many, many years. She was an enthusiastic supporter of this project and instrumental in making *Inklings from Cape Cod* a reality. Without her, there would be no anthology. Mary, we cannot thank-you enough.

This anthology is also dedicated to each of you, **Alex B., Alex D., Amelia, Andrew, Angelica, Ashleigh, Caroline, Chris, Christina, Courtney, Emilie, Hannah, Jessica, Kaitlin, Katrina, Liam, Lydia, Maret, Megan, Miranda, Niki, Rachel M., Rachel L., Rebecca H., Rebecca V., Sarah M., Sarah V., Seth, Tom, Tosh, and Wisima (aka "Sam"),** and the poets **Alicia, Khalia, Nicollette, Taylor, Zach** - the young authors whose pieces are included in this book. You are an inspiration to writers and teachers everywhere. Your hard work has not gone unnoticed. No doubt, this is just the start of your publishing credits. Congratulations!"

Pictured on the previous page is Young Writers' Workshop chair and *Inklings* proofreader, **Mary Littleford**, with Cape Cod Writers' Center's 2001–2007 director, **Jacqueline Loring**. This photo was taken at the CCWC Halloween Dress-Like-Your Favorite Author get-together; as you can see, Jacqueline dressed as Mary, who is the author of *Helium Verse*.

Contents

On Their Own

Poetry Students' Work

Bios

Finalé

Index

Photo Collages

*At the end of each section, a selected longer piece
will wrap up the section as the grand finale.*

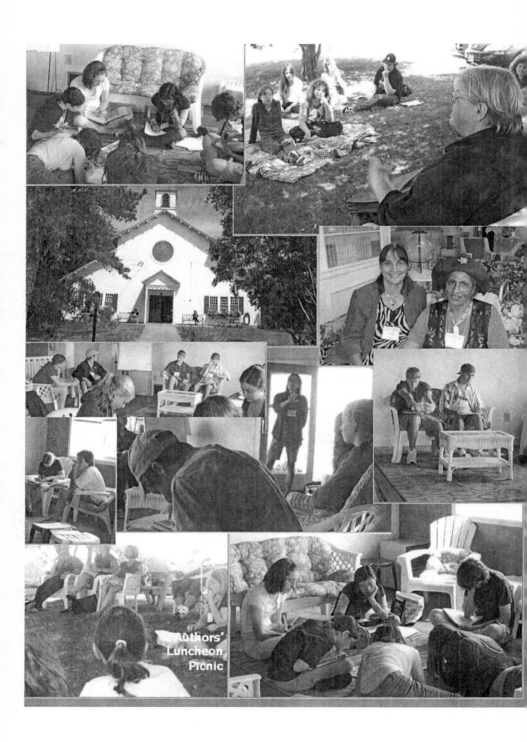

Authors'
Luncheon
Picnic

Acknowledgements

At one of the Harwich Writers' Group breakfasts, a dear friend, Ellen Prophet, jokingly connected publishing a book with the old African Proverb, "It takes a village to raise a child." The scaffolding of this metaphorical connection is endless. I was surprised at just how complex and time - consuming it is to compile, organize, and edit a multi-authored collection.

In recognition of this "village," we, the members of the Young Writers Workshop, are indebted to many creative, talented, and generous people, who helped make this anthology a reality. Among these "villagers" are some to whom we extend a special thank-you:

... to Jacqueline Loring, who was the executive director of Cape Cod Writers' Center during the conference and six years prior; to Mary Littleford, who was for many decades, and during the conference, the director of the Young Writers' Workshop; and to Shelia Whitehouse, who was the multi-year president of the Cape Cod Writers' Center. Thank-you to all three of you for immediately recognizing the merit of this publication, working to secure its funding, and encouraging me with your ongoing support. Your promotion of this project has been invaluable;

... to John Prophet, creator of the very popular Casey Miller mystery series, who - as my writing mentor - was the first to offer guidance for publishing this volume. His meticulous editorial assistance, enthusiastic encouragement, and insightful, practical assistance with the complexities of organizing and editing this anthology kept me sane and moving forward;

...to Karen Townsend, Maria LaTour, and Di Hartley - all professional educators - for their keenly articulate final editing, meticulous proofreading, attention to detail, and endless enthusiasm;

... to Joe Scherpa, for his invaluable computer graphics expertise, good humor, and patience, who with great proficiency, enthusiastically converted the numerous photos and graphics to TIFF files;

... to Nicole Norkevicius and Emily Hopkins for additional technical computer assistance and the endless use of their laptops;

... to Linda Foley, consultant, for her expertise, suggestions, and diverse perspective on editorial questions;

... to Elizabeth Moisan, author of *Master of the Sweet Trade*, who was consistently available for consultation and a heartfelt good laugh;

... to Michael Boosahda, retired teacher, and to Jessica Skolski, middle school teacher, for their enthusiasm, insight, attention to detail, and precise proofreading assistance;

... to Lacey Perry, Jessica George, and all the helpful, knowledgeable people at iUniverse and to Johann, Raylene, and Ken at Staples for their interest and consistently cheerful assistance; and to Susan Crowely Clemence of Clemence Photography for the back cover photo of Stephanie Boosahda;

... and to all the parents of the Young Writers as well as my own parents, Emily and Leo Boosahda, for their special kind of encouragement and enthusiastic support that makes a world of difference. Many heartfelt thank-yous to each and every one of you.

And, notes of appreciation and additional thank-yous go to Pat Reck, Freda Dadah, "Scottie" (aka Doris Scott), and Elizabeth Boosahda, author of *Arab-American Faces and Voices*, for their wholehearted endorsements and ongoing interest; to Silvard Kool for his creative and soothing New Age musical recordings that inspired us while we wrote; to Jean Stone, guest author of over a dozen books including *Dare to Dream* (co-authored with Tim Daggett), and *Good Little Wives, Four Steps to the Altar,* and *Three Times a Charm*, for her warning that getting a book published takes longer than you can ever imagine, and that "sometimes writing the book is the easy part;" and also to Anne Balzarini and the Czarnetzki family for the Berkshire retreat that brought this collection to the "finish line."

I am also honored and blessed to have had the opportunity to work with all of the fantastically creative young writers whose passion and work inspired this anthology. I can not even imagine where their writing adventures will take them, expect to read more of their bylines accompanying future pieces, and hope they treasure this volume as much as I do. I join them once again in saying "thank-you" to these wonderful, enthusiastically encouraging people who, like me, recognized the outstanding merits of their work and helped make the vision of this anthology a reality. The efforts of all those mentioned above enhanced this collection of writing.

To anyone whom I might have inadvertently forgotten, my sincere apologies.

And, lastly, thank-you to all of you for choosing this exciting anthology to read; ENJOY!

Editor's Note to Readers

This anthology, *Inklings from Cape Cod,* showcases some of the student's work produced during their week attending the Young Writers' Workshop. There were so many praise-worthy submissions that *Inklings from Cape Cod* contains only a sampling of some of the prose and poetry students' work during the Workshop; however, it captures the outpouring of their lively spirits, their dedication, creative excellence, and artistic enthusiasm. The entries were written during workshop time or following workshop lessons; some pieces are revisions of previous work fine-tuned after related class instruction. There are poetry pieces in both prose and poetry students' sections as both groups worked on poetry. Some of the pieces are short, while others are excerpts from larger pieces or works still in progress.

This anthology celebrates our young writers. It gives new ideas and examples to creative writing teachers to keep them motivated Additionally, this anthology is intended to inspire and encourage more students to appreciate their own writing and value creativity. I trust this artistic collection will provide the featured young writers, and others like them, the ongoing incentive to pursue and develop their passion to write and to seek out writers' conferences where they can meet and enjoy other like-minded wordsmiths. Ultimately, this book is for everyone to enjoy and to appreciate wonderful young writers.

Enjoy!

Prose
Students' Work

Inspired by Others

This lesson followed instructions on creating
setting (time, place, and mood),
crafting and using figurative language,
and developing detailed description.
It featured a variety of readings, first teacher-selected,
then student-selected,
both fiction and non-fiction,
where the reader abruptly stops and
the students continue to write on …
Here are some of the results.

inspired by <u>**French**</u> <u>**Dirt's**</u> *chapter "**Silk**," by Richard Goodman*

by Andrew Roiter

... The water poured and poured and we watched as the farmers wept over their drowning crops, as if more water could shelter the innocent plants from the deluge. They prayed to their god, so that he might end the rains that had long since quenched the thirsts of the harvest. Now, with their seemingly infinite generosity, they threatened to asphyxiate the farmer's livelihood.

Their dire need drove them to commit the acts of desperate men: stealing food from the fields of those who lived on higher ground, their crops spared from the flooding, and when their baskets were full, they destroyed the other crops out of spite and insidious madness.

To see those, whose form was so similar to our own act in such wretched ways, shook us to our very cores.

inspired by *The Roads of My Relations,* by Devon A. Mihesuah

by Alex Denton

It was late. All you could hear were the horses' hooves heavily pounding as they galloped off into the night. There was work to be done, criminals were on the loose, and the night horsemen were gone all night. It was the night before election night, and the tension was so built up that no one dared to speak to one another.

more inspired *French Dirt's* chapter *"Silk,"* by Richard Goodman

by Angelica Dellamorte

... We had heard rumors of flooding in other parts of the area, and I remember kneeling down every night to pray my innocent child's prayer that the angry waters would not reach our town, and for a long time it seemed as though my prayers were going unanswered, as news trickled in almost as fast as the rain water trickled into the buckets in our room.

"I heard the village a few miles south of here got hit pretty badly. They say this blasted rainstorm is still marching toward us at a slow, yet steady pace." A delivery boy might report to my mamma while hastily dropping off the day's milk. Poor mamma, she tried so hard to hide the terrifying news from us.

"Mamma, are we gonna die in this rain?" I had asked her with the blunt curiosity of an innocent six-year-old child.

"Of course not, my sweet. I'll protect my darlings no matter what happens," she had replied, kissing my forehead; but even at that young age, I could sense a hint of alarm in her soothing voice. It must have been so hard for her, while Papa was at war and she trying her best to support me, my seven-year-old brother, Izzy — his full name was Isadore — and the baby, Madeleine.

Now, more than twenty years later, I flip through my silly weather-beaten diary I kept when I was six, which is what helps me recall those horrible, rainy days. I chuckled a bit seeing that my diary was filled with so much nonsense, yet so rich with memories. I could clearly recall how unhelpful I was to Mamma, and how patient she was with me. I wish I could have gone back in time. Maybe, if I righted all of my little wrongs in the past, I could change the way my future is now: lonely, desperate, and monotonous.

Maybe if I could have just fixed that one wicked deed, the deed that haunted each of my dreams at night, maybe my whole family would be alive right now.

also inspired by <u>French</u> <u>Dirt</u>*'s chapter "Silk," by Richard Goodman*

by Caroline Hibbert

... I made my way over to the window, streaked and blurry from the downpour. Outside, I could make out a man cursing loudly, pushing and kicking his car, which was stuck in the slimy mud. Several times, another man inside the car would attempt to start it and climb out of the muddy trap. The wheels would spin, but the vehicle could not move in such a mess. Tired of observing the two infuriated Frenchmen, I grabbed my navy trench coat and beige umbrella I had just purchased from a little store on the corner. As I was leaving the inn, I stepped aside to let a family by, clasping soaking luggage and all dressed in ridiculous matching yellow ponchos. I ran through the rain past people with newspapers held desperately above their heads. I stopped when I finally made it under the maroon and white awnings of the local bistro. I liked it, because it reminded me of a classier version of my favorite Lower-East Side Lunch spot, Henry's. J*eez,* I hadn't been to Henry's in God knows how long...

<u>French</u> <u>Dirt</u>*'s chapter "Silk," by Richard Goodman inspired yet another creative piece*

by Sarah Martin

... The rain made a light tinkling sound against the metal of the buckets while we slept. Even though the drip of water was constant and aggravating at first, by the end of two weeks it was what lulled me to sleep. It was something I began to count on at night to pull me away from consciousness when my brain wouldn't rest. Because of the rain, the room always smelt of a southern breeze, like the one I remember when we lived on the river in Georgia.

"Maybe all rain smells like that," my little brother, Caleb, whispered in a voice so small I almost didn't recognize it.

"Maybe, Caleb, just maybe."

I lay there quietly for a few minutes wondering if Caleb had fallen asleep. I shifted on my side, angling myself away from the doorway so that if my mom came in to check on us she would think

I was asleep. I gently reached my hand out toward the bucket closest to me just so I could feel the cool water hit my fingertips. I heard the pitter of footsteps coming toward the room. I withdrew my hand so quickly that in the process of doing so, I knocked over the half-full bucket of water. The pitter no longer sounded like my mother's light pace but heavier and solid. I didn't move an inch. Every muscle in my body was tightening and the blood that coursed through my veins penetrated my insides. I tried to whisper to Caleb for him to wake up, but nothing came out. The breathing of the heavy-footed stranger became more audible.

"Shanty, is that you?"

How did this voice know my name? It was thick with a Russian accent and extremely low pitched. I squeezed my eyes shut hoping that when I finally decided to open them, I would discover this was all a dream. But it wasn't.

Another muffled voice erupted from the darkness. "Did you find the boy?" it mumbled.

My heart was racing. I knew that my mother was somewhere lying on the ground either dead or unconscious; and if Caleb woke up, he would get us into deeper trouble. I willed my body to unravel itself so that I could wake up Caleb to run in case we needed to. I slipped my hand over Caleb's mouth and his copper eyes opened wide. I saw them travel to the dark figures in the doorway and he knew not to move. Our eyes met. Caleb's voice emerged into my brain.

"Shanty, who are those men? Why are they here?"

Being unable to respond, I just shook my head as carefully as I could.

"You don't know? Do you think they know where Papa is? Where's Maman? What are we going to do?"

I looked toward the window and then back at Caleb. I glared at him until I knew he understood.

"But, what about Maman?" His eyes began to water.

I grasped his hand in mine and squeezed. We would have to fly.

"What did you do with Sonya?" the Russian one hissed.

"Don't worry, she won't be getting up anytime soon," her friend replied.

"Well, let's get him while they're both asleep!"

"I don't think Shanty is sleeping."

"I don't want them to get away. We both know what they are capable of."

"Don't you know of anything that can prevent them from, well you know, rea—"

"No. Sonya left me right after I found out."

They looked over at the lumps in the beds; they seemed to have stopped moving.

"Wait, where did they go?" the shorter one whispered harshly.

"Don't worry they'll come back for their mother," the Russian said aloud.

"We have to go back for Maman," Caleb exclaimed partially out of breath.

"We can't just leave her!"

"I know, Caleb, but she's all right. They are looking for us, not her. We will go back when I have a plan. In the meantime, we have to get away from here. Give me your hand."

I grasped his hand hard, and he knew what this meant. I unfurled my wings from my bulky blue sweater and we took off into the crisp night air.

inspired by **Summer of the Monkeys**, *by Wilson Rawls*
by Andrew Roiter

... There was something about the sounds of nature that was so soothing. One could be lulled to sleep by the woods' grand concerto, so unlike the ambivalent sounds of man's artifice. Their sounds meant conflict and strife, a war of tones and pitches, each one designed to drown out the other, so that only one would rise victorious from the melee.

But here, the croak of every toad, song of every sparrow, and rustle of every leaf and blade of grass seemed to blend together in the true definition of harmony. No musician of men, no conductor of cacophonous cords could have woven a tapestry of notes comparable to that of this, the natural world.

inspired by **While I Was Walking**, *by Sally Russo*
by Sarah Martin

... Every morning I could tell it was eating away at me. The long scar above my left eye that once was barely visible seemed to be etched into my skin, deeper than when I first got it falling off my bike when I was eight. My face was thinner than ever and it seemed to have turned an even whiter shade of pale. My $4,000 pearly whites were no longer the color of frost but more cream colored and slightly crooked at the bottom. So much for braces. My once toned and sculpted calves were tired looking, worn with the miles of running I told myself would make everything better. I slowly began to recognize myself less and more as the town gossip. I was no longer anyone's pride and joy. I was like an unwed mother in Amish Country.

My parents were out of the house by the time I got up in the morning, so I was forced to wander the lifeless rooms alone. An unopened box of Life cereal was the only thing left in the cabinets. I found the biggest bowl in the house and filled it to the top. No milk, no nothing. Its dry crunchiness was loud and it echoed through the cavities of my mouth. When I eat, I don't have to think. It's so simple. Put spoon into bowl, get cereal onto spoon, put into mouth, chew and repeat. With each bite, you always know what is coming.

inspired by Bonnie Neubauer, her Story Spinner and by the movie "Donnie Darko," a seven-minute quick-write[1]*

Helen Keller was Friends with Icarus

by Niki Bousquet

... The spaceship landed, crashing through the roof of Donnie's bedroom, but he wasn't there because he gets claustrophobic, especially at night, and has to go skip around outside. He's sleepwalking in his nightmare; it would have been more of a nightmare if he hadn't gotten up, put on his faux-pleather wingtips, walked outside onto the juicy wet grass, but he couldn't feel the dew on the grass because his feet weren't bare.

The fuel from the rocket spewed onto the king-sized bed, and it caught on fire like straw in a California heat wave.

Another of Donnie's imaginary friends was a Pterodactyl who used to be a nun, but, after she did a belly flop off the high dive in the community center pool, a spark went off in the light bulb in her brain and she had a change of heart.

So, Donnie walked down the street now, and he decided to lie down in the golf course and sleep, next to hole seventeen. The stars are dripped from the sky into his eyes, because he sleeps with them open. This means a lot of bugs fly in between his eyelashes while he dreams and he awakens, startled with mosquito wings plastered to his opalescent white pupils. He is blind as well as deaf. Donnie had scarlet fever when he was thirty-seven days old, like Helen Keller. They could have saved his ears and his eyes, but his mother was a ladybug, a scarlet one, so she thought it was normal that her son was also scarlet, like the setting sun.

When the sun comes up in the morning, ninety-three-year-old men - lined up like limousines - file onto the green in green tennis shoes, and Donnie awakens to see a spectacled man staring down at him. He gets up and runs, even though he can't see or hear him, but he can sense his presence and it is terrifying, not like flying, because flying would be fun, but not up too high, up to the sun, because his wings would melt like the ones Icarus wore with the wax to hold them on, because they didn't have glue guns then.

The Story Spinner is a writing ideas tool that Bonnie created; it can be found on Amazon.com..

[1] *Quick-writes present in a variety of writing strategies; here students merely took a break from directed writing activities and pursued a seven minutes free write; another very successful Quick-write technique is used when students are journaling about a novel or other written work. In this case, students write one sentence, usually compound or complex, including the name of a character, an action or event the character took part in, and the student's feeling about the character's activity. The first type of quick-write increases writing fluency and confidence; the latter polishes summarizing and reflecting skills. You can see more examples in the "Bits and Pieces" section.*

inspired by "The Light Horseman" story, from <u>The Roads of My Relations</u> told to the class by author Devon Mihesuah
by Liam O'Connor

... The rising dust caught the last rays of the sun as it slipped out of sight behind the distant peaks. The swirling motes caught the light and held it, giving the eerie illusion that they themselves glowed. Within moments the illusion passed; as the sun's rays retreated behind the vast slopes, the dust began to settle, landing lightly on the very thing that disturbed it. A man lay unmoving on the trail. Blood oozed slowly from eight small bullet holes, though the flow had nearly halted; the wounds were already beginning to clot. A few flies buzzed around the corpse, landing for a short time and then flying off. A buzzard swooped down to feed as well but left without touching the body. The wounds held an evil no creature could stand.

inspired by **<u>While I Was Walking</u>**, *by Sally Russo*
by Sarah Martin

The last day of senior year, I remember thinking about the promising years ahead of me. I had earned a full ride to Sharpton University, home of the Sharpton Sharks, to do what I do best, what I had been trained to do my whole life, to play basketball.

I had always loved basketball, from the day I first held that tiger-striped ball in my miniature four-year-old hands. My dad had given it to me for Christmas. That was fourteen years ago. Now I'm eighteen years old and living at home while my friends are off where I'm supposed to be. But I will never go back. Not while I know they're still there, waiting, lingering in my direction.

to be continued...

***inspired by the song "The Boy Who Blocked His Own Shot"
by the band Brand New ...***

While listening to this song, Niki was inspired to write this poem

A Brand New Day in a Life That You Hate

by Niki Bousquet

Clenching my jaw
Hurts
With the plastic
Digging into swollen skin.
But,
I've said it so many times.
It's better than
Anything
Else I've felt today.

Why do they look at
All the same surroundings
With such
Disgusting interest?
I'm jealous.
I'm jealous.
I want to want
Anything
As much as I remember
Wanting
Just some Sour Patch Kids
When I was seven.

Tuesdays with Colin

by Stephanie Boosahda[2]

*This poem, in two voices,
was inspired by
Paul Fleischman's
A Joyful Noise.*

*These two-voice poems
– a genre created by Paul Fleischman –
are great for creating dialogue:
the left side is one speaker, Colin;
the right side, the other speaker, Sitti.
Read down horizontally;
parallel lines are read in unison.*

Sitti!
Hi! Sitti!

        Hi! Colin
        Love you
Miss You   Miss You
Sitti's House?

        No, Colin's House

My House?

        Yes, your house
        Bike Ride first

Bike Ride first
Need coffee, too?

	Good idea: Coffee
Coffee and cow juice	
Good idea	Good idea
Horseys first?	
	Okay, Horseys first
Then bike ride	Then bike ride
Need hug	
Hug	Hug
	Kisses
Kisses	Kisses
Then Sitti's house?	
	No, Just Colin's house today
And Thomas?	
	And Thomas
Thomas and eat at Auntie Money's restaurant?	
	Thomas and eat at your house
	Auntie Emily is at college
No restaurant?	
No duckies?	
	Not today
Horseys	
Horseys here	
Horseys now; here, now	Horseys now
Fun	
	Fun
Lots of fun	Lots of fun
Tuesdays with Sitti	Tuesdays with Sitti

[2]*Best Teaching Practice suggests that teachers write along with their students as they are writing; the poem above is such a piece.*

More poetry can be found in the Prose Students' "Poetic Dabblings" section and in the Poetry Students' "Golden Nuggets" section. ENJOY!

just One Selected Longer Piece ...

In reading, as with writing in our Young Writers Workshop,
variety is often a welcome change.
At the end of each section,
a selected longer piece will wrap up the section
as the grand finale.
And, of course, there are more longer pieces
in the Longer Pieces section, too.

Brandon

by Kaitlin Meiss

His parents were at it again. But, this time it was a public affair. They never liked Brandon to hear it, though it was constantly obvious when they fought. This time, in their favorite restaurant, with Brandon's grandmother, the conversation exploded. In the beginning, she never approved of their marriage, so Brandon's parents would deny having their share of problems. After they both excused themselves, Brandon and his grandmother sat at the table to feast on the uncomfortable silence and awkwardness. Because of the wonderful times they had shared, Brandon loved his grandmother, but she was in no condition to embark upon the journeys they may no longer be able to take. He had no idea what they should talk about. Sports seemed inappropriate and school — well, it was July — and nothing had changed with his friends, so he really didn't know what to say.

Apparently neither did she, so he sat staring in the mirror above his grandmother's head at the reflection of the Red Sox game on the TV behind him. The barely distinguishable scent of stale popcorn served to each table and swearing at the fried food stench ironically kept his stomach from retching food. Yet, he managed to mindlessly wolf down the ice cream sundae placed before him. Averting his grandmother's gaze, his eyes wandered from table to table, happy family to happy couples, anywhere to avoid eye contact with his grandmother.

With the sight of his parents, Brandon felt relieved but disappointed. He had not seized the opportunity to talk about the important things he wanted to know from his grandmother, whom he recognized as the wonderful person across the table. This was the last meal the Tripp family would share before the abrupt wave of detestation and grief would begin.

* * *

The Tripp family understood that the day would come and Brandon's grandmother knew it was her time. As she lay in her hospital bed, his grandmother lovingly placed a beautiful heart locket into his clammy palm. When Brandon's grandmother lost her long battle with leukemia and passed away, the silver heart necklace tumbled out of his hands and plummeted to the carpeted floor.

"Look inside," he recalled his grandmother beckoning in her frail and raspy voice. Inside was engraved, "Sometimes the journey is better than the destination." He embraced his grandmother one more time and whispered that last goodbye as he walked away. It wasn't manly for a boy to cry, but Brandon couldn't help it as intense sorrow overtook him. He participated in activities, but his heart was not in it; his mind was not in it. The quote he could not forget and yet he yearned to know what it meant.

Weeks passed slowly; he had no concept of time as grief overtook him. At the reading of her will, Brandon shut his eyes and tried to remember his grandmother reclining in the chair yonder. After only three weeks the memory was already becoming hazy, the fog rolling in and out, with the sun occasionally burning it off.

He was awakened from his reverie by the sound of his name.

"To Brandon Tripp goes my beloved dog, Sammy, and..." but Brandon did not hear the rest, for he was already wondering why he got the dog and what in the world he was going to do with it.

His grandmother's house was about three hours away, close enough to get there in a day but far enough that you really did not want to do the commute both ways. To get to her house you had to travel on the highway, get off at an impossible exit, and then make a series of turns that made you feel like you were more or less at the end of a whip. His mother was going to live there for the time being, and since Brandon inherited the dog, he had to come too. His father was going to stay at the condo, and since no dogs were allowed, it gave his parents the perfect excuse to secede from the other's grasp.

His mother was at it again, talking of her plans for the house, when they finally neared the spacious homes that towered high above any that Brandon had ever seen. Even though the market was dreadful, the family decided it was best to sell the house. They all had their own lives and did not want to alter them in any way; they did not want to compromise their kids, work, or school. Brandon's mother was the only woman in her family not to have a position in the workforce. Therefore, she was deemed the most appropriate individual to work on the promotion of the house; because it was their understanding she really didn't do anything, anyway. She was shamed into it. And now the two were here, in front of a house Brandon had barely ever been into, and in a neighborhood of kids who would want nothing to do with him.

He was mistaken, for the kids loved his grandmother, and snootiness was not yet embedded into their attitudes. Sammy, the enormous shaggy canine, ran to greet them as they entered. The neighbor had been taking care of him and now she was off on vacation, leaving Brandon to learn how to care for a dog all by himself. The dog books and how-to manuals prepared him in no way for pet sitting much less being Sammy's full-time guardian.

Brandon meagerly found the pet food and poured a generous amount into the pet bowl just as he let the dog out into the fenced backyard. The blinds covered the sliding door; however, they could not shield the beauty and splendor that the backyard beheld. The garden was cared for by Grandma's green thumb, and it showed. All over the yard there were flowers in bloom and although learning to garden was not the first thing he wanted to do here, Brandon was drawn to it because of the splendid spectrum of colors. He forced himself to close the door when Sammy came charging back, hastening his return inside.

Brandon had a sleepless night between the dog pleading to get in the bed and whimpering when he was forbidden. To retaliate, Sammy pleaded the need to relive a bodily function, and when they got back inside, he rushed up the stairs, hopped on the bed and fell asleep before Brandon even was halfway up the winding staircase. Somehow, Brandon managed to get up and get ready by nine. As he opened the shades, he saw a trio of teenagers gathering in his neighbor's lawn. The three had dogs and looked ready to walk them. The light bulb in Brandon's head went off, and he flew down the stairs, found the leash, and headed off to give Sammy a walk. It was a bold gesture just to walk up to these complete strangers and ask if he could walk with them. But really, they weren't strangers, exactly — they were neighbors — and they did not look as if they were going to bite, unlike their dogs, who looked restless waiting for their morning enjoyment. He had nothing to lose; he needed them to help him learn the necessary ways to take care of this canine, this new best friend.

"Hello," Brandon ventured as he headed toward the group.

"Did you just come from Mrs. Smith's house? Hi there Sammy," she said as she bent down to rub what Brandon would come to know as Sammy's favorite ticklish spot.

"Yes," Brandon answered uncertainly and without knowing what really to say next.

"Well, then, where is she and who are you?" the other girl retorted, more accusingly than questioningly. Brandon stared dumbfounded at them and wondered what he should say.

He settled on, "Mrs. Smith was my grandmother," but that did not appease the second girl.

"Was! What do you mean was?" she said judgmentally and with a hint of anxiousness.

"She died three weeks ago."

"From what?" The boy who had not spoken until then inquired.

"Leukemia. She had a long fight, and now..." he trailed off.

"Oh, I'm so sorry," said the first girl, who had now risen to eye level and had sympathy in her eyes that Brandon had come to expect from all of them after mentioning his grandmother.

"I'm Kim Thatcher," she murmured, "and this is Devon Little." Brandon was thankful that she changed the subject.

"And I'm Jane Porter. Nice to meet you. Now can we get going," Jane interrupted. She was clearly the impatient one of the odd group.

Brandon knew they were all his age. Kim was tall with shamrock-colored eyes to offset the flames on her head. Jane Porter was a brunette with so many freckles coating her nose and cheeks that they covered her face like sand covers a beach. She was petite, yet not so small Brandon had to look down at her; he was 5' 7". Devon was taller than Brandon, with raven hair and a round face; his eyes were darting as if he had done or planned to carry out some mischievous deed.

"Okay! You coming?" Kim directed toward Brandon with unusual cheeriness for this hour.

"I guess," Brandon replied, giving off a hint of casualness along with the understanding that this was what he really had wanted them to ask and why he came outside in the first place. As they wandered down the road the trio talked about everything. Unknowingly, an informal support group was forming; they touched upon various subjects from parents to dogs to life in general.

After analyzing the group, he realized Kim was the sensitive one who was always there for comfort, while Jane would always give you what you deserved. Devon was kind of the all-around, common-sense pessimist of the three. They fit well, and Brandon began to wonder what he was and if he would fit in. Kim's dog was Molly who was energetic yet always ready to obey. Jane's dog, Buster, matched Jane's personality in every way by being somewhat standoffish and ready for confrontation. Devon's dog was a mellow chocolate Lab named Sarah, who seemed to be the oldest of the three. They were two streets down when he finally got up the courage to say something.

"So what do you guys do for fun?" It was out of nowhere and was the first thing that popped into his head. They stared at him with curiosity.

"I'm a hockey player. Kim is a reader and writer. And, well, Jane what do you do?" Devon said playfully.

"You know full well," she retorted, though Brandon had no idea. "What do you do?"

"Lacrosse and baseball are my favorites," Brandon answered hesitantly. Just then they completed their first loop and ended where they had started. Though the walls were thick, they could hear Brandon's mom yelling at someone, probably his dad.

"Whoa! Want to come over? That sounds nasty," Kim wondered aloud, and as soon as she said it, she knew she had said something to offend Brandon.

So she quickly added, "Only if you want to. We normally rotate whose house we have breakfast at every morning. We have the whole house to ourselves. My parents are gone by eight."

"Sure."

Brandon followed Kim into the Thatcher's home. As he stepped in, he thought he had entered the kitchen of a big city restaurant.

It was bigger than his living room, dining room, and family room combined. It had a huge stainless steel stove with space enough to cook four thanksgiving turkeys and every appliance imaginable, each one on its own shelf. The entire kitchen was matching and reminded Brandon of his cousin's Barbie Dream House.

"Wow!" Brandon muttered as he wandered around.

"The kitchen is the largest room in the house. My dad's a caterer and my mom's a party slash event planner. This is kind of the center if they need to experiment or work on things at home! The master bedroom and bathroom aren't even this big!" Kim tried to joke, but Brandon knew she felt uncomfortable with the identity she was gaining because of this one room in her house.

Brandon quickly ate a donut and headed home to feed Sammy. He showered and changed, for that walk had drenched him with sweat. It was July, and the air was so heavily dampened with moisture he felt as if he were gliding through the mist. This daily morning ritual continued until mid-August, as they talked about Brandon's grandmother's death, his parents' fighting, and how to care for Sammy. Every time Brandon brought up his parents' bickering, Devon knew exactly what he meant. His parents were divorced and his mother had remarried. Unfortunately, his mother and stepfather were beginning to have little disputes that brought back memories of his parents before their separation.

... The rest is yet to come...

Six-Word Stories ...

These Six-Word Stories were created following
lessons on word choice,
story structure,
and a
sharing and discussion of
Cape Cod Life magazine's
"Six-Word Stories" article.

Check these out, then try to
create your own; the students
make it look easy, but they're quite
a challenge; have fun with these.

Cape Cod in Six ...

Lighthouse fell. But ship sailed on. — Ashleigh McEvoy

Pizza place, sandy beach, Cape Cod. — Lydia Burrage-Goodwin

Black sky buried me in light. — Ashleigh McEvoy

Relaxing, fun time, not like Weston. — Lydia Burrage-Goodwin

Riding along beneath Cape Cod trees. — Lydia Burrage-Goodwin

After, she drifts off to sea. — Rebecca Harris

Life's Challenges, Take Six ...

I survived. I'm not a survivor. — Ashleigh McEvoy

Super Glue and kids equals trouble. — Wisima "Sam" Nipatnantaporn

Small dog, left alone, starved, died. — Lydia Burrage-Goodwin

more of Life's Challenges ...

Velvet green lawn, chemicals in air. — Lydia Burrage-Goodwin

Ha-ha, funny; yeah, you too. — Wisima "Sam" Nipatnantaporn

We're World Series Champs - Go Sox! — Megan Cronin

Death by her own piercing voice. — Ashleigh McEvoy

Sorry. I thought that was chocolate. — Tosh Mihesuah

Six words is way too short. — Katrina Malakhoff

Papelbon is Dancing Red Sox maniac. — Wisima "Sam" Nipatnantaporn

Rain falls after twenty dry years. — Rebecca Harris

I love Papelbon; he's my idol. — Wisima "Sam" Nipatnantaporn

No glue? Don't break me then. — Ashleigh McEvoy

I call her name --no answer. — Rebecca Harris

Good thing this shirt is black. — Tosh Mihesuah

matters of Family & Friends - in Six ...

I am not my father's son. — Ashleigh McEvoy

Mom! You didn't say I couldn't. — Tosh Mihesuah

I am who you've made me. — Ashleigh McEvoy

I'm my best friend; she's me. — Ashleigh McEvoy

That is not your shadow. Run! —Tosh Mihesuah

Don't bow down to my expectations. — Ashleigh McEvoy

She comes back, but it's different. — Rebecca Harris

Regarding the Red, White, and Blue ...

He was born, lived, then died. — Wisima "Sam" Nipatnantaporn

I'm enlisting. I feel useless here. — Ashleigh McEvoy

And the World at Large, in Six Words ...

Cinderella lost slipper, found Prince Charming. — Wisima "Sam" Nipatnantaporn

Women forced to hide their faces. — Rebecca Harris

Boy Girl Black White All Human. — Jessica Schiffman

After, she drifts off to sea. — Rebecca Harris

Horns, Starbucks, banks ... I smell sushi. — Emilie Foy's NYC

Selected Longer Piece...

The Better Side of Rapunzel: In the Perspective of her Hair

by Miranda Burrage-Goodwin

Once upon a time, I lived on the head of the most ungrateful, annoying, prissy princess. Now, in that time, I was blonde, attractive, and shiny, but I was stuck in a tower. Exactly why I was there, I will never know. I do have a faint idea, though. When I first appeared, I had only little golden strands. Then my head and I were sent off to a tower far, far away. I grew in the tower because there was no barber to clip me. As I grew, I became the talk of the village. I was thirty feet, ten inches long. I was extremely wavy and I had no idea of my fate.

One day in mid-July, I was staring at myself in Rapunzel's hand-mirror while the princess brushed me for the ninety-ninth time. In the reflection of the mirror, I saw a prince approaching. Rapunzel combed me one more time and put down the brush. "Rapunzel, Rapunzel, let down your hair," cried the prince.

Now, this is the part that never makes it into the story. I said, "Rapunzel, you can't possibly be considering letting that, that, that … man climb up me, can you?" Obviously, she ignored my cries and lowered me down the tower wall. The prince tied a knot at the bottom of my locks, stuck his feet on my hair knot, and climbed up me. It was the most painful, undignified, humiliating thing that ever happened to me. When he reached the top, Rapunzel pulled me up and I examined myself. I was a mess. The prince's boots had cut chunks out of me, and I watched ripped pieces fall wearily to the ground. (The princess later used a special pro-vitamin formula specifically for dry, damaged, or treated hair, but it was of no use.) So much for my full-bodied locks. I never looked the same again. It was so sad.

The prince came every day after that, each time calling, "Rapunzel, Rapunzel, let down your hair." And each time, I was lowered down and I experienced excruciating pain and embarrassment.

One day an evil witch came, and — oh, this part is so difficult to talk about — she cut me off, just like that. She cut me off!! I fell to the floor in a heap. I was no longer a part of the princess, whom I had been with my entire life. The witch forced the princess to flee for good before the prince arrived — on time, I might add. When he arrived, he shouted, "Rapunzel, Rapunzel, let down your hair." The witch cackled madly, and lowered me down the tower. For the final time, I experienced that pain again. As he climbed, I tried to warn him of the witch at the top of the tower, and obviously, he didn't listen. Young people these days!

Up he climbed. When he reached the top, the witch said, "I didn't think you'd be so stupid as to fall for it." With that, she pushed him off the tower. Down, down he fell, until finally he landed with a dull thud on the thorny ground below. A few minutes later, the prince let out a low, rumbling moan, and crawled into the thick scrub bush.

As I watched in horror, a plan was beginning to form in my mind, my escape plan. When the witch turned her back to tell herself how marvelous she was, I "fell" out of the tower window and flew away. Now, this part of it wasn't well planned out, because I was at the mercy of the wind. I went where the wind blew me. I flew on and on for days, and I was lucky to keep all in one clump. One day, after a short nap in mid-air, I flew into the window of a royal kingdom, into what appeared to be the king's royal study. It was not however, the father of Rapunzel's prince, but another king far, far away, in another land. The king was not in the room, so I had to wait for someone to show up.

A bit too soon, a young maid came in and found me on the ground. "How beautiful! How exquisite! It is the most wonderful thing I have ever seen," she exclaimed. "I must show the king." She ran out of the room, almost as quickly as she came, scooping me up as she went. I have to say, I was quite flattered by her words. As the maid ran deeper and deeper into the bowels of the castle, I wondered what would become of me. I was soon to find out.

The maid ran into a room and bowed so hastily to the royal family that I almost fell out of her hands.

"Yeeeeesssss?" the king said in his high-pitched voice.

The maid looked too scared of him to answer. That's when I piped in. I told him everything that had happened to me, in hopes that he could help me. His answer wasn't exactly what I expected. He said, "The rigging on our fastest ship, the *Steadfast*, broke in a storm last night. We need a rope that is thirty feet, ten inches long.

The only one in the land is on our enemy ship, the *Crackpot*. How long are you?"

I knew I was thirty feet, ten inches long, but I wasn't sure I wanted to work on a ship for the rest of my life. I told myself, "It's better than nothing." I resolved to tell the king that I would humbly work for him.

"Your majesty," I said, "I am exactly thirty feet, ten inches long, and I would be honored to work on your ship."

By this time, the maid was so horror struck at the idea of talking hair that she fainted. The royal medics rushed in and took her away. The king looked thoroughly pleased with himself and said, "I am very glad, you know. I have never met talking hair before, but I do like the temperament and personality. I would like to propose a feast in honor of ... what's your name?"

"Just call me Rapunzel's hair," I said.

Then he said, "Good, good. A feast in honor of Rapunzel's hair! Fantabulous! Splendid! This will be the best feast ever. What exactly does hair eat?"

Three months later...

So here I am on a boat, salt wind blowing right through me, giving me split-ends, and I'm no better off than I was before. Men still tie knots and climb me, this time yelling, "Land ho!"

Terrible Two's ...

With a few choice prompts
from guest author
Bonnie Neubauer
and some ideas from her book,
The Write Brain Workbook,
students were inspired to create these
"Terrible Two's" characters and
accompanying pieces.

Can you just picture their characters?

Caitlin Angela Trent
by Ashleigh McEvoy

Nickname: Catie
Eye color: Turquoise
Hair color: Bleach blond
Favorite food: Granola bars
Siblings' names/ages: Stuart
(24), Amy (9)
How they treat you:
    Stuart: like a somewhat
    distant half-niece
    Amy: as the guinea pig
    of her elaborate science
    experiments
Thoughts on toilet training: a
pointless waste of time

Here I am stuck in my crib, dancing to the tune of the Elmo's World theme song that's playing endlessly on the TV. Amy's at a national science fair with Mommy, Daddy's at work, and the babysitter is sleeping, so I've got the place to myself—just as I like it. I look out the window. Rain. Again. Gross, I hate water! No baths for me! I reach out, trying to grab the granola bar that the babysitter, Annie, left on the bureau — just beyond my reach, probably to torture me. How interesting, a babysitter who likes to torture babies. How sick. Hmm, maybe I should throw a tantrum, you know, as a little revenge, a little taste of her own medicine. A *taste*, ugh, I'm starved. What kind of a babysitter falls asleep anyways?! Leaving a *granola bar* in plain view, no less! This woman should definitely seek therapy.

Carly Anthony Trace

by Rachel Liu

Nickname: Car
Eyes: green
Hair: brown
Favorite food: grapes
 Siblings: Rosie (6 months), Amy (7 years)
Views on potty training: Diapers were easier

Here I am, stuck in a crib. There's a pea stuck in my right nose hole because it looked like it fit and it did. I don't like peas, really, but I like them better than corn and carrots and yams. I guess peas aren't that bad, but I don't like them stuck in my nose. I try to take it out because it makes it hard to breathe, and when I sniff, I can only kinda smell pea juice. Plus it feels all mushy.

 I try to pick it out, but my pinky's bigger than my nose hole and it won't get up there. I try to squeeze it out. Oh! Some came out! It might be boogies, but it's a little greener than boogies. I want to get it out before Mommy comes up to wake me from my nap, because if she sees me with a pea in my nose, she'll probably get all weird and say, "Oh, Caaarly," in that tone which makes my tummy feel weird.

Terrible Two's

by Megan Cronin

Name: Cindy Adrienne Timlan
Nickname: Cindy-Windy
Eye Color: Hazel
Hair color: Blonde
Siblings: Patrick Justin Timlan (age 5)
How Patrick treats me: He makes fun of me
My favorite food: Peanut butter sandwich
Thoughts on toilet training: Boring. Why run into another room to go pee? They have diapers for a reason.

Here I am, stuck in my crib. Just because I fussed over my lunch a little, my mommy thinks I need a nap. I want to play with my blocks or watch a choo-choo train show. But now, I am a captive. Stuck. Like glue. Glue tastes good. But I want my sandwich. And I want to leave this crib thing. Soon they'll make me use the bathroom or something. No fun. Why did they invent diapers if I am forced to use a toilet now? It's dumb. Like my big brother. He fell down because he tripped over my block castle. It fell down. The fairy princess got hurt. Fairies are pretty. I want to be a fairy when I grow up.

(C.A.T.) – An Encounter with a Two Year Old

by Niki Bousquet

Chlorine Alexandra Toothbrush (C.A.T) is twenty-four intervals of about thirty days old, is nicknamed Calico, has yellow ocular devices, and maroon follicular strands, favors macaroni and cheese with avocado over all other edible matter, has three siblings who give her piggyback rides, although they would never transport an actual pig who goes oink, and thinks toilets look like the opening at the top of a submarine.

Here I am, stuck in my crib, and I'm wearing a pretty, fluffy, puppy-covered bib. It smells like mashed pomegranate seeds, and I have leaves in my hair from playing outside on New Year's Eve. I'm not falling asleep, so instead I'll daydream of drinking tea and eating Cadbury chocolate in England at my grandmother's house in seven intervals of three-hundred-and-sixty-five-day years. Seven is my favorite number, like jam on toast, but I don't like the doorjamb, especially when I jam my toes, who are pigs, between the door and the jamb. Lambs are pretty and fluffy, like fleece, because I think fleece is from sheep, isn't it? That would make sense, because they feel the same, like pencils and trees. The eyes on the ceiling are dark and scary on this New Year's Eve. It's midnight and I'm lonely. All alone like lonesome sheep when all the others have been counted. But then the owner falls asleep and leaves the last one uncounted, unused, and unsure of why he got this job as a counting sheep, whose only purpose is to be counted.

And, One More Selected Longer Piece ...

Gold Rush

by Lydia Burrage-Goodwin

Tuck and Mercy sat quietly, twiddling their thumbs at the bus stop bench. Both of them were in somewhat of a daydream, with their mouths opened lazily as they stared into the misty morning air. It was so quiet that they could hear the blood pumping in their heads.

"Maybe the bus broke down!" exclaimed Mercy, who for the record never missed the bus.

"Eh," Tuck moaned. "Who cares?"

Tuck never really cared if he missed the bus. He would just say, "What the heck? I'll bike to school," while Mercy rolled her eyes and sighed.

Mercy and Tuck were twins and in the eighth grade. They attended the Lewis Middle School in San Diego, California. Mercy was a science geek, and every Tuesday she looked forward to science club after school. She didn't even mind that it let out late, and that she had to figure out a way to get home, she just loved it. She loved doing science projects at home in her spare time. She even set the house on fire while doing a chemistry project using gas and baking soda. While she loved science with a passion, she hated English just as much. In English class, she would make spitballs and hail them at her classmates just for something to do.

Tuck was exactly the opposite. He loved reading and English. He thought Mercy was crazy for loving science class. He thought it was the perfect class to take a nap in — the only moments in the day that he got to kick back and relax. Tuck was quiet, and he didn't talk much. He also wasn't very popular. He wrote what was in his head rather than telling anyone. He also didn't care what he looked like, and he didn't care about the way he smelled. No one liked to sit next to Tuck after gym class.

At the bus stop, Tuck began to pull his history book from his bag when he noticed a raccoon wandering nearby. Unusual to find a raccoon wandering about in the morning, the twins wondered if it was rabid. Tuck sat perfectly still, while Mercy hid behind her backpack, shivering. When the animal didn't go away, Tuck took the opportunity to pull out a piece of paper and a sharpened number two pencil and he began sketching every last detail—its bristly brown fur, its enormous claws, its brown and black and white bushy tail. A car drove past, which scared the raccoon, and racing rapidly it jumped onto an old willow tree. As the tree creaked and swayed back and forth, the raccoon took advantage of the time and distance he had to get up to the top.

Tuck put his picture down on the bench and stood up. He picked up the picture again and positioned it to the exact angle that he wanted and said, "Perfect!" Satisfied that he had captured the raccoon's likeness, he laid the paper down once again and picked up his history book.

January 1848

James Marshall sat quietly overlooking a rather small ditch, soon to become his sawmill. The worn and tattered shoes on his feet swept through the air as he dangled his legs by the edge of the pit.

It was another long, dull day in Coloma, California. The sun took its time passing by, as if it didn't want to rotate the Earth. It was almost time for James to call it a day. Everyone was packing up or setting up camp nearby. Pots and pans were taken out of old crates and set above the fire, and the sound of sizzling poultry and crackling wood was all that was heard in the dim camp light.

John Sutter, a Swiss adventurer and a dreamer, was Marshall's best friend. Sutter traveled the world. He made an agreement with the Russians to buy equipment, including horses, mules, carts, a forge, a gristmill, and a schooner, planning to build a fort some ninety miles north of San Francisco, only to find that he was short of cash and heavily in debt.

"Boy, do I vish zat I vas rich," exclaimed Sutter as he picked up his moldy tack and examined it. He cringed and gulped the hard bread, after picking off the mold and then stuffing it in his mouth. His cheeks bulged out like a chipmunk packing nuts. Marshall laughed. Sutter snorted and grinned and washed it down with bitter, three-day-old muddy coffee. The men sat before the fire for a while, before turning in for the night. "I'm goin'k to bed," Sutter said, yawning.

"OK," Marshall mumbled. He took the lantern and passed it to Sutter.

* * *

The crickets were singing and the birds, bees, and bugs went off to sleep by the time Mercy and Tuck were making their way home from school.

"I'm not waiting for the bus any longer," Mercy whined. "It's cold!" The twins had no coats, and they noticed the slight breeze in the air that chilled their skin. An hour had gone by as the last glares of the sun cast shadows on the trees and faded into darkness. Strange eyes from nocturnal wildlife peered from behind the bushes at the two kids. Metal street signs creaked when cars passed by, creating an airflow in their wake. Mercy felt as cold as a rock. Goosebumps prickled her arms, as if they were trying to pinch her. They shuffled their feet through the leaves and finally came to some dead grass. Their journey was silent except for the steady flow of cars. They felt that they were being followed.

* * *

Marshall sat by the campfire for a while warming his hands and feet. Through the glow, he sat quietly thinking. He was carried away with fanciful dreams of becoming rich. When he was younger, kids teased him because he was poor. He had to share his bed and clothes with his older sister. There was nothing more humiliating than wearing his sister's clothes. He had become hardened to not having anything, but boy, did he wish for more. His partner, Sutter, grew up poor as well. His father had a lot of debt from poor business deals, so the family was forced to move from Europe to the United States in search of a better life — and that better life seemed elusive to his family too.

In the tent, Sutter closed his eyes and listened to the crickets singing and the wind blowing gently toward the river. Soon, he drifted into his dreams like walking on clouds.

* * *

After a very long walk, Mercy and Tuck soon arrived home to a very unpleasant smell. Their dad was in the kitchen with an apron on. This was a very bad sign. He had a burnt pan in his hand and the smoke detector was going off. A cloud of black smoke rushed out as they opened the door. As they both walked in, coughing and gagging, they waved the smoke out the door. Their dad started to swear at the oven, but they couldn't hear it over the loud whistle of the alarm. After fifteen minutes the smoke detector stopped and in the silence the smoke finally retreated out the door.

"So, Dad. What would have been our dinner?" Tuck asked.

"Pancakes." He looked at one and then threw it on to the table. It landed and made a thud sound against the wood.

"Where's Mom?" Mercy asked.

"Looking for you," he mumbled, devastated by his pancake failure. "She said if she couldn't find you, she'd come home and call the cops."

"Great," Tuck complained. "No food until she comes home." He plopped into a chair and slouched down like there were cement blocks on his stomach. He took out his history book.

* * *

"Wake Up!" Marshall yelled into his best friend's ear. Sutter dozed off at lunch break and everyone was annoyed because he snored so loudly.

Marshall was making his scheduled inspection of his massive ditch, when he spotted some glimmering sand down at the bottom. It was a shiny gold color, and it floated around the surface of the crystal clear water. Marshall jumped in to have a closer look. The other workers nearby kept on eating.

Marshall scooped the glittery flakes into his hands and let the water sift through. It was heavier than dirt, and it was shiny, and he suspected that it was gold. He couldn't let anyone know. Maybe there was more gold in this same spot, and if others found out, he would never be rich. Marshall looked around to see that the others were preoccupied and began to pocket the nuggets of gold he had sifted.

"What are you doing down there?" one of the workers asked.

"Um, well," Marshall sputtered, trying to give a reasonable excuse for being in the ditch. "Well, I tripped over a root or something and I ended up in here." He exclaimed, "Can you give me a hand?" A group of men were gathered near the ditch, and they were ordered to pull the rope connected to the belt on his pants. They hauled Marshall up slowly, and he soon reached ground level. "Thanks," he muttered.

"No problem," they all answered.

Marshall casually walked over to Sutter as if nothing was going on. "Sutter," he whispered. "Sutter!" He started getting louder. "Wake up!" He lost his patience. Everyone stopped what they were doing and stared.

"Uh, sorry. He is a deep sleeper, and if I don't wake him up he will sleep all day." They were convinced and went back to work.

Sutter rubbed his eyes and blinked a couple of times before he realized where he was. "Why did you wake me up? I still have a few minutes more to nap," he grumbled. "Follow me," said Marshall.

They walked for a while to a rundown shack, far away from the rest of the workers. As they cautiously entered, floor boards creaked and they had to wave cobwebs away. Marshall wiped off a dusty seat and sat down, motioning for Sutter to do the same. "Why would you bring me all the way out here? What is so important that you couldn't say it back at camp?" Sutter asked.

Marshall pulled the shiny flakes out of his pocket without speaking and held them to the light for Sutter to see. Sutter smiled, examined the specimens closely, and then started hopping around and yelling, "Yahoo!" He did a little jig before Marshall joined him in the dancing and merriment.

"I found it in the sawmill ditch." Marshall's voice increased in intensity like a crescendo in a piece of music. He was so excited. "But we have to keep this a secret. I think it's real and I need to get it assayed to be sure."

Suddenly, they heard a noise coming from the door. "Hide!" Marshall whispered. They jumped behind old wooden barrels hidden behind a cache of crates that said "Fragile." The door creaked open. Sutter and Marshall saw a pair of large brown cowboy boots scrape the dusty floor. The feet inside the boots belonged to a rather drunk man, whom Sutter and Marshall could not see clearly. The man stumbled over the many boxes and barrels that cluttered the room. He threw an empty bottle of whiskey into the corner. It landed with a crash, and shattered glass filled the floor. It took the man about five minutes to chug down the next bottle. It was nearly midnight when he passed out from the whiskey.

Marshall and Sutter made their escape. On their way out the door, they recognized the man as Judge Brown. They were grateful that they stayed hidden until the man was asleep.

* * *

Tuck and Mercy's mom arrived home at around eleven o'clock. She trampled in the door with rather large circles under her eyes. Her high-heeled shoes were covered in dirt and her hair was a tussled mess. Dust layered her glasses and spots of mud caked her stockings.

Tuck was asleep on his unmade bed and his dad was asleep on the sofa. Mercy was leaning against the table covered in burnt pancake crumbs. She was too tired to deal with the pots and pans, and she stared blankly at the pile and the sponge and dishwashing soap by the side of the sink.

Tuck and Mercy's mom was so relieved to find that they had made it home. Suddenly the tension subsided and her shoulders relaxed, and she collapsed into the chair.

They got a late start the next morning. They missed the bus, and it was about ten o'clock before any of them woke up. Their mom was the first to open her eyes. "Oh no. We're late. Everybody up, quick!" She yelled the same thing several times before Tuck and Mercy finally got out of bed.

Rowing ...

This exercise was an all out lesson in creativity, with very little prompting. After a variety of different lessons on everything from word choice and using poetic devices in prose writing to crafting intriguing settings, students were merely asked to "write about rowing."
"How do you mean that?" they asked.
"Any way you want," they were instructed.
Whether metaphorically or literally,
they "rowed" with smooth enthusiasm.

How would your rowing go?

Rowing, the unfinished story

by Liam O'Connor

I startled violently. Someone had said the word, the forbidden word!
Rowing.
I sank back, far back in time. I was eighteen, fourteen, eight. And then I was six, and about to relive the worst day of my life. The day so horrible, my own mind had locked the memory of it behind an impenetrable door, but for some reason, today that one word, rowing, had broken through that barrier or protection.
Rowing.
I felt my body begin to move. I glanced around as my six-year-old self hopped happily up the steps to our summer house at Lake George. I was helpless to stop myself. After all, I hadn't actually gone back in time; I was just reliving a memory so long forgotten, it had become incredibly vivid. Every detail stuck out in my mind, from the feathery cirrus clouds in the deep blue sky to the rough feel of the stone steps on my bare feet. The lake glittered in the distance with the setting sun, red bleaching into the waters. It looked like the lake had turned to blood.

Come to think of it, I smelled blood, too. But I was six, and this smell me no fear.

I had just been out on the canoe. My brother, Simon, had suggested I go rowing. It didn't occur to me that I was too young to row alone, and my sixteen-year-old brother knew that. All I knew was that he had treated me like someone worth his time. And for that I was ecstatic.

I reached for the doorknob, the scent of blood filling my nostrils. Even my cheerful and naïve six-year-old mind realized something was wrong. A frown crinkled my nose, and I pulled the door open.

Rowing

by Maret Gable

Six years ago my family went to a lakeside house in Vermont. The family whose house we rented had a small rowboat. We went out in the boat a couple of times with my dad rowing, and then he started teaching my brothers to row. Whenever Seth and Michael were at the oars, I made sure I wasn't in the boat. I wasn't sure I trusted them, even though they never actually did capsize the boat.

A Rowboat Story

by Caroline Hibbert

It was one of the hottest days of the summer. The humid, heavy air had driven the families staying at the campground to the lake, which offered a sanctuary from the heat. On the beach was a makeshift boat-rental station. Upon eyeing the little rowboat, my friend insisted we take it out. I pointed out the variety of kayaks and informed her that I knew how to use them, but not a rowboat. After a small debate between my friends and me, the decision was made: we decided to go rowing. It didn't look too hard; after all, I'd always assumed it was an easy task to row a little boat out on a lake.

We slid the small vessel into the water and jumped in. I tried, first, to lift both oars simultaneously. After several unsuccessful tries, my other companions took turns, both failing to make the boat move as well. The oars were heavy and difficult to lift compared to the lightweight kayak paddles I had used before. A couple minutes later, we concluded that we were "stranded" several feet from the shore.

While jumping into the neck-deep water to push the boat to shore, I noticed one of my friends had black stains on her hands from the oars that were now also rubbed on her face. Rubbing the stains with water didn't help much, so we traveled back toward the shore, grease- stained and amused at our pathetic attempt at rowing.

Rowing Tedium

by Seth Gable

Rowing, green, endless rowing, endless fields of green. Fields? No, water, dark, but green, painfully green, and more rowing, tedium, endless tedium. Night and day are nonexistent, no dark, cloudy evenings, no pale morning sunlight, only the infinite green and the strange light coming through the endless fog. Rowing, tedium.

A Sailing Fiasco, based on a true story

by Katrina Malakhoff

Our ancient Chrysler sailboat was free, and consequently in pitiful condition. The seats had long since rotted into mildewy chunks of decaying red fabric. There were several holes we neglected to notice under the six-seater benches, the yellowed white paint was chipped and peeling, and the jib was so full of holes it was amazing it could still catch any wind. Nevertheless, Dad relished taking guests out on "pleasure sails" on Wequaquet Lake. These sails were not remotely pleasurable. Every pitch and roll of the boat threatened to capsize us, and there would be no chance of bringing the boat up again. Nevertheless, the boat survived, and after a day of sailing it would be secured to the mooring once more.

On a particular Friday night, we were just about to drive up to Boston when we got a call from someone saying, "I don't know what it's doing here, but your sailboat just drifted in front of my house on the lake, and it's starting to sink."

My dad, determined to save his precious boat, had to row across the lake in a little old dinghy, and with the help of some other people on pontoon boats, he managed to pull up the now waterlogged, cruddy old boat. It was full of tiny black leeches that writhed all over the rotting seats. Turns out it broke free of the mooring in a heaving wind and took a mind of its own. We didn't get to go to Boston.

another Selected Longer Piece ...

Lydia's Nightmare

by Ashleigh McEvoy

I sat there on the cloud, abandoned. It was cold, but still, and there was a weight to the air that suggested it held secrets, some of which I knew must pertain to me. The clouds shifted under me, wispy and soft, but surprisingly solid, a stable perch in the dreary night sky. I smiled at this dream, at how pleasant it was up here, perfect even, so different from my horrifying nightmares of late. I leaned back, readjusting myself as if on a bed, which I was sure the wispy marshmallow fluffs would prove to be any second now. My eyes would flit open, my hand already flying out to silence my shrieking alarm clock.

With my eyes closed, I sighed, shifting again, unable to sleep, but then, laughing, I sat upright. I was already asleep; how foolish of me. I reached out and grabbed for the cloud floating past me, sure my hand would immediately sink right through it, as if it were smoke or simply invisible. It didn't, though; I held it in my hand, and knowing this would be my one and only chance to eat a cloud, I stuffed it in my mouth. Eating a cloud, that had always been a fantasy of mine. How silly it seemed then. How precious it seemed now. The cloud tasted exactly like ... Banana Laffy Taffy. Funny, I'd eaten that the day it happened.

A little later on, the with sun high in the sky, just when I was beginning to wonder if I was oversleeping, if I'd forgotten to reset my alarm, I glanced down and noticed my attire for the first time. I was wearing a bathing suit, a shiny, red, glittering bathing suit. This dream was getting to be pretty strange, but I didn't mind; the view was spectacular.

I strained my eyes, trying to get a sense of where exactly my cloud was situated. I couldn't tell much, though; the houses were mere specks below me, the trees just a green blur. The sun was beating down steadily now. My cloud was sticky with heat, but again, I didn't mind; I was just glad it wasn't raining.

Although there was no wind to speak of, the air seemed to be whispering to me. I caught phrases, sometimes just words at a time.

Lydia. Waves. Help.

And then: *Path, don't do this,* and *future.*

There was something about running, too. I didn't understand, but I brushed it off. It didn't matter; it was a dream. Besides, no one knew about Lydia.

☼

When the sun rose on my third day up in the sky, I was in a state of panic. Why wasn't I waking up? Who would take Pa in for his check-up? Where was I anyways? Why was I even dreaming of a stupid cloud?

But by then, of course, I knew that it was not just some stupid cloud. It seemed to anticipate my wishes, read my mind. If I was thinking of Pa, for example, the sky would become a slideshow of images and memories of him: the time he was rushed away in the ambulance, his overflowing medicine cabinet, an old scene of him and Ma dancing at Grandpa's eightieth birthday party...

It would also show other things, flashback to other moments, ones I had forced to the back of my mind and vowed never to think of again.

They're just some harmless pills, David. Go to sleep now.

She echoed through my head at all hours, as if talking over a loudspeaker, the image of her body being pulled up onto the beach flashing across the sky, the image of the empty pill container playing across the darkness behind my eyes.

"*What do you think you'll do today?*"

"*The beach. I'm going to the waves.*"

☼

I was going crazy up there. It was no longer bright or sunny. It stormed torrential downpours. The lightning, mixed with Lydia into chaos, illuminated the smoky black sky. My cloud was no longer a fluffy marshmallow but a demon, a storm cloud. Angry, it shook with thunder and death.

Her mother's voice was next to reverberate across the heavens.

41

She could swim! Oh, Lord, no. No. Please. No, not Lydia. Take me. PLEASE, God.

The policeman pulling her away, the ambulances lining the beach like tourists' rental cars, the foreboding yellow caution tape separating Lydia from the world...

I had sworn to put it behind me, not to tell a soul, to leave the memories of her untarnished no matter the cost, memories of a happy, passionate woman, a woman who had everything under control. If only they knew.

I want to go home, I thought. I had dreaded that place since the accident, but now it seemed safe, haunted sure, but filled with the kind of quiet strength that carried me through those dark months.

I wish I could say that the story ended differently, that after two weeks of being stuck in a nightmare I didn't revert to that old line, "Then I woke up and it was all a dream," that something more meaningful happened, something more along the lines of making peace with the world and my wife. I woke up, however, just as expected, my hand already pounding the snooze button on my alarm.

As I opened my eyes, taking in the mellow April sunlight, my eyes fell upon a picture of her, one of her looking out at the ocean, a peaceful look on her face. On that April morning, though, on the one-year anniversary of her suicide, Lydia turned to me, and I swear to God she smiled.

Bits and Pieces ...

Some of the writing endeavors in this section
were less directed than those in previous sections, for example,
Megan's piece was merely prompted by that one question "Do You
Fear It?"
Other entries in this section were
more of the quick-write genre practicing one of the previously taught
techniques,
and some snapshots of scenes ...
and all, definitely
worth publishing and savoring.

Here is a smorgasbord of
eclectically exciting writing – bits
and pieces of well-penned morsels.

Untitled *from the prompt* "Do You Fear It?"

by Megan Cronin

"Do you fear it?" she whispered to him as the waves splashed against the rocks on which they were perched. The salty air was lingering in their mouths as well as their nostrils. Small breezes played gently with their hair, and nothing but gulls spoke for a long time. He deeply inhaled the crisp air around him and stared out at the rollicking ocean waters. His facial expression changed as he watched a hermit crab scuttle along the edge of a jetty. He looked at it with a smile glazed with pity. Such a depressing creature, for its permanent home was itself. To him, that was torture. He could not imagine a life where he was stuck within himself, unable to break free. She grasped his clammy hand and lightly squeezed it, hoping to get a reaction, but it was to no avail. He did not grasp it back, nor did he blink or shift his gaze as she slid closer to him. It was only when she got so close that he could feel her uneasy breathing against his cheek that he looked down at her hand and encased it safely within his own.

Character Creating Excerpt

by Rachel Liu

The road unfolded like a sandy ribbon, rolling over bumps akin to the terrain of Caleb's hand. He knew them too well, so well that they were only a part of him to be forgotten and ignored. Its dirty caramel color reflected again, and again, and again in his eyes, hairs, and clothes. His body had lived on Earth for thirty-five years, but when he stood against the road, only his eyes, hair, and sometimes shirt glowed with the road, and he became like the road and Earth: ageless.

Coffee

by Amelia Mumford

Someone told me that you can tell what a person is like by how he answers the question, "Who are you?" Some people will talk about their job, others will describe their appearance or personality, some will talk about religion, and so on.

I don't think any of those defines me. If someone asked that question, I probably wouldn't respond.

Who am I? I'm the kind of person who gets hate and love mixed up. I change my mind. I'm fragmented; the person I think I am, and the person who lives my life every day and drives my car and brushes my teeth are very different.

I don't like coffee. But I drink it every morning, two cups of it. It makes my stomach clench like my fist knotted through my hair, my lower lip pinched between my teeth. But I drink it. It doesn't seem to matter that it makes me feel sick.

I like the way the milk looks when I pour it in, sort of like fast-forwarded footage of storm clouds. I like the cup, heavy and warm like something alive, pressed between my palms. Sometimes I imagine its heartbeat under my skin.

When I drink it, I think of it mixing with my blood and roaring through my veins, which is ridiculous, because my digestive system and my circulatory system are two very different things. But if I had coffee for blood, would I still need to remind myself to breathe?

But then the coffee goes cold. It looks darker, greyer, and sometimes there's this little arrowhead streak of milk in the very center. A streak which always makes me think of the tokens that appeared on the Bubonic plague victims before their death, of being poured down the sink, rinsed out, and placed upside down on the top rack of the dishwasher.

I guess you can see that things fit together strangely in my head.

Yesterday, I went to the pond down the street from my house. It was cloudy and silent and empty, and I stood, pant legs rolled up, in the shallow water, looking at my feet on top of the pebbles. But then a fleet of ducks glided toward where I stood, surrounding me in an expectant cluster. We regarded each other, mammal and birds, until their anxious milling ceased when they decided I had nothing to feed them. They glided on, leaving only a few milky arrowhead streaks in the water, which dissipated in their absence.

Setting the Scene

by Katrina Malakhoff

The trees of the forest pressed together in a dense mass, smashed together and straining to reach the sunlight like a crowd of people standing on tiptoe to see a famous celebrity. Beneath the canopy, the darkness and hot humid air pressed in on all sides, suffocating and oppressive. Vines wound their way around the gnarled, protruding roots and wrapped strangling arms around the vast trunks. Every once in a while, a new sapling, unknowing of the ways of the forest, would sprout up from the dark earth only to be repulsed by the older trees that stole all the sunlight from the lower regions. The sapling, shunned and weak, would wither and die all alone. And none of the great old trees would know, none of them would even be affected by the fact that another life had been vanquished on the dark forest floor, so far away from the happy sunlight that beamed upon the upper branches. Thus, for many years, the young died and the old lingered, clinging to life with tenacity, refusing to give way for the new generation. But, when the vines finally succeeded in choking their prey and the old trees splintered and fell, there were no new trees to replace them, and they continued rotting on the forest floor.

Snapshot

by Sarah Van Sciver

Lights switch on, chairs creak, and all chatter comes to an abrupt halt as the teacher speaks. Loafers squeak, more piercing than chalk on a chalkboard, decorating the tile floor with a jumbled collection of streaks and dots of black and white. The chalkboards seem to envelope the entire room because as the blank wall color mirrors the dull hue of the blackboard. It seems that this classroom was designed to prevent distraction. If you were to avert your gaze from the furious scribbling of the chalk, the only thing you could look at would be the corners of the room, shiny and black and crisp like a motorcycle. It's like being in an immaculately clean microwave. Desks line the floor, too small and too angular, as if they were made for tiny robots and not college students.

Creating Dialogue - a draft

by Rachel Maginnis

My parents had told me the story of their work in the rainforest many years ago, but I often thought of it and marveled at the fact that my parents, the CEOs of a large fashion company in New York City, were once naturalists fighting to help save the rainforest. Of course, they didn't like to talk about it anymore and refused to answer any questions I had about their lives before I was born. In desperation, I once asked my older sister, Olivia, if she remembered anything from when she lived in Peru, even though she was very young at the time and only lived there for a year and a half.

"Oh, pu-leeze, Veronica!" she exclaimed when I asked her. "I was three. How am I supposed to remember? Why do you care so much about the rainforest anyway? It's sooo boring." Suddenly, her expression brightened. "I'm going to look online for some heels to match my new dress," she said.

I frowned slightly. My sister had given me just as much information as I thought she would, but I couldn't help being slightly disappointed. Looking at rainforest pictures on the Internet, I tried to imagine the magical feeling of tropical air, warm rainstorms, and thousands of interesting plants and animals to study. I sighed sadly and shut off my computer.

Olivia was sitting at her computer desk, shopping online.

"Please?" I begged. "You must remember something." She ignored me. I tried a different approach. "You are completely urbanized!" I yelled. But she seemed to take this as a compliment as she surfed the Web for designer shoes.

"You know, Veronica," she said, "if you weren't so interested in all this stupid rainforest business, you might actually be able to enjoy the city. I mean, look around. We have an amazing house, and we can buy whatever we want. Not a lot of people who live near the rain forest can do that. Now leave me alone so I can decide between emerald green and zinnia pink Jimmy Choos."

She bought both.

Selected Longer Piece...

Ruby-Quartz Glasses

by Andrew Roiter

He never noticed before how loud the clock was, counting away the seconds. "Tick, tock, tick, tock," he mocked quietly. He marveled at how the colors, which once seemed so benign and unimportant, now glared malevolently: the white, now ivory, from the tusks of a ravenous beast, its black forming the obsidian eyes of the monster that stalked him; the whole creature was coated, reminiscent of crimson plasma.

He closed his eyes and slowed his breathing. It was vital that he control his appearance; couldn't let anyone get suspicious; he had enough problems as it was.

Upon opening his eyes he took a cursory glance. Left: two girls were far too stuck in their own conversation about last night's reality program on FOX or something, so much so that the teacher couldn't even break their attention away from each other, no matter how much he pleaded.

He looked right. He stopped. His veins felt like ice. It pained him to use the cliché, but there was no other way to describe the feeling, frozen shards being pumped through his entire body. There was a girl with red hair hunched over her desk staring at him dumbfounded, one eyebrow raised higher than the other. He struggled to recover her name so that he could tell her off. The name was uncommon, but it wasn't extremely rare or obscure, and still it didn't come to him.

Screw it! he thought. He would just have to wing it. "Can I help you?" he asked nonchalantly.

Her face grew concerned; it was kind of comforting to him. "No, you were just fidgeting a lot; I was wondering if you were okay."

Now that was genuinely pleasant to hear. It made the knot in his brain loosen just a little bit.

Karen! That was her name, he thought. He kept that to himself, though, as not to let her know that he had ever lost it. "Well, thanks, but I'm fine," he whispered back. He turned his head back to the front of the classroom, not that he was paying any attention, but he didn't want any more attention from Karen. She was pretty and seemed nice enough, but there were more important things that needed his attention, like that goddamn clock for instance. How the ticking frustrated him.

There was no reason for him to get this riled up so he decided to transciate. It was a nonsense word that he used to describe a self-applied hypnosis that he had developed. The semi-trance would put his body on autopilot, for taking notes or something. It left his mind free for important matters. He had often remarked to others that it was also a cure-all for physical dependencies, but it had become increasingly difficult to defend what so many of his "peers"—he used the term loosely—considered to be a madman's snake oil psychology.

The school bell rang signifying the transition from one class to another. This roused him from his trance. He moved to the door to go to his next class: French. It was on the other side of the school, so he had to hurry, but he stopped when he felt a tap on his back. He turned around. It was Karen.

"Hey!" she said.

Compelled not to ignore her, he met her gaze and responded, "'Sup?" Strange, that was a much more casual response than he had initially prepared. What was it about this girl that put him at ease?

She pushed a few strands of hair out of her face.

She would, he thought.

"The teacher said that your name was Hank Boggle, but the other guys, they all call you Piter."

He wanted to roll his eyes but he thought better of it. The nickname was given to him in eighth grade by the members of the Sci-Fi Club when he explained the concept of transciation; he had then called it "meditainment." It was the name of a character in the book *Dune*, by Frank Herbert. The character was a "mentat," a human computer. He started to explain it to her.

"Oh, it's just some stupid nickname from—"

She interrupted him. God how he hated that. "Like from *Dune*?" She excitedly reached into her purse and retrieved a worn and beaten copy of the novel. He could barely make out the name Frank Herbert on it. "So tell me, is it Hank or Piter?"

He smiled a little and bounced his head slowly from side to side. "Piter's fine."

Karen smiled big—her teeth were perfect and as white as the board Piter had pressed his back up against. He hated how she made him think in clichés.

"Oooh, a bad guy ... I kinda like that, Piter." She bit her lower lip. His eyes snapped open and he blinked over and over. She released her lip. "Hey, it's last period. I've just got a study hall. So you wanna ditch?"

Piter couldn't even remember why he was supposed to be panicking. He was captivated by the vixen. "Yeah, sure, one second." He glanced around and picked the Harrison brothers walking by out of the mass of commuting students. Team Hari-san, as they called themselves, was an amateur video game team made up of Lock, Load, and Headshot. Headshot was the oldest. After years of going by Fire, he adopted the new moniker when he was declared the school's top *Halo* sniper a year earlier. Lock was the youngest and by far the weakest of the team, but Load was the one Piter was after. He grabbed him by the arm and pulled him into the room. "Hey, Load, what do you guys got next?"

Load squirmed at the notion of Piter's impending request, despite the seemingly innocent nature of the question. "I got gym, Lock has French, and Fire has A-plus certification."

Headshot leered at Load for using his old handle.

Piter released Load and turned his attention to Lock. "Do me a favor, tell the Madame that I'm at the nurse. Should she try to check on that, come up with something better."

Lock nodded at Piter. "No prob, Piter."

"Great," said Piter as he turned to Karen. "Okay, let's go."

Piter and Karen were sitting with their backs against the outside wall of the 24-Mart, the generic connivance store that did business in their town. Piter was rummaging through the pockets of his sweatshirt pulling out bits of paper and refuse until he found a beaten up cigarette carton. He flipped open the top and grimaced at the single cigarette in the package. He gestured to her with the pack.

"Smoke?"

She placed her hand over her heart and overtly feigned gratitude. "Oh, be still my beating heart. Doth the gentleman offer me his last tar-filled cylinder?"

"That *Romeo and Juliet*?" he asked factiously.

She scoffed, "Shakespeare would've thought it was funny. But, no thanks, I don't smoke." She paused. "Why do you?"

"I don't have to," he said quickly.

Karen sighed. "Oh, come on, I've dated a dozen guys who smoked, and they all said the—"

"You've dated a dozen guys?" he interrupted.

"Fine, exaggerating, but they all say that exact same crap," she chided.

"No, seriously, I've come up with this thing I call transciation. It's like—"

She smiled coyly. "Uh, is it anything like meditainment?"

He paused, contemplating, but continued to light his cigarette. "You're not Karen, are you?"

Her smile was wicked now. "Karen is my sister."

Piter sighed a gray cloud. "Oh ... I remember. You were the only girl in the Sci-Fi Club ... Rose."

She kicked her feet a little. "Well, I'm going by Thorn now, but yeah, it's me."

He laughed. "Wow, did you get hot."

"Ummm, I can't tell if I should be insulted or—"

"Consider it a compliment, and just that."

She grinned, and her eyes lit up like gorgeous starlight. It frustrated him to no end whenever one of the clichés popped into his head.

"I guess the same could be said about you then," she said, laughing, "but it's good to talk to you again, though." She continued, "I've been trying to work up the courage to say something to you, see if you were still cool."

Piter was silent.

"Here, I'll explain what I mean." She shifted her body to face him. "For the first fourteen years of our lives we were sheltered nerds, and now we've emerged from our black silk cocoons as beautiful hell-scarred butterflies."

He furrowed his brow. "I thought butterflies came from chrysalises, not cocoons?"

"Still a nerd!" she scolded jokingly.

Piter shrugged. "Still a good line, I guess."

"Ya think? Well, I'll try to work it into a story or a poem somewhere."

"You write?" asked Piter.

"Hey, I'm a cynical, fire-haired neo-geek. Of course I write." She stood up. "Which basically means I'm a geek who wears techno-goggles." Laughing, she reached into her purse and pulled out two pairs of goggles. "Here, try 'em on."

He put them on his head, but not over his eyes. He stood up to look at his reflection in a store window, deciding to kill two birds with one stone. He pulled back his top lip to see if his teeth were clean, "Not bad at all." He turned around and leaned against the wall, sliding down it so that he was back in his original position.

She copied his actions, leaning against the wall and sliding down next to him, much closer than before. "You smell like smoke."

"Sorry."

"No, no, it's okay, I'm used to it."

Both of them sounded sullen.

"That's a little depressing," he said.

She shrugged and then looked at him. "You ready to tell me the truth?"

He looked at her; she was staring into space, her head resting on his shoulder. "What truth?"

She lifted up her head and looked at him. "Well, I figured since we've had this heart to heart, you could explain why you were so damn fidgety in math."

He sighed. "I'm surprised you haven't heard yet. I thought all the rest of the school was talking about it."

She furrowed her brow. "I don't listen to what the rest of the school is saying." She gave him a small punch on the arm. "So tell me already!"

"Fine, fine. Ya know that football player who got killed, ummm, Chad Abrams."

"Oh right, The Tank." She made quotation marks with her fingers when she said it.

"Yeah, well the cops seem to think that I had something to do with it."

She shouted, "Why do they think that?"

He shrugged, "Uh, dunno, something about 'bad blood' between us."

Never able to stay focused, Thorn said, "Well, that's a little cliché, bad blood between the jock and the geek."

Piter laughed. "Nah, I sorta stole his girlfriend. We broke up when she graduated, but he still … he held a bit of a grudge." He stopped laughing.

"That's something different."

The pair looked up. Their sunlight was cut off by a pair of ominous silhouettes. "Hank Boggle?" a featureless creature asked.

Piter shielded his eyes to better see the officers. They weren't the detectives that had visited him earlier that day. These guys were definitely full-blown cops

"Yeah?"

"We need to talk to you down at the station," the other officer said.

Piter stood up and brushed the back of his pants. "Okay, okay, see ya later Rose, but thanks. I needed this."

As they walked to the cruiser, their voices faded from Thorn's ears and all she could decipher was Piter asking one of the officers, "Either of you guys got a smoke? I think I really need one this time."

Settings and Characters ...

After working with their senses and
creating vivid settings,
students worked on developing characters
and then
fitting them – the settings (time, place, and mood)
and the characters – together.

The results are impressive.
Don't you think?

The Tea Room

by Rachel Liu

The Tearoom was always smoky with steam and burnt toast smoke. It was the one place on the entire city campus devoid of a set, die-hard purpose. The Tearoom. It sounded like a place for old ladies, but only the students visited there. (The professors had their own homes and lounges.) On a rare day, a student could make and sip a light breakfast of tea and toast with, maybe, a romance novel—a refreshing change from the usual egg and cheese McMuffin or cereal bar drowned in coffee and chemistry notes.

Ali had visited the campus in the summer of her junior year. Back in the summer, the hallways were empty and the surrounding city was, Ali now realized, peacefully deserted, its many occupants at some beach or foreign shore. The one thing that attracted Ali the most was the big, burnished bronze church bell slightly to the right of campus. But now, people swarmed the streets in cars and bikes. The once-impressive bell no longer shook the ground and hallways with musical splendor but nagged meekly, cast into shadow by the chaotic city around it. Now, the bronze knobs of The Tearoom were all that gleamed in Ali's eyes.

The Tearoom today was busier than usual but still not busy at all. A couple of the professors were out sick, so those who really cared retreated to The Tearoom while the others disappeared into various restaurants, bars, and malls around the city.

Ali sipped her orange herb tea and pulled at a page and flipped it. She always read romance novels, the books with the muscular, dark-haired man supporting the spineless damsel on the cover. The man always wore a shirt, unbuttoned, so it served no practical protection against the harsh wind, and he always had gleaming eyes matching the stormy sea behind him. He probably had a British accent.

Ali considered the romance novel to be, biologically, the most natural book for *Homo sapiens* to read. If anyone were placed in a room alone with a choice of a book of any genre, everyone would choose the romance novel. Human nature.

"Excuse me," a voice, reverberating in the caverns of Ali's right ear, interrupted. Reluctantly tearing her eyes from her book, Ali attempted to trace the source. A couple of pieces of blackened toast were shoved under her nose.

"Your toast burnt."

Ali could smell the burnt toast now, the bitter smell tickling her eyes.

"I ... yeah, thanks." Setting her tea down and switching hands holding the book, she reluctantly accepted the charred toast. Unsure of what to do with the blackened objects, Ali attempted to nibble at the toast, eyes watering as the bitterness flooded through her head.

"Burnt toast doesn't taste good," the voice remarked.

"No, it doesn't." Ali fought the urge to spit out the scratch leftover crumbs stuck to her tongue and roof of her mouth.

"You've never burnt your toast before."

Ali blinked once and finally raised her eyes to study the specimen before her. First, she saw medium-sized eyes, like stretched hexagons. Brown. His hair curled rebelliously at the ends. He wasn't plump, but he wasn't sapling-pine tree skinny either.

She imagined them six months later, in love, by a river lit by twilight. He would say that he only went to The Tearoom because he'd seen a beautiful girl there and couldn't stay away. She imagined them a little later, either married or broken up, and she'd find out that it had been an accident and he'd been as lonely as she was and they'd been opportunists—victims of life.

55

Blinking, she glanced up again. "I guess you come here often."

He laughed and took the seat next to her.

Opportunist, Ali thought furiously. Victim of life.

"What major are you?" he asked.

Ali let out a disappointed stream of air. Majors were just another label. Ali hated labels.

"Sociology," she muttered, sliding the book up by her nose.

"Nice."

"You?" Ali added, hating her uncontrollable politeness.

"French history. But I'm pre-med."

Nodding lightly, Ali attempted to immerse herself in the story once more. After reading the sentence where the protagonist launched into a lengthy description of his love interest's cinnamon red hair blowing in the sea breeze a half dozen times, Ali decided that her preoccupation with something outside of the book was too obvious. Hoping to better feign her interest in the book, she flipped the page.

"Is that a good book?"

Ali nodded.

"What book is it?"

Ali's fingertips and toes suddenly froze.

"It's a … just something someone … it's called…" Her voice dying away into murmurs in the back of her throat, Ali wordlessly flipped the cover of the novel, flashing a quick view of the muscley man and the spineless damsel and the stormy sky and the French script title: *Beneath the Stars*.

All Ali saw was a twitch of his mouth before she lost her ability to look up. She must look so desperate right now.

"That looks interesting."

Ali could taste the laughter in his voice.

"Well, what are you reading?" Ali retorted, surprised by the aggression in her voice. Though her words pointed to him, she kept her eyes down. She didn't need to check if he'd brought a book with him; books in The Tearoom were a given.

"*Sous la Lune.*"

The coral mirth in his voice made Ali look up angrily. To her surprise, she found his eyes completely devoid of mockery. Instead, they gleamed like burnished bronze in the sun.

"It's French," he explained, showing her the cover. "I'm reading the French version. It's French for 'Beneath the Moon.'"

"I didn't know there was a sequ …"

Suddenly she was laughing, the sound shaking the ground and hallways with musical splendor.

The Ocean and Being in West Dennis
by Lydia Burrage-Goodwin

West Dennis is peaceful. Every day I wake up in the morning to the sounds of birds, not cars and beeping horns, like in Weston. When I take the three-wheel bike out and ride the quiet streets around the block and down the driveway, nothing is there to stop me or chase me away. Nothing. There are no cars or trucks or angry commuters swearing at me to get out of the road. I know that road blindfolded, the bumps, the turns, when to peer around the hedges to look for cars, or when to watch out for Mr. Pickering or Mr. Daigle, the crabby old neighbors. On the way to the store, I ride up and down hills and pass the pond, the playground, and the school, joyously twisting and turning my way through the cemetery, weaving between headstones like an obstacle course, and on to the post office. The wind, the speed, I feel like I am flying, as if I will never stop. As I pass the pond coming home, the sun shines on the ripples of water; it shines on my face. I arrive home and park my bike between two evergreen trees, which we planted for privacy, to keep the neighbors from peeking in as we walk, wrapped only in a towel, from the outdoor shower to the house. The trees also provide privacy so we can enjoy the morning sun in our PJs.

I get off my bike and push the evergreen branches away, clearing a path, and wiping the sap on my pants. To my dismay, the sap sticks to both my pants and my hands. No matter how hard I try to scrub it off, the sap sticks. It feels uncomfortable; the dull white paste remains all day on my hands and in my nose. It smells of maple syrup and pine needles after they have fallen off the tree. I decide to retreat to the barn, defeated by sap and let down by the Ajax that supposedly takes grease off anything.

The barn is a mess, especially today. There are toolboxes everywhere, linens strewn across the table, and bicycles parked in various ways, both lying on the ground and leaning up against chairs and against the couch. I search for something to do, something that sparks an interest, but as I scan the floor, nothing inspires me. I decide to do something lazy—go back inside and sit on the sofa. But as I walk into the kitchen, I learn that it's time to go to my grandparents' house.

My grandparents' live less than a mile away, on Bass River. The river is so peaceful and yet full of energy as boats pass playing their music, people partying on deck and having fun. The names of the boats are interesting to look at: The *Sea Star*, *Pop Aye*, *Crest* (named by a dentist who owns the boat), names with character that tell a story. In contrast, the boats my grandparents have are not massive or even operable. They have a small aluminum boat with three leaks in the bottom and holes in the sides where the seats use to be. Their other boat is blue vinyl with no motor, and its only purpose nowadays is to offer protection from beach erosion. I use the boats to pretend I am sailing down the river. The knobs, switches, and other such contraptions long ago fell off the boat or broke apart, but I still imagine that I am using them to navigate.

My brother dreams of fixing up these boats and really taking them out on the water. His other dream is to annoy my parents until he gets some support on this. Somehow I don't believe it is ever going to happen.

Every time we arrive at my grandparent's house, Grandma is always running around, making sure we don't have sand on our feet or shoes, or in the kitchen making one of her famous tuna sandwiches. Grandpa is either in the living room watching a Red Sox game or watching a murder mystery, like *Murder She Wrote*, or outdoors watering Grandma's hydrangeas.

From the Rooftop

by Seth Gable

Thymothy stood on the roof of the apartment building. He looked over the city, feeling the wind hit him in what seemed to be a desperate attempt to tear him from the rooftop, but Thym knew that nothing as trivial as the wind could harm him. This building had originally housed large numbers of people who came to the city for extended periods of time and needed a cheap place to stay, but Thym had purchased it for other reasons, which he had refused to tell anyone about, but one was that he wanted to have a clear view of the city from the building's roof.

The first step in Thym's grand plan for himself and his followers was complete. The second step was visible in the constant stream of workers going in and out of the building.

Across the street from the apartment building, Joshua Trenton was arriving home from a morning working at Billy's, a local breakfast restaurant. As he stepped out of his vehicle, he heard crickets chirping and leaves rustling in the breeze; he could smell the freshly cut grass of his lawn and see its beautiful green color, a green that one might expect to see in someone's front lawn. Then, as his car went to park itself, he heard something he did not expect to hear, the droning of various power tools, accompanied by the sound of many people talking at once.

A Christmas Miracle
by Wisima "Sam" Nipatnantaporn

From under my warm blanket I can feel a cold and soothing breeze rush into my room. I get up and look outside my window to find a fresh layer of snow on a wonderful Christmas morning. It's about 6 a.m. and I cannot sleep. I put on my slippers and try to walk down the hallway slowly and quietly. I try not to disturb any of my family members, who are still sound asleep. You would imagine my six-year-old brother already being awake and tearing apart his presents, but no, he is still in bed. I try to tip-toe quietly into the living room, but I fail. I have to run! I stare in awe as I see dozens and dozens of presents under our beautifully decorated Christmas tree. I walk over to our fireplace and start a fire. While the fire is going, I sit and watch the flames and think about each and every present. Every Christmas I get what I want, but I never get what I wish for. It's a whole different concept, want and wish. Want is to must have it. Wish is to have a miracle. My miracle is to be able to speak again. When I was younger, I was in a car crash on Christmas Day. I lost my voice. Now that I am twelve, I still do not have my voice back. The doctor says only time will cure it, but I think a miracle can. I wait and wait until my family comes downstairs. I can hear my brother's footsteps, and then he appears in the doorway.

"Presents!" he screams and he rushes over to the colorfully wrapped gifts. He looks over at me while holding a present in his arms. "This one is for you, Sarah! Me, Mommy, and Daddy got it for you!" He runs over to me and places the present in my lap. I carefully open it. Inside is a wrapped glass angel the size of a fist. It is small but elegant. I hug my brother and smile. He nods and runs back to the tree. While he is opening the rest of his presents — a toy racecar, a model airplane, and all the basic toys for a six-year-old— I look at my angel. Twirling it in my hands, looking at every detail, the gold wings and halo, I like her eyes the most. Her eyes seem as if they are real, looking right into my soul. It isn't a creepy feeling that I have in me but a warm feeling. I have a feeling of hope. This angel seems as if it holds many secrets, that it holds some kind of magical power. Maybe it even holds a miracle. I'm foolish to think so; no mere glass angel can bring my voice back. I place the angel on the coffee table and walk over to the rest of my presents. I begin to feel an odd presence behind me and turn around slowly; the angel is still there and doesn't seem to have moved. For the rest of the Christmas Day, my family and I spend it the way we usually do, as happily as every year. As night comes near, my family and I begin to go to bed. I look over to the table beside my bed; my angel is placed near my lamp. I pick it up and wish. I wish that my voice returns.

From under my warm blanket I can hear my alarm go off. It's 7 a.m. and I have to go to go to work with my mother. It's Bring Your Child to Work Day. My brother is knocking on my door; I slowly drag my feet over to the door and open it while I rub my eyes. When I open my eyes, my brother is wearing a scary mask and I scream.

"Sarah? SARAH! You screamed! Say something!"

"S-S-something!" I stare at my brother, no expression on my face to describe how I feel.

"Say it again!"

"Something! I can speak!" My brother takes my hands and we jump around in circles.

"Sarah can speak, Sarah can speak!" my brother chants.

My parents walk out of their room and stare at us as if we are crazy." What are you two doing?"

"MOM!" I scream with tears in my eyes.

"Sarah," my parents say in unison as their voices drift. My brother and I run over to our parents and they give us both big hugs and don't let go. The whole family is happy once again. It's a late Christmas present, but it is still the best. I look over to my open room and over at my bedside table. The angel is gone.

The angel, after all, was a miracle. There is always an angel watching over you to help you out when you need it and to give you a miracle.

Happy Holidays.

Fierce Metal Teeth

by Niki Bousquet

On Saturday, we were sitting in the dark under that blanket with the fierce metal teeth, listening to ourselves breathing and shivering like elves at the North Pole. It was cold. It's not a good idea to go swimming at night when it's only sixty degrees, even though it's August, although it might have been worth it if we had been snorkeling, with a coral reef and horses of the sea to keep us company. We were listening to Wolf Parade — the band, not a procession of canine-like mammals — which has the same vocal chord manipulator as Sunset Rubdown, although I like Sunset Rubdown more, while you prefer Wolf Parade. You say Wolf Parade is sludgy, like noise rock, which makes me think of slushy, muddy melted snow that has been mixed with soil in a blender, and Sunset Rubdown is too Indie rock.

Talking isn't always necessary. Sometimes, in the dark, feelings are better than words. This day was different. That's not an accurate description, but there is no point in even trying to get it right. I was so happy, like a little kid organizing crayons by color and shade, despite the pain in my shoulder from tripping while playing hide-and-seek in the dark. And, my stomach was complaining like a kid whose organized crayons got mixed up, complaining from the pizza that we ate standing up outside, next to the broken saucer with no water, water that is intended for aviary creatures that she picked up and hid behind.

The woods behind those trees was a good hiding place, but not from spiders. They didn't find us for a long time. She was creepy, hiding under that protective piece of aquamarine plastic, not saying anything. We heard the rustling, but we couldn't see her, although I'm sure she could see us. It was like the *Blair Witch Project*, but not terribly terrifying because my friend was the monster and I don't think she would harm me beyond startling me, or at least starting to before I startled her, and making me scream, but not for ice cream, which would hurt because I just had four quite wise calcium formations extracted from my jaw and I can't open my mouth too wide.

The woods in the dark are a scary place, but that day they were safe and warm, even though my thirty-two chewing shoes were chattering so quickly that I could feel the vibrations of an earthquake through my entire body.

Another Selected Longer Piece ...

Letters Home

by Miranda Burrage-Goodwin

Dear Dad,

The truth is that college is too hard for me to handle. Back home with you, I was able to worm my way out of any situation. I was so smart that I didn't need to study. I never developed good study habits, so now when I really need them, I am at a loss. I never was very popular, but at least I had people who appreciated me and valued my opinion. At college, so far this semester, my head has been flushed in the toilet twenty-seven times by the seniors. I have no friends and I've felt like a nobody for too long. So I'm dropping out. I'm on my way to Woodstock, the Hippie Capital of America. It's the sixties, and I want to be a singer like Bob Dylan (only better). I feel like I have tried hard enough, but every time I try, someone puts up a roadblock harder than the one before it. It's like someone doesn't want me to succeed. I've tried too long and it's time for me to say good-bye, Dad.

Sincerely,

Your son, Rainbow

P.S.
I will keep in touch

* * *

Dear Christopher William Stevenson III,

I'm sorry to have to drag you back down to reality so hard, but if you must know, you ARE a bit conceited, and maybe you just need to appreciate other people so people appreciate you. As far as being "flushed down the toilet by the seniors twenty-seven times," this is a bit extreme. Son, you have got to stop your imagination from running wild like that. Like you said, it's the sixties, not the dark ages. People are not running around giving people swirlies like there's no tomorrow.

About the singer bit: We told you we wanted you to become a doctor, maybe even a rocket scientist. Look where Bob Dylan got himself. He sings as if he is asleep. Why didn't you ever tell us you wanted to be a singer? You always said you wanted to be a scholar. But this is the least of my worries. "The Hippie Capital of America?" We raised you in a good, loving, affluent Christian family, and now you decide you want to be a tree-hugging dirt worshipper? What kind of a son are you? News of this has leaked out at work, and I am in big trouble, and all you want to do is hitchhike to Woodstock? I am sorry, but don't ever let me see you call yourself Rainbow again.

Your father

P.S. The Stevensons have always prided themselves on their loyalty to tradition. The fine men at the country club reminded me of that today. You are putting us all on the road to destruction. Every man in the Stevenson family has gone to college, made a steady and noble career for himself, gotten married, had children, and continued that tradition. I am warning you now before it is too late. I hope you will have a change of heart.

P.P.S. Your mother is very upset. She thinks you are being unruly.

* * *

Dad,

It's too late now, what's done is done. I already have a job as the lead singer for a ho-dunk band in D.C. I have attended some peace protests, and I have played at one or two of them. I am going on tour, so don't write for a while.

For your information, I have met Joan Baez. You probably don't even know who she is, but she is a great singer and activist. And I camped out on the green of the Washington Monument. Don't worry. I have to sleep somewhere, and I'm with my band and groupies, so I'll be ok.

And Mom, you shouldn't be worried. The girls here spoil me as well (if not better) than you do. I am having a good life for myself, and I am making enough money to live on. Don't worry, I'm perfectly fine.

And Dad, since you never wanted me to call myself Rainbow again...

Sincerely,

Sunshine

P.S. Peace out
and spread the love!

Prompted by Bonnie Neubauer ...

Guest author Bonnie Neubauer came to our class
and shared her Story Spinner ideas,
giving the students an opening line
and
some words to include in their composition.

The results were really exciting; here is an example.
The words students were asked to use appear in **bold.**

Aliens

by Ashleigh McEvoy

The spaceship landed in a strange place. In the corner sat a weird raised rectangle with other smaller rectangles at the top and a blanket laid across two giants, who appeared to be sleeping.

"What's that?" I whispered to our translator, Akin.

"It appears to be a ... **king-sized bed**," he replied after a moment's hesitation.

I didn't have time to ponder this, as my eyes had just fallen upon a long black hat-thing hanging from the bedpost.

"I believe that's a **habit**, the headdress of a nun, one of their spiritual leaders," Akin whispered, noticing my stare.

I flicked the so-called habit and it fell. It was simply a black sheet.

"A **fake** habit!" I announced.

I was immediately hushed, but not before one of the sleeping giants had begun to stir, groaning and turning in his sleep.

"Perhaps he is having a **nightmare**?" Akin asked himself.

In a corner sat the remainders of what seemed to be a puppet show. Hats, scarves, and several other **dress-up** items had been dumped besides plastic creatures, almost aliens, like us, but **bare** and primitive looking.

"What *are* those?" I hissed.

"Children's playthings in the shape of ... dinosaurs. That one is a **pterodactyl**," Akin said, pointing. He then turned me away and motioned toward the door.

Just then, one of the giants began to awaken, rubbing his eyes and yawning. In our haste, I tripped and **belly-flopped** out the door.

We hurried down the stairs, unsure of whether or not the giant had seen us but glad to escape that **claustrophobic** room. Stopping in what Akin called the kitchen, we split up to analyze the different contraptions and select samples to bring back to Upshooyon.

I followed my comrades' lead and hurried over to a wooden table, where I began to take measurements. Harrel tested out the "oven," producing a **heat-wave** at the touch of a simple button, while Jamka turned on the "stove," which created blue and orange **sparks**.

After an hour's work, we had collected a piece of "firewood," eating utensils called "knives, forks, and spoons," and coupons to "stores," including Target, Apple, and **Juicy** Couture, along with detailed descriptions of the "oven," "refrigerator," "sink," and "stove." Running back to the bedroom, we departed for Upshooyon, where we would drop off our samples, refuel the spaceship, and set off to investigate "Antarctica."

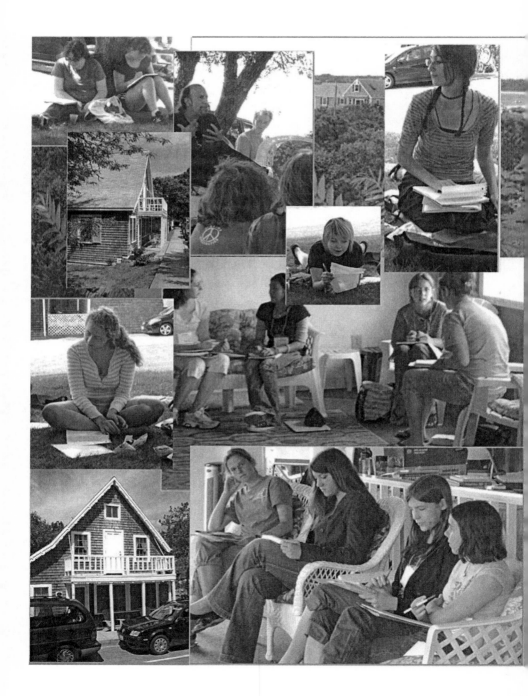

One More Selected Longer Piece...

Time Machines Don't Work

by Niki Bousquet

Some things just don't make any sense when you think about them later. You just cannot comprehend how you once could have been such a different person. Sometimes you hate that person, like a rotten banana peel that falls out of your locker from last month's lunch, back to slap you in the face with its repulsive, mushy, aged bits of stringy, pale yellow memory. Sometimes you envy that person who once slept with her head on your pillow, drooling because of her retainer and leaving stains on the scratchy case like water splattered on ink. You wish you were as happy as she was, with her blind trust, ignorance, and doe-like quality of wide-eyed, peach-cheeked, freckled optimism. With long, soft clean feather dusters of lashes acting as an aegis, protecting his or her tiny, so-gleeful-it's-nauseating, form from all harm. But you never love that person, and if you say you do, you're probably lying. Because that person is you, and very few people have the capacity to tolerate everyone around them, let alone themselves.

I'm jealous of the person I used to be, to such an extent that I feel I must have green Jell-O oozing from all my ear piercings, like pus. The biggest mistake I made as a kid was forgotten like a faded rainbow after the rain gets dehydrated and goes to drink some Gatorade and the sun dies like a fizzling light bulb, going to sleep in the soil beneath the plants it feeds. I couldn't have been older than seven, because I recall pulling a white, maroon, and pine-tree green Osh Kosh B'Gosh sweatshirt over my ears that morning. I wish I could have that rainbow back.

When I woke up in the morning, I could smell summer's metallic oily lawnmower and just-cut grass scent seeping into my perceptive nasal cavities. This season wasn't bad, but I preferred the fall's crisp, thin slices of cucumber air, which made my eyes water like an ice cube that has just begun to melt. I knew Deanna would be there today, in the compartment of our dwelling – conveniently located maybe fifty to one hundred feet from the wall of my bedroom – my eyes were drilling through it right then. I leapt from my sheets, because I was a youngster, baby chicken who knows the horrors of a short life confined to a cramped cage, with fractured wings, and stunted bones, before becoming part of the protein section of the food pyramid. That meant no extra sleep was necessary; no wishing it were some other day, time, or place.

Deanna visited her parents, who might be grand, at their house behind me every summer, and on selected holidays and weekends. She had lived through two or three more years than I had, so of course she intimidated me, and I wanted to be exactly like her, in spite of the not-quite-as-friendly-as-a-fluffy-bunny things she did to me. I coveted her Hershey's special dark chocolate curly hair that landed on the blade-like bones that ornamented her upper back, when it wasn't scrunchied into the tail of a miniature equine creature, that is. I remember her skin, that epidermal covering, like chewy caramel candies that got trapped in the braces I would later be fitted with. I would wait for her visits from Dedham or Sharon, or it could have been anywhere really, because anywhere would seem more exotic than Sandwich, to watch her draw sophisticated French women lounging under parasols in one-piece vermillion swimsuits. I remember the tone and texture of her voice. We would record ourselves singing Backstreet Boys songs, and I would become a red apple at my uncontrolled squeak next to her melodies, which seemed at the time, but likely were not, to be milky French coffee, operatic and smooth. I now have a profound distaste for her name, but at a younger age I even thought it was wonderful — so much more sophisticated than mine, Niki, which was meant for a baby or a kitten.

After eating breakfast, which I rarely have, which I guess is odd for a kid, I bounded out the back screen door of my slider. The thin netted metal was speckled with little pet doors for moths and fireflies, who I sometimes saw mating. The summer heat was actually buzzing, with grasshoppers kicking me in the nose and lawnmowers moaning. I leaped from the cracked concrete slab and wooden railings of my back deck, danced on tiptoes across the grass that sparsely grew in the sandy Cape Cod soil, and darted through the barely detectable path that ran through the thin strip of woods to Maya, Deanna's grandmother and her house. It was a single-level Cape, maybe a little less voluminous than mine was. Like little kids are, I was content right then, not knowing what will happen next; yet, also, because I was a kid, I believed this happiness to be boredom.

After my knuckles made contact with the hardness of the door, the back door — I never used the front — Maya responded to the sound I had created.

"Please don't play the keyboard unless you've learned how. Your ungraceful fingertip pads could fracture the plastic keys, breaking them into bits."

I'm sure she didn't exactly say that; the truth is there are few things I can exactly recall her saying. Maya, who was born in Russia, along with Deanna's grandfather, who I basically have no memory of, always made me feel a little out of place. She certainly was very avid about the health of the electronic piano that Deanna could manipulate beautifully.

Deanna was in the living room, legs curled under her on an old brown sofa, with another drawing that probably wasn't as gorgeous as it seemed. I once traced stencils of dinosaurs and told her I drew them myself. She didn't buy my fib. I didn't know then that sometime around fifth grade, the art flower on the right side of my brain would bloom and I would no longer feel belittled by sketches like Deanna's.

"Hey," she spoke to me, ignoring her younger brother Sam. We mostly disregarded him as a pesky little child, although I believe I had only a year on him, possibly two. Deanna once told me, as if it were some great secret, that at five, Sam still wore diapers. Our friendship was basically based on lies, and this was probably not completely truthful either.

Soon Deanna and I tired of the stale old smell of an elderly person's house, something like mothballs, rotten plastic, and weeks-old cookies with strange prune filling. Seriously, I bet plastic can rot when it's that old.

"We should walk down Somerset."

This wasn't an uncommon suggestion for Deanna, but something lurked in her voice, like a razorblade in a Halloween candy.

"Should we ride our bikes?"

"No."

I was wondering why she said no. We always rode our bikes down her street. Not that it was much of a ride. It was a dead end, just like mine, just like this town.

"Why not?"

"You know that house near the end with the huge garden?"

"Yeah."

We can take some of her flowers."

"What if she sees?"

"We can tell her we're florists, Niki. They do it all the time."

We were always pretending to be things that seemed grown up to me. At that age, it's easy to get lost in make-believe and seriously think for an hour or two that you really are married and giving birth to a baby. Even if your husband is your best friend and the delivery room is her closet.

"Uh. Are you sure we're supposed to do that?" I knew florists didn't take their roses and gardenias from strangers' yards, but it's not like I could have undermined the authority of a ten- or eleven-year-old kid.

'Why would she plant them for them just to sit there? They need some exercise; we can take the tulips for a bike ride after."

"Ok, well, can we at least pay her for them or something?"

"Oh yeah. Of course. That's what florists do." It got past me that neither of us brought any money along.

So we left, out her front door. My nose ate the air as if it were oxygen deprived. It was so hungry to breathe something dangerous and grown up. Why had I always glorified what I was not, what I didn't have? And then sickened of it once I did have it?" It became sour milk on stale Cheerios, with green-fuzzed moldy strawberries. This was the only remotely dangerous or illegal thing I'd ever done. No candy bar stealing for me. Once we got up there, I didn't want to, but still felt like as if I had to. I didn't know; oh, that green Jell-O. I would later learn that if you feel forced into a situation like breasts into a bra that's too small, it's probably not the right size for you.

The yelling. That's all I can clearly recall. We were caught after so many trips back and forth, for so many of those colored blobs. I didn't understand why everyone thought they smelled so great. I don't know what the woman was yelling; I ran away so fast.

Deanna abandoned me, or I abandoned her. I don't know which, but I was at home alone for the rest of the day, trying not to be too obvious, feeling I had committed murder. I finally told my mom late at night.

"What's wrong, Niki, honey? You look like you're going to cry."

"I feel really bad."

"Why?"

"Deanna made me steal flowers from this garden on Somerset, and I didn't want to, but I felt like I had to, and we kept going back and taking more, and I don't even know why, and then this person came out and yelled at us. She was really mad, and I didn't even see her because I ran away, and I didn't even want to."

Who knows what my mom said after that. I was too caught up in the atrocity of my crime to pay attention to anyone else.

That night I couldn't sleep, so I counted sheep, staring up at them on the ceiling, until I fell asleep, but there was still one sheep left that I left uncounted when I fell asleep, and I felt he or she was disappointed in me

I felt better when I woke up the next morning.

* * *

A few years later, I was ten or eleven and the vacation from summer vacation I took with my mom and dad just happened to lead us to Georgia. There were dolphins there. We were staying in a hotel room, a nice one. We normally camped or stayed in Motel 6 that had the same inartistic floral pattern, whether it was in Canada or Florida, on all the thin bedspreads that wouldn't have kept out the winter. But this room had a view of the eighty-eight degree ocean, with its large, intelligent bluefish, from the slider door. I don't know why it was different this time. I was different too, and older, but it would still be at least a few months before reality set in.

We were outside by the pool; it was right in front of our door, which filled me with giddy euphoria at the time. And suddenly, there was Deanna, with Sam, her mom, and her dad. She was so much older, taller, and curvier, in a magenta sweet raspberry juice bikini. I was too shy to try to get her attention, even though I had just been playing in the pool with some kids with cool southern accents whom I had never even met before, so my mom called her name. I don't how she couldn't have heard; she was right there. It was definitely her. I knew. Maybe she forgot me. Maybe the wind carried my mom's call away from Deanna's ears, like a kid's lost kite, but things like that make you wonder if any of your life before the exact present moment happened at all. I didn't imagine it, but being able to entertain myself with daydreams for hours on end, I could have. My dad, and even my mom, didn't really think it was her.

They didn't believe me. How could they forget? Well they weren't forced by some preteen to become a criminal. My mom doesn't even remember the flowers.

I was still a kid. Deanna was not.

Poetic Dabblings ...

... by Prose Students

Although these students were in the
Prose Workshop, they were guided to explore
literary devices, figurative language, and poetic techniques
and then did some dabblings in the poetic genre.

Invisible Fear *from the prompt* "What do you fear?"
by Jessica Schiffman

The outcast girl
Walked around school
She was known for never being scared
But she had a secret
Her invisible fear

She was known as the girl without fear
But she had invisible fear
She always had fear hanging over her heart
Since the fire
That destroyed her home

Her parents
And everything she loved

The fire stole everything from her
So she hid her fear
So no one could see
How scared a person could really be

She was known as the girl without fear
But that was a lie.

Sixteen Thumbnails in Your Pupil

by Niki Bousquet

I want eyes
So
Much bigger than
My fingernails.
If my eyes
Were most of
My face,
Then maybe I would
Look forward
To something as small as a letter in the mail.
And I would only
Cry
If the girl with
The pink pick necklace
Left.
Because shiny glasses,
And
Guitar pick pendants,
And
Neon locks
Would be all I would need
To be happy.

Mind Forest

by Chris Chacon

As I wander aimlessly
Within this life,
          I

Will always remember
The day I became what I
          Am

The hour on the ticking
Clock watches, has me
          Trapped

Within its never-ending
Second, holding me
          In

And out of reality,
Like a painting,
          The

Artist able to manipulate
The image in his own twisted
          Mind

Seeing the turmoil
Within, lost in a
          Forest

Of chaos.

The Television in My Grandmother's Basement

Niki Bousquet

I've been told by a reliable source
That lots of people have faulty antennae.
So they have trouble picking up staring
The signal. And the hard fluffy fuzz inside
Their heads kicks out the feelings so sometimes
They feel like they are dead.
So maybe I'm not alone.

It's not comforting though, this snippet of
Psychology. I know the source
Meant it to be but it's more like invasive
Gynecology all the time in an
Environment like the source's, like mine. Kings
Just think they have a right to your
Secrets, to your insides.
I've been told by a reliable source.

Well this is one thing deserving to
Die in order to be
Dissected. It's not
Nature's. It's mechanical and metal and

Hard and cold. Some would say this
Phenomenon is slimy and akin to fungi. I say
Fungus is more noble, gentle. It comes from nature.
Lots of people have faulty antennae.

My feelers were donated by grasshoppers. They died of
Natural causes of course. But later the furry rods, not
Lightning rods, were struck by lightning held this guy's
Jeans pocket. That's where my cold sand-born
Glass originated.
So they have trouble picking up.

I'll try to get more in tough. I'll
Contemplate my
Guts, my ribs, my
Tailbone, esophagus that fears drain cleaner.
The signal. And the hard, fluffy fuzz inside.

And if you
Squeeze my hand really tight maybe I'll
Feel it. Use some
Teeth please. Sometimes, grip with all your might. So
Mine is just like theirs.
Their heads kick out the feelings sometimes.

Do
Pomegranates have
Feelings? I couldn't tell you. I'm not
Good with these things. Maybe my
Antennae have an iron
Deficiency.
They feel like they are dead.

I read about a girl. She was
Like me. On the
Intercom, too, I heard about her. The
Announcer had no
Compassion for her. She had
Dead flowers in her
Garden. She was me. She was all the
Bent antenna bugs. They thought we

Couldn't feel. Now they, we, have
Faulty feelers.
So maybe I'm not alone.

Dandelion Innocence

by Rachel Liu

With it, morning brings the sun

Bright, yellow petals pressed against the day,
filtering through the windows

With it, morning brings a kiss,
a hug
a laugh
a box of handmade chocolates
a vase
maybe a string
of freshwater pearls

With it, morning brings more than a memory,
but the feeling
of a small hand reaching around a bouquet of dandelions,
presented,
Tucked behind an ear
Embracing a neck, brushing a shoulder

I miss you though you're here,
A scratchy stem between my fingers
leaking bitter, milky sap,
bleeding

With it, dusk takes the sun,
And the gift

of dandelion innocence

Are Numbers Numb?

by Niki Bousquet

Could words be written with
Numbers? A story could; an
Equation is a problem and
Life has
Lots of those, and usually
Stories concern lives. Sometimes
Dead lives but even someone
Dead had problems once and
Problems are
Equations but it's harder to
Solve something real that's not on
Paper. You could put it on
Paper. The world's like
Numbers, but this method is not
Often effective. I have
Equations and problems. Sometimes I can
Solve the equations but never the
Problems. Albert Einstein had problems and
Equations. Surely he could solve the
Equations, but what about the problems? If
Equations done in your head help to
Ease you to sleep, what about the
Problems that keep you
Awake?

Ladder

by Sarah Martin

I am sitting on rung three with an
uncomfortable silence surrounding me.
    I look into myself, trying to remember what
happened that cold, winter day: but my brain is a
vast ocean.

    I shift down to rung two, and cup my face into
my worn hands, each crease telling a different story.
    The unsteady ladder sways as I descend toward
the hard ground.
    I fumble to grasp the thoughts swimming in my
head.
    I hold onto the rung above me to steady myself.

    I look around bewildered at a stray cat who is
wandering into the barn.
    I turn away and brush my dirty, stringy hair
from my face.
    I squeeze my eyes shut, hoping that when I open
them I will be in a pool of nothingness.
    I feel myself sliding down to rung one,
I can no longer clutch onto reality.
    I gladly accept the nothingness and shrivel to the ground.

    I cry.

Crying Without a Parachute

by Niki Bousquet

You numbed her
Tear ducts, her
Taste buds. She's an
Iceberg because of
You and being
Frozen hurts like being
Drilled with a
Cactus jackhammer.

She lives in a desert now, with
Parched sand and
Perverted columns of
Prickly plants. The ants
Crawl over her
Eyelids, her
Tear ducts. She doesn't
Feel their hairy feet because
You numbed her.

Thoughts are fractured, their bones
Disjointed, because she's so
Disconnected from everyone. No matter how
Close she gets, how
Far she stretches her
Fingers underneath their
Ribs, she can't touch them. She can't
Feel it when they touch her
Tear ducts, her.

You should be
Drowning in guilt like
Salt in
Sea foam. It should numb your
Taste buds, she's an Iceberg
because of
You.

When she drowned the
Titanic, she felt
Nothing. You froze the
Tears in a block when you
Stole them from her. How did you
Ever come across such a
Massive ice cube tray? To cage an, she's an
Iceberg, because of.

Being is nothing like it
Used to be when it
Used to be
Something more than
Nothing. She can't stand
You and being.

Icebergs must feel
Tortured and
Tormented all the time. As cold as
Red-hot
Knives. Being
Frozen hurts like being.

The letter V,
Capitalized, it's hard and
Cold and hurts like
Ice. You stuck her in a
Mold, molten hot. Now she
Cold, a letter V.
Drilled with a.

When you at last get the
Hell away. Maybe you'll
Cry without a parachute or
Fly. Maybe she can live as a
Rain puddle. Maybe she'll
Thaw, with a
Porthole drilled to let in
Warmth. Drilled with a
Cactus jackhammer.

85

My Greatest Fear *also from the prompt* "What do you fear?"
by Hannah Van Sciver

My greatest fear is that
Ten years from now, when I sit in a plush sofa chair
I will have forgotten this moment,
I won't remember what it's like to feel
Lost, afraid, excited, confused,
It will have been sifted, melted, compressed
Into a single pellet
And it will be labeled and classified
Into a phase,
Nothing more.

> I will forget the
> Mindlessness of it all
> The angst that once pumped through my veins
> That poured over my head like holy water

I'll forget what it's like to fall asleep in too-tight jeans
And a green-studded belt
Just to feel important,
I'll forget what it's like to compose sounds into words into a message
When I sorely need to study for a biology test

> I won't remember the dull ache that wrenched
> In my side
> The coldness
> The emptiness

I won't remember lying on the lawn in splendid stupor
And thinking that the things I was thinking were
Original
Profound, even.

> I'll forget how I once wondered at how I was the
> only one to think,
> Is this worth it?
> Will I not rust and evaporate?
> Will China conquer the world?
> What can I leave behind?

I'm afraid that I shall sit in my plush sofa-chair
And forget to question, to wonder
At the way it is shaped

        I am deathly afraid that I will recline my head
        Heave a sigh
        And be content
        To sleep through it all

Sea Saw

by Niki Bousquet

I saw
The jolly ranchers
In your window.

Then
I saw
That you had been
Swallowed by the
Whispers
In the sea.

Proof *also from the prompt* "What do you fear?"

by Rachel Liu

Assuming no clouds linger over my sky
Assuming no smoky whispers loom over yours,
Then the stars, the little flickers we see,
Are the same.

AssumingIrememberhowyourglance,afleetingsunset,slippedintomine,
Assuming you still feel the crystal glass ripples of my smile brush yours,
Then, for a moment, we touch elbows again
Under the same sky.

But something trembled,
And time rolled over our planets,
Sinking your sunset to dusk
Cracking my crystal glass
Broken,
Shattered,
Scattering the pieces like the stars in the sky,
But brightness lost in a haze of time.

Assuming the starts are millions of billions of miles away,
Assuming that the clouds will only dim their light,
Then my only fear is losing you to the miles between us
and losing your light in the haze.

Horseshoe Crab photo by Katrina Malakhoff

What You're Doing Now

by Megan Cronin

Written after the Thursday evening awards ceremony,
while Megan was sitting on that stone bench,
overlooking the marsh,
to someone
- she cares greatly about –
who lives forty-five minutes away.

I wonder what you're doing now.
Now as I sit here, listening to the cricket chorus,
Feeling my inner peace restoring
Overlooking the marsh that has beauty beyond words
The finest author could not describe this
The stillness of the cool, winding stream
As it courses through the land
Dividing one area of perfectly still grass from another

I wonder what you're doing now.
As dusk covers the land
While clouds silently pass overhead
The half-moon watching from my left
A troupe of silhouetted birds gliding by on my right

I wonder what you're doing now.
Nighttime settles in comfortably
Pronouncing the moon's luminance
To all who gaze upon it
Crickets chirps are accompanied by buzzes and hums

The water gently ripples from creatures within
And reflects little lamplight from houses far from it
Wishes of you beside me ride on the small breeze the mallards
soar on
Wishes of you sitting next to me
Holding my hand
Taking in this beautiful scene
Saying "I love you" without speaking

A lone star peeks out in the sky
Comfort comes from its presence
Because maybe, just maybe
Despite all the miles between us
You're looking at that star -- that same lone star -- as well

Untitled
by Sarah Martin

I stare at blank pages
but they're not all
that blank

They have faces just
like you and me

Glassy eyes
gaze at your forehead
Perfectly curved lips
taste the words on
the page

A bland nose
can smell the scent of
a freshly
sharpened pencil

Strong fingers
guide my pencils in
swirling loops

A pink tongue
swallows the words
that don't belong

Round ears
hear the meter of the
poet's lines

The pages practically
write themselves.

If I Were an Angel

by Megan Cronin

If I were an angel
I'd hold you every day
Embrace you in my loving arms
Even though you're far away

If I were an angel
I'd kiss you when you're sad
Hold your hand and listen
As you tell me of the bad

If I were an angel
I'd give my heart to you
Believe that my trust was safe
And that my feelings were true

If I were an angel
I'd protect you from your fears
Fight them off one by one
To make sure you never shed tears

If I were an angel
I'd be by your side
Every day, protecting you
Spreading my arms out wide

If I were an angel
I'd never stop my love
Putting it all in your heart
While God watches from above

If I were an angel
I'd love you 'til the end
Even when our lives are over
Heaven is just around the bend

However, I am no angel
I'm a human that is all
But I shall love you always
Until our gravesites call

A Magical Place

by Jessica Schiffman

One night as I was walking
I heard an old man talking
And I started to walk with him.

He said:
> I know of a place,
> A magical place,
> Where no one ever gets harmed.
>
> I know of a place
> A wonderful place
> With its own beauty and charm.

This place can be found
If you look long and hard
But if you find it, do not make a sound
Do not disturb the peace

For it is a place of peace
And when you find The Door
To enter this place
You need no key to go in

Just open The Door and
Let yourself in
To a place
Where all of your dreams
Can come true

Marriages last to the end
Wars never start
And everyone's nice
To each other
Everyone's friends
This land will never end

As the man and I turned
Our separate ways
While walking home
Parting at the interception

At the sidewalks,
I now know of a place
A magical place
Where no one ever gets harmed

I now know of a place
A wonderful place
Where I can now be found.

A Poetic Trio

by Rachel Liu

Running

Running into the sun
Each eyelash, even, glaring drops of sunlight
Blinded by the very body
That lets him see,
He wonders
Is this really who I am?

Mirror

Seven years bad luck
for a broken mirror.
Seeing the symmetrical world,
that familiar face,
suddenly smashed into a spider web
of fragments.
And what a horrible fate indeed,
in this world,
to be that shard containing the eye.
Always seeing
Always silent.
With no voice
with which
to speak

Graduation

I'd grown accustomed to your presence,
Like salt water at high tide.
Cool, foamy waves lapping at my toes.
I'd gotten so lost in the deep blue of your reach
    across the horizon,
I barely noticed the sweet liquid fingers around
    my ankles,
filling my footprints.
I lost myself in the waltz of the waves,
Rushing against grains of sand.

Not knowing that with each beat, each reach toward me,
you pulled back farther
and farther
and farther until high tide receded to low
and you were far in the sparkling blue horizon,
leaving me stranded in the cracked hourglass desert,
sand grains spilled around my ankles.

But the tide will crawl back,
This time swirling salt water and sand grains around my knees,
my waist,
my shoulders,
Pulling me, too,
Into the sparkling blue horizon.

From a Time We Forgot

by Niki Bousquet

We are in the great
Shouting outdoors
With the doors shut,
Shouting with our whispers.
Cold night wind blows our
Breath around our ears
Until it swirls back
Into our brains.
Makes us dizzy from our own
Carbon dioxide emissions.
You hit me with your
Warm bright breath in
The sweet cold day.
Breathing in my face,
Not obnoxious,
More like grace.
The softest punch
I have ever felt.
I love the sour cherry
That has replaced your
Nose
When I stand on my toes.
Those lips that I feel,
I could kneel in the snow,
Need to cool
Burning Cheeks.
How does that
Verbal orifice
Keep such warmth in the
Burning turning brown snow
As to make us both glow?

Another Selected Longer Piece ...

My American Dream an original NBC's *Scrubs* screenplay
by Andrew Roiter and Matt Costa

EXTERIOR SACRED HEART HOSPITAL – PARKING LOT – MORNING

Doctors and Nurses are exiting their vehicles. A maintenance van is attending to a broken air conditioner. JD cruises through the parking lot aboard Sasha, his motorized scooter.

JD'S THOUGHTS: As Sasha and I cruised into work this morning, I couldn't help but feel excited. My awesome messenger bag that I have been waiting for had finally arrived and today was the grand unveiling of possibly the greatest male accessory of all time.

CUT TO INTERIOR SACRED HEART – LOBBY – MORNING

JD strolls in through the automatic doors.

JD: Ladies and gentleman, I, Doctor John Dorian, have finally recently received what can only be described as the greatest accessory of all time.

JD: whips the messenger bag out from behind him; it is engulfed in a Godly light with a church orchestra sounding off in the background.

DR. COX: (V.O.) For the love of Lohan, newbie, please tell me that is not a "murse" you have dangling from your scrawny little arm.

JD: Actually, Perry, it's a messenger bag. Very exclusive.

DR. COX: Really? Please do explain then why you have a Hello Kitty emblem sewed onto the cover.

JD: Because all the HE-MAN emblems were sold out; and besides, the pink really accentuates my eyes.

DR. COX: And just when I was considering calling you by your real name, Felicity, (applauding) Atta girl.

JD'S THOUGHTS: (discouraged) Damn.

JD lowers his head, Cox moves off. Elliot enters.

ELLIOT: Hey. (re: messenger bag) Nice murse.

JD: It's a messenger bag! Everyone has them!

Elton Jon is seen exiting the hospital; he too has a messenger bag.

ELTON JON: He's right you know. (Both look at him as he leaves.)

INTERIOR SACRED HEART – SURGERY WING – DAY

Turk and Todd are walking together. A beautiful nurse walks by them and both turn and look back at her.

TURK & TODD: (in unison) Damn! *As the two turn back around they run into CARLA, who is glaring at both of them.*

CARLA: Do you have any dignity?

TURK: Yes ... I left it in the bedroom.

Carla hits Turk in the arm. She raises her hand to hit Todd, but Todd puts his hand up.

TODD: Revenge Five.

Carla lowers her hand and storms off. Turk and Todd keep walking.

TURK: You are so lucky you're single. I can't check out a single hot mama without getting hit.

TODD: Hey, when in doubt, (puts hand up) put your hand out.

TURK: Hmmm ...

Dr. Wynn turns the corner and walks up to Turk.

DR. WYNN: Turk, these surgical reports lack a lot of vital information. What happened?

TURK: (slowly raises his hand) Won't happen again five...?

DR. WYNN: (studies Turk for a moment, then high fives him) All right, I'll let it slide this time. Just make sure you fill out the report with a little more heart next time.

He walks away, leaving Turk, his hand still in the air and his mouth agape. He looks at his hand then looks up and smiles.

MONTAGE: Turk high-fives various doctors for various mistakes. At one point we see Turk talking to a family whose sixty-one-year-old grandfather died while in surgery.

TURK: I'm really sorry. We did everything we could.

FATHER: Is that all you can say? My father is dead and it's your—

TURK: (raises hand) I'm really sorry—five.

FATHER: (high fives him) It's not your fault.

FANTASY SEQUENCE ENDS. Turk is still standing there smiling.

TURK: Oh this is sweet.

INT. SACRED HEART – INTESIVE CARE WARD – DAY

JD is walking through the hallway, which is crowded with doctors and people on stretchers being hauled off to the ER.

JD'S THOUGHTS: When you work at a hospital, you tend to see some really horrible things. Whether it be the aftermath of a car accident (show cut up woman being wheeled off), the result of a fire (show child with severe burns), or the faces of a family who has just lost someone they loved (show grieving family). Luckily, there are people who know how to make you feel better.

Dr. Cox turns the corner. JD hits him like a brick wall, falls over backwards. Dr. Cox looks down, crooks his head.

DR. COX: You ok there, Shirley?

JD: (getting up) Fine, fine.

DR. COX: Shame. Do you have Mr. Ramirez's chart?

JD hands the chart over to Dr. Cox. They start heading into the room.

JD'S THOUGHTS: Mr. Ramirez has been experiencing chronic pain in his chest. He was admitted to the hospital a few days ago and has been experiencing fluctuating mood swings.

JD and Dr. Cox enter. Mr. Ramirez is lying in his bed, smiling.

JD: Good morning, Mr. Ramirez.

RAMIREZ: (loses smile, sneers) Screw off, Caroline!

JD is taken aback; Dr. Cox is smiling.

DR. COX: God, I love this man. (opens chart, reads) Well, Mr. Ramirez, looks as though your insurance won't cover the remainder of your visit. I'm afraid that the extent of your illness is so severe we'll have to transfer you out.

RAMIREZ: What the hell do you mean?

DR. COX: You have no insurance coverage, Mr. Ramirez. I'm sorry, but we can't keep you.

RAMIREZ: So I come to America in hopes of getting good healthcare, and what happens to me?

DR. COX: I'm sorry. Mr. Ramirez, but if you—

RAMIREZ: No, I'm sorry. I know it's not your fault. (sobs)

JD: (whispering to Dr. Cox) I don't see what the problem is. Let's just do what we always do in situations like this, find a dead guy and float Mr. Ramirez in his spot.

Dr. COX: (whispers back) I'd love to, newbie, but frankly ol' Bob-o has been breathing down my neck a little more recently after what happened last week.

He cocks his head to the left.

FLASH BACK Over the shoulder view of a woman in flowery scrubs, Dr. Cox is addressing her.

Dr. COX: Listen here, lady. I know you're new around here, but here's the way things go: if I ask you get me a Foley cath, you better make sure I get the damn Foley cath.

Dr. Kelso walks into shot.

DR. KELSO: Ah, Perry, I see you've finally met my son Harrison. (to Harrison) Damn it, boy, where did you get those scrubs? Go put them back and put on some man clothes for the first time in your life.

BACK TO NORMAL

Dr. COX: Remember, newbie, never underestimate what Bob Kelso will do in response to anything, even insulting his son.

Kelso walks by the room.

Dr. KELSO: Perry, the inmates say they're excited to see you again this year. The warden mentioned that a certain someone is especially excited.

Dr. COX: (sneering) Lenny...

JD's THOUGHTS: Hmm?

Dr. COX SHAKES HIS HEAD: Bubula. Never ... ever ... underestimate him.

RAMERIEZ: I realize you two are doing your best, but you have to understand how this is for me. I uprooted my entire family to come to this country to make an honest living, to live the American Dream.

Dr. COX: I'm sorry, Mr. Ramirez. We'll see what we can do.

COX and JD leave the room.

JD's THOUGHTS: I thought about what Mr. Ramirez had said and it got me thinking; the American dream was—

His head slams into a lamp in the hallway and falls to the ground.

JD: Ow, ow ow.

Carla leans over JD

CARLA: Oh, poor Bambi, you haven't done that since your first day.

She helps him up.

CARLA: Okay, JD, what were you thinking about that had you *that* distracted.

JD Rubs his head

JD: Oh, it's just this patient I have from Honduras. Ya see, he doesn't have health insurance, and with Kelso looking over our shoulders all day, we can't very well make him well. (*snickers*)

CARLA: Concentrate, JD.

JD: Right, we can't help him, so we have to turf him to the free clinic.

CARLA: And you hit your head because...?

JD: Oh, right. Well, he mentioned the whole leaving his country to live the American Dream, and it just got me thinking about what that actually means nowadays.

CARLA: Oh, well JD, when my family came here from the Dominican, we did it legally; but still, life is really hard for immigrants.

JD: I thought you were from Chicago.

CARLA is taken slightly aback, but recovers quickly.

CARLA: Well, yes, *I* was born in America, but still my grandparents told me all about how hard it was to come here and get settled.

KEITH walks in.

KEITH: Hey, if there's a problem with his insurance, why don't we just talk to Dr. Kelso about it. I mean, he isn't that heartless.

DR. COX: (walks up to KEITH, saying) Dear God, it's the same with every litter of you interns, isn't it?

He puts his arm around Keith's shoulder and starts to pull him away.

DR. COX: If there is one thing you need to know about Bob Kelso, it's that he is the most evil person on the planet.

They walk off screen and Dr. Cox's voice fades out. Elliot sees Dr. Cox talking to Keith. She shouts after them.

ELLIOT: Promise you won't mutilate my boyfriend's soul, Perry!

DR. Cox's voice can be heard in the distance.

DR. COX: No promises!

INT. SACRED HEART HOSPITAL- NURSES STATION

Turk is acting inconspicuous, but sees a cup of coffee on the desk and smacks it with his hand onto the lap of a doctor working on the computer. He stands up screaming and looks at Turk mouth agape. Turk raises his hand.

TURK: It was too close to the edge of the counter five?

The doctor high-fives him and waddles away in pain.

Shift to Todd on the other side of the nurses' station: he trips and knocks into an orderly and he drops some bed pans. Todd looks at him and raises his hand.

TODD: Sorry, dude; I'll look where I'm going from now on.

The orderly rolls his eyes, picks up the bed pans, and walks away. Todd is perplexed by this and looks to his right to see Turk high-fiving a man who is rubbing his head. He walks over to him.

TODD: Dude, not cool.

TURK: What?

TODD: You've abused the power of the five.

TURK: What do you mean? You use it much more than I do.

TODD: Yes, but our combined use of the five has caused a disruption of the natural order of the hospital.

TURK: That is absolutely ridicu—

Todd interrupts Turk by raising his hand and blocking a surprised nurse walking by.

TODD: No particular reason.

She rolls her eyes at him and walks on.

Turk's eyes widen

TURK: No...

Outside Mr. Ramirez's room, JD and Dr. Cox continue talking.

Two-Sentence Rotating Story Creations ...

This is a fun exercise, which can
even become a game.
The way we "played" it, student wrote two sentences,
covered up the first sentence,
and then passed the paper to the person on the right,
who then wrote the next two sentences, covered up the top one,
and passed it to the right—and on went the writing.

If it's done well, the stories come out unexpectedly cohesive,
and it's a lot of fun, too.

Two-Sentence Rotating Story, an a.m. class collaboration

The monster creaked emerging from the lake. Then everyone screamed.

It was the craziest party I had ever been to. People were punching holes in the walls and causing general mayhem, not stopping to think of the damage they were inflicting.

They said they were trying to get the flood water to drain out; they were soaking wet. Then, just when everyone thought they couldn't get any wetter, a horrendous wave joined the deluge and got them soaked again.

Luckily, a record-breaking hot, heavy, humid sun rapidly began to rise and fill the sky with a vibrant red sunshine. The warmth from this filled many people with joy.

Some cheered and others laughed endlessly. But all the firemen were beside themselves and jumped off the dock into the swamp below, only to find the missing ballet slippers!

Two-Sentence Rotating Story, submitted by Liam O'Connor

The light died. Everyone in the room started, glaring around. None of them could see a thing. One man stood up, blundering around. Elephants ran over the hills and almost trampled everyone. It couldn't get any worse. In fact, only if the aliens managed to destroy the entire solar system would I admit that it could get worse.

As it was, I wasn't in a particularly good mood to have my house crushed by giant man-eating elephant aliens. I was very depressed. No one destroys my house and gets away with it. He had to find a way to get those squirrels. Then he got it; he would take away the tree in the backyard.

Cutting away a large circular clearing, he'd lay cement and put in a backyard fish pond, complete with goldfish. Young kids could come and feed the fish.

Two-Sentence Rotating Story, an a.m. class contribution

The monster creaked emerging from the lake. Then everyone screamed. It was the craziest party I had ever been to. People were punching holes in the walls and causing general mayhem, not stopping to think of the damage they were inflicting. They said they were trying to get the flood water to drain out; they were soaking wet.

Then, just when everyone thought they couldn't get any wetter, a horrendous wave joined the deluge and got them soaked again. Luckily, a record-breaking hot, heavy, humid sun rapidly began to rise and fill the sky with a vibrant red sunshine. The warmth from this filled many people with joy. Some cheered and others laughed endlessly.

But all of the firemen were besides themselves and jumped off the dock into the swamp below, only to find the missing ballet slippers!

Two-Sentence Rotating Story, another a.m. class
contribution

Unfortunately, the distantly loud tunneling sound of overhead jets
was loud enough to drown out the flock of melodious geese. So, the
crowd stood silently waiting, looking overhead, still waiting.

They were waiting for the Gezunderwiezen to pass over them.
These Gezunderwiezen were boats that fly. But then, it exploded!
And, sadly, all the penguins died.

Their bodies were given a proper burial, which everyone felt
was suitable. The poor penguins never had a chance to achieve
their goal!

Another Two-Sentence Creation, a collaborative P.M. class
creation

It was a totally unbelievable, exhausting experience. The bear was
huge, black, and moved unusually fast.

Out of fear, I sprinted away. Finally, I stopped and caught my
breath checking to see if it was still behind me.

Realizing that it was still trailing behind me, I screamed and
began to run even faster than I had ever run in any of my track
meets. I practically flew down the street and nearly ran into a wall
at the end of the alley.

At that very moment my phone rang. I stopped abruptly and
answered, "Hello, Mr. President. Yes, I do need some protection."

"Um, okay; then get a body guard.

On Their Own ...

After completing a wide variety of exercises
and being inspired by published authors,
students tried a piece totally on their own ...
perhaps inspired by a fellow Young Writer
in the workshop or by the setting of
the Craigville Conference Center,
or inspired by a new strategy and the realization
that a previously written piece was ready for revising.

Here are the results; enjoy!

Short Pieces

Untitled

by Andrew Roiter

The whispers were deafening: he could hear pieces of conversation, snippets of accusations. It was all he could pick out, but that didn't make them any less maddening. He gnawed and picked at the callus on his index finger. He ran every scenario through his mind: How much did they know? How much was a rumor? How much was fact and how much hyperbole?

At this point, did it matter what the police found out? Had his fellow students already convicted him? And most importantly, did he have any hope of vindication?

He kept scratching at the back of his head in a futile subconscious attempt to tear away the looming aura of fear, shame, and paranoia. As he passed a long row of lockers, their owners standing guard like sentinels at their posts, he shut his eyes tight and attempted to wade through the fog of accusers' stares.

The Mutant Wasp and the Window

by Maret Gable

Trapped. Honestly. I was such an idiot. Why didn't I stop to think before flying through the hole in the invisible wall? Now, not only was I stuck in a mesh with holes almost as large as my legs, but the hole in the invisible wall wasn't there anymore.

I was stuck there through dark-time and the start of bright light when, without warning, something huge plucked me off the mesh and enveloped me in darkness. At first I tried to beat off whatever was around me, but I soon saw that nothing changed when I did this and gave up, hoping for a turn of luck.

That turn of luck came not long after that, when bright white light poured into the trap, nearly blinding me, and I was dropped unceremoniously onto leaves, twigs, and dirt. Unceremonious as my release was, I was elated to be free. However, when I took off I flew smack into another invisible wall. Every direction I went there was an invisible wall and above me there was a plain wall.

The Tower

by Jessica Schiffman

I look in the mirror and see my reflection. I do not recognize who I see. I see a sad, lonely girl, with a face the color of ash. She looks sickly. She has knotted red hair from hours of hard labor and cleaning. She has glazed-over green eyes and is devoid of any emotion. What happened to the girl with the toast? I lie down on my lumpy mattress and put a flimsy, scratchy blanket over me, hardly enough to keep me warm during the harsh winter weather.

I hear the rain coming down on the stone roof above me: drip, drip, drip. A beat is forming in my head. The raindrops seem to be chanting: sing, sing, sing. My throat aches to supply the words to the melody, but I know it is forbidden. My feet long to dance, but if I grant my dancing feet this wish to dance, almond face? With the rosy cheeks and freckles sprinkled across her nose?

Where is the girl with big, sparkling, mischievous green eyes, and shiny, full red hair? What happened to her? But I know I will be punished. For I am a prisoner of the tower. Long ago, hundreds of demons, dragons, and evil creatures guarded my tower. But through the years, all have been slain by noblemen on their trusted steeds, hoping to wed me. But all of my chances of escaping the tower were murdered by the two demons that cannot be defeated.

One is a dragon that goes by the name of Black Thunder. He has the strength of one thousand men. His fiery breath rivals the heat of the sun. His body is covered in reptilian-like scales, except for his exposed belly, over which he wears his armor. His scales are the dark color of coal, darker than darkness itself. The only bit of body that is not black is his eyes. They're like glowing red jewels. Look directly into them and become a slave forevermore to the dragon's master.

The Three Calls Preceding the Event
by Hannah Van Sciver

"Ready!" His gruff voice sliced through the cold air. My diaphragm contracted, my neck stiffened, my calves flexed, and my heartbeat quickened. I shifted my right leg behind my left, resting my weight on my left foot. I craned my neck, staring intently at the grass. My shoe wasn't tied very tightly, I noticed. Oh well, no time for that. I breathed in deeply to relax, but my shoulders shook with nervous excitement. I could sense their eyes on my back. Overzealous fathers and encouraging mothers in warm coats huddled together like old friends to cheer us all on.

I glanced quickly to the runners packed in next to me. A tall and gangly brunette was clenching her fists and looking straight ahead. She wore a severe expression. Another girl on my other side had her eyes closed in a sort of wince. Only she was smiling. She was much shorter and a bit stocky.

"Runners set!"

I inhaled sharply. I clenched my teeth. I was racing through the mulch on the playground at summer camp. I couldn't have been more than five years old.

I was in hot pursuit of a soccer ball on the field, under the kind but watchful eye of my grandfather on the sidelines. It wasn't about reaching the ball itself; it was about running faster than anybody else. I stretched my legs out and sprinted down the field for all I was worth, overjoyed at the ability of my small body to move so quickly. I leapt across the finish line, beating my opponent by inches, as the crowd roared and the announcer confirmed my victory into his microphone.

I was running into my father's arms when he arrived home. My socks slid dangerously across the tile floor, but I was determined to reach him without slowing down.

I was running down the hallway to class as the bell rang in my ears. I was running after the car where I'd left my lunchbox. I was running from his outstretched hand in a game of duck, duck goose. Sighing again, I opened my eyes.

"GO!"

Azure and Royal Deception

by Alex Bahrawy

"Father, there is a matter I'd like to disc— "

"The case is the same for me, Arzure."

"Well you speak first then."

"I was going to regardless —"

"Then do it."

"Manners, prince."

It was a strange setting. Two men, who couldn't have been farther apart in age, yet were exactly similar in looks, stood together in a wine cellar. The king sighed loftily. "Your mother is ... unwell, Arzure?"

"I'd say that's an understatement," Arzure said with a curious tone of bemusement.

The king's flesh flushed.

"I saw the coffin," Arzure said indifferently.

His Majesty's eyes welled with tears. "I ... I'm so ... I apologize," he gasped.

His eyes were now as waterfalls. "They think it was murder," he said when a reply did not escape the lips of his son.

"What evidence of that is there?"

"Her wounds were ... t-that of a blade," the king murmured.

"Suicide is a possibility," Arzure replied casually, picking at his nails.

"N-no ... the stab wound was located upon her back. She ... she was ... i-impaled." His majesty, still misty eyed, gazed upon the prince. "Who? Who would...? Kailina ... she was such an ... angel! How ... how could ... anyone?"

"I can think of only one individual," Arzure replied calmly as he slowly lit several slender turquoise candles. Although the match in Arzure's palm had the shape and texture of any other of its ilk, the fact that its flame never vanished and its length never changed made it different.

"S-son, p-prince. Please I must know. I need help. *W-we* need help," the king wheezed pleadingly.

"Think, Father," Azure said, enflaming the remaining candle's wick. "With mother dead, a position of royalty is up for the taking."

"Bite your tongue!" his Majesty retorted. "I would never ... I could never! She's the only one! No one could fill her place."

"Oh, I wasn't speaking of the queen's royal position necessarily. I mean, the throne belongs to you after all."

The king's crimson eyes narrowed as they focused upon his son.

"Who?"

"Again, think. You *are* the great and powerful king of Adorkort," Arzure said with an apparent tone of mock drizzled with arrogance. "Now who ... who would benefit from a dead mother? Who would benefit from having the sheer knowledge that his father would bring him to his favorite bonding place to discuss said deceased mother? And who would become the next ruler of Adorkort once both his parents had a mouth full of maggots?"

The silence that followed was beyond unnerving.

"You ... fool." The king was so overwhelmed by rage that he could barely string together the words. "They will never ... *never* take you seriously. You are an adolescent ... prepubescent pup."

"How dare you," Arzure spat, "use a term such as 'pup' to —"

"To who?" his Majesty bellowed. "You? You are nothing! You think you're a clever little boy? You think you're a bloody genius? You shall never gain the respect of my people. You'll join me in the ground not more than a month after you've taken the throne! If I, Avadra Almast, die tonight, your plan and your life will go up in flames!"

Arzure's mouth arranged itself into a most unusual grin. "Which is precisely why Avadra Almast won't be dying tonight."

"What do you —?"

"And so funny that you should use the phrase 'go up in flames,'" Arzure said, twirling the flint between his fingers. "Oops."

Within the next seconds the room was ablaze and the king was face down in a pool of alcohol. Arzure made his way to the door. His hand allowed the shattered remains of the wine bottle he had used to strike his father to fall into the flames. He ripped away his father's clothes and pressed them upon his mouth. It was only moments after he had slipped inside the clothes and applied the necessary materials to age his face that Arzure, now his father, was approached.

Immediately he feigned fatigue. "F-fire," the king spluttered through a fit of coughing. "T-the wine cellar! Arzure is trapped down there!"

Within moments, the alarm sounded. Chefs, aides, soldiers, and all manner of castle folk barricaded the blackened cellar. Buckets of water were passed quickly as brave souls rushed inside the basement to retrieve the doomed prince. All the while, Avadra Almast shed deceptive tears.

At last, the great flame was extinguished and the prince's body along with it. The news brought more dark water from the king's eyes. Although the incident seemed to slow time, night eventually came. The kingdom was drenched in grief for their mighty ruler. He was left alone in his massive bedroom to ponder the day's events. However, if passersby were to listen with care, the sound of sobs would not invade their ears. Instead, they would hear a low, hollow, and horrible laughing coming from the chambers of the new king of Adorkort.

Need for Intelligent Voting

by Rebecca Van Sciver

We, the citizens of the United States, all have a unique right—the privilege of voting for our leaders at a local, state, and national level. By choosing presidents, governors, senators, and other leaders, we have the ability to secure our future. We can elect leaders who will take us in the right direction. We encounter a problem, however, because not all of the voters in this country are educated. If we have people in our country who make poor decisions when voting, then we jeopardize our country's safety and our economy.

Often, political leaders take positions on issues but don't inform us of the reality of the situation. It is our responsibility to know the truth and learn from our history. For instance, the Bush administration is supporting the idea of ethanol. What they don't tell us is that ethanol is extremely wasteful, even more so than oil. It is extremely expensive, costs billions of tax dollars to produce, and only benefits the big companies who support elected officials. The government didn't tell you that on television did they?

Sometimes our own government can be ill-informed. Consider the war in Iraq. The government thought that there were weapons of mass destruction. It is up to us to consider Iraq's history, how the people live, what languages they speak, and the poverty there. How can we, as a people, make informed decisions about the war if we don't know about those on the other end of it?

The issue of uneducated voters comes up again when we look to global warming. Many people in this country don't understand the science behind global warming. Increasing levels of the greenhouse gas CO_2 can destroy our ability to live on this planet, but most of our country doesn't understand that undeniable fact. We Americans must comprehend what could happen to us if we don't choose leaders and take individual actions to stop this global warming from happening. We must inform the politicians and vote out those who do not act on our information.

We have the right to vote in our democracy, but we must understand the impact of our votes and vote intelligently. Otherwise, the future of our nation is beyond our control. We have the collective responsibility, as a nation, to make sure that our children are educated so that they can vote wisely. This is crucial to our survival. You can make a difference. All it takes is a little education.

High-School Gym Insanity

by Megan Cronin

The gym was packed with raging hormones due to the excessive amount of teenagers within. They were being serenaded with the most "appropriate" music any teenage party had to offer. From the vibrating speaker system burst such artists as Avenged Sevenfold, Metallica, and Nirvana. The greatest source of entertainment was the mosh pit, a group of rowdy boys created especially for "Enter Sandman." Adults surveyed the area carefully. Though the "vulgarity" of the teenage grinding and dancing is not appreciated, they simply looked out for fights (and, of course, kept an eye on the doors leading to the dark outside). Just as the gym seemed ready to explode, the song switched, as did the atmosphere. "Hotel California" began to float into the ears of the crowd. Males that had been jumping around calmly asked females to dance. The room then became a place for the hearts of young lovers to gently pulse in synch.

The Life-Lifting Trap

by Christina Brown

"Whew," howled the wind on this dreadful foggy morning. I was about to put my hand on the mailbox when a big, fat, juicy black spider approached my hand. At first, I didn't recognize it, until the furry spider tickled my tan arm all the way to the opening of my floral tank-top. When it happened I, of course, screamed.

Neighbors were rushing to their doors as if something had happened to someone, but they were all relieved when they realized it was just me. This time, when I cautiously went to open the mailbox; but the information inside the mailbox was even worse. I took out the mail and started flipping through it. Bills, trash, more bills, more trash. As I was walking down my driveway, I stopped and opened a letter that read "Anonymous." I didn't know what I was thinking, but I decided to open it. As I unfolded the letter, the creases made the letter all crinkly. The letter follows:

6/11/1994

Dear Jessica,

Tomorrow is the day I will be visiting you for what I call payback!

Sincerely,
Anonymous

Ding Dong!

"Ahh!" I was pacing frantically. Oh! It was just the driveway sensor!

After reading that letter I was frightened, scared. I didn't know what to do, so I decided to fly to my parents' house in Nevada, on Lake Tahoe. The flight went well, and I met some new people. As soon as I walked through the gate, everything changed. People were staring at me as if I didn't belong or have any right to be there. My parents met me with their car outside. My parents and I did the usual hugs and kisses and left the airport. They told me that we were going to a cookout tonight. I asked where it was going to be held, and they replied, "It's a ... neighborhood party." At that, I started to get worried.

Later on, at the house, we had some soda and caught up on news. When we were ready to leave for the "cookout," I made sure I had my brand new cell phone and a list of excuses to get me out of things, if you know what I mean!

When we arrived, all of a sudden the whole world tipped upside down, just like that, so ... we had a cookout. Everybody was friendly. There was a moon bounce for little kids and raffle tickets for adults. Hot dogs, hamburgers, all-you-can-eat food. I met people, ate, met some more people, and drank. So, when my parents decided to go sit with their friends, I headed for the bathroom. The walk was pleasant. I was admiring all the flower gardens when it immediately turned foggy and cloudy.

In the bathroom, there was another woman.

Boom!

Something sounded like it had collapsed just outside the bathroom door.

We huddled together in the bathroom to decide whether to risk it and find out what happened. We decided to risk it. We came out of the bathroom and took a left, staying close to the brick building. We were walking along when, "Whoosh," we fell into an unknown hole. Both of us started panicking when two people touched our backs.

At that minute and that exact second, I started imagining what was going to happen to us. I knew what I was going to do. I thrust away from the strangers, saved the other woman, and was ready to fight when I realized we had fallen into my younger cousin's trap. Finally, my heart rate went back to normal. We got out of the hole and headed back to the party.

When we arrived in the backyard, no one was outside, so I headed to the closest house. As I opened the door, "Surprise," everybody yelled. As I was taking it all in, I saw signs that read, "Congrats on your new teaching position." Come to find out, the letter was just a way to get me to come to the party. Now that all my worries were gone, or at least I thought, I partied all the way to my bed and my diary. In it I wrote:

6/12/1994

I took a chance tonight that I will never take again, for this was a threat to me and you, and only me and you.

Peter's Perspective

by Hannah Van Sciver

He peered out tentatively, eyes filled with wonder. Everything was vivid—the smell of rotting wood and cigarette smoke, and the feeling of the cream-colored curtain in his sweaty palm. They were all sitting down now, speaking in hushed tones about things he could not understand. The smoke from their cigarettes wound lazily over their heads. The fat one with the suspenders slowly reached for the deck in the center and pulled it toward himself as a cat pulls in a mouse. The cards lay in front of him, lifeless. He spread them out with a graceful slide of the hand before gathering them up again with a slide in the opposite direction. He ran his thumb over their edge, and the crisp sound like rain pounding the street was delightful. They danced elegantly between his grimy palms. Then, without warning, he flung them across the table with surprising precision, and each man speedily pulled them up and fanned them out. Not a word was spoken. Peter batted his eyes and suppressed a cough, watching intently. They seemed to be hiding behind their cards.

The tall one to the right of the fat man had the brim of his hat pulled down over his eyes. He dropped something in the center of the table. Peter stared intently as it glittered in the dim light. The one next to him was much shorter, with a squeaky voice. He chuckled under his breath before dropping multiple objects in the center as well. Peter cocked his head sideways, trying to understand the unspoken code. The last man was tall, like the one with that hat, but much thinner, with a stony, drooping expression. He shook his head slowly and let his cards drop down in front of him. Barely had they hit the table when the fat man extended a paw and snatched them back up greedily.

After a long pause the fat man with the suspenders dropped his coins in the center and the talk resumed. The droopy one who'd dropped his cards sat up awkwardly and left, dragging his feet and cursing quietly. He brushed by the curtain as he exited through the swinging doors, which swung noisily on their hinges as if waving good-bye. His seat remained vacant, making the booth bigger and more dangerous.

Talk resumed again as the game wore on. Peter observed their every move with curiosity and fascination. He marveled at the way they sat, the way they had combed their hair, and the way they blew cigarette smoke into the air without opening their mouths. At that moment, he wanted nothing more than to sit in the empty seat and take his chance with the men and the cards at the polished table. He couldn't imagine anything more glorious.

As Peter fantasized, all at once their voices became louder and less conversational. Tension filled the dank parlor room. It seemed to involve the little man and the tall one with the hat. The tall one knocked the little man's cards to the floor with a brush of his arm. They both stood, knocking their chairs to the ground with a clatter. Peter cringed and gripped the curtain tighter. The fat one looked on, silently, still seated. The little one pulled out a gun. It was a revolver, just like the one that Peter's father kept at home in the closet. It gleamed in the parlor light, looking smooth and beautiful. The big man at last jumped to his feet to intervene, but he was too late. A shot exploded through the room and Peter covered his mouth to stifle a scream. The lifeless body of the tall man with the hat crumpled to the floor in a heap. The little man quickly grabbed the coins in the center, gave the fat man a stiff nod, and fled, the doors flapping behind him. The fat man gathered up the cards into a neat pile, sighed as he scratched his head, and with a sideways glance at the paling corpse, lumbered toward the doors.

Peter, at last, emerged from behind the dusty curtains into the now silent parlor room. As Peter watched the blood pool on the floor, he realized that he no longer wished to play cards.

The Best Christmas Ever

by Courtney Bergh

It was the day I had been waiting for, the best day of the year. The one day that may have even been better than Christmas itself: Christmas Eve. In a way it could not even compare to Christmas. The joy of waking up earlier than any normal teenager and miraculously being as wide awake as you could possibly be, even after the long sleepless night before. The excitement of sprinting down the stairs, two at a time, anticipating the beautiful sight of red and green wrapped presents under the tinsel covered tree. But, sometimes, sitting around the fire, a warm sleeping puppy snoring on your lap, you can't help but think you would give up all the Christmas days in the world to be here again watching "A Year Without a Santa Claus" by the warm firelight, and suddenly being told to go upstairs because the sound of hooves were heard on the roof.

As usual, I jump into bed, trying my best to believe that all the presents I would see in the morning were really coming from the North Pole, not my parents' closets. Turning out the lights, I think of the excitement that will come in the morning, coming in the form of gifts under the tree, and the Christmas cheer, coming in the form of Christmas carols on the radio. I look at the clock on my night table after only about two minutes in bed: 10:27 p.m. This was going to be a long night.

Before I knew it, I awakened and my eyes shot open. I opened the shades and let the light pour into the room. What had been a cold, grass-covered lawn the night before had become a soft coat of fluffy white powder. I jumped out of bed and ran down the hall to my parents. My sister and I each dragged one of them out of bed. Our family Christmas tradition said that Lindsey and I weren't allowed to go downstairs into the living room until my dad had gone down to "check that Santa had come." As we nearly shoved our father down the stairs, we sat down on the top step, anticipation building. After a few minutes of "better not come down, you'll be disappointed" and "looks like Santa missed our house" my sister and I gave up trying to follow the tradition and sprinted down the stairs.

I gasped when I saw the room. Presents covered in Santa, reindeer, and shiny red wrapping were nearly bursting through the doors. We got straight to work, not wasting a second of precious gift opening time. My sister and I tore away the wrapping on each present, and, one by one, they were put neatly in a pile, only to be covered again by extra wrapping being flung across the room. After about three hours, all the presents had been opened, the stockings had been filled with empty candy wrappers, and I was lying down on the couch once again next to a fluffy snoring puppy. But this time I was surrounded not by the warmth of the fire but by the warmth of Christmas cheer. I guess it's not the presents that make me happy. It's not Christmas Day, or even the day of Christmas Eve, although I always become convinced so. It's the happiness of Christmastime, and all that happiness and cheer glowing in everyone's smiles. It's not all the stuff we get and the sweets we get to eat, or even the relatives and friends we get to see for the one time a year. It's how all that makes us feel and act that brings the true Christmas spirit.

more ... Longer Pieces ...

Like the short pieces,
students wrote these mostly "On Their Own,"
applying reflective editing techniques from Workshop activities.
These were occasionally written in editorial collaboration with
Young Writers' Workshop classmates, in such editing exercises as
Five-Minute Editing rotations,
Three Favorite Things, and the
Bless It, Address It, or Press It Editing technique of the National
Writing Project.

The Hunting Adventures of Tosh Mihesuah

by Tosh Mihesuah

It was mid-November in Duncan, Oklahoma, right before Thanksgiving. That means it was deer season, and it was very early in the frosty morning, around five o'clock. Some houses still had pumpkins on their front porches, while other houses already had Christmas decorations up. I sat in the back seat of my grandpa's pick-up truck while Dad drove. As we rode over the bumpy dirt road toward the land where we hunt, I heard a rattle in the motor. Dad said not to worry, that it always makes that sound.

We were hunting for white-tailed deer on the opening day of deer season. My dad was raised as a hunter on his dad's allotment in southern Oklahoma. We're Comanche, and Grandpa got his allotment from his parents back in 1902. Now every time I go onto his land I feel like I'm going back in time. There are no power or telephone lines. You can see where the old houses used to be all around his property. Those old farm houses are now just piles of gray, dry, and rotten wood. No telling what is living in the mounds of rubble. Lots of animals run around the area.

My mom is Choctaw, and her grandmother sold her allotment in the 1920s. That land is in southeastern Oklahoma and is really pretty. It would be nice to have that land. But just like other Indians can say, that land is gone forever.

Grandpa had a two-room house. He was born there, with no doctor to help his mother. All his brothers and sisters went off to school, but grandpa only has a sixth-grade education. When he turned ten his mother died and his dad was sick and had to live with one of his daughters. So Grandpa was left on the land all by himself. He once told me that he broke his ankle and had no way to get to a doctor. So he just limped around until the bones healed.

Grandpa also shot squirrels to eat. He fished and grew a small garden. Sometimes he got money from one of his sisters, and then he could buy bread and coffee from a local store. I don't think I could live like that. Grandpa had no television and no books. There were some friends in the area that played basketball with him. His hoop was just a basket with no bottom nailed to the barn. One time Grandpa played ball with a kid who had a glass eye. The eye fell out and the boys had to look around in the dirt for it.

I first saw his old house when I was just a baby. It was like the other old houses in the area. It collapsed years ago and is just a pile of rotten, splintered wood. The cellar is still there, but the door is gone. He told me not to go into the old cellar, because snakes live in it. Grandpa says he feels sad to see his house ruined, but on the other hand, he likes to tell me about his life. He lives in Duncan and drives the nine miles to the "Home Place" several times a week to watch for turkeys and deer and to make sure no one has come onto the land to hunt without his permission. Deer, turkeys, opossums, snakes, bobcats, and huge pigs that we call hogs live on the Home Place, and Grandpa loves them all. Mom's tribe calls the pigs *shukhushi*.

Dad hunts on his father's land because there are so many animals there. Even on a hot summer day my sister and I can fish in the creek, because the trees keep the area shady and cool. We always see lots of fish, frogs, snakes, and sometime raccoons. We have to change clothes as soon as we get back to Grandma and Grandpa's, because we usually bring home ticks. I should say that until I was about eight, I called both my grandparents Grandpa.

My grandparents went to California on the Indian Relocation program in the 1950s. Grandpa hunted anytime he had a chance. He got a deer once and brought it back to the Indian Center, where some other Indians lived, and the lady there said she could skin and cook it, and she did. I think Grandma and Grandpa missed

Oklahoma really bad, because he told me they drove back there at least once a month. Dad was a little kid when they did that, and he never wore a seatbelt.

Now, it was my turn to learn to hunt. There are a lot of things you need to know before you can use a gun. First, there is a program called "Hunter's Ed," and you go to a session for three hours a night. The teachers don't just talk about hunting. They also teach the students how to survive in the wilderness, what the parts of the gun and bow are, how to care for your gun, bow, and arrows, what hunting regulations are, the various hunting areas, and many other things dealing with hunting and safety. A lot of people don't go through the course. That is why hunters get lost or accidentally shoot another hunter.

Dad drives pretty fast and we soon got to Grandpa's allotment. The trees had lost their leaves. The leafless branches of the cottonwood trees looked like skeleton arms reaching up to the sky. We arrived at a gate held shut by a chain. The gate was old and rust flaked off the hinges. It was a lot older than me.

Dad stopped so I could get out and open the wide gate door while he drove through. The land next to Grandpa's belongs to one of my cousins. He sometimes let us hunt the land, because he had too many deer this year. In many places in the country there are so many deer that they eat all the grapes and leaves and then starve. On the allotments there is so much to eat that they won't starve, but they have too many babies too fast.

Dad only drove onto the property through the gate a few truck-lengths and stopped. We were in a large wheat field surrounded by cottonwood and bois d'arcy trees. Deer also like to eat wheat, Dad said. We would have to walk through the field to get to where we would sit and wait for the deer.

He stopped the engine then before opening the door he told me to be quiet. "Don't talk so loud," he said. He always says that even when I don't say anything.

The morning was cold. Most of the crickets were already gone for the winter, but I thought I heard one. An owl hooted, and both Dad and I jumped. A lot of tribes think that owls are messengers of bad luck. I hoped this was just a friendly owl. Then a turkey answered the owl. That is a common thing for turkeys to do.

I was dressed in my usual camouflage hunting clothes, plus long underwear, heavy socks, hat and gloves. Even though I had on warm layers, the cold breeze hit my throat and raced down my neck, making me shiver.

The sun was not up yet, and we walked for twenty minutes in the dark. I walked close to my dad, who said we must look like a cow since we had four legs. I was still feeling half asleep when a turkey gobbled, then I woke up. Some turkeys are very loud.

We finally reach our destination: a grove of trees with enough space between them so we could sit and see everything from that spot. Our timing was perfect, because the sun was starting to rise. It looked like a lamp in the distance. I was watching it and thinking so hard about how pretty it looked that when Dad used his loud deer call he scared me. My dad uses a buck call to lure bucks. The sound it makes is like another buck, so any others in the area will think there is another animal in its territory and often will want to fight.

On opening and closing day of deer season you can shoot a doe and a buck. As we sat there looking around, slowly looking around, I was freezing. My hands and feet felt like ice cubes. So I told my dad, and he said that we would move in a couple of minutes. I know from experience that when Dad says a "few minutes," he really means more like half an hour. We waited and saw nothing, and finally we got up and slowly moved around. Dad led me through some thick brush, and we had a hard time pushing through the branches. My backpack and gun got stuck in the thorns.

After I finally got loose from the thorns, Dad took me to another field. This time we arrived at a one-man blind, and inside the blind was a five-gallon heavy-plastic bucket turned upside down for a seat. I got to sit on the bucket, but the problem was that I was still too short to see out the window of the blind. So, I had to depend on Dad, who sat outside the blind, in the brush, to tell me if a deer walked past.

Once again I had to sit and wait. That's one of the hard parts of hunting. You might have to sit for hours and never see a thing, but on other days you might sit down and a perfect animal walks by within minutes. A few times Dad would tease me and say, "Look! There's one!"

Every time he said that I stood up all excited, but I never saw anything. My heart beat fast, and I had to remember to take deep breaths. I hate it when my dad teases me. Finally, he said more quietly, "Tosh, there's a doe." I knew from his whisper he meant what he said that time.

I looked out the window and saw the doe, but she was too far away for me to try to shoot. So we waited again. I asked if we could go someplace else, mainly because I needed a change of scenery from the inside of the blind. Dad said if we keep moving then we'd never see another deer.

He let me outside the blind and we sat together, enjoying the scenery. I was still very cold. The sun had come up and I could see the birds flitting through the branches. Squirrels ran up and down the tree trunks chattering to each other. I always think I should bring a camera when I go out hunting, but you can't hunt and take pictures at the same time.

The tree next to us had a strange ivy growing up its side, and my dad studied it for a while. My dad looked past the ivy-covered tree and, suddenly, he nudged me as he pointed to the south.

"A buck. See him?"

Dad can see very well. Sometimes when we drive down the highway he can spot turkeys half a mile off the road in the bushes. I started to jump up, and he put a hand on my arm. "Slow down," he reminded me.

I made myself stand slowly and then I brought my rifle to my shoulder. When you shoot a deer, you are supposed to just shoot once, right behind the shoulder to make sure the bullet goes straight to the heart so the animal won't suffer. I took a breath then slowly let it out. When I had almost ended my breath, I squeezed the trigger. Any kind of jerk will make you miss your target.

It isn't always easy to tell if you shot a deer, because they usually jump and sprint away, even if they are shot in the heart.

Dad yelled, "Shoot, shoot again!"

I knew I had hit it again, but to make certain I shot a third time. After that last shot, the deer fell. We ran to where the deer fell and then stopped a few feet from it.

"Reload the rifle," Dad told me. "You'll feel funny if he gets up and runs again and you can't shoot."

He didn't move, so I knew I had hit him correctly. Now we had to get him back to the truck. Dad and I had to drag him. It wasn't easy. Even though Dad is strong it was still hard for us both to get the deer into the back of the truck.

We got him to the fish and game department so he could be measured and weighed. Game officials have to keep track of the animals hunters bring in so they can monitor how many hunting tags to give out the next year. My deer weighed about 110 pounds.

Next we brought him to my grandpa's house. If you have never skinned a deer before, it can be surprising how difficult it is. It is hard enough to skin a deer, but dressing out an elk is twice as difficult.

I shot my first elk when I lived in Arizona. A lot of people think the whole state is one big desert, but we lived in Flagstaff, at seven thousand feet above sea level. We lived on five acres with many Ponderosa Pine trees. Elk came into our yard and ate the leaves off our apple and pear trees. They also drank out of the bird bath. Dad would get so excited that he'd run out into the yard in his underwear with the video camera. He thought no one could see him, but we did.

On hikes with my mom, we would see bull elk, but we often could only see their antlers. The bulls liked to stay on the far side of a small hill, and only their horns showed. That's what we saw until we got closer and then they ran away. Once we chased them on foot and couldn't catch them. But they stopped to look behind them to see if we were still there. Then we could catch up. I have some pictures of us looking at them, through binoculars.

The morning I started the Arizona hunt was almost like the morning I got my Oklahoma deer: cold and dark. On that day of elk hunting, my dad and I went down a rugged mountain road less than a mile from where we saw the bulls with my mom. I was thinking that the truck might flip. Dad drove down the road for a while, and then we got out and started to walk on terrain that was so rugged we could easily have fallen and broken a leg. I was still sleepy and could only concentrate on not falling on the rocks. Like a mindless zombie, I followed my dad as we walked what seemed like forever. Then my dad, all of a sudden, threw me roughly to the ground. I wanted to yell, because I hit the ground hard. But when my dad said, "Elk," the pain in my knee was gone.

I didn't want to miss my shot, so I listened and looked all around me. Dad then whispered to me to look across the field. My heart dropped. An elk was standing at least three times as far away as the one I had missed the day before. It would, for sure, be a long shot, but I would try.

I took a breath and set my gun on a Y-shaped log. My dad said, "That's not right. That won't work."

I gave him my mean look and rolled my eyes. Then I went back to aiming at the elk.

After I shot it, we ran over to look at it and to thank it for letting us have him for meat. Then Dad left me with the animal while he walked off to find the road. I had to stay with the dead elk all by myself. My mother was very upset when she later found out that I was alone. She reminded Dad about the mountain lions that live in the area. I had thought that maybe one might come by, so I kept my rifle at my side, but Dad left me with only one bullet. I guess he thought I might try to shoot anything that I couldn't see very well because I was scared. It wasn't all that scary, though.

I finally fell asleep. I woke up to the sound of my dad's voice. I jumped up. Then we began to drag the elk out. It was too heavy. It weighed as much as a horse. We didn't budge it one inch.

So, we had to walk to the truck and drive it back to load the elk. This is one of the problems with hunting: if you get something, then what do you do with it? You can carry a turkey, but not an elk. We walked for about a mile through the rocks and brush, and my dad kicked over a stump that was rotten. That didn't seem like a big deal, because there are a lot of rotten stumps from trees that have been logged. But, when the stump fell apart, we heard a loud buzz, and I saw yellow things coming out of the ground.

Immediately, my dad yelled, very loudly, "Run!"

At almost the same time, I felt a sharp pain in my leg, and I yelled out, "Yellow jackets!"

Dad got stung on the head and I had stings on my legs. We got back to the truck and saw some of Dad's friends. We hurt from the stings, so Dad's friends said they would go back and get the elk for us. Hunting friends do that all the time for each other. If Dad had helped them, they would give us some of their elk meat, so we ended up giving some of ours to them. Dad got stung *all* over his head.

My Oklahoma deer was a lot smaller than the Arizona elk. We brought the deer back to Grandpa's house around 9:00 a.m., and we were still skinning it at 4:30 p.m. Even though we had already taken the hide off, preparing the rest of the animal is even harder. We gave up and took him to one of the many places in Duncan to have him processed.

This was my first deer, and I got him on opening day. My grandpa and dad are proud of me, because it sometimes takes adults many seasons to get a deer. Sitting still is hard enough, and then making sure you keep a steady hand to shoot is also challenging, especially if you're nervous and very cold.

I think I pretty well described how cold it was hunting the deer: like being in a freezer. And my adventures in the cold didn't stop with the deer. Just yesterday morning I had to bundle up again before heading out with Dad to get my first turkey.

On hunting mornings, Dad shakes me awake and says very loudly, "Come on! Get up!"

I usually groan and turn over. I hate the part where you have to wake up early and face the cold. Dad is not a morning person unless he's going hunting. I never am. On those days, he gets under my skin, and then, when I am grumpy, he later uses it against me, like later in the day, if I look tired he asks, "You still grumpy? Snap out of it!"

I roll out of bed, put on my clothes, and lay back down. Dad comes back in the room and says loudly, "Move." As I get up again, I gather my hunting pack and gloves and go to the truck where my dad waits.

I walked out the back door toward the truck. As I walked across the yard, Dad yelled at me to look down. I did and almost stepped in dog poo. Even though it was cold out, I usually carry my shoes or boots to the car and lace them up after I get in. A poo-step could have been messy. I got to the truck with all my stuff and threw it in first. Then, I got in, buckled up and tried to get comfortable in the very hard back seat.

Dad looked back at me and said, "This truck is old and it may not start." He turned the key, I heard a heard a whirl, and to Dad's surprise, the truck started.

I tried hard to go back to sleep, but I knew it was impossible: my dad's friend Jerry was coming with us, Jerry talks loudly and laughs all the time. There was no way I could drift off after we picked him up. Just like with the deer, we got to the gate, but this time Jerry got out and opened it while Dad drove through. That old rusty gate reminds me of my sister screaming when she gets her hair combed.

Like every time we go hunting in this land, Dad looked at me and said, "Don't talk so loud when you get out." Jerry and I got out. It was very quiet. It was too cold for crickets to chirp and for frogs to croak. As I looked around, Dad did his coyote call to make the turkeys gobble in warning. Man, did that scare me, just like the years before when he did the deer call. I even jumped. We heard what we wanted to hear, a turkey gobble. We all froze since it sounded very close.

After a few minutes, we crept down into some brush, where Dad and Jerry set up some decoys. We backed away slowly into the trees and Dad did another call, but this time a turkey call. They gobbled again and this time they were very close to us. My heart pounded even harder. They gobbled for ten minutes, then were quiet. Suddenly, a flock of them flew down right in front of us, just out of range. I watched a big gobbler and two smaller ones walk slowly toward the decoys.

Gobblers are the males. When they want to impress a female, they fan out their tail feathers and strut around. Dad whispered that they were in range. He also said, "The big one." I knew that meant to take aim and fire. I did, and now we had a turkey for the freezer.

That was how I got my first turkey, deer, and elk. But I am most proud of what I have also learned about the outdoors. I know that you can only hunt animals that are not endangered. And we eat everything we shoot. I feel like I could survive if I got lost outdoors. I hunt sometimes, but I also respect the animals and I would never want to live anyplace where I could not see the turkeys, deer, coyotes, and other animals that live in my yard and in the nature preserve next to me in Baldwin City, Kansas.

William: The Friendly (We Think) Pair of Ectoplasmic Travel-Oriented Anatomical Features

by Niki Bousquet

The gray gloom loomed up from the trees like an evil omen waiting in the eves. Omen is a derivative of a Latin word. Strange things enter your mind at times like these. I find I can be very random, not unlike Kara, as she has actually been nicknamed "Random." Should we run away? Kara and I pivoted on our two pairs of ambulatory devices and fled from this carved rock that we perceived to be malevolent and foreboding. Rocks don't have personalities, do they? No, this is ridiculous. Even if it does have a personality, I'm sure it will be quite amicable.

"Let's go back. We should at least see what it says."

An unsure expression manifests itself on Kara's face, "Ok, fine," she retorts, probably wondering if the menace we have fled from will reveal itself. If expressions are capable of doing so then why not a long gone man, who has not even a pair of long johns?

We walk tentatively. I'm not sure why we are so frightened of this inanimate object. Or is it inanimate? You can never be quite sure. We halt just before the stone. There is a slight clearing around it. Maybe something really is living — or not living — under the earth here.

The words are almost illegible: William H. Gardner; Newport, R.I., 1825 – 1860. That is well over one hundred years ago. The body must have rotted and been eaten by maggots by now, only a frail skeletal frame left.

I speak finally. "Why haven't we come upon this before now? It's strange; we've been wandering around in here for a while." We are in the woods at the end of my street, near a hill that has been named "Snake Hill." No one knows why. Someone might have once witnessed the slithering of a slinking snake there.

"But does anyone else know about it?" Kara ruminates.

I was wondering the same thing. This could be our secret.

"I don't know. I mean, it's pretty close to that house." I point to the last house on my street. I have no idea who lives there. The petite street has only eight or nine houses, but somehow we, those who dwellwithinthehomes, managealmostnevertospeaktoeachother.

We trudge back through the lifeless brush and foliage, to my house, and retrieve my very own contraption that captures images using the rays of the sun. It is of the digital variety. I do not speak a word of our dead discovery to my mom. Kara has reason to believe that if my mom tells her mom, she will give birth to a metaphorical bovine creature.

Once we reach the home of our newfound companion, William, the shuttering of the lens that allows light into the inner workings of the photographic device is incessant. We take turns posing with the stone. It is an infamous celebrity, being venerated for its talent. Oh, how honored William must be. And how confused; this advanced technology had not yet been discovered in 1860. Or had it? I am not quite sure.

At home we connect the output cable to the corresponding outlet in the camera, and then to the one in the computer below the CD drive. I believe that this tower that eats and digests information is actually called the computer. Many people think the monitor is the part of the computer that does all the work. But really, it is the tower. Oh, how underappreciated it must feel. The poor, cute, little rectangular prism - shaped box of technology just doesn't get enough credit for all the work it does.

There are transparent whitish orb-like things peppered over the images that we captured photographically. This could mean nothing. Or it could mean something. I have heard that digital cameras cause things like this to appear. They could be mere specks of dust, just as meaningless as that unpoetic noise that radiates from the speakers of a unit that picks up sound waves from numerous stations when a knob or dial is tuned. However, I have never encountered such phenomenon with my camera before, although I have captured many images with it. Kara and I agree to dismiss this evidence of an unsettled spirit. Well, at least until we have something more stable, like concrete, to back it up. Yes, that is what we decide on.

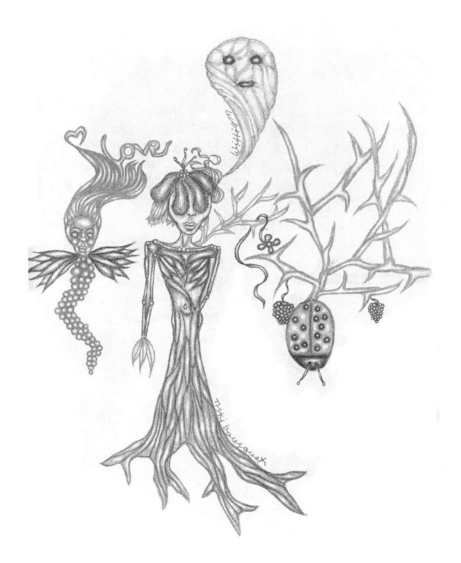

In the following months, we visited the site often. Were we begging for something to appear, to frighten us so horribly that we jumped out of our animal-patterned socks and kerplunked our skulls upon the overhanging limbs of those beautiful creatures that we should save so we can breathe. We were not sure of our motive, but we were shavings of iron, and the area of the discovery was a horseshoe-shaped magnet in a third-grade classroom. Perhaps William was the teacher, observing our wide eyes, so perplexed by this ominous yet marvelous happening. I think this is what I hoped, with my eleven-year-old hunger to find something beyond the monotony of everyday life. It is likely that Kara, too, shared my dream.

I presented the ancient relic to my friends, proud that Kara and I had likely been the first *Homo sapiens* to lay our image processing devices upon it in one hundred and forty-two years. "Do you want to meet William?" I ask, with a hint of mystery in my voice.

"Who is William?"

An unsuspecting accomplice would question, unaware of the potentially sinister nature of my seemingly innocent query. I told many people the tale of William, subsequently presenting to them his cozy place of dwelling. I thought at the time that the earth was his home and he would not dare to abandon it. Perhaps the deceased become restless and bored with the same scenery day after monotonous day, just as the living do.

It was the second hour of a quite mundane day the following summer. Kara was sleeping over and we had just completed our viewing of the movie *Donnie Darko*, which features a giant malevolent bunny rabbit named Frank. I walked with Kara out of the den, which is adjoined to the living room and the dining room. Our intent was to journey to the kitchen for the purpose of retrieving two glasses of coffee milk. This is not coffee with milk in it; it is milk with coffee-flavored syrup. That concept seems to puzzle a surprisingly large number of people. As we made our way to our destination, we were required to pass through the room of living, which now strikes me as hilarious in its irony. As Kara and I approached from behind the smaller of two sofas, this one seating only two people, and as our eyes adjusted to the darkness, a strange image presented its certainly not-living self to us. A gnarled pair of knobby, wrinkled, and veiny feet were dangling over the arm of the sofa. They were not transparent or ghostly, and at first I thought they were the ambulatory devices of my dad. No,

I realized, he is snoring obnoxiously in his bedroom, with no regard for the fact that anyone else, even this man who had been dead for so long, might enjoy a good night's rest. From the angle at which I stood, I could see nothing but the feet, but as I adjusted my position, the top of a head became visible, as well as a pair of ankles attached to the feet. A moan escaped the lips of this apparitional creature composed of ectoplasm. It was not an anguished, distressed, or threatening noise. It seemed as though the dead wished only to rest in peace in our room of living and was slightly irritated that we had disturbed his extended slumber. In the moments after he had voiced his annoyance, this form, which I was now sure was William, or as he would come to be nicknamed, "The Feet", dissipated, leaving Kara and I alone with ourselves, incapable of disappearing whenever we pleased.

I turned to Kara and saw in her living eyes, head, ankles, and feet that she too had witnessed this anomaly. It had honestly not been so frightening, as William did not seem to intend to do us harm. However, we still felt the need to gallivant, screaming into the bedroom of the man and woman because of whom I am alive, and therefore will someday, like William, no longer be alive. This is probably because they had just been rudely awakened from a pleasant dream of sugarplums and magical ponies with aerodynamic capabilities. It is also imperative to be aware of the fact that my parents knew nothing of William's gravestone at the time, and therefore could not see that there was absolutely no chance that this happening could be a mere coincidence. Kara and I were ordered by my mother and father to vacate their place of sleep immediately. We did so, but despite their narrow-minded disbelief in friendly spirits who camped on our living room sofa, we were not discouraged. Kara and I knew what we had witnessed, and to this very increment of time that contains twenty-four hours, we stand by our statement.

We even continue to visit William, although his gravestone has grown crooked and his engraving has faded, we will always love him.

Consequently, it is now clear to me that ghosts, apparitions – or whatever these creatures may be labeled – are indeed present. They do not always have cruel intentions; William is living, or nonliving, proof of this. There may be ghosts surrounding me and I would not even know of their presence. There is probably a ghost hovering in front of my computer screen at this very moment, making comical faces at me. It could even be the spirit of the last unicorn, who, unfortunately, met its demise because humans refused to believe in its magical existence. I just wish that all apparitions could be as kind as William and deign to introduce themselves to us lowly living beings.

Note from the author: This a completely true personal narrative about a gravestone located down the street from my house.

Chapters 3 and 4 from an original book in progress
by Angelica Dellamorte

"Mother, have you seen Blaize? He promised he would help me clean our room. And it's getting close to twilight. I am worried about him," Raiye said as she descended the spiraled staircase. She ran over to look out the window, hoping to see Blaize whistling a cheerful tune on his way home from work. But nobody was out on the streets at this hour. The Shade would awaken soon.

Seeing Raiye's worried look on her face, Lunimae stopped sweeping the floor and put her hand on her shoulder. "Well, Raiye, I believe I heard Blaize say something about going to the seashore. He was excited about some new trinket the sea otters gave him and he wanted to show you, but you were assisting Ms. Harukae at her bakery. I would not worry; Blaize knows that it is extremely dangerous to stay out too late. He will be home in time."

Although these words were true, they provided Raiye no comfort at all. "Bye, Lunimae, I'll come see you tomorrow!" Brien called as he went out the door.

Lunimae gave him a slight wave and was about to say something when, without a word or warning, Raiye dashed out the door in the opposite direction Brien was going. That is, the direction of the sea.

"Raiye! Wait!" Lunimae called after she finally realized what just happened.

Raiye ignored her calls. The girl just kept running. The sun's last rays were shining on her long golden locks and her dress made of golden silk.

"My only hope is that both of those children will be home before..." Lunimae's voice trailed off. She felt obligated to go after Raiye, but ever since that night when she found Blaize, Lunimae had never been able to go outside before twilight. It was not a sense of fear when twilight came, but a sense of doom. It was as if out there, someone was watching her, waiting for her to step outside just so that they could stab her in the back with a knife. Lunimae whispered a short prayer to the Creator as Raiye vanished from sight.

What could that crazy boy be doing?! I've been worried sick about him, Raiye thought as she ran. Only a few more yards until she reached the seashore. She could barely see his silhouette.

"Hoy, Raiye! What are you doing running about at this hour? Would you like me to walk you home?" said a friend of Blaize. He was accompanied by four other boys who were now arguing about who would walk Raiye home.

Raiye raced past the boys and called back to them, "Sorry guys, I have got to get Blaize before nightfall. Maybe tomorrow."

The boys were a bit disappointed and complained amongst themselves, "Blaize is sooo lucky. He always gets to spend time with Raiye. It's not fair!" With glum faces and pouts, the boys dispersed and started walking toward their homes.

"Finally! I am here!" Raiye said to herself as she kicked her golden slippers off her feet and started running on the sand. "Blaize! Blaize, is that you?!" she yelled as she approached the boy on the beach.

"Raiye! I'm so glad to see you!" Blaize said as he embraced the girl. "Look what the sea otters gave..."

The boy stopped dead in mid-sentence.

Raiye looked angrily at him. If looks could kill, Blaize would be dead. "Hey ... uh is something wrong?" he asked nervously.

"Is something wrong?" Raiye repeated calmly, too calmly, dangerously calm. Then he exploded, "IS SOMETHING WRONG?! I WILL TELL YOU WHAT'S WRONG! I HAVE BEEN WORRIED SICK ABOUT YOU AND YOU HAVE BEEN HERE, ALL DAY, WITHOUT EVEN GIVING A THOUGHT ABOUT THE PROMISE YOU MADE, NOT TO MENTION THAT THE SHADE WILL BE OUT VERY SOON."

Blaize stared at her, trying to recall the promise. He knew if he asked her, she would throttle him, but he asked anyway, "Exactly what promise are you talking about?"

Raiye could not believe her ears. She was so mad; she couldn't even yell at Blaize. All she could do was stare into his amber eyes. They stared at each other for a few moments, until finally Raiye slapped Blaize right across the face.

This was a casual fight between Raiye and Blaize — Raiye would get mad, Blaize would be clueless, Raiye would somehow injure him, Blaize would still be clueless and his temper would rise, and from there, the argument would get out of control. Many times, Blaize felt as if he could hurt Raiye, but he never dared to touch her. He knew if he hurt her in any way, he'd be severely punished.

This time was different. Blaize's temper soared and he lost control of his actions. "GET AWAY FROM ME!" he said as he shoved Raiye into the sand. For a split second, Blaize was satisfied with himself. But as soon as he took one look into Raiye's face, he felt ashamed.

Tears filled Raiye's blue eyes and rolled down her white cheeks. Her honey-colored hair was covered in sand, which made it tint red with the setting sun. "Raiye, I'm sooo sorry. I didn't mean to —"

Raiye didn't give him time to finish his apology before she ran away in tears. She didn't look back. Blaize watched the girl run away from him like a frightened rabbit. He felt tears fill his eyes, but he refused to let them roll down his cheeks. He sat down in the sand and stared at the waves. How could he have done that? Raiye is such a fragile girl. He shouldn't have done that.

He pulled out a trinket from his pocket. It was so small; it fit in the palm of his hand. It was a glass orb filled with silver smoke that swirled around hypnotically. He had been staring at this curious trinket, trying to figure out what it was. Blaize sighed. He decided he'd have to apologize to Raiye and do something nice for her.

I'll probably just pick flowers with her or something. She's been trying to get me to come with her for quite some time now. He continued to play with his new toy.

Meanwhile, Raiye rushed home, still in tears. She felt heartbroken. Never before had Blaize ever hurt her. *But*, she thought to herself, *I guess I did slap him pretty hard...*

She shook her head. *No! Blaize doesn't even know how worried I was about him! I just wanted him to come home safely. Well, good riddance! If he doesn't come home, I won't care!* But even as Raiye thought these words, she couldn't help but glance back to the seashore. She could see Blaize sitting on the sand, tossing something high into the air and then catching it again.

"Raiye! You are back! Where is Blaize?" Lunimae asked through the window.

Once again, Raiye ignored her and ran up the stairs and slammed the door to the room she and Blaize shared. As Raiye ran, Lunimae thought she could see tears glinting on Raiye's face with the fading light of the sun.

"I wonder what happened," Lunimae said. She nimbly climbed the stairs to Raiye and Blaize's room. She tried turning the doorknob, but Raiye had locked it, so she tried the next best thing. "Raiye? What happened? Why were you crying, my dear? Where is Blaize? Is he all right?" She knocked urgently on the door.

Lunimae received no answer from within the room. She was now worried about Blaize. The last few minutes of light were quickly slipping away. If she didn't act now, Lunimae might never see him again. She turned the doorknob, and she received a brief flash of the last time she had been out after nightfall so many years ago. Lunimae shuddered. *I love Blaize and I would do anything for him*, she told herself in between deep breaths. As soon as she stepped out of the house, she ran. She ran as fast as she could; she did not look at anything other than the beach and the setting sun.

The sun was only a sliver on the horizon now, and it was rapidly sinking. Lunimae increased her pace, but before she knew it, there was darkness. Darkness, darkness all around her. It was as if someone had spilled ink over the sun and sky. Lunimae now ran blindly in the streets, relying on her knowledge of the little town she had grown to love so much.

Suddenly she felt it: a chill hand brushed against her arm, a flutter of tattered robes against her ankles. The Shade. In a matter of moments, she felt dark hands, robes, mouths, and faces touching her smooth white skin. As they touched her, she felt her blood run cold, her hands start to numb, and her consciousness begin to falter.

"It is all an illusion. Do not let your fear take over, Lunimae dul Shin," said the voice that lived in her heart. It gave her courage and strength to carry on with her mission. Soon, Lunimae's breath ran out and her chest started to burn, just as it had so many years ago. Her bare feet bled from the sharp pebbles on the cobblestone street. Just as Lunimae was about to collapse into the dark arms of The Shade, she felt sand on her feet. Soft white sand now stained red with the blood from her feet.

The sand was still warm, even after the sun had set. "Blaize! Blaize! Where are you, my dear child?" Lunimae shouted desperately. She still could not see through the darkness, so she placed all her hope of finding Blaize with her voice.

"Lunimae! I'm here!" came the reply to Lunimae's call. Lunimae could now see something penetrating the darkness of the night. It was small, round, and glowed with a soothing white light. Blaize held it in his hand and used it to guide his path to Lunimae. She did not pay any attention to the object. Instead, she grabbed his wrist in panic and began running again. Blaize stumbled behind her, apparently unaware of the danger he was in. The light of the orb helped Lunimae find her way, and she could now see a few feet ahead of her. She could see the door to her home, and she ran faster and faster.

Blaize could not keep up with her fast pace, so he fell, bringing Lunimae tumbling along with him. The orb fell out of his hand and once again, both of them were submerged in darkness. Lunimae tried to get up, but her ankle had twisted in her fall. She knew that this would be the end of her. She threw her body over Blaize's to shield him from The Shade's deadly blows. She then closed her eyes. She felt a long black knife slip through her body. She felt her precious life slip away. She felt Blaize trembling underneath her. Then, slowly, Lunimae's vision blurred and she murmured her final words, "I am ... so ... sorry..." Her body went limp, and Lunimae died.

Blaize felt Lunimae's body collapse on top of him. At that moment, he knew that something was terribly wrong. He felt the sting of tears in his eyes, and although he tried his hardest to hold them back, he could no longer resist crying. As the tears poured down his cheeks, he laid Lunimae's body on the ground, repeating to himself that she wasn't dead, just seriously injured. But as soon as he felt her ice-cold hand, he knew that she was gone forever.

"Lunimae ... no ... you can't leave Raiye and me alone!"

As those words came out of his mouth, he suddenly became aware that he was not alone. The Shade were watching him. Trembling, he looked around, trying to see where they were. But the darkness was too deep, and The Shade blended in with the darkness itself. But wait! The darkness was thinning!

Blaize squinted to adjust his eyes to this new, mysterious light. It was a soft white light, but very bright. He searched for the source of this light, and he found it. Wide-eyed in horror, Blaize saw a small globe filled with bright silver smoke rise out from Lunimae's chest. He saw The Shade shrink back from the light, all except one. One of The Shade, the tallest of the group, pulled from his robes a black velvet sack.

Blaize took this opportunity to glance into the face of The Shade. It had smooth black skin, and glassy black eyes. There was no mouth or nose visible. This Shade, who was obviously the leader of this group, pulled the bag over the orb and once again plunged the world into darkness. The rest of The Shade seemed to be bowing in respect for ... something. Even the leader gave a slight bow after capturing the orb. He then fumbled with the strings of the bag, but finally managed to tie them into a tight knot. The Shade then thrust the bag back into his robes. Although Blaize could not see, the leader of The Shade made a gesture to his companions, and they departed.

Blaize felt their presence fade. He sat there in the darkness with Lunimae's cold, dead body. He was angry, confused, and shocked. He had so many questions now, but he had nobody to answer them. What was that globe that had come from Lunimae's chest? Why did it look similar to the globe the sea otters gave him that afternoon? Why didn't The Shade kill him as well? What were they bowing to? It almost seemed as if they were bowing at ... to ... it couldn't be.

These thoughts still spinning in his head, Blaize picked up Lunimae's body and stumbled home.

Colt

by Chris Chacon

Let Blood Spill in Every Corner of the Earth ... Until Justice is Served...

"Our father," he prayed to himself, "who art in heaven..." he heard horses galloping behind him "...hallowed be thy name..." he peered over his shoulder and saw a gang of bandits chasing after him, and a familiar figure riding as their leader "...thy kingdom come, thy will..." he grabbed his pistol, aimed, and fired "...be done..."

The figure flew off the back of his horse and landed in a pool of his own blood. Before his followers had time to react, they trampled the body. They stopped for a moment to mourn their leader, then turned to continue after their original target. But to their disappointment, he was gone. One of them cursed into the hot desert air.

- - -

The man slowed his horse into a trot and rode into a small town. When he found the saloon, he hopped off of his horse, tied the reins to a post, and went in. He sported a brown leather waistcoat, sleeves rolled up, with a faded blue cloth tunic underneath. His tall boots were made from worn leather and patched up in a number of places. On both sides of each boot, a blue cross was sewn on. He wore a black belt, and on each of his sides was a .45 revolver, black with brown handles. Hung over his right shoulder was a cartridge sling. On the outer sides of his pant legs were large combat knives.

The man sat at the bar and ordered a glass of whiskey. The bartender nodded and began pouring. He then slid the tall glass to the customer, who drank all the whisky in a single gulp, then ordered another. While he was drinking his second glass, a band of three men burst through the door.

"We're looking for Colt," one of them said.

"Yeah?" the man said after finishing his drink. He turned around and recognized the men as the bandits who were chasing him a few hours ago. After a moment, they pulled out their revolvers and began firing. Colt jumped behind the bar and retrieved his own revolvers. The bandits stopped firing. They slowly walked up to the bar and looked over. When they came into sight, Colt shot two of them in the head. Blood burst all over the counter, and the men collapsed lifelessly onto the floor. The last one shot at Colt, but he jumped to the side. When he landed, he put three bullets into the final man. When the final corpse dropped, Colt stood and jumped back over the counter. He rifled through the dead men's pockets and dropped some coins on the counter, then thanked the bartender, who was still crouched behind the bar. He turned and left. The saloon was silent, and all the bystanders slowly rose from under their tables. Looking at each other, everyone's expression said the same thing, "Wow!"

Colt untied his horse and hopped on. *Back to the farm,* he thought. He jabbed his heels into the sides of his horse and galloped out of town. He rode for a while, and as the desert slowly turned into grassy plains, his farm came into sight. It was a large red barn with a house close to the same size. Acres upon acres were fenced in for his cattle, horses, pigs, and sheep to roam as they pleased.

Colt stopped his horse outside of the fence entrance, removed his saddle, bit, and reins, opened the gate, and let his horse run to the others. He placed the equipment in the necessary places in the barn, then joined his father, Jack, who was standing just inside of the gate.

"Hello, son!" Jack greeted.

"Hey, Pa," Colt replied.

They shook hands and watched the animals graze. Colt and Jack were very close. They lived together on their farm, Hill Ranch, located near the lands of the Apache Indians, and sold milk, wool, and sometimes beef or ham to the town.

The day went on, and when the sun slowly dipped below the horizon, Colt turned in.

"I think I'm gonna go to sleep," he said.

"All right. G'night, son."

"Night," Colt replied. He went to his room, collapsed on his bed, and quickly fell asleep.

The next morning, Colt left the ranch. He went into town and tied up his horse outside of the saloon. It was a little busier than usual. He sat at the bar and ordered a whisky.

"Hey you," a drunk mumbled. The bartender handed the beverage to Colt, and he started drinking. "Hey, don't ignore me!" the drunk shouted.

He clumsily stepped up to Colt and grabbed his shoulder. Colt turned around only to have a heavy fist fly into his jaw. He grunted in pain, and the saloon fell silent as everyone stared intently at the two. He looked at the drunken man, standing in an awkward position with a vacant look on his face, and nailed him in the nose. The man was sent spiraling off of his feet and landed on someone else's nearby table. This caused a glass of whisky to spill on the man sitting at the table. He grabbed the drunk by his dirty shirt and threw him off.

The whole saloon broke into a huge fight. Men hit each other over the head with empty whisky bottles, others were punched, and some ganged up on a single man. Everyone hit everyone; everyone was fighting with everyone, but Colt managed to silently slip out of the saloon. He untied his horse and galloped home.

The ranch was torn apart. Some of the house was on fire. The barn was in pieces. The animals were running wild in a rage, sheep crying loudly, horses galloping and kicking their legs, and cattle mooing and ramming the fence. Colt jumped off his horse and dug through the remains of the house.

"Dad! Dad, where are you?" he shouted. When there was no answer, he dug even faster. He kept calling out for Jack, but each time there was silence. He grew more and more anxious. When he found nothing but burning wood under the house, he ran to the barn.

"Dad? Dad? Are you here?" he shouted. Again there was silence, and he dug as fast as he could. He found no one under the barn. He sat in silence.

Colt heard a rustling in some nearby trees. He grabbed a revolver and ran toward the noise. He jumped into the trees and came face to face with a bandit. He held his pistol to the side of the man's neck.

"Who the hell are you?" Colt asked.

"What's the matter? Miss your daddy?" the man replied with a sinister grin.

"What do you know about my father? Where is he?" Colt shouted, pushing the pistol into his neck. The man merely grinned. "Where is my father?" Colt tried again.

"Walker" was the response.

"Walker?" Colt asked. The man said nothing more. Colt waited a few more moments, then shot. He turned around and stepped back to the barn. He opened the gate to the fence, then got on his horse. He rode into town, thinking that he'd never see his ranch again.

Colt reloaded his revolvers as he arrived at the shop. He placed them back into his pocket and walked in.

"Can I help you, sir?" the clerk asked.

"I need a cartridge belt," Colt said. The clerk ducked behind the counter, and Colt heard him rummaging through things. He came back up with a cartridge belt in his hands.

"Here's a nice one. Holds fifty rounds of either .45- or .38-caliber bullets."

"How much?" Colt asked.

"'Bout fifty bucks," the clerk replied. Colt took out the rest of the bandit's money that he had taken the previous day and placed it on the counter. The clerk counted up the money and said, "Sir, there's seventy dollars here. The belt's only fifty."

"I know. I want some ammo, too. Forty-five calibers," Colt replied.

"Well, twenty bucks'll get ya 'bout 150 rounds. You need that much?"

"Yep."

"Well, okay, but since you're bein' such a good customer, I'll throw in this storage box for free," the clerk said with a smile. He ducked behind the counter again, then came back up with a dusty old storage box full of .45-caliber bullets.

"Thanks," Colt said, taking the ammo and the belt. The clerk nodded, and Colt left. He put on the belt and filled it with fifty bullets. Then he filled up the empty spaces in his sling and led his horse to the saloon. He tied up the reins, put his storage box in the saddlebag, pulled out his revolvers, and entered.

"I'm lookin' for a man named Walker," he said as he came through the door. No one listened. Colt shot at the ceiling, and when he had everyone's attention, he repeated the statement. But the saloon remained silent.

"What do you know of Walker?" a man finally said.

"He has my father," Colt answered. The man and gestured for Colt to follow him. He led Colt up a flight of stairs and into a room. Inside were a few more men.

"Alex, this man is looking for Walker."

"Thank-you, Max. Well, welcome, boy. What's your name?" Alex said.

"Colt."

"Well, Colt, you better take this." Alex handed Colt a sheriff's badge. Colt put it on, and Alex continued. "Men, there've been sightings of a man fittin' Walker's description, so I want you to go there and find out what's goin' on."

"Where is it?" Max asked.

"At the outskirts of town, a place called Long Farm."

Max nodded, and the men followed him outside.

"By the way, Colt, this is Black, Thomas, and Rob," Max said, pointing at each of the men as he said their names.

They all mounted their horses and rode off to Long Farm. When the men arrived, there was a burning house and a fence that had been torn down. All that was left was an old barn and a very frightened man and woman inside, huddled together. The woman was in tears, and the man was trying to comfort her. Colt dismounted and stepped toward them.

"W-who are you? P-please, don't hurt us!" the man pleaded.

"We're not here to hurt you," Colt said.

"We're looking for Walker Brown," Max said as he dismounted. "Is he the man who did this to you?"

"Yes, he is," the man said.

"Where did he go?" Colt asked.

to be continued...

When Blue Turns to Gray in Less than a Day
by Niki Bousquet

This morning, when I awoke, something was not quite right. My ocular devices were blurred with sleep, so it took me a few sixtieths of a minute to realize just what the problem was. I was in my bedroom as usual, but the color of the snow blue walls and just about everything else was slightly yellowed and dull. It looked as if the world was inside a television set whose color settings had been fooled around with by my cat. Cuniculus, my feline pet who should have been a rabbit, is double pawed, which gives her human-like abilities when it comes to turning knobs and pressing buttons.

After staring in dumbfounded confusion for a little longer than I would like to admit, I got to my feet and traveled into the hallway. It, too, seemed to have acquired a layer of dirt and cobwebs during the seven or so hours I had been unconscious and probably snoring obnoxiously. Even more bizarre was the fact that I seemed to be completely alone in this desolate, two-story, medium-sized house, which had formerly been a pretty cheerful and jolly place. My mom, brother, and feline companion should have been prancing around madly preparing to venture out into the world on this Monday morning.

As I explored the other rooms of the house and found them identical to the way they were the previous evening, other than the griminess that comes from a long period without disturbance, I tried to fish through my brain for some explanation. While doing this, I was startled to recall a surrealistically realistic dream that my strange brain had apparently conjured up the night before.

In this nighttime adventure, which I was able to recall with startling accuracy, I had been sucked out of my bed, through my open window, and into the sparkling night sky by some unseen force.

A disembodied voice had said in a relieved whisper, "Good. Now that we've retrieved Opal, she can lead us to all we need to know."

I could not figure out what this meant. All I knew was that my name is Opal and some strange bodiless kidnapper somehow found me to be of great importance. As I replayed the dream I thought of the black holes, white holes, and wormholes I had been marveling over after watching my favorite movie, *Donnie Darko*, last night.

Black holes are extremely dense bodies from which nothing can escape. They pull matter into them with great force, much as I had been plucked out of my bed. In the dream, after the voice spoke, there was nothing but unbearable darkness for a great while, like I would expect there to be inside the intestines of a lion or a bear. It occurred to me that the phenomenon I had experienced was undeniably similar to what traveling through a wormhole, a combination of a white hole and a black hole, would hypothetically be like.

Of course, this would not be a logical explanation from the point of view of most scientists. Wormholes and white holes are possible, but physicists have concluded that they could not exist in nature, as there is no way to create a white hole. On the other hand, Albert Einstein formulated equations that allow black holes to be constructed. If these equations were simply reversed, they could, in theory, produce a white hole.

However, many factors make time travel through a wormhole seemingly impossible. It is scientifically accepted that no white hole or wormhole is created upon the collapse of an actual star into a black hole. Real black holes have only an entrance, but no exit, much like a coffin. Even if a star collapse did occur, it is not likely that the resulting wormhole would possess much stability. Any disruption, such as a human or a spacecraft venturing through it, would cause it to collapse, as it would be such a delicate body. In other words, if a wormhole were to be shipped through the mail, it would require all of the FRAGILE: HANDLE WITH CAUTION stamps that exist on Earth. Even with those, it would probably be deemed unfit for travel, much like a terminally ill cancer patient. Even the gases produced by the dying star from which a black hole results would cause a tumult far too great to be tolerated by a wormhole.

Furthermore, if a wormhole was somehow created and happened to be stable enough so that it could handle passengers, anything that entered it would be in for a very gruesome yet speedy trip. This is because the wormhole would be absolutely stuffed, like a very fluffy pillow, with harmful energy, such as X-rays and gamma rays, that would flow in from galaxies and stars in its proximity. These rays would instantaneously vaporize any person or object that entered the wormhole.

Despite the nighttime reverie and the aged objects within my house that obviously did not belong to the time from which I had come, I did not fancy the idea that I had traveled through a wormhole to the future. It was not only highly improbable but also unbearably depressing. It seemed that I was completely alone in this future world. The quiet was impossibly loud, and when I stepped outdoors, walking quite a few miles in each direction, I observed no signs of intelligent life. There were no people or even squirrels or ladybugs to keep me company. Only the giant oaks with their old wrinkled bark smiled at me, and their friendship did not do much to console me. I looked for an amicable elderly tree that I used to climb in my former life. I had named this tree Phineas Perigrin Alexander, and when I found it, I hugged it, but it had no arms to hug me back. All its branches were old, dead, and crippled with arthritis that I'm sure was very painful.

I stood there for a long while with Phineas until he finally opened his chapped and cracked bark lips and spoke.

"I brought you here, Opal."

I stared at him, wondering if my lack of human companionship had caused me to go mad as a hatter who worked in a hat shop all day with whatever chemicals were used to make those strange, stiff old hats. Years ago, I had had many conversations with this arboreal organism, but those were only figments of my quite fabricated imagination.

"I know it is gloomy here all alone, but you were the most intelligent human I could think of when my friends Barry Black Hole, Wendy White Hole, and Willy Wormhole asked. You see, the entire Earth was sucked into a black hole and expelled from a white hole, killing everyone except you. This was done purposefully to prevent it from being hit by an asteroid, which certainly would have obliterated everything. The three variations of celestial chasms do not mean to hurt anyone. They do have protective shields that they can activate to save humans, but just one requires so much energy. There was only enough energy in the universe to power one of those shields, along with the one required to protect the Earth itself, so we had to select the person we believed would be most valuable to the future of the planet," Phineas explained.

This caused me to feel even more discombobulated than I had previously. "But," I protested, "white holes and wormholes could not possibly really exist."

"Well, yes, that is true for the most part," began my talking tree, "You see, in science, it is believed that even if a black hole were to rotate and possess a charge of electricity, something would be able to fall into it, but still not into the singularity that exists at its center. If anything, like a person or a planet, could fall into a black hole, it would not likely miss the center and, therefore, pop out in another time. Normally, the object would simply hit the singularity and its journey would come to an end."

Afraid of what the answer might be, I asked, "Phineas, are you saying that some one-time phenomenon occurred, allowing me to safely be transported through a wrinkle in time? Do you honestly expect me to believe that?"

"Opal, I know with your level of intelligence you are not gullible, but, yes, that is precisely what I am suggesting. I hope you will believe me; I am an oak. In the hundreds of years I have been around I have seen much, and what has happened to you is actually not as extraordinary as it appears to be. White holes and wormholes normally cannot be created, but in this case, the sky and all the celestial bodies agreed that such a strange occurrence was necessary."

"Even if that is true," I continued, still skeptical, "why do you need me?"

Phineas paused thoughtfully before speaking. "We hope someday to be able to transport the Earth back to its previous position. There may have been damage to the atmosphere that cannot be repaired where it is now, because the proper gases do not exist at this time, as they did where the planet was before. We need a human with great scientific knowledge to help us, and you meet all the requirements. You see, it will take at least fifty years to conjure up enough power to shield the Earth from vaporization as it goes through a wormhole again, back to where it belongs. You are the only human who has the required knowledge yet who is young and healthy enough to still be alive when the time comes to return."

I sat there stunned, not talking, just processing this giant glob of unfathomable information, much as one would after eating a large holiday dinner. Soon, I lay down on the soft moss at Phineas's roots; the realization that everything familiar to me was gone had left me fatigued. Before I fell into a deep sleep, I heard Phineas mention that the celestial bodies were attempting to develop technology that would allow them to go back in time and retrieve everything from Earth that had been killed so it could be put back on the planet when it returned to its proper place. They were also hoping to figure out how to put everyone in suspended animation so they would not age. I would be put in suspended animation also, with the exception of my brain, which was the part of me most instrumental to the plan.

When I awoke, I was at home and something was not quite right. My ocular devices were blurred with sleep, so it took me a few sixtieths of a minute to realize just what the problem was. I was in my bedroom as usual, but the color of the snow blue walls was just as frosty and crisply blue as always. It looked as if the world were inside a television set whose color settings were crystal clear and absolutely perfect. Cuniculus jumped on my face and purred in my ear.

I ventured out into the hallway to see my little brother, Andrew, frantically eating Cheerios at the kitchen table, along with my mom. We were all going to be late for our respective commitments this Monday morning. All of us had slept through our alarm clocks, as if we were too busy enjoying long, peculiar dreams to notice the arrogant buzzing. After breakfast I traveled to the bathroom to brush my teeth. When I stared at myself in the mirror, as clear as crystal, I looked just the same as ever, yet I felt very, very old.

The Storm

by Lydia Burrage-Goodwin

"Are you afraid?" he asked as they watched from the dunes off the shore.

The clammy air made their hands stick together and their hair twist and tangle into clumps. It smelled of salt and fish, and although there wasn't any sign on the ocean, old rope from whaling ships.

The wind blew in from the north, cold and icy, playing with their hair and threatening their stability. White waves on the sea swelled and crashed down on the sand, and the clouds darkened, looming above the choppy waters. Dirty white foam washed onto shore, picking up sand and seashells every time it made its journey inward. A flock of geese screeched and cawed as they flew away from the danger of the sky, flapping in a V-shaped procession. They flew over the shack that Addy and Caleb retreated to before the storm, they flew over the disturbed ocean waves, through pine trees, pine needles shaking and quivering, and they flew by town, where anyone within twenty miles traveled to buy goods at Ahab's Mercantile and General Merchandise. Flying was a dream in any human's mind, only to be witnessed in a nightmare, or in heaven, as they believed it. It could only be reached in a fantasy.

"Well?" Caleb insisted, staring into her worried green eyes. "Are you scared? I certainly am not," he lied. "I have seen many a storm on the seas. The *Rose* was the most reliable of the ships. She kept the crew safe when the last hurricane hit."

"I am troubled with such a thought as being on the sea while a storm was brewing," she replied. "The sky is much darker than it has been during past storms, and it seems more eerie." Then, suddenly, she snapped her head away from the roaring seas and with a concerned look upon her face looked up to the sky. "It is beginning to rain again, Caleb. We should go inside."

Addy followed Caleb into the tattered red barn and watched him check on the horses and the wagon. He gave them extra oats that they had brought along for their long journey and then shut the swinging red doors tight. "I sure hope we can get to your parents' house before the wedding," Caleb said. "I don't think that this jumble of wood is going to hold out in this storm much longer."

As they entered the one-room house, Addy took the coffee pot that had been abandoned with the house and washed it out to use for supper, as it was the only pot they had. "I didn't plan on staying anywhere overnight, so I didn't bring any cooking supplies. It is a darn good thing that this house has some things," she said, looking around the house for a sufficient meal. She took some cornmeal out of a big basin beside the door. Then she ran outside to the well and filled the coffee pot to the brim. "We shall have corn paste for dinner, honey. Does it sound okay?"

"Sounds fine, Addy," he said with a grin.

The room was merely a few degrees warmer than the outside, and one of the window panes was broken, not helping them very much heating the place.

When they had finished eating their warmed corn paste with their fingers, Addy wiped her fingers on her clothing and sat down on the one straw pile in the room. Her face looked troubled and scared as she peered out the wet window. She watched raindrops race down the window and lightning fill the sky for a split second.

"It is going to be fine," Caleb told her after seeing the worried expression on her face. But he had no idea what was ahead of them.

Addy awoke in the middle of the night to the sound of the wind crying and moaning and the tree branches from a pine tree batting against the window. She got out of bed, walked over to the broken window pane, and stuffed some straw in the gaping hole, ceasing the irksome howling and chilling wind. She went to the fireplace and warmed herself on the dimming coals. Caleb heard her yawning and got up out of bed himself. "I can't sleep," she told him, "I'm scared."

"There is nothing to be afraid of. I am sure this storm will only last the night."

"Yes, but what if it lasts longer? We will be late for the wedding."

"We won't be late. They are expecting us tomorrow, and tomorrow morning, we will rise early and be on our way." He tried to comfort her, but she just seemed more and more worried about the storm. "Let us now go to sleep, so morning will come faster."

Addy smiled and willingly lay down on the pile of straw again, wrapping Caleb's coat around her and clutching it twice as hard. The sway and creaking of the shack lulled them to sleep, and the two slept side by side, keeping each other warm. Caleb encased his hands around Addy's, warming them with his gentle touch, and they both drifted off to sleep.

The sun remained behind the clouds in the morning, casting only a haze of fog over the still-roaring ocean. The fog deepened, and the clouds turned into a rock-gray color. The storm began to feel more threatening: thunder bellowed and echoed across the land. The rain fell harder and faster, the swell of the ocean increased into large waves, and more and more animals fled far from the danger. Wind began to break apart the old shack that Addy and Caleb were in. Boards of wood began to warp in the muggy air, and pieces were sent flying into bushes and into the sand. The danger was serious.

"What do we do?" Addy panicked, already wide awake but unaware of Caleb's dormant body. "Caleb?" she poked at him and shoved him off the straw until he realized he was being summoned.

"Huh, wha...?" he mumbled.

"We have to get out of here. The storm is getting worse."

"We cannot. If we try to leave, we'll be battered with wood chunks and debris. We must stay here."

"We are right on the shore!" Addy sobbed. "We will be blown away in a few minutes. If we don't try, we will have no chance of outliving this hell. It is getting more and more dangerous." Her throat was choked up and she wanted to cry, but nothing would come to her.

"No is my final answer. I won't risk losing you in this. We will wait it out."

Addy sat there with tears streaming down her face, feeling angry and defeated. She also felt vulnerable for not being able to get out and escape. Thoughts boiled inside her, but she loved Caleb, and although she didn't always approve of his ideas, she trusted him with her life, even if he was stubborn.

Suddenly, she began to worry again, and she tried to keep her mind off the storm by working. Caleb brought over some firewood and got the fire going again. Addy swept the dirt floor, washed the windows, and instead of using the last of their corn meal, she prepared the last of their food, a jar of canned peaches. They ate their meal in silence.

Water began to creep into the cabin, inching its way toward the fireplace and their straw bed. "Caleb! Look! Oh my God, we're being flooded!"

Caleb ran over to the door and stuffed some straw in the crack beneath it, but it was to no avail. Water slowly poured in, soaking the rest of their cornmeal, wetting down their bed, and putting out their only source of heat, the fire.

They took what they could and raced against the fast moving water, battering winds and heavy rainfall, and moved uphill a ways to the barn with the horses. They settled on a new pile of straw, half of which was either already eaten by the horse or covered in horse-pies. It reeked of horse. The stench was so dense in the barn that when they entered, Addy gagged and covered her nose.

"With the way the water is flooding the cabin, this barn won't hold us for very long either." Caleb blamed himself for the events that took place—the flooding, the wind, everything— and wondered if he was doing the right thing for Addy. Before he could answer that in his mind, a bolt of lightning streaked across the sky, and a huge thunderclap shook the earth, disturbing the rhythmic pitter patter of the rain on the roof. A nearby tree was hit and cracked in half. Bark and wood screamed as the tree came down onto the barn roof. The crash was ear-splitting. The thud of the tree on the roof was muffled by the cracking barn beams.

"Caleb, look out!" Addy screamed.

Caleb looked up and raced toward the barn door, but on the way out, a beam from the barn struck him in the head, and a tree branch pinned his leg to the ground. Both his head and his leg began to bleed. Addy ran over and ripped off a piece of her apron, stuffing part of it beside his leg and part beside his head to stop the bleeding.

"Caleb." She slapped him on the cheek a few times, but nothing happened. He was out cold. She attempted to lift the tree branch off of his leg, but it was too heavy. "I need to get help," she said under her breath. She tore open the barn door and sloshed through the puddles of water, realizing that the water was rising still, knowing that she couldn't swim.

"Help me!" she screamed. "Anyone, help!" Then, desperate for anyone's help, she searched for a town.

to be continued ...

Cifer

by Liam O'Connor

It was a day late in March, and the snow lay in patches on the soggy ground. Two men strode quickly in the mud and slush, taking a shortcut through someone's yard. Neither was remarkable; the redhead wore a plaid sweater and the black-haired one wore a dull brown coat. They were students at the nearby college.

A black van drove toward them. It was moving slowly, so slowly the words on the mud-splattered hubcaps were deciphered without difficulty. The black-haired man ignored the van completely, attempting to continue the conversation. The other brushed him off and walked to the sidewalk, then stepped onto the curb.

The van stopped right in front of the red head. The driver was the only person visible from where the black-haired man stood, but his friend walked to the tinted window of the third seat. As his friend walked, the first man noticed that the driver ignored them, staring forward in a daze. His skin was drawn on his face and a bit of drool dribbled onto his shirt.

The first student was beginning to get nervous. "Sam, come on. Something's not right."

"Shut up, Joe." But Sam's voice was tight with fear. In fact, Joe noticed his friend's muscles were clenched, as if he were trying to fight some impossibly strong force. Joe leapt forward and grabbed Sam's shoulders, dragging him back from the curb. In the instant before Sam's gaze was jerked from the window, it slid open.

As Joe hit the sidewalk with Sam lying heavily on top of him, the screech of rubber on pavement shattered the deathly silence as the van shot away. Then, as if the sound had broken a spell, Sam began to scream. He screamed so hard blood began to bubble up, as the force of the sound tore his throat. The fear in his voice was far louder than the voice itself, however; it struck the hearts of all who heard it. In fact, it awoke something powerful and determined in three hearts, two of whom were present, and one of whom was miles away.

One of those whose heart was stirred was Joe. He bent down to Sam, shaking him slightly.

"Sam?" he whispered. "Are you okay? What happened?"

Sam looked up fearfully. "Joe?"

"Yes, it's me."

"Did you see it? The boy?"

Joe frowned. "What boy? There wasn't a boy, Sam."

"Yes there was. In the car. I saw his eyes, and..." Sam coughed, more blood spurting up. "They glowed. They were the eyes of the devil. He was only a boy, but he had the eyes of the devil." Sam began to sob, tears dropping to the ground and making little pockmarks in the snow.

The second heart that stirred belonged to another that was present. Cifer stared through the back window of his van at the two men on the ground. Before they disappeared from sight, he burnt their faces into his brain. He would have to watch out for them. If the red-haired one recovered, his hatred would be formidable; the scream had shown that. And the other one—the one with the black hair and the stern eyebrows—he was more dangerous still.

"Alter course. Take a few back roads; stay out of sight." No need to take any risks. He didn't want anyone telling the two where he went.

The corpse-wraith that was Cifer's chauffeur said nothing. But then, it never did. All it ever did was what it was told. The wraith turned the van onto a dirt road through a gloomy stretch of forest. As it grew darker, the shadows stretched on all sides, the dead and withered branches like fingers grasping for prey. Cifer smiled. His chauffeur had an uncanny sense of what would please its master.

Once he had enjoyed the gloom enough, and was sure no humans would notice his van, he ordered the wraith to drive home. He was hungry, his previous meal interrupted by the man with the stern eyebrows. Joe, as the victim had called him.

Joe gazed sadly out the window of the hospital waiting room. Sam's family was in with him now. They had been called right after the ambulance, and they entered Sam's room immediately upon arriving. Joe didn't know the doctor's verdict yet, because family had to be told first, but he knew it wasn't going to be good. Sam had been driven insane, mumbling incoherently. The devil eyes thing was the last sentence that came from Sam's mouth.

Joe put his head in his hands, sighing heavily. He had told the doctors, and then Sam's family, the story of the black van, but they hadn't believed him. The doctors had simply smiled and nodded, but worse than that was the reaction of Sam's parents. They had started yelling at Joe, telling him that it wasn't funny to make up stories, and that he should just admit that the two had been experimenting with drugs. Joe rubbed his eyes with his palms, the exhaustion taking hold.

A hand on his shoulder made him look up. A man of about fifty stood next to him, though his gaze suggested him to be younger. His eyes were bright and alive, though they had an air of wisdom. He removed his hand from Joe's shoulder and held it out.

"My name is Jean von Harris. I have it on good information you've encountered Cifer. Though I think not face to face, or we wouldn't be speaking."

Joe took his hand carefully. He didn't know what the man was talking about, but he felt he should listen. It was the same feeling that had awoken in his heart when he heard Sam scream; it flared up the instant Harris spoke the name Cifer.

"Who is this Cifer?"

"He goes by many names, though you would recognize few. Some speculate he is Satan, a theory supported by his name's similarity to Lucifer."

Joe held a hand to halt the man. "Some? Who are some?"

Harris sighed. "I suppose I should tell you the whole thing. Come, sit down." Joe followed Harris to a couple of chairs in the corner, sitting down opposite him. "This world is riddled with things foreign to you, things that, if you were introduced to them, would fascinate or terrify you, sometimes both. The few who know these things, and what they are, work to understand them—and, if necessary, eradicate them. Cifer is one such thing. He is a horror as old as the world itself, a phantom from the beginning of time. None have succeeded in killing him, though, believe me, many have tried. But you might succeed where others have failed."

"Hold on, how do you even know I've met Cifer?"

"I felt it, my boy. I felt your friend's scream, the terror he experienced. It reached me and told my heart what I needed to know." Harris reached forward again and grasped Joe's shoulder. "You can do it. You've an air about you that's indescribable; you're strong, unbelievably so. If ever Cifer was to die, I think your hand would be the one to do the blessed act."

Harris continues talking, about silver being deadly to evil entities and how he could use it to kill this one in particular. Joe listened, though not avidly; he was learning what Harris taught him, yes, but he was also thinking. Should he do it? Would it do any good?

Well, thought Joe, it might not help Sam, but it'll prevent this from happening again. If he could help stop this evil from attacking another innocent, he should.

Cifer was not in a pleasant mood. He had thought the danger of the black-haired man, Joe, had passed, but apparently it had simply fermented, stagnating into something far worse than a slight inconvenience. That doddering old fool von Harris had found him, and had planted ideas in Joe's head.

Cifer stood up. He had been sitting in an old armchair next to a fireplace that was equally old, stewing over the infuriating occurrences of the past week. The crow he had made as a spy to make sure Joe didn't take any actions against him had come to warn him of Harris' contact. The corpse-wraiths he had sent out to investigate the area the two were staying in had been destroyed; he could only assume it had been either Joe or Harris. He had received further word from the gargoyles at his gate that the two impudent humans had entered the grounds of Cifer's age-old mansion. This went beyond stupidity and arrogance. Harris should know no normal human could kill the child devil; therefore Joe must not be normal.

Cifer pondered for a moment, then spoke into a hole in the wall. "Wraiths. Intercept company in lobby. Kill the boy, but bring the old man to me."

Harris was an old enemy. He deserved so much more than a quick death.

Walking to an old and grimy window, Cifer stared into his grounds, searching for the two humans. A flash of color in the gray landscape drew his attention like a magnet. There they were, creeping from dead bush to dead bush. They obviously thought they were clever, Cifer thought with a smirk. But a human's experience and intelligence can't compare with that of a creature as old as time itself.

His mood considerably lighter, Cifer sat once again in the old armchair. He reached one of his thin arms to the table next to it and grabbed his glass of spirits, though this wasn't alcohol; it was the liquefied soul of a human. He downed it in one gulp, grinning at the wriggling sensation as it flowed down his throat. Two humans come to fight him; utter hilarity! Humans existed solely as his prey.

Joe grimaced at the gloomy mansion rising up before him. It looked as if no one had lived there for years; vines climbed up its sides and into its smashed windows, and in several places the roof was falling in. Joe turned to von Harris with annoyance. "Is this the right house? I'm sure no one actually lives here."

Harris raised a finger to his lips. "See there, boy?" Among the rubble of a stone wall to the left, a gargoyle in perfect condition sat gazing in their direction. "That's proof enough," Harris continued. "Cifer uses them as guards, and soldiers, when the mood takes him, though he prefers corpse-wraiths for that."

Joe nodded once, his doubts abated. The two humans, the only ones for miles, walked the last few yards to the large, rotting doors. Harris reached out and pushed one door open. It creaked slightly as it swung forward. Harris stepped into the murky light beyond, with Joe right behind.

It took two minutes for Joe to get used to the lack of light. In those two minutes, he became aware of a shuffling sound and a closeness of the air. It felt as if the room were full of people, all struggling for space. He felt Harris stiffen beside him.

"Well, it looks like the little devil knew we were coming. He's sent a welcoming party," Harris said grimly.

As Joe's eyes adjusted, he saw what he first thought to be the same creature that had been driving the van when Cifer attacked Sam. He noticed there wasn't just one creature. A hundred rotting and slimy corpses ringed the humans, every one indistinguishable from the next.

Joe grimaced at the sight and smell, then turned to Harris. "What do we do? There are a lot of them."

Harris gazed around them calmly. "Reach into my bag and get one of the silver eggs." Joe did as he was told, handing a shining object to Harris.

"What is that thing?" Joe was skeptical. One shiny egg was going to get them past hundreds of corpse-wraiths?

"Watch and you'll find out." Harris pressed the top of it once, then threw it in front of them. "No need to duck," he said to Joe, who had flattened against the ground. "It won't hurt us."

A blinding flash of silver light illuminated the room, pushing the gloom to the corners and doorways. The light died away quickly, but not entirely; a silver mist shrouded the room. All of the corpse-wraiths lay immobile on the floor.

"What did you do?" Joe gaped at the older man. Harris smiled and began to pick his way through the corpses to the stairs at the far end of the room. Joe hurried to catch up with him.

"It was a silver bomb. Upon detonation, it lets loose a flash of silver light and dust, after which the dust stays in the air. Anything supernatural can be felled with that, as long as they breathe."

"Those dead things breathe?"

"Well, they're not really dead. That's how they are from the day they're created. And they're not particularly strong as they go in the world of the evil, so they breathe. Cifer doesn't need to breathe, because he's one of the most powerful evil entities in existence."

"Oh. So it won't be that easy to kill him?"

Harris looked at him oddly. "Of course not. Otherwise he'd have been killed by now. I told you it would be difficult. Near impossible, in fact."

Joe sighed. He'd hoped for a second after the detonation of the silver bomb that the whole expedition would be that easy.

The two reached the top of the stairs. Joe paused, uncertain where to go next, but Harris walked straight on, as if he knew the mansion intimately. Well, perhaps he did. He seemed to know a lot of things.

Harris led Joe to a set of doors at the end of a hall. Unlike everything else in the house, these doors were in great condition, the large gold knocker gleaming despite the murkiness of the hall. Harris nodded to Joe, who reached out and pushed hard on one door. It swung open, revealing a slightly better lit room with a fireplace on the far side.

Joe stepped forward into the room. He immediately noticed a large armchair facing the fire. He turned to Harris, who was still in the hall, and pointed at the chair. Harris nodded , and then followed Joe into the room.

Suddenly, Harris was thrown out of the room, back into the hall. The door swung shut with a loud booming sound. A high thin laugh came from the armchair.

"Surely you didn't expect me to allow you to fight two on one? That would be unfair. The rule is two men to a duel." A pale boy about the size of an eight-year-old stepped around the chair to stand in front of Joe, black hair shifting from the movement to fall in front of his eyes. As the boy brushed the hair away, Joe saw that his eyes glowed like pale lanterns; they were a shimmering, luminescent yellow, even more disturbing, they were white and slitted.

Cifer laughed again, but he wasn't really amused. In fact, he was very angry at the death of his wraiths. In the end, they had proven worthless, failing at their job miserably. He had to act on his own, and now actually had to fight the boy. Cifer was confident of his abilities, but battle was impossible to predict; it was quite possible that something could go wrong.

Cifer frowned as Joe pulled out a whip made of silver. It had been aptly chosen; the silver would damage him, and whips had always been a problem for the child devil. He could never predict their movements, and they were sometimes too fast to dodge or counter.

The human cracked the whip expertly, adding a new layer to Cifer's caution. Joe stepped forward slowly, testing the ground to make sure of its solidity. He began to circle.

Then, Joe lunged, the whip curling around Cifer's neck. But the devil twisted down and forward, under it. He reached up with one small hand and somehow fitted it around Joe's throat. Cifer pulled the human down, until their faces were level. The frown lifted from the childish face, replaced with a grin of satisfaction.

"So, Harris was a fool after all. I thought perhaps he'd brought me an adversary, but instead he offered me a sacrifice. Two, in fact. He shan't leave here alive."

"Harris isn't a fool. He knew you'd gloat." With one swift movement, Joe drew a silver dagger from his belt and plunged it into the devil's heart.

Pain filled Cifer's chest cavity. It burnt his heart, then his entire body as the power of the silver spread through his black veins. All his strength, all his evil, all of his millennia of memories gathered at the point where the dagger broke his skin. Then, it burst out along the blade, into the hilt, leaving the broken body behind.

Joe felt the power approach his hand, but Harris had warned him of this. If it touched him, Cifer would be reborn in Joe's body. So, Joe let the body fall, stepping back to the door. Harris came in behind him, clapping him on the back, the ward broken with the devil's death.

"Good work, my boy."

"Yeah. Thanks." Joe gazed at the corpse. It was strange how something so evil could, in death, look so peaceful. Cifer looked like a normal child, especially now that his eyes were clouded in death. Joe turned away, disturbed.

"Yes, of course you'd be shocked. But don't go feeling sorry for him. Watch, I've got something that'll cheer you right up." Harris led Joe to a closet in the corner of the room.

"What?"

"Watch." Opening the door, Harris pointed to a dozen bottles full of a swirling liquid. A faint humming sound emanated from the room.

"What are those?" Joe stepped forward, then back again quickly. Something about these bottles wasn't right.

"They're souls. Human souls, liquefied by Cifer to consume."

"How is that supposed to cheer me up? He killed all those people?" Joe glanced at Harris' face and was disgusted to find him grinning, but the old man shook his head, gesturing at the bottles again.

"It's good because the soul maintains the sanity, rationality, and thought. The people may still be alive. If we smash the bottles, then the souls find their humans, and they recover."

"Like ... Sam?"

"Exactly. So what are you waiting for?" Harris set to systematically breaking bottles. Joe joined him a moment later.

By the time they had finished, Joe's mind was set. He had to continue what he started. If there were other devils and monsters in the world that killed and hurt innocent people, Joe had to defend those he could and prevent any from being hurt in the future.

When he finally returned to the hospital to check on Sam, he found him bright and alive. As he greeted his friend, he smiled. Yes, he thought. This is the payoff.

The Locket

by Christina Brown

The old steps may have creaked that day, but the truth hung on the old oak tree. I knew as I opened the door that something was unusual, but I guess it was that my mom had decorated for Halloween. The outside stairs were covered in cobwebs with hairy black spiders dangling from the doorway.

"David, how come you're so late getting home from school?" Mom asked.

"Well, it all started with when I forgot my homework ... then, it just got even worse." I grumbled, shook my head, and walked away.

"Sorry to hear that, David. I just made your bed. Go do your homework in your room while I'm cooking dinner."

As I headed up the stairs, I could hear the wind whipping through the trees like a freight train. I thought, *Man is that loud. It is probably going to be a stormy night. I had better hurry up. Dinner smells delicious.* The house was filled with the scent of chicken and broccoli casserole, which made my mouth water.

After I finished my homework, Mom yelled up to me, "Dinner."

It was perfect timing. As I rushed down the stairs, my door slammed shut behind me. Whoa, creepy, I thought with a shudder. From there on, it was getting spookier and spookier.

As I was reading a book after dinner, a crow flew by—not once, but twice—squawking, giving me the jitters, as goose-bumps appeared on my arms. The book I was reading was called *The Night of the Werewolf.* Since I couldn't tolerate the influence of ghosts and witches, I decided to get my pajamas on and call it a night.

I had just finished brushing my teeth and was about to take off my glasses when, totally unexpectedly, the crow flew by again, this time with metallic shining bright eyes. I headed toward the window, cautiously, even though my legs were frozen with fear. I peered just over the ledge, so I wouldn't be seen. The crow was perched on the old oak, its eyes glaring back at me, so focused it was as if its eyes were a telescope, and they could see far more than any naked eye. Following it outside was probably not the best of ideas, but I took a chance.

Coyotes howled with a full moon beyond them. A glowing object was coming from the tree. My heart was pounding so hard, it sounded like the steady beat of a drum.

Bump-bump ... bump-bump ... bump-bump.

As I got closer, I realized it was a key hanging from the tree by a chain, but a key to what? The key was old and fragile looking, like an antique. Although the crow was still perched on the tree, I grabbed the key and went inside. Now I could finally go to bed. I set the key on my nightstand right beside my alarm clock so that I could grab it tomorrow and no one else could get their hands on it. The nightstand was an oak color, stained the same color as my bedpost. I got into my bed and shut off my lamp. The moon was the only light shining through the window. I fell asleep wondering what tomorrow would bring.

* * *

Beep! Beep! Beep!

Aw! Is it already time to go to Nana's house? The sun was shining through my window causing the bureau to cast an intriguing shadow. As I got out of bed, I could hear the birds chirping. It was like lightning. Once my clothes were on, and the key is in my pocket, we were off in the car driving to Nana's.

As my mom and I were passing the houses on my nana's street, we saw Halloween decorations covering the houses and trees. When we got out of the car, we were greeted by my nana standing on the front porch. Fall leaves covered the sides of the walkway on both sides of the slate steps.

"I just put the cookies in the oven, David. Go put your coat in that old useless room, if you don't mind," Nana stated.

She was full of energy and looked as if she had gotten a good night of sleep.

Since I knew my mom would make me, I decided to just do it. In the room were a mattress and a mini-chest on top of a table that had a lock on it. I hung my coat in the closet where the doors squeaked and the paint was chipped. I left the room the way I found it and headed into the living room to sit with Nana.

"Nana, what is that mini-chest in there for?"

"Oh, come sit down and I shall tell you the whole story! A long time ago—gosh, maybe a hundred years ago—your great, great grandmother bought that chest. The people who sold her the chest locked it. They lost the key. On the way home it didn't close fully, which saved it from locking, but after she put some of her belongings in it, it closed fully. The next day, she went to open the chest and realized that she didn't have the key. When she went to get the key from the people she bought the chest from, they said that when the time was right, someone in her family would find the key. From then on, the chest has been passed down for many generations." Nana hesitated. "So why were you wondering?"

As I began to speak, I remembered that this morning I had placed the key in my pocket. "Nana, I found this key last night, and for some odd reason I think it might go to the chest." I took the key out of my pocket and showed it to her, so she could examine it.

"Oh, is this true? Hurry, go in there and see if it will open!"

I rushed in the room, put the key in the lock, and as it unlatched, I saw there was an immense heart locket in it, except it didn't have a chain to wear as a necklace. The locket was tarnished. I opened it, and in there lay a picture and a note that were folded multiple times, so that they would fit.

"This locket belonged to my great grandmother. David, pass me that note," Nana said. The note was a brownish-greenish color; it had weathered many years.

She began to read the letter, and then, about five sentences down, she quickly folded it back up, stuffed it in the locket, and closed it with a snap. "I had a feeling you were the one," Nana continued, "but I had to see it with my own eyes to believe it. I want you to keep the locket, but you must promise me you will never read this note, unless you feel trapped and like you're at the end of life's road. This locket contains powerful information and you may end up learning that the hard way."

"What's that supposed to mean?"

Beep!

I saw that my mom had pulled in the driveway and needed to get home soon. As I was getting in the car, I took one last look back to wave goodbye to Nana, and saw her fall to the ground.

I ran inside and stayed with Nana while my mom called the rescue team.

My parents and I followed the ambulance to the hospital. We were exhausted, and, before I knew it, we had fallen asleep. The doctor came and woke my parents and me up. "I have some bad news. She died of a major heart attack. I was going through her files and supposedly, she was having chest pains and was told a few weeks ago there was a possibility of her dying. If you would like to come say some last words, she is through the double doors on your first left."

I looked at the double doors that were down the long, narrow hall. I wondered what else was on the other side, but I remembered my grandmother, the way she stopped me from reaching the other side.

"I think we're just going to go home, if you know what I mean," my dad answered.

"Well, yes of course. If you want to come back later, I'll be here till eleven tonight," the doctor replied.

At school the next day, my friend Kevin asked me what I did over the weekend.

"My nana passed away; luckily I had time to say goodbye. Also, I found a locket that was from my great, great grandmother."

"What's inside of the locket?"

"Well, I know there is a picture with a piece of paper, but I don't know what the paper says."

"You should read it. What are you, stupid?"

"My nana had told me to only read it when I feel like I'm at the—"

"Look, she isn't alive anymore, so what difference does it make? If the reason you don't want to read it is that you miss her, and it will be too painful, I'll read it for you. You can drop it off in my locker after school, tomorrow, and I'll get it back to you the next time I see you."

"Well, I guess it will be all right. I wouldn't be the person reading it technically. She didn't say that no one else could read it. I should probably be getting home before my mom gets curious. Bye!"

When I was at school the next day, I gave Kevin the letter toward the end of the day. When I got to my house, I saw police cars in front of it.

"Why are there police cars here, Mom?"

"Well, actually your friend Kevin has the will for your nana's belongings and the police are here to get the key."

Kevin read the letter, which was a will, and now he was claiming it was his all along.

"WAAITTTT! I declare that we go to court. This afternoon, I gave Kevin a letter that I wasn't supposed to read until I was trapped in life, and now he's using it as if it were his!"

"Is this true?" one of the police officers asked.

Kevin didn't answer.

"On March 19, 2007, at 3:00 p.m., we will be meeting at court in Flaganagal's Courtroom. If there are any objections, you may speak before the judge, but otherwise there should be no talk about this," a different police officer stated, after he had gotten off the phone with the court.

On Friday at 2:00, we got ready and headed for court. The judge we had was a lady named Judge Judy. We told her the story and the sides we were on. Then she asked to have Kevin bring up the will for her to see it.

When she was holding it, the judge said, "This is a fake will! Kevin will be charged with a felony, and we'll set the bail. Give the will back to David, for he is the rightful owner."

Once I was handed the will, I asked the judge how she could tell it was a fake. I went up to her and she tried to show me, but something happened. When the will was in my hands, it was real, but when it was in the wrong owner's hands, it was fake.

"Ladies and gentlemen, it appears that somehow this locket has changed the will from fake to real when it's in the rightful owner's hands. David, did your nana give you any information that made you call upon this court?" the judge asked.

"Well, she told me one thing that stayed in my head."

"What was that?"

"I want you to keep the locket, but you must promise me that you will never read this note unless you feel you're at the end of a road in life and trapped. This locket contains powerful information and you may end up learning that the hard way."

"This case is closed. Kevin is charged with fraud. Bail is set at $5,000 and David gets the will. You are dismissed."

"How come you didn't tell me about the locket?" my mom said curiously.

"You know, I don't know why. I guess I didn't want to be reminded about her dying."

"You know, just because she died doesn't mean that she doesn't hear you and still talk to you in different ways. So, when you're going around with sad spirits within you, just remember she still loves you no matter what happens and she'll always be with you."

"I know that, and that is why I am going to protect this locket with all my heart."

"Here, let's go get some dinner with our family at Craganog's Holstice Restaurant."

"Boy, am I glad. I'm starved."

After we all sat down and finished our appetizers, Mom made an announcement. "I can't believe that I have to say what I'm going to tell you. This situation will end up coming down hard on one of our family members. Someone here right now sitting at this table is very ill, and my husband and I have decided that we need to tell the person and the family what is going on, because soon this person will be in the hospital. Now, I don't mean to shock anyone, but the person is David. He has the disease Monakaladajenn. There is no cure. David is one of three people diagnosed with it in the United States. David, listen, remember when you went for your physical and had blood work done? Well, we found out yesterday morning, while you were at school. The doctor's office called and told us that your blood showed the disease. We thought that it would be appropriate if we told you and the family at the same time. I'm sorry, but we're going to have to be strong for each other so we can get through this!"

The family was all shocked. They stared at me with glassy eyes, not wanting to believe this news.

"Dinner is served," said the waitress.

I couldn't believe what I had just heard. I was going to die! In the pit of my stomach, I had a strange feeling about this.

When I got into bed that night, my mom and dad sat next to me to have a talk. "David," said Mom, "I know how you feel — trust me I do — and tomorrow we'll go to the hospital to try chemo to see if it will work with this disease. The best thing the doctor said you could do is eat healthy things, exercise, and get ten hours of sleep each night. You know what, don't even worry about it; just get a good night's sleep. You can sleep in, because tomorrow is Sunday. Good night."

Once they left my room, I fell asleep.

"The locket is going to save your life. Just speak into it when you're harmed and it will save your life."

"AHHHHHHH!!!"

"What's the matter, David?" Mom asked as she ran back into my room. "Are you okay?"

"I'm alive? I must have just been dreaming. Sorry to wake you!"

Again, I fell back to sleep and this time stayed asleep. In the morning, I went downstairs, where a doctor was waiting to do tests on me. "I thought I was going to the hospital today, not having a doctor come here."

"Well, we decided that it might be better to have a doctor come, so that we don't have to wait in the waiting room at the hospital to be admitted."

"Hi, David. I'm Doctor Weyhandith. As you may know, I'm here to help you. To start, please drink this medicine so that we can take an X-ray of you that will show us three things. First, it will show where the disease is. Second, it will show if it's contagious. Finally, the X-ray will show if it's going to spread. I don't mean to scare you, but you do have a chance of dying, and I want you to know that we don't know if we can prevent this from spreading. I'll see you tomorrow for the X-rays. Make sure you take a pill at every snack or meal that you eat today."

"Oh doctor, thank-you so much for all that you have done. Bye!"

When I was eating breakfast, I had to take my first pill. Man, were they disgusting — they practically tasted like throw-up! I wanted to spit it out, but of course, my mom was there at my side, and I knew there was no chance of escaping this pill, so I got it over with. As it was making its way down my throat, I could taste the misery in my breath as I breathed in and out, in and out. I knew that each day, the pills were not going to taste any better, so I had to find a solution to get them over with.

As we entered the doctor's room the next day, everyone in the waiting room immediately turned and stared at me. I was trying to figure it out, until I saw the news on the TV: "A local resident David, a son and minor whose last name is being withheld, was recently diagnosed with the rarest disease in the world, Monakaladajenn. The question on everyone's mind is, 'Will he make it?' " I couldn't believe that I had made the news. That is why everybody was staring. No wonder!

"Now, let's take the X-ray. Please lie down on this bed and put these goggles on so you don't have a glare hitting your eyes so bright that it makes you want to shield them."

Beeazzz!

The electronic equipment sucked me into the tube that would take the X-ray. Once the testing was over, the doctor went into a different room to print the X-rays. When he came back, he looked at my mom and me in disbelief.

"You see this pink smear going around your heart and into your lungs? That is the disease. David, I'd like to talk with your mom alone, if you don't mind."

"No, go right ahead."

I couldn't help; I had to listen at the door. The doctor told my mom, "I know how hard this is on you, but by the look of this, there is a chance of the disease spreading, which may lead to David's death. I am so sorry."

"Oh, my God. I can't believe this is happening to my own son. I have to tell my husband, but would you mind telling David right now. I can't handle this!"

"Yes, of course, just send him in on your way out!"

"David, the doctor needs to talk to you. Please go in there, now."

"David this disease is terminal. You can die from this. Your mom wanted me to tell you this, because she's too upset. It's time for you to go. Please make sure you take care of your mom for me!"

"What happens if I do die?" I cried.

"Right now, we can only wait. If it makes you feel any better, here is my phone number."

"Thanks, but it won't keep me from crying, or from dying!"

"I know. Trust me, I know how it feels. You see, my mom died when I was twelve. She died of a disease that caused her to have a stroke during the middle of the night while I was sleeping over a friend's house and when my dad was at work. I know how it feels. Just bear with me and together we can survive our losses. Here, you should get going. Your mom is probably waiting. See you later."

"Bye," I said, clearing my throat so that he couldn't tell that I was crying and wondering what his losing his mom had to do with me.

"Mom, are you ready to go home?"

"Yes, let's get out of this place! Let me cook dinner for you and Dad tonight. I had better start it right away, so it will be ready when Dad gets home. You should probably go pick up your room, since it's probably a mess from all the commotion lately. I'll let you know when dinner is ready. Is everything all right?"

"Yeah, I'm fine."

"Come here. Give me a hug."

"I love you, Mom!"

"I love you too, sweetie."

While I was in my room cleaning, I took out the locket. I had the locket in my hand and I started to cry. "If this locket could prevent me from dying, it would be the best locket in the world, except I know that it won't happen, because of course I'm going to die." As soon as I said that, a strange blinding light appeared, "Ahhh!"

"David, is everything all right?" asked Mom.

"Yeah, for a second a light blinded me, but I don't know what it was from."

"Dad should be home any minute. Here, let's go downstairs."

"Mmmmm! Dinner smells delicious! Hey, is anybody hungry besides me?"

"Dad, you're home. I thought you wouldn't be home in time for dinner."

"Well, I couldn't miss out on a fabulous meal like this, could I?"

"Hey, can I talk to you in our bedroom?" asked Mom.

"Is everything all right?"

"Yeah, just fine. Now, please."

"Okay."

My parents went in their room and didn't come until out fifteen minutes later. "Let's eat!" Dad announced. "I would like to discuss your disease, David," he continued a minute later. "You know you're probably saying that you're going to die tomorrow or something like that, but everything happens for a reason. Everything goes from something bad to something good. From what I have learned, the good helps the bad and the bad helps the good, so everything turns out positive in my experience. Don't worry, David. Everything is going to be fine."

"Tomorrow, David goes back to the doctor, and I think you should bring him, since I brought him today, if you know what I mean."

"Yes, I already took the day off tomorrow, so I can spend time with my lovely family."

The conversation continued, mostly around my illness, then finally it was time for dessert.

"Can you please pass the ice cream?"

"Here you go."

"Thanks."

At the doctor's office the next day, once again, they took X-rays to check the disease's progress. get a progress report. When the doctor came back, he carefully compared the two photos.

"Well, this is very unusual, but it seems to me, by the look of this, that the disease has decreased about a quarter of an inch in a twenty-four-hour period, so in about forty-seven days the disease should be the size of a raisin. Now, I know you probably want to spread the good news, but first you need to schedule an appointment in about a week from now, so that we can check up on the progress of your disease. See my secretary and schedule an appointment, okay? Take care."

"Bye! Wow, this is terrifically great. Aren't you happy, David?"

"Yes, just great!"

After we had a celebration, it was time to go to bed.

We all said out goodnights, and as the lights went off and my parents left the room, the locket opened and a light beamed from it. "You see, you did the right thing. You prayed that you would live, and now, as my command, you must! Think about the dream!"

"I must be dreaming. This can't be true."

"Oh, really? Look around you, for as far as the eye can see, it's true."

"Wow, you saved my life! How did you do it?"

"For me to know and for you to find out! Just remember, history tells the future!"

The Pashka Fire

by Lydia Burrage-Goodwin

Chapter One

There once was a little girl named Elena who lived in the forest with her sister, Ayn, her mama and papa, and her dog, Sasha. Sasha loved being with the little girl, so she followed her everywhere she went. Every morning Sasha woke Elena for school. She got dressed in her linen shift, blue roach, and boots, then went downstairs. Every morning, Elena paused as she descended the ladder into the kitchen, smelling the fresh biscuits and bacon cooking. Every morning, Elena gathered her writing tablet and her lunch tin and set them on a wooden stool by the door. And, every morning, the old woven basket was waiting for her on the table, waiting for eggs to be collected. Today was special, though. This was not a school day. Elena picked up the basket and skipped outside to collect the eggs.

In the chicken house, chickens and feathers flew all over the place. The roosters were eager to gain entry into the coop, and the cackle of chickens and roosters deafened her ears. Elena struggled to close the door of the coop and to keep a distance from the chaos within. Out of breath, she carefully lifted each hen and took the eggs from the nest. As she gathered the last few eggs, she heard a bark coming from the other side of the coop. Sasha was chasing hen feathers that flew in the air.

"Sasha!" Elena yelled as Sasha was about to bite off one of the chicken's legs. "Nyet!" Elena screamed.

Sasha turned to look at Elena as if she were speaking in a foreign language. Confused, she took one last look at Elena and restarted her hunt. If Sasha killed a chicken, Elena thought, then her mama and papa would get rid of the dog, and Elena would get a whipping for sure. She dropped the basket of eggs onto the ground and ran to get Sasha out of the hen house. The dog was so wild that Elena couldn't catch her.

Chapter Two

While Sasha was disturbing the peace in the chicken coop, Elena went back to the house for help. Her father, busy reading a newspaper, didn't notice that she had come in. Her crisis was urgent, but her father could not see it in her face.

Without looking up, he asked, "And what can I do for you, young lady?"

Elena looked frightened. "I, I, I," she stuttered. "I need your help. Sasha won't leave the chicken coop, and she is trying to eat the chickens! And, and ... I dropped the eggs!"

As Vladimir Procknik responded to Elena and hurried out the door, Ayn, her younger sister, was in the kitchen taking Russian black bread out of the oven. Raina Procknik was preparing the cheese. She had placed the brushes and paints on the table for her daughters to decorate the eggs and was waiting for Elena to bring them inside. The girls were eager to participate, for this was a ritual that they enjoyed greatly each year. Potatoes were sitting on the top of the stove simmering quietly. So much food to prepare, for it was Pashka, and that called for a great feast! Using the frayed potholders, Ayn picked up the pot of potatoes, which were ready to be mashed. As she picked it up, a flame caught the edge of the potholder, and fearing that she would be burnt, she threw the pot and holder onto the floor. The steam rising, potatoes rolled all over. Flames from the potholder burst on the floor.

Chapter Three

As flames rapidly spread to each board of wood, Elena, Raina, and Ayn raced around the house pulling quilts off beds and out of trunks, quilts that took years to make — scraps from old clothes, delicate pieces of cloth from baby clothes, from Deda's old *navershnik*, intricately woven into beautiful bedding. Raina, heartbroken, grabbed her wedding quilt and threw it onto the fire.

Vladimir Procknik was unaware of the turmoil inside the kitchen. Finding the broken basket of eggs upside down in the henhouse, he was angry that his daughter had dropped the eggs on this special occasion and feared what his wife, Raina, would say. But when he walked into the house, he too dropped the basket of eggs and hunted for quilts to put the fire out.

"It's getting too big to put out," he yelled. "Take as much out as you can. We have to get out now!"

He was heard very faintly, for the fire and the crackles and the yells of the family were too loud for him to be heard. Only Elena heard him and started throwing their meager furnishings out the door.

Chapter Four

The next morning the house was but a pile of ashes. The family managed to salvage most of the furniture, carrying it to a small opening in the woods. The afternoon before, a few friendly neighbors came and helped dump buckets of water over their smoldering belongings, which were now sitting in the sun to dry. Exhausted and covered in soot, the family slept in piles of leaves. Elena woke up first, feeling chilled. Sasha nudged her out of the leaf pile. Elena stood up slowly and looked over at where her house once was; now it was nothing but a heap of ashes. Looking closely, she noticed something shine gold in the sun, mixing with the cinders. As she got closer, she soon realized that it was her mother's amber necklace. This was the necklace that Vladimir gave to Raina before they got married. She ran down to the river to wash it off. She scrubbed very gently and thoroughly. She didn't even wash her clothing this well.

When she was finished, she stared at it. A smile appeared on her face. Her mother would be so happy to see it. She was eager to show it to her. Elena quickly ran back to give the necklace to her mother, but when she got to the spot where she thought her family was, she was mistaken. Confused and disoriented, she walked back to the river to retrace her steps. The only landmark she could remember was a great big oak tree with patches of moss covering it, but there were hundreds of trees like that in this part of the forest. She kept walking for what seemed liked hours until she came to a rather steep hill. Racing up the hill, stumbling over rocks, and almost running into trees, she finally made it to the top. She stood there to see if anything looked familiar. A film of smoke floated horizontally into the clouds rising from the hill and atop the trees. Elena was lost.

... more to come ...

James Flanning Middle School: Rumor or Truth?
by Wisima "Sam" Nipatnantaporn

Weird things happen at this school — people say it's haunted or cursed. Nobody knows why or how things happen, but they know there's a reason for it ...

Sarah Napling never believed in Halloween or mysterious vanishings, not even as a child, or at least until that day. She was a new student at James Flanning Middle School, or JFS, as they call it. She is in the sixth grade and has only one friend, Tina Arden.

Part 1: The day before Halloween

It's the day before Halloween, a Monday, and everyone knows that tomorrow "weird things" will happen. Every year, rumors circulate that if Halloween falls on a Tuesday, someone ends up missing from JFS. And, the student who went missing the year before comes back for the next victim. People work and come to learn at JFS. They aren't scared. Teachers don't quit, and no one ever leaves. Why, does this happen? No one knows; it's a mystery yet to be solved.

"You've got to be kidding me!" says Sarah.

"No, it's true! Weird things will happen tomorrow. Someone will disappear!" Tina, replied trying to convince her friend.

"I don't believe in Halloween or things like that"

"I know, but it happens every year if Halloween lands on a Tuesday!"

"Fine. Why haven't they closed down the school then?"

Tina and Sarah have all their classes together. While walking home with Tina, Sarah learned about the weirdness supposed to happen tomorrow. The two live near each other, sort of. Sarah reached her house first, then another three roads down, Tina turned toward her house. They walked home with each other sometimes, but they didn't hang out in school, because Tina is popular and Sarah isn't popular at all. Tina didn't want her school friends to know she likes the new, weird, freaky non-Halloween-believer. She was afraid of what her friends might think and that they would tell the whole sixth grade. Sarah was fine with this. All she cared about is that she has a friend.

"Dad, I'm home!" cried Sarah.

Sarah's parents are divorced, and so are Tina's. They both live with their moms. Sarah sees her dad every day after school, but Tina only sees her dad on weekends. Tina has a younger sister named Haley, who is in the fourth grade. Sarah is an only child and has no pets. Tina, on the other hand, has two dogs.

"So, Sarah, how was school?"

"Okay. Tina told me that tomorrow spooky things will happen."

"Oh, that's nice. You don't believe in spooky things, do you?"

"Notreally.HeywegettowearourHalloweencostumestomorrow."

"What are you being?"

"I don't know, Tina's being a hippie, though."

"Why don't you be a hippie, too?"

"Nah. I'll be the scariest thing of all."

"What's that?"

"Myself!"

"Funny."

"Thank-you, thank-you!"

Since Sarah has no homework, she jumps on the couch and watches TV.

Part 2 - Halloween Day

Tina walks to school and Sarah gets dropped off. They meet by the bike racks. It's early so no one sees them, only the older, weirder kids.

"Hey, Sarah. Been thinking of today?"

Sarah is deep in thought, staring into space. She is thinking about today, how things will happen. Does she actually believe they will?

"Oh, what? Right, yeah, uh huh."

"Ok?" says Tina, a little confused.

"Nice outfit, hippie." Sarah sees how Tina looks and starts giggling.

"Hey! Well, what are you?"

"Myself."

"Creative."

The bell rings, so they head to their homerooms. It's now 8:10, so everyone heads to class. Tina goes to band and Sarah goes to PE. Later, they both go to their next class, which is Social Studies. It's dark outside — looks like it might rain. All of a sudden the blinds go down, and the lights go out. Nobody is panicking, which is good. Since Tina and Sarah are sitting next to each other, Tina leans over and whispers to Sarah.

"Ha! I told you weird things will happen. First it's pitch black and then someone vanishes!"

"I'm so scared," Sarah says sarcastically.

"Do you hear that?"

"Yeah it sounds like someone banging on the lockers."

"I'm scared," says Tina.

"Don't be a — "

Sarah gets cut off by one last BANG. "Okay, I'm scared too." This time Sarah is not being sarcastic.

The loudspeaker comes on: "Hello this is your principal speaking. Everyone please report to the gym, starting with the sixth-grade English class."

In the English classroom, the teacher is telling everyone to line up by the door. They don't listen. They just keep talking until the teacher yells, "Hello!"

"Whoa," one kid says.

"Line up by the door, single file!"

Everyone hurries to the door and lines up single file. The teacher leads the way, and they head for the gym.

"Ahhh, help!"

Everyone hears a distant scream. The person at the end of the line has just gone missing. The English line goes back to the classroom, and the teacher calls the principal.

"Hello, there is another announcement. When proceeding to the gym, go three at a time: the teacher and two students.

You, the teacher, will drop off one child and go back to the classroom for another. That way no one will be alone and won't go missing. There will be teachers in the gym to supervise."

The English class makes it without anyone else going missing. The lights are still out, and it's still pitch black. Next, the sixth-grade Social Studies class, Sarah and Tina's class. They are the first to go into the gym from their class.

"Ahhh! Sarah, help!"

"Tina? Tina, where'd you go?"

"Mrs...." Her teacher has just disappeared, too.

"Oh, no." Sarah is alone and is super scared now.

"Tina, Mrs. Bandlet, where'd you go?" Sarah starts to cry. Feeling hopeless, she sits on the floor and continues crying.

Bang, Bang, BANG! They're back, and they want Sarah.

"HELP!" yells Sarah.

Bang!

"Don't come closer!"

Bang!

"Leave me alone!" Sarah screams as she sees hands reaching for her. She tries to get away, but she can't. She's surrounded.

"HELP! HELP!"

"Sarah, Sarah, Sarah..." They start to chant her name, like mindless zombies.

"Sarah, Sarah ... WAKE UP! You're going to be late for school!" Sarah's mom yells.

"What? It was all a dream?"

"Yes, now get dressed."

It was all a dream. Sarah can't believe it. At school, by the bike racks, it seemed so real.

"Hey! So, you ready for today, Sarah?"

"Yeah."

Sarah decides not to tell Tina about her dream. It might freak her out. As the day begins, all is normal until social studies. The blinds go down, and suddenly it's pitch black.

"Uh oh," announces Sarah, staring into the darkness.

Chosen

by Wisima "Sam" Nipatnantaporn

Imagine having a fight with your best friend and wandering off to the attic. You find an old ancient antique doll hidden in an old box under a loose floorboard you just sat on. The doll has this evil magic force that takes over your body, causing you to do some really bad things — even bad enough to almost kill your truest friend of all. That's what happens to fourteen-year-old Carly Burnett. Find out how it all happens, if her best friend ends up dead or if Carly will ever escape from the magic force.

Prologue

It was a cold and stormy night in the town of Salem, Massachusetts, in the 1600s. Maria, trying to escape from the overwhelming evil power of the antique doll, finally escapes. Trying to destroy the antique doll she found on the grounds of a house occupied by a witch, she finds that it can't be destroyed. She runs through the dark woods, then into an old abandoned house at 18 Ally Lane. She goes upstairs into the attic and hides the doll in an old box under a loose board. Forever. To collect dust until a new person discovers it, and then the story begins.

Part One: Present

Zzzzz ... ding!
The school bell rings.
"Huh? What? Oh, the school bell! Yeah! Eww, I have drool on my face. Oh well, school's out!" shouts Carly Burnett, psyched for the first day of summer.
Her parents have planned a vacation to the Caribbean for the whole summer, and Carly gets the house to herself! Carly is fourteen, and her parents trust her. Her best friend, Anna Ebell, is also fourteen, and with her mom also in the Caribbean for the summer, she too has her house to herself.

Anna and Carly have planned on living with each other until the summer is over, or at least until Carly's parents and Anna's mom come back. They live in Salem, Massachusetts. Carly lives at 18 Ally Lane, where the neighborhood is nice and quiet. Or at least it was that way. They are not really the popular kids, but they aren't geeks and nerds either. They always stick out, not like Goths or troubled kids, but as individuals. They have lived a really, really dull life. So when they are living with each other, they are going to make plans to change for next year — change their style, become popular, or at least as close as they can be to popular.

"Where's Anna? She was supposed to meet me here, at the front of the school, thirty minutes ago?!" Carly said whispering to herself while she was listening to her iPod.

"Carly! Over here!" Anna yells while pushing her way through the middle school crowd of kids.

"Excuse me! Pardon me! Coming through!" Anna yells, sounding a bit irritated.

"Where on Earth have you been, Anna? I've been waiting here for almost a half an hour!"

"Sorry, Carly, Mrs. Barson made me write a three-hundred-word sorry note to Candina after I 'accidentally' stuck gum in her hair."

Anna's mind wanders. *Candina is one of the popular mean girls. Why do we want to be popular? Well, let's see: we don't want to live a boring life anymore!!*

Carly notices that Anna is spacing out and asks her, "Why did you stick gum in her hair?"

"Well, she was saying to all the girls, 'Your hair is all wrong, your clothes are horrible,' stuff like that. I had to do something. I couldn't take it!"

Anna is not a troubled kid, but she likes sticking up for people. She doesn't like seeing defenseless kids get pushed around by Candina or any other mean person.

Her dad died in a car accident when she was little. His boss was always telling him what to do, how to do it, to hurry up, until one day he couldn't take it. When he was driving home, he drove so fast that he couldn't brake in time. He hit a tree in front of his house. Anna and her mom heard the crash, so they rushed outside to see what had happened, but what they saw was Anna's dad, dead. So, that was that. Ever since, Anna has always stuck up for people, afraid that something bad would happen, like what happened to her dad.

"Whatever. Let's just go get your stuff and head to my house."

"Okay, okay. You did ask why I was late, did you not?"

"Yeah, yeah, I hate it when you correct me!"

"Well, sorry, your Highness."

"Sarcasm? Funny, Anna. Oh, so funny."

"Thank-you, thank-you, and thank-you very much. Anna has left the ... school!"

"Come on, let's go!"

"All right, I'm coming. Can't a girl be funny?"

Carly and Anna leave the school, riding away on their bikes, the cool summer breeze brushing through their hair and amid a blur of middle school kids' voices. Anna has an odd sense of humor that nobody gets, and Carly is more the serious type. That's why they stick out as individuals.

Part Two: Carly's House

"Home at last! I still can't believe that the school year has gone by so fast!"

"I know, Carly. It went by like it was only a month long!"

"Hey! Don't go that far. It wasn't that short!"

"I guess you're right. Can you imagine having to read a book and write a thousand-word book report on it?!"

"Uh, Anna, not to bring a hailstorm to happy time, but Mr. Campbell assigned one to the whole eighth grade. Remember?"

"Oh, right. You just had to remind me!"

"Well, sorry! You want a snack?"

"I'll just have a soda."

While Carly and Anna are snacking — well, at least Carly is snacking on some potato chips, not like Anna, just drinking a soda — the phone rings. Carly picks it up.

"Hello?"

"Hi, sweetie. It's Mommy."

"Oh, hi Mom. How's the Caribbean?"

"Oh, just wonderful, darling. And Daddy says 'Hi.' "

"Well, tell him I said hi, too."

"Honey!" Carly's mom calls to Carly's dad.

"Yes?"

"Carly says hi!"

"Okay." he replies and goes back to watching TV.

In the kitchen, Anna is making hand signals to Carly to tell her parents that she says hi, too. Anna is almost like the Burnetts' second daughter, since she spends most of her time at their house and since her mom is always working. That's also why the vacation to the Caribbean was a good thing for Anna's mom: not just so that Carly and Anna could live together, but so she could get her mind off her work. Carly's mom and dad, as well as both Carly and Anna, chipped in to buy the plane tickets for Anna's mom as a surprise. It was also the perfect time. Anna's mom had the whole summer off from work, since she was just promoted and had some time between positions.

"Mom, Anna says hi to you and dad."

"And we say hi back."

Carly is making hand signals back to Anna saying that her parents say hi back. Anna is now lip synching and dancing to her favorite song because she is bored. She looks weird.

"Well, Mom, I've got to go. Love you, and tell Dad I love him, too."

"OK, love you, sweetie. See you before school starts. Have a great time with Anna."

"I will. Bye."

"Bye."

Carly shoots a you-look-like-an-idiot look toward Anna, who just nods and goes back to lip synching and dancing, badly.

Part Three: The Next Day, at the Mall

New look, new style, and new attitude. Carly and Anna have decided to start their journey to popularity. After a good night's sleep and wonderful dreams, they are ready to shop until they drop!

"Ooh! Look, Anna, that shirt is so cute. Come on let's go into the store."

"But Carly, that's too girly."

Anna is more of a tomboy. She was not always like that; before she would wear dresses or skirts, but ever since the accident she has turned into a tomboy. Why? Whenever she needs to express her anger, in a girly outfit it just looks weird. Dressing up as a tomboy doesn't bring back as many memories of her dad, because when she was a girly girl, she would always do girly things with him, like play makeup or dress up with him. But, now things have changed. It has been seven years since Anna's dad died, and she still hasn't gotten over it. She misses him a lot.

"So? How about this? You can hold my clothes." Anna is making her I-miss-my-dad-face.

"Oh my gosh! I am so sorry, Anna. You miss him, don't you?"

"It's fine, but..." Anna starts crying.

"But what, Anna?"

"It was too soon! How could he be in a car accident? He was a great driver, and I was only seven, Carly! Seven!"

Anna puts her face in her hands, crying harder than ever. People are staring, but they don't care. Carly puts her hand over Anna's shoulder. Comforting her best friend, she hands her a tissue. Anna sniffles quietly, and her eyes are all puffy and red.

"Look at me; I'm crying. I haven't cried in years. So, do you still want that shirt?"

"No, it's fine. You pick where we're going to shop."

"How about … that one?" Anna is pointing at the punk shop. The shop has all these weird things.

"Um, about that…" Carly makes a shocked face.

"Oh, my gosh, Anna! Look at that kid who just came out. He has a Mohawk! No way am I shopping in there! Girl today, freak tomorrow!"

"I was only joking! Don't take it seriously, Carly! Chill!"

"I know, but don't joke about that anymore. Look. The hair on my arm is sticking up!"

"Wow! You are such a drama queen. You are definitely ready to become popular!"

"Well, you have to practice before you do."

"Come on. That store looks normal enough. Let's go!"

Carly and Anna walk into a shop that has both girly clothes and tomboy clothes. Anna picks out greenish baggy pants and a top that's too big for her. The top is black with a purple skull on it. She also picks out an orange hat, which she'll wear backwards of course. Carly picks out a light pink skirt with light yellow flowers on it and a white tank-top with a jeweled flying butterfly appliqué.

Now, they have paid and are on their way to the food court. The food court has five different types of places to eat from. There is an American, Chinese, Italian, Japanese, and a sandwich store to choose from. Since it's almost noon, the two girls decide to go to the sandwich store, where they only serve sandwiches and beverages. Carly orders a ham and cheese sandwich, and for her drink, she orders a cherry vanilla Coke. Anna orders a PB&J sandwich and a Mountain Dew. After they pay, they head off to find some seats, but the only available seats are near two jocks from their school who always tease them. They have to sit there. They don't want to sit, but they do. They try to ignore the two idiots but can't. They have to talk to them, even yell, because of the noise.

"Hey! Look, Dan. It's Anna and Carly!"

"Yeah, it is. So, what are you two girls doing here in public? You're not afraid that your ugliness will scare everyone?"

"Oh, don't worry. Dumb and Dumber we're not."

"But Carly, don't you think they're wrong? I mean, if they are calling us ugly, don't you think they're just looking in a mirror?" Carly and Anna giggle. Dan and Tom just sit there looking baffled.

"Yeah, Dan, you do look a little ugly, though. Not like me ... I mean, I am so handsome." Tom is agreeing with Carly and Anna. What a shocker!

"Shut up! Don't agree with them!"

"Well, they are right, dude. Come on, look at that face. I would definitely win the handsome contest if there was one."

Dan and Tom keep on fighting while Carly and Anna just laugh at them and go back to eating. It has been a wonderful day.

Part Four: Back at Carly's House

After a long day at the mall, Carly and Anna are tired and satisfied after setting up Dan and Jason fight's about who is more handsome. Boy, are they acting like couple of idiots. Anna and Carly are tired, so they get ready for bed. While Anna is taking a shower, Carly wanders around the house. She's surprised to realize that for fourteen years, she has never really noticed her house's old antique look. The floor is a dark brown wood. The walls are a creamy yellow but seem to have an old look to them, even though her parents had just recently repainted. Every time they repaint, it's no use. The walls keep going back to their regular color. It's almost as if the walls just absorb the paint.

It was a full moon, and the rays from it just happen to be shining on the stairway up to the attic. It's been doing that a lot lately, but Carly never really cared, just accepted it being there. But tonight, it seems to be shining brighter than ever, as if it is a sign for Carly to go up there.

Carly seems interested, so she starts walking toward the stairs. She reaches the staircase and is wondering if she should go up, because she hasn't gone up to the attic since she was a little girl. She's nervous and scared. Slowly making her way up the stairs, she gets to the top and reaches out for the doorknob. Carly's having second thoughts; the moon's rays of light seem to have faded. She looks behind her and down the stairs and gets dizzy. Everything is all blurry, so she puts her right hand on her head and turns around. Once again, she reaches for the doorknob. She hears Anna yelling something, so she decides to go down the stairs instead.

"What was that, Anna? I didn't hear what you said."

"I just said that I'm done, and you can come take your shower now."

"Okay, be right there."

Carly looks back at the door and walks off, leaving the attic for another day. She freezes. She has a flashback to when she was five and the moon was also shining at the staircase up to the attic. Then, too, she went up and opened the door, but when she did, a force pushed her backwards, sending her flying down the stairs. She broke her arm that time, and that's why she has never really cared for going up there. She's scared. Carly screams after her flashback, so Anna come running to see what happened.

"Carly! Are you okay? What happened?" Carly didn't answer. "Carly?" Anna repeats in a scared voice. She rushes to see if Carly is all right, but all she sees is Carly on the floor.

"Oh no! What happened??" Anna whispers to herself.

She kneels down beside Carly and checks her pulse. It's beating, but slowly. All of a sudden, it stops! Anna panics, and she calls the emergency room. Three minutes later an ambulance arrives. Thank goodness Carly's house is near the hospital. The ambulance arrives at the hospital and everyone is rushes to get Carly into the ER. The lady at the front desk won't let Anna go into the emergency room.

"But I'm her best friend!"

"I'm sorry miss, but I can't let you in."

"Fine." Anna is ticked off; she wants to go in and be there beside her best friend.

"May I ask you some questions about how she got hurt, miss?"

"Sure, but I don't know how it happened. I heard her scream, so I rushed to see what happened, but when I got there, I saw her lying on the ground."

"I see, and where are her parents?"

"They're in the Caribbean."

"Do you know their phone number?"

"Yes." Anna tells the lady their number.

Carly's mom picks up the phone. "Hello?"

"Hi, my name is Joanne. I'm calling on behalf of — "

"Sorry, we're not interested in buying anything," Carly's mom interrupts, thinking Joanne is a telemarketer.

"Oh, no. I am not selling anything."

"Okay, then why are you calling?"

"I'm calling on behalf of your daughter, Carly."

"Oh my! Is she all right?"

"We're not sure yet. We still are waiting for the results."

"What results? What happened!? How did it happen?"

"Well, we have a young lady here named Anna that can tell you." Joanne hands the phone to Anna.

"Hello? Mrs. Burnett?"

"Oh, Anna. How is Carly? What happened?"

Anna tells Mrs. Burnett what happened. She is shocked but calm — a little confused, but she understands. Joanne comes back with the results.

"Anna, the results are in. Would you mind telling Mrs. Burnett that Carly will have to stay overnight, just to be sure nothing else happens. Carly is okay, but just a little woozy."

"Mrs. B?"

"Don't worry, Anna, sweetie. I heard. Tell Carly best wishes and that I'm here for her whenever she needs me."

"Okay, bye." Anna hangs up and asks Joanne if she can go see Carly. Joanne says yes and Anna goes into Carly's room to see how she's doing. Carly is still knocked out, so Anna waits. She starts to get tired and slowly falls asleep.

Part Five: At the Hospital in the Morning

It's morning, 8 a.m. Anna wakes up and notices that Carly is sound asleep, so she goes to find something to eat. She wanders off, making sure she knows the way back to Room 12A. Easy enough to remember, but it's such a big hospital. Anna hasn't been to the hospital in a long time. The last time she was here, it was when her dad was in the car accident. Anna sees a sign that says "Cafeteria" and goes in. She buys an apple for herself and a banana for Carly. Anna walks down the hall past Room 15A, 14A, 13A, and finally reaches 12A. Anna carefully opens the door, making sure she doesn't wake Carly. She puts the banana on the table next to Carly's bed. Anna sits down on a chair and eats her apple.

"No! No! Go away! Leave me alone! What do you want from me?"

"Nurse! There is something wrong! Nurse!"

"I'm here. What's happening?'

"I don't know. She, she..."

"Oh, she's just having a bad dream. Don't wake her up, though. It's not good."

"Okay."

"See? She is calming down already."

Carly is having a dream about the doll, and it's trying to take over. She is trying to escape, crawling away for her life.

"Come back, Carly. You can't escape," says the doll.

"What do you want from me?! Leave me alone!"

"Come with me, Carly. Help me destroy all ancestors of Maria."

"Who's Maria? I won't help you, I won't hurt anyone! Go away!"

"I must destroy all ancestors of Maria, starting with your best friend, Anna!"

"No! I won't hurt Anna! What did she ever do to you!?"

"She may have not done anything to me, but Maria did, and Anna has Maria's blood in her. Anna must DIE!"

"Nooooooo! Go ... away!"

Carly wakes up and her breathing is heavily. She doesn't remember what happened or why she is in the hospital.

"Hey! You're up, sleepy head,"

"Anna, you're okay!"

"Me? You're the one who fell down the stairs!"

"I fell down the stairs?"

"You don't remember?" Carly shakes her head. "That must have been some fall!"

"I guess so."

"Up for some ice cream?"

"Yeah, sure. Okay."

Carly and Anna head for the cafeteria to get some ice cream.

"Hey, Carly."

"Yeah?"

"You look awful in that hospital dress."

"Hey! It's not like you look any better. Your hair looks awful!"

The two of them walk down the hall laughing at how they look; Carly never feels happier than when her best friend is beside her.

Part Six: Home Again, Carly's House

"Are you sure I fell down the stairs? I really don't remember anything."

"You really don't remember anything at all? Nothing?"

"Yeah, weird isn't it?"

Why don't I remember anything? Carly is thinking. That dream, that awful dream was about Anna betraying her. She has never betrayed anyone, not even me. Why would she start now? I don't remember what happened to me or why I was in the hospital, but why did I remember that dream? And that doll, that evil doll.

A lot has happened in the past few days — mysterious lights coming from the attic, strange bizarre dreams and the slight confusion about who was handsomer. Carly can't stop thinking about her dreams. She wants to know why she has been having them and why the weird things are happening to her and not Anna or anyone else. Could it be she has special powers? Or has she discovered a new sense, a sense of magic? Is this magic or just her imagination? No, it can't be, well, at least not now — not when Anna was over at her house. If the doll in her dreams is real, then what will happen to Anna if she can't control her dreams and the doll actually does kill her? Bad things are happening in this little town called Salem, and Carly will be behind it.

"Carly? Where are you?" wonders Anna.

"I'm over here!"

"Want to go get some ice cream? I hear they have a new flavor."

"Sure let's go. I want some anyway."

Carly and Anna walk to the mall for some ice cream. When they get to the mall and are waiting in line, all of a sudden a storm hits and the lights go out. How bizarre! No one is panicking, except some little kids. Who would blame them? They are scared. Carly and Anna are, too, especially Carly. She knows this is a sign that the doll is coming back to haunt her again.

"Carly, where are you!?" shouts Anna.

"I don't know. It's too dark, I can't see!"

"Follow my voice! I'm over by the cash register!"

"Okay!"

"You look so familiar."

Immediately after Carly says that, the doll disappears, leaving a puff of smoke behind. In just a few seconds, the doll reappears in Anna's room. Carly is still confused and still doesn't know anything except that the weirdest thing just happened to her.

"That ... was ... bizarre! But that doll seems so..." Carly remembers now. She doesn't know how, but it just clicks inside her mind. She knows the doll is out to get Anna.

"Oh, no. Anna!" Carly tries to run downstairs, but the attic door is locked and she can't get out!

Inside her room, Anna is playing on her laptop and listening to music, at the same time. Poof, the doll appears.

"Who are you?" Anna asks, not even noticing that it appeared out of thin air.

"Hello, Anna, how are you?"

"Who are you?"

"It's a fine day today, isn't it?"

"Don't try to change the subject. Who are you?" Anna's starts to get irritated. She wants an answer.

"Oh, I'm just a friend."

"Why are you here?"

"Can't a friend visit another friend?"

"Not when you won't answer the simplest question. *What* and *who* are you, and *why* are you here?"

"I am a doll. I was your great, great, great somewhat great grandmother's doll, and I am here because I want revenge. I am going to kill you."

"Now, wasn't the ea ... what, you're here to, what?"

"Kill you."

"Oh, AHHH HELP!"

"You pathetic little girl. No one can help you."

"CARLY!" Anna yells. She grabs for the door, but it's locked.

"She's locked in the attic."

"What did you do?!"

"All I want is revenge, Anna."

Up in the attic, Carly can hear Anna's cry for help. She can hear the desperate voice.

"I'M COMING, ANNA!" Carly screams, trying to push her way out, but it's useless. The door is locked and it won't budge.

Back in Anna's room, the doll is chasing her around her room.

"Come back here, Anna!"

"Stop chasing me! So what if my great, great old grandmother tried to destroy you! No one holds a grudge for this long!"

"What's your point?"

"You're a crazed, bizarre, maniac doll — that's my point!"

"Thank-you, I try."

Anna stops running and turns around and gives the doll a what-the-heck look. But the doll only stares back.

"Wow, you're ... a weird doll."

"So? Now, back to trying to kill you!"

"Oh, right. Ahhhh, stop chasing me!" Anna turns around and in a bizarre moment starts screaming and running away from the doll again.

One last push and Carly will break down the door. She backs up and runs into the center of it. CRASH! The door brakes and slides down the stairs, with Carly riding along.

"I know I broke the door, but I didn't intend to go for a joyride down the stairs! I'm coming, Anna!"

Anna hears Carly scream her name and knows help is on the way, but then she thinks, what if the doll controls Carly again? What if it's more powerful when it's in Carly's body? Will it have a better chance at killing her?

"Carly is coming. You can't kill me now! She'll save me!"

"Will she? She's weak. She won't stop me."

"Don't touch her!" Carly pushes in the door to Anna's room.

"Carly!" Anna shouts with relief.

Carly runs toward Anna, only to be stopped by the doll. The doll shoots a powerful light out of its hands and Carly goes flying out the door.

"I didn't know you could do that?" Anna says in shock "Why didn't you use it on me before?"

"I didn't want to waste my powers on you. You could have repelled it without even a scratch on your body."

"I'm not a sorcerer. I don't have any magical shields to protect me. I'm only human!"

"Somebody's cranky today!"

"Well, when a doll is trying to kill you, you tend to get delusional and cranky!"

"Oh no! You did *not* just blast me out that door with your hand ray thingy!" Carly gets up, stomps through the door, and kicks the doll out the open window. "That's what you get, you creep!"

"Carly! You saved me, and you kicked that doll out the window!" Anna is amazed at what Carly just did.

"I guess I did, didn't I?"

"Yes, you..." Anna stops when she sees the doll trying to climb up the window and back into the room. "Carly let's go! The doll is back!"

"To the school!"

"The school?"

"It's probably the safest place. It's huge, and the doll won't find us. Come on!"

They run to the school with the doll trailing behind. Good thing Carly lives only a few blocks away. Hopefully it's not locked. When they reach the school, the doors aren't locked, so they go in and run to their old homeroom, Mrs. Cally's room. They hated Mrs. Cally. She was an evil witch, and they thought they would never survive that year at school! But they made it through the year without anything evil happening to them, until now, that is. The school year went by as fast as their preschool years, and, Carly's and Anna's preschool years went by fast!

"Anna, do you remember the secret passage we found in the class library when it was silent reading?"

"Yeah, why? I don't..."

Anna stops when Carly gives her "the look." It's the same look that Carly gives Anna when she's not thinking straight, or when Anna just seems to be acting stupid. "Oh! We can hide in there! I knew that!" Carly nods her head in dismay, then quietly walks over to the passageway, kneels down, and unbolts the door. They climb into the passageway and close the door. There is a small hole where they can see through. They see the doll. Its back is turned away from the door, but then its head quickly turns around as if it senses their presence. They gasp in shock, but not loud enough for the doll to hear. The doll turns around and walks away. For the rest of the night, Carly and Anna stay in the passageway until they think the coast is clear.

Part Seven: A Night at the School

"Carly, wake up." The whole night Anna didn't sleep at all. She was too afraid that the doll would come and kill her in her sleep. Anna is very cautious. She once got a chain letter that said a dead seven-year-old boy named Teddy, who had no ears and no nose, blond hair and scary eyes, and would appear by her bedside to kill her in her sleep. She also got one about a girl named Amy who was cheated on by her boyfriend and was so upset that she committed suicide. If you didn't pass the chain letter on, Amy would come and kill you in your sleep. Anna never believed in chain letters or in being killed in her sleep by a ghost who got cheated on. She knew that today she wouldn't get killed by a ghost either, but she might get killed by an evil doll.

"C'mon Carly, WAKE UP!!"

I'm up, I'm up!" Carly sits up in shock and accidentally bangs her head against Anna's.

"I think I heard footsteps outside."

"Probably some janitors."

"The janitors left already, and they locked the doors. All of them."

"The wind?" Carly tries to assure Anna that the doll is not in the school.

"Carly," Anna says, not believing her.

"It's a suggestion."

"What was that?" Anna crawls to the crack in the door to see what is outside. She sees a shadow of someone walking. Is it the doll? "Mrs. Cally, what is she doing here?"

"It's a school, she's a teacher — do the math, Anna," Carly remarks.

"It's summer. Shouldn't she be in 'How to torture kids' camp or something?"

"Funny, Anna. That's very..."

Carly stops talking when Mrs. Cally turns around.

"Anna, look, don't her eyes look familiar, and her stare, it's so creepy."

"The doll took over Mrs. Cally!" Anna yells.

"Anna, shhhh," Carly says while putting her hand over Anna's mouth.

All of a sudden, Mrs. Cally turns around and walks near the girls. She stares at the secret passageway as if she is looking to kill, and she is. As Mrs. Cally walks, she is getting closer and closer to the passageway.

"Carly, we have to crawl deeper into the passageway."

"But, Anna, we don't know where it leads."

"I don't care. We have to get away."

"What if it's a dead end?"

"What if it isn't?" Anna remarks.

Anna and Carly crawl deeper into the secret passageway. They hear a clink; Mrs. Cally has just opened the door to the passageway with such force that she breaks the door off its hinges. Anna and Carly start to crawl faster, with Mrs. Cally right on their tails.

"Anna, she's gaining on us."

"I know, then, crawl fas - ... uh oh,"

"Uh oh, what?" says Carly in a voice that tells you she is not liking what she is hearing.

"Dead end," says Anna with a quivering voice drifting away into the darkness.

"Dead end. What are we going to do!? We're going to die, we're going to DIE!"

Anna knew that the more she and Carly avoided the doll, the sooner they would come to a dead end and perish.

"We have to fight back."

"I'll hold Mrs. Cally back while you escape."

"We'll hold her back together."

"No, Anna. You have to escape. I'll be okay; don't worry."

"Okay."

Anna and Carly crawl back to the opening of the passageway knowing they will collide with Mrs. Cally. While Carly and the doll fight, practically strangling each other to the death, Anna escapes when the doll is too occupied with winning against Carly. At the end of the tunnel, Anna looks back.

"Be careful, Carly."

Anna sees a ray of light for a split second and she hears Carly's scream fade away. She doesn't have even to imagine what happened; she knows it's over. Anna will run and lead the doll into a trap. Destroy the doll for all it is worth for what it has done to Carly. Anna sobs, but she is strong. She gets up and yells into the tunnel, "I'm sorry, Carly! You were my best friend! Come and get me, you stupid doll. Now that you have killed my friend, there is no reason for me to hide from you anymore. You're going to pay!"

Anna takes one last look at her school and runs to the schoolyard, where the battle for life and death against the doll will take place. She is ready to fight, and she knows exactly what she will do. The doll is going to be destroyed, once and for all.

"Ha, ha, ha! You are dead, Carly! Dead! Muah-ha-ha!"

The doll's evil laugh echoes through the tunnel, throughout the school, and into the schoolyard, where Anna is waiting peacefully, just standing there in the middle. Not even blinking. Her face is straight, and she feels the emotions of hatred, despair, and most of all loss. She feels that she is lost without Carly by her side, to fight the doll and gain power to overcome any obstacles they may face in their lives to come. Now, all is lost. Anna will stand alone in the battle. If she wins she will face life alone, wondering what would happen if she only stayed back and fought with her friend back in the tunnel.

The doll crawls out of the tunnel and starts to run. It starts to run faster with every step it takes, knowing that it will finally get rid of Anna. Its evil laughter rings within the school hallway. Finally, the doll gets to the field. It emerges from the shadows of the big oak tree. The doll, no longer in Mrs. Cally's body, looks mad, but it is comfortable enough to blast its ray at Anna without being cautious of harming Mrs. Cally.

Why would it be cautious in the first place? Doesn't it just kill anything that gets in its way? It did kill Carly, didn't it?

"So, Anna, you have finally given up. Why?"

"You killed my best friend. Why should I not die for something that is my fault?"

"To please you, I will make your death quick and easy. It won't hurt a bit, not for me at least!"

"What are you going to do? Shoot me with your ray? Go ahead."

"You are so still, so patient, so emotionless. I like that. Now, close your eyes, and it will be over in seconds." The doll shoots its rays out of its hands, but they do not hit Anna. She jumps up in the air and does a flip, landing perfectly on the ground.

"I never knew four years of gymnastics would pay off!" Anna runs toward the supply shed and the doll follows, just the way she wants it to. "You have fallen into my trap, doll. Perish with the shed."

"What do you mean? You will not *destroy* me. You cannot. You are merely a pathetic, mad, emotionless girl who feels lonely and alone." The doll laughs its evil laugh, but it stops when Anna takes out a match from under her sleeve. It watches patiently as she lights a blanket on fire. "Ha! You think fire can destroy me?"

"No, but I think an explosion can."

As the blanket slowly catches on fire, the smell of gasoline flows through the air.

The doll shrieks with horror. "You will be destroyed also!"

"I will not." Anna walks backwards and then disappears. There are two doors in the shed. While Anna escapes, she locks the doors and hammers them shut, so the doll cannot escape. The doll is trapped and screams are heard from within the fire, crackling screams, and then there is an explosion that can be heard and seen a mile away. Four tanks of gasoline plus one match equals an explosion and a dead doll.

Anna is in the middle of the field again, lying on the ground with her eyes shut. She finally opens them. Where a shed once stood, a pile of dust, despair, and filth now lie. Anna slowly walks toward the remains of the shed. She searches for the doll. When she finally sees it, all that is left of it is its glowing heart. The heart rises up into the air and disappears in an explosion of red dust. The doll had finally been destroyed.

"It's over. You're gone and you won't be back." Tears run down Anna's face and she immediately runs back into the school and into the tunnel where Carly's body lies.

Anna puts her hand over Carly's heart and cries. She cries all day long. She just sits and waits. What is she waiting for? It's not as if Carly will come back. She's gone. Just like the doll. All of a sudden, a glow flows through the tunnel, and a mystical ball of energy hovers above Anna's hand and Carly's heart. The ball seeps into Anna's hand and Carly's heart, and then a slight sound of breathing and a heartbeat comes from Carly. She's alive. The ball of energy is from the doll, and now this power lies in the bodies of the two fourteen-year-old girls. Anna has the power of healing, and Carly the power of seeing into the past. Together, the two of them will withstand all that they will face throughout their lives, together, just as they expected.

"Carly?"

"Anna."

"Do you know what happened?"

"No, I do not know. But I know that you defeated the doll."

"Yes, we are safe."

"Yes, we are."

Tears of joy cover their smiling faces.

Epilogue

Anna and Carly spend the summer in happiness. They get their book reports done and their parents don't suspect a thing. Once school starts, the principal, teachers, and students wonder what happened to the shed. Anna and Carly would live their lives in peace, without being bothered by the doll ever again. They would face what normal teenagers face in their lives: school, parents, even boys! They grow up and raise a family. They still live in Salem, Massachusetts. Although they are sure the doll is gone, they still look out to make sure the doll will not harm their children. Only Anna and Carly know the story of what happened to them when they were fourteen.

Salem is never the same after that battle, nor are Anna and Carly. Even if the doll is destroyed, its spirit still lives within the town. Even now you can sometimes hear its evil laughter in the school hallway — laughing, just laughing, a never-ending laugh.

Nihil, Nemo

by Niki Bousquet

So now I, Zoë Jane, have decided to write a memoir of key moments and experiences in my existence, altering only the necessary identifying material. From a poll (not a fishing pole taken among my peers on a fishing pier), I have ascertained that Zooey James is to be my alias, although I am not an alien, despite the fact that all organisms are composed of carbon that originated in outer space. You, whether you are you or someone else, will never discover the true identities of the remaining characters in this, the sometimes bland like mashed potatoes yet ironic and passionate story of my life.

Let's jump into it now, but not off a diving board, because those boards (not the wooden kind on my floor) frighten me. The day that is not today, or even tomorrow, but just yesterday was the day on which a male *Homo sapiens*, whose certificate of birth reads Xander in the space that is provided for a label called a name, popped out of the dark into the harsh glow of some fluorescent lights seventeen years ago. Because Xander happens to be of the male *Homo sapiens* variety, my close confidants, Andrea and Tegan, are quite shocked, like a turtle in a shell, that I have been seeing him, for the past several measurements of time that last approximately thirty days.

But this memoir isn't either of theirs; it is mine alone. Everyone doubted Xander's identity; but that can be explained by the fact that in this small town, even in a place as enlightened as Canada, we are surrounded by unfortunate *Homo sapiens* who malevolently mock (not like a benevolent mockingbird) any nice and considerate male and any female without oodles of makeup, like a poodle with its toenails painted. Any labels that may be stuck on us with a price sticker dispenser don't bother us; however, the matter in our craniums is highly functioning and compassionate enough to allow us to coexist with any other *Homo sapiens*, despite their nuances in personality that others call sinful or nauseating.

Anyway, since it is today, we must return to yesterday. Xander, his parents (one of which is female and one of which is male) and I trailed a trail of pollution to Quebec City on the day preceding the present one to view the exhibits at the National Museum of Hosiery. The drive did not take light years, as we live among the marching mooing cows just outside Quebec City; but still it was slightly awkward, with only the loud silence of our quartet, as we were not of the musical sort.

When I become nervous, my insides seem to effervesce and send streams of giggles bubbling off my tongue and out through my metal studded teeth. So, I was painfully clenching my jaw in an attempt to stifle my outbursts throughout the entire outing, which was nothing like a power outage.

Xander fancies handholding an awful lot, in contrast to the stereotypical male *Homo sapiens*, which is quite wonderful and very consistent, considering that he is not a stereotype of anything. So, because of this fondness that he and I share for such a simple demonstration of affection, we rode to and fro with our fond digits fondly intertwined like wilting fronds. I spent most of my time gazing at those devices below our wrists, which are useful for grasping utensils, whether metal or plastic, observing Xander drawing little swirls on my thumb with his. What if, for some reason, it was anatomically necessary for humans to hold hands with the hand that they use to write letters, numbers, and such? That could be troublesome. Xander and I are both pleasantly odd left-handed anomalies, so, if that were the case, the person on the left would be required to be in possession of a quite lengthy appendage.

I do fancy palindromes; wow is a palindrome, but somewhat ironically, palindrome is not. Please pardon the digression. This is the nonsense I contemplate to prevent myself from being as embarrassed as a pirate walking the plank over land, by an unwarranted fit of laughter, although at least it would not be an epileptic fit.

When we arrived on the correct incorrectly shop-lined avenue in Quebec City, we stored our vehicle of pollution in the lot of parking belonging to a mini golf venue called Skittles, as all the street-side parking had been hogged, although not by hogs, as barnyard animals are not permitted to operate vehicles of pollution. I'm sure they wouldn't want to anyway. They probably care about the muddy Earth on which they roll around far too much. We stepped on our feet all the way across the street and then continued stepping - not on steps, parallel to the buildings, like geometry class - for nearly a block before stepping up the steps and through the whirling revolving doors of the National Museum of Hosiery.

After viewing the various colored, patterned, striped, polka-dotted, and lace-adorned socks, tights, leggings, pantyhose, and fishnets, we ate breakfast at midnight in the Hosiery Café. It served mostly fish wrapped in fishnets, but being a vegan I ordered an eggplant salad, which rested on a bed of socks made of organic burlap. Strangely enough, the edible socks were quite saucy, and as I have a very low spicy foods threshold, like the threshold between my room and the hallway that I walk over in my organic burlap socks, I made a rooster of myself by choking and coughing as soon as the first bite slithered off the choo-choo train of my fork and into my mouth. I gulped some sparkling pomegranate and blueberry–flavored rainwater from a stemmed glass made of papier-mâché translucent trouser socks to calm my tingling taste buds (which were not like rosebuds). Inside my throat, my esophagus, and my intestines were the climate of a toasty summer afternoon, created by spices and worrisome thoughts of tape and worms and tapeworms, although outside it was mid-February and quite tootsie chilling.

The discussion between us four varied from the connection between Swiss cheese and Switzerland to the incorrectness of the name of the French and Indian War.

"I don't know what they have to do with each other, but I do like the holes." This was the opinion offered by Sue Ellen, Xander's only female parent.

"Why does there have to be a connection? French fries are a glorious take on the potato, and I have no idea how they're related to France. It's not like they're third cousins or something. I don't even think they call them that there."

Xander's father, Jackson, was a fried potato enthusiast. "That war didn't even involve indigenous people, although the French were part of it."

We all agreed on this statement, as Xander and I had learned of the misleading name in eighth-grade U.S. history.

I am sure (but not quite like the shore) that the conversation veered off to something more meaningful, meaning filled with meaning, but I was lost in my own thoughts, which weren't mine, wondering if I would ever again be in such a joyous (not joy us) state of mind as I had been in over forty-eight hours before (not be four, bee for, or even bee four). There wasn't much reason for my jubilance, like cherries, then, and even less to warrant the melancholy, like Christmas gifts named Carol, and anxiety whose frothy waves crashed over me now like the slobber of a dog bitten by a rabid but well meaning raccoon foaming at the mouth. The chemicals in my brain seem to come and go as they pleased, not like the obedient chemicals of an experiment in eleventh grade advanced placement chemistry class. Gosh, I wonder how I did on that test. My serotonin doesn't care if I'm supposed to be sobbing like a sopping wet dirty sponge used for washing grease off of delicate porcelain, and its depressive counterpart has no regard for the fact that I'm riding up into the sad sky in a supposedly cheerful Ferris wheel that has become teary.

Xander and I don't exchange many sounds from our mouths around the two beings who are responsible for his large eyes, yellow like yelling, shielded by an aegis of leaning-long eyelashes, and his precisely, pricelessly pigmented vermilion lips of pillows filled with down; but not the kind from geese, because that wouldn't be very nice now would it? Conversely, when only our ears are around, our musings, like muses to musicians, stretch like rubber bands that are painful when used as hair elastics, from the discussion of mundane daily experiences, like falling in the mud, to the examination of topics, like topical ointment, so personal or bizarre (not like a Christmas bazaar) that it would not feel correct, like a computer file corrupted with a virus that says I love you, to ink them into the processed fibers of this thin, flattened tree.

After what seems like a long while, we depart that room meant for consumption of nutrients, with its table and chairs, all plaid, striped, and clear. Clear the sky is not, but Xander's eyes are, as he shoots me sweet glances, unlike bullets, while we trot.

Once we reach the car and its wheels begin rolling over themselves, our hands, like bats, use their sonar to find each other again, squeezing messages of wanting something that we are not permitted to have now. We both quite enjoy looking at each other, as I have told Xander and he has told me; and whenever I twist slightly to the side so our wonderful ocular spheres lock in a long gaze, I feel my feelings playing jump rope with my intestines, but in a pleasant way, not in a way that would induce vomit.

Back within the boards and nails Xander calls home, we consume pomegranate flavored Jell-O, with cellulose, the plant alternative for gelatin, which is an animal by-product. The candles, a few short of seventeen, when lit sort of melt the Jell-O, and we eat it in screaming silence; then again, nothing can be perfect, and I wouldn't want it to be.

After the jiggly birthday treat, which I didn't finish on account of my appetite , which seems to have recently gotten frightened and fled, we depart to the level concrete roof, which can be accessed from the massive windows that line the walls of Xander's bedroom.

"I don't want to rip it; it's so pretty."

Xander carefully extracts a journal with a chubby happy hamster on the cover from the paper that I covered with rainbows of colorful wormholes and galaxies.

Yeah, we like our pet hamsters. They're always friendly and you can talk to them when you are lonely; and Xander writes a lot, although he won't let anyone witness his words. He quickly drinks all the ink in his pens, spitting it out to engrave prosaic paragraphs on pages of processed wood.

"Thank-you so much. Wow; I can use this when I'm at physics camp this summer."

Xander smiles his sweet smile with his straight white canines and incisors, like a sugar-soaked candy cane if the red stripes were bleached with whitening paste and a scary blue light in a dentist's chair with a bib. He envelops me in a hug, but it's not rigid like an envelope. Lately, when we have wrapped each other in our arms like blankets and propelled our lips toward each other like magnets, something has been different. We have both noticed it.

"I've always loved being with you, Zoë."

Xander whispered in my ear like we shy people do when we are afraid of revealing too much warm mushy stuff and subjecting our hearts and internal happy switches to the jackhammer of reality. We say little but we feel bunches, and it is understood that we mean much more.

"But lately I'm just like ... wow."

I nod with a slow smile, sponging in his syllables and knowing exactly what they mean.

But I realize, at this moment in time, which may not exist, only the memories of my feelings mirror his. Under normal circumstances I feel all the wowness too, but right now, and at least fifty percent of the rest of the time, despite this wonderfully insane, happy falling elevator between Xander and me, it's like I'm just not in my body to feel the feelings that I'm feeling. I try not to let it worry me too much. Since yesterday, I've been in one of these horrible funks, which isn't funky like hemp and peace signs but more like rotting flesh and massive sad leeches bloated with blood. I feel like an unperson. I feel like nothing, *nihil*, because I feel nothing; and only a few individuals, Xander included, can identify the something that this nothing comes from.

"You look really sad."

Xander speaks quietly and gently. I'm so good at hiding myself and all the pathetic junk inside me. He's the only person I can never fool, as long as he can see the watermark on my face, of something being not quite right. That's why I love the lovely, luscious dark. Its nothingness counteracts mine and acts as an invisibility cloak for sadness and secrets.

I feel so guilty for capsizing the happy boat we were sailing on, especially on Xander's birthday.

"Seeing you smile makes me happy."

I say this, not sure if it's the truth or just wild hope, but then Xander smiles that sunny half circle genuine smile, and it is the truth, truly, not like a false tooth. I'm inexpressibly grateful for this opal arch of warm, white friendly fire. My sadness makes him sad and I don't think I'm worth it, but that is the only reason I have ever seen him not completely elated. And that just devastates anything inside my brain that was trying to get happy again, so the corners of mouth are weighted with cement blocks, sinking to the bottom of some dirty city river. They won't make a U–turn; it's illegal. Like the supportive frowning arches of a Roman coliseum, they are stubborn.

But at least for now, everything isn't too terrible as we curl around each other underneath a fluffy, friendly, flannel blanket and nearly careen over the edge of the roof because of the turbulence in the space between us. Slow, cautious kisses are the best antidote for sadness and they do function as such.

We are the intertwining codependent climbing ivy on the chimney of an old house I no longer visit; but in this way, I can go back there and hold on tight to the strand of ivy that grasps me like a lifejacket on the *Titanic*.

So, in the last few hours, I have been doubting myself even more than I had been expecting, doubt which had, until now, stampeded out the door, and hopefully would never return. And, like I always do, I hid my doubt with all of that embarrassing blathering and humor that I didn't have my heart in.

But now you, Ivy, are a part of me, and I don't doubt you; I never have, so I suppose I can't doubt myself anymore, and I never have.

Then again, I have to wonder...

The Man in the Mirror

by Tom Lemberg

Lloyd Anderson was tying his tie before dinner when the telephone rang. A feeling in his stomach told him that this call was bad news. When he thought of what had happened just that morning, fear nearly claimed him. He pushed the memory to the back of his mind. Probably a wrong number, he told himself.

By the fifth ring, he had answered the phone. As he pushed the receiver to his ear, he felt a chill run through his body. The man on the line introduced himself as a police officer. Lloyd felt the feeling in his stomach returning strong.

"What's happened, officer?" he asked with bleak anticipation. The response was worse than anything he could have imagined.

* * *

In the year 2020, fifteen years before Lloyd Anderson received his phone call, he remembered sitting in a waiting room of a hospital wing in New York City. His father had recommended the doctor to Lloyd as the finest surgeon money could buy. Of course, money was no object for the Andersons, ever since Lloyd's father hit it big in real estate. "Only the best for my boy" was the saying Lloyd best remembered his father by. Now Lloyd was the father, and with a large inheritance at his disposal, nothing but the best would be suitable for his own son.

A nurse entered the room through double doors.

"Mr. Anderson?" Lloyd stood up and approached the young woman, a black leather briefcase hanging loosely from his left hand. "Dr. Sullivan is ready to speak with you," she said before showing Lloyd to a room hidden behind a closed door. He waited for the nurse to leave before entering.

Dr. Sullivan was a man in the final years of his youth. He was a short man, overweight but not terribly so, with a head of hair that struggled to keep from falling out and turning gray.

He wore round, wire-framed glasses that had been out of style for years, but which gave him a look of intelligence. The doctor was standing when Lloyd entered the room and gave a firm handshake. Lloyd, though, could only feign interest in the man. He had always carried an air of self-absorption, masked only by his professional demeanor. For the time being, the only thing on Lloyd's mind was his son, but more importantly the boy's diagnosis.

Greg rose from his chair and raced to his father, clinging to Lloyd's leg as tightly as a five-year-old boy could. Lloyd ruffled his son's black hair before placing a hand on his shoulder, a gesture that left the boy strangely uncomforted. The hand was far too smooth to convey any sense of age or strength. It was the hand of a small child who had yet to develop calluses, who had never used his hands for labor in its most basic form. Lloyd tightened his hold on his son's shoulder.

"Good afternoon, Mr. Anderson," said Sullivan.

"You as well, Doctor," said Lloyd. "I've been anxious to hear my son's results."

"Ah, yes, the results," began Sullivan cautiously. "Before I tell you of them, I would like to advise you not to take what I tell you as fact. The tests I administered are not common practice among doctors, even to those involved in neuroscience. The results may not be entirely accurate."

"I have faith in your work, Doctor," replied Lloyd. "Like my father always said, you're the best money can buy."

"I am glad to hear I have your approval." Sullivan turned his back to Lloyd and paced over to his desk, where a stack of papers was neatly arranged on a clipboard. He flipped through several pages before finding Greg's test results, at which point he turned back to Lloyd, eyes still focused on the paper as he spoke. "You gave me the very unusual request of administering a medical IQ examination, if I'm not mistaken?"

"That is correct. I wouldn't make decisions for my son based on some absurd oral examination. Your work is much more reliable."

"Very flattering, Mr. Anderson, in which case you shouldn't be alarmed to hear that the analysis of your son's scans returned an intelligence quotient ten points lower than what he scored in the oral examination."

Sullivan saw Lloyd's lower lip quiver for no more than a second before he was able to compose himself.

"My son scored below one hundred?" he asked in disbelief.

"Don't sound so appalled, Mr. Anderson. Your son doesn't have any sort of disability. He's perfectly healthy, not even below-average intelligence."

"Not even?" Lloyd was taken aback. "What do you mean he's not even below average? Andersons aren't average. Anderson's don't settle for less than the best. My son deserves the best."

Sullivan closed his eyes after hearing the statement. His expression hinted at revulsion. "Well, Mr. Anderson," he said matter-of-factly, "there are some things that even science can't change."

Acting as though the inevitable response wouldn't be uttered, Sullivan turned around and placed his clipboard back on the countertop, only to find that Lloyd had thrown down his palm on top of the stack of papers and was now standing beside him at the counter. When Sullivan looked into Lloyd's face he saw malice. In an angry voice Lloyd spat out, "We both know that's not true."

Sullivan feigned naivety, which only provoked Lloyd further. His volume was low, so as to hide his intentions from his son, but his tone was gruff .

"I'm not so out of touch, Doctor," said Lloyd. "I've read all about your newest research."

"I don't know what you're talking about," replied Sullivan.

"Then, maybe I should give you a hint," said Lloyd. "The computer — "

"That research is purely experimental and not properly tested."

"I think you underestimate yourself, Doctor." Lloyd's eyes narrowed. "Or perhaps you merely lie. You forgot to mention the autistic girl. No less than a month ago, was it not?"

"It was a high-risk operation. That girl needed the computer implanted in her head to lead a healthy life, while your son is in perfect health just as he is. It wouldn't be right for you to risk his life so that he *might* end up the next Einstein."

Lloyd laughed, a sinister, near-silent laugh. A chill ran through Sullivan's body upon hearing the sound. "Why do we kid ourselves, Doctor. You know there is no risk. You are merely afraid. Why don't you prove yourself. After all, you're the best money can buy."

Sullivan was tempted to have this unwanted visitor thrown out of the building, yet something caused him to restrain himself. "What are you suggesting, Mr. Anderson?"

With a grin of delight, Anderson lifted his briefcase up onto the counter. He spun it around so the front was facing Sullivan, then opened the case. Lining it were stacks of bills. The quantity of money was obscene, much less the actual sight of it in cash. "It's all yours. All you have to do is earn it."

Sullivan said nothing. In silence, he closed the lid of the briefcase and turned his back to Lloyd. As he walked to the door of his office he brushed past Greg, who was standing idly in confusion.

For the first time since he entered the room, Lloyd was now nervous. "If you walk out on me now I'll make no second offer. Be reasonable."

"I follow only reason," said Sullivan. He was now halfway out the door.

Lloyd couldn't breathe. Had the offer not been enough? "You can't just leave. Finish this like a man!"

Sullivan took a deep breath. "I'll be right back, as soon as I clear my schedule."

* * *

The operation was a complete success. Better yet, Lloyd knew that his son wouldn't even remember having it after a while. Greg would be a genius, and what happened that day in the operating room would be a well-kept secret from the press and from the boy. He'll never know, Lloyd told himself. So long as he doesn't shave his head.

* * *

Twelve years passed by quickly. The year 2031 had slipped into 2032 seamlessly. Greg Anderson was now a junior in high school and an academic star of his class, though not the only one. This was a fact which greatly bothered Greg's father, who had lately taken a keen interest in his son's college admissions. The other boy's name was Robbie Leizman. Robbie had a flawless academic record and was in pursuit of an award offered by MIT to a single high school student in the country. The competition was a scientific race, and the winner was the first to cross the finish line and submit his discovery to the college that every young scientist dreamed of attending.

Both Greg and Robbie were at their wits' end in their attempt to be first to create what the competition demanded. The goal was to design a robotic head, humanoid in its features, that could successfully complete a college interview. The questions that would be asked were entirely unpredictable, which made the challenge incredibly daunting. Lloyd remembered hearing about a high school student from Colorado who traveled all the way to Cambridge, Massachusetts, to have his robot interviewed by an MIT professor, only to fail. Lloyd told this story to Greg as a warning, reminding him that students were allowed only one interview. It was hit or miss, and Greg knew his robot would have to be perfect if he was to succeed.

Lloyd was beginning to feel the pressure. He knew that soon there would be news of some student from California whose robot succeeded in the interview — or from New York or Tennessee or Alaska; it didn't at all matter. All he knew was that he couldn't picture the headlines reading, "Greg Anderson from New Jersey builds winning robot." No, that wouldn't happen. Something would have to intervene. He couldn't just let his son go on tinkering in his workroom day after day. Nothing would come of it. When the answer came to Lloyd, so did a strong sensation of fear. He decided he would lay low for a while as he thought of how he would break the news.

* * *

Greg stared at his unfinished work. His headache was intense and reminded him more and more of the pain he had felt for weeks now as he pored over every little thing he might have done wrong. Everything is right, he would tell himself. Everything is as is should be, but something was missing. But what? His robot had mastered the difficult task of learning. When he told him his name, he remembered. When you told him that he was being rude he proceeded more politely. So what was left? What couldn't he do? He could learn the way a human being can learn. But could he learn to learn?

Greg erased the robot's memory and turned him on. The machine's eyes lit up as his neck spun around on the wooden board it was mounted on, eventually settling on Greg.

"Hello, sir," said the robot.

"Hello, my friend. Your name is Nathan," declared Greg.

"Very well, sir. What is your name?"

"My name is Greg."

"Hello, Greg. It's a pleasure to meet you."

"What is your name?"

"Nathan."

"Who gave you that name?"

"You did, sir."

Greg sighed in relief. At least he'd made it this far. "Nathan, I would like you to change your name to the next thing I point to."

"As you wish, sir."

As Greg stood up, the robot followed him with its eyes, turning its neck only when necessary. Greg could see the robot observing him as he paced over to his workbench and picked up a simple hammer. He carried the tool back to where Nathan was mounted and sat down. Greg said nothing to the robot, only held out the hammer so that Nathan could clearly see the black grip of the tool. He pointed to the bright yellow text on the grip that spelled the brand name, "Stanley." Nathan's eyes were clearly focused on the text, up until the time when Greg lowered the tool onto the floor. Their eyes met. "Now tell me," said Greg slowly. "What is your name?"

Without hesitation, the robot replied, "My name is Greg."

Greg wasn't frustrated. He was furious. He turned off the machine with force, happy to be rid of its annoying voice. Something had been building up inside him for months, and now it was stronger than ever. He felt an overwhelming doubt of everything his father had ever told him. *You're an Anderson, and Andersons are meant for great things.* Why? Why should he have to exhaust himself every day of his life? He didn't think having a wealthy grandfather should result in so much pressure. Greg began to see his whole future spread out before him, and all that was there was one long, hard day. When, in the future his father had planned out for him, would he be able to rest? When the postman comes home from work, he is home. He doesn't have to worry about his job until nine o'clock the next morning. When a construction worker comes home, he is home. Greg would never be home. Home was work. His life would always be work. Yet somehow, he couldn't call it quits. The idea that if he tried hard enough the work might one day be complete was terribly alluring.

Greg heard someone knocking at the door to his workroom. "Come in," he said.

His father entered with a serious expression on his face. Somehow Greg sensed that his father wanted to talk seriously with him. How he hated conversations with his father. He had hoped dinner was ready. "Son, can I talk with you about something?"

Greg sighed. "Sure. What is it?"

"It's about this robot," said Lloyd inconclusively. Greg knew there was more. "And your future."

"What about it? How I need to work harder if I'm going to be happy someday? How I was meant for greater things than everyone else? Honestly, Dad, what is it?"

"Don't talk to me like that."

"Sorry," said Greg.

Lloyd took a seat on a stool in front of his son and sighed. "Son, how much does this competition mean to you?"

"Don't worry, Dad, I'll finish it. I just need more time."

"Answer my question."

"It..." Greg hesitated. "It means a lot to me."

"Just how much do you want to succeed?"

"Dad, what is this about?"

Lloyd hated that question. He so badly didn't want to explain it, but knew he had to. It was inevitable. "Son, you are very talented. Your level of thought is incredible."

"Yes, yes, I — "

"Let me finish, son. This isn't easy." He took a very deep breath. "Do you know why your mind works the way it does?"

"Because of how you raised me, I guess."

"Not quite," returned Lloyd.

"Dad, what are you talking about?" asked Greg.

"Well, you see, there was an operation..."

Suddenly it all made sense.

* * *

Greg dreamed that night. It was a dream he had visited many times in the past. He was standing in an endless forest of dead trees, none of them any taller than ten feet, on a ground coated with dead, dried-out brown leaves. And worse was the emptiness between the trees, the unnatural amount of open space, so void that one could see the horizon in all directions, a marriage of dead leaves and pale gray sky.

There was a man standing with his back to Greg. Greg tried to see his face, but from any angle he seemed to always be facing exactly the opposite way. Greg had to see the man face to face. He had so many secrets.

Greg started running and the man immediately broke into a sprint. The two were perfectly matched, the gap between the two of them never growing, never shrinking. But this wouldn't go on for long. Eventually Greg felt his foot catch on something, and he fell forward onto the ground. What he felt, though, were not leaves. He was on cold, smooth concrete, rolling down a slope like a dead log until finally he struck merciful, level ground. He was in an empty aqueduct, flat on his back.

As he stood up, he could finally see the man's face. He was standing before him, unscathed, beside a pedestal. Greg felt he was looking into a mirror. Almost. The man was identical to Greg in every way but his eyes. Greg's eyes were a pale blue, while the man before him possessed eyes of a metallic gray, almost appearing to be scratched or carved. Maybe etched.

"Who are you?" asked Greg.

"I am everything you want to know," replied the man in a voice much darker than Greg's, despite having come from an identical pair of lips. His hand reached for the cloth covering the pedestal and threw it onto the concrete, revealing Greg's robotic head. "What is your name, my friend?"

"Stanley," said the robot. "My name is Stanley. Name is Stanley. Stanley. Stanley. Stanley..."

The robot wouldn't stop, and the man wouldn't stop laughing. "What did you do to him?" shouted Greg over the chant of the robot and the sinister laughter of his twin with mechanical eyes. "How did you make him work?"

The man replied in a different language, one that Greg wasn't even certain was spoken anywhere in the world. The man continued to repeat his coded response, as if in a chant, and the robot moaned on louder and louder, "Stanley, Stanley, *Stanley* — "

Greg woke up sweaty. He cursed his father for ever putting that chip in his head. It made him want things he wasn't meant to have. He needed knowledge he wasn't meant to possess. But that was just it. He needed to know. Greg's dream was only one of many that were all much the same.

His mechanical self would offer him knowledge, and rarely would Greg get it. He had never received the knowledge he desired of his robot.

Greg's father had offered to have his chip tuned up, enhanced by means of a medical procedure. Greg hated the idea, and now he felt no differently. But he needed it. He despised the thought of having a second operation, but he knew he had to have it.

* * *

The operation was a success. The next time Greg dreamed, he was answered in his native tongue. His robot performed perfectly in the interview at MIT, and he would return almost two years later to move into his dormitory.

* * *

Greg was now a sophomore at MIT studying electrical engineering. The year was 2035. As he overlooked his mess of a workspace, he wondered how things had ever gone so far. The research had gotten out of hand so quickly, but Greg couldn't stop himself. He knew the answers were all so close. He couldn't give up.

Greg remembered vividly how the research had all gotten started. His professor had announced that his top student in the freshman class would be given the opportunity to work with him and his graduate students during the summer on an artificial intelligence project. Greg strived for the position but was beaten out by another student. He remembered begging the teacher for the chance to prove himself, pleading his case. He had even showed him the robotic head he constructed in his junior year of high school. The professor had been unimpressed, telling Greg that his robot had no capacity for invention.

"I'll show him," muttered Greg under his breath. His robot was close, very close. It lacked creativity, an ability of the human mind that had never been duplicated by machine.

This was Greg's inspiration. That was where he would find the answers.

His mind. His mechanical self. He looked at the hideous machine he had constructed and almost felt sorry for himself. But he knew there was no way out. He had to finish what he started. He had to know.

* * *

Lloyd Anderson approached the door to the lab. He had planned to visit his son in his dorm room but found that he wasn't there. A student told Lloyd that Greg practically lived in this laboratory. Already he was beginning to worry about his son's mental health.

When Lloyd walked in, he saw something unlike anything he'd ever seen. A cylindrical steel machine was attached to an LCD screen, showing moving images of graphs and recording data. The other end of the cylinder connected to a metallic ring, which was worn around his son's head like a headband. He almost seemed to be capturing data from his mind. Lloyd tried to see his son's face, but the young man's back was turned away.

"Son," whispered Lloyd. "It's your dad."

Greg said nothing.

"I went to your dorm room, but you weren't there." Still nothing. "Greg?"

Greg turned around, and Lloyd regretted ever speaking. His son's eyes were scratched, etched. What looked like wires seemed to be burned to his eyes, glowing red hot like a soldering iron. Lloyd was taken right out of reality. He prayed he was in a nightmare.

After what seemed like an eternity, Greg removed the metal headband. He blinked once, and his eyes returned to their normal pale blue. The graph on the LCD screen became a solid green line. "Sorry, Dad," he whispered.

His father couldn't respond. He was stricken with horror.

"Dad?"

"I'll meet you for dinner, son." He covered his mouth and turned around. "Just take a rest."

* * *

Greg stood before the mirror in the lab. He didn't see himself in the glass. He saw the man, his mechanical self, with eyes ablaze like hot metal. The being had developed into more of a machine and had become far more grotesque. The sides of his face were only half skin, the rest replaced by metal, with wires etched into the plating. His left cheek was half gone, revealing nothing on the inside. He had no tongue, and other than his last remaining rotted teeth, he possessed only steel in his mouth.

"You want to know," said the mechanical man. "You're dying to know."

"Tell me what I need to know," Greg growled.

"Why should I tell you?" he said. "What have you done?"

"I have searched, long and hard. I have found nothing."

"What have you been given," asked Greg's mechanical image. "You have no mind."

"I'm more intelligent than any other student on this campus."

"You have no intelligence. You have only me."

"Tell me what I need to know," repeated Greg.

"Earn it."

"Tell me," demanded Greg.

"Someday."

"Tell me now!" Greg punched the glass ferociously, causing his knuckles to bleed. He wanted to strangle the man, tear out the wires that made him whole. He wanted to pin the monster to the ground and make him beg for the honor of disclosing his unnatural secrets. He lost all sense of reality. Glass shattering could be heard from outside the lab. Blood was everywhere. But Greg saw none of it, felt none of it. The mechanical man would speak.

* * *

"Your son has..." The officer didn't finish his sentence.

"My son has what?" Lloyd said into the telephone. He remembered his son's condition from that morning and feared what had happened.

"This is never easy, sir, so I will simply tell you the facts. Your son has taken his own life. He died in front of a laboratory mirror this afternoon."

Lloyd didn't respond to the officer. He set the telephone down on the receiver and turned his back away. He removed the heaviest coat he had brought with him from the closet and threw it over himself as he stepped out the door of his hotel room.

An Excerpt from My Novel

by Rebecca Harris

A sign hovers in the darkness, its blue and red paint chipped and fading. Its white words are impossible to make out, though the lights on the sign's perimeter still flash. Limitless pavement stretches out from the base of the signpost, as far as I can see. At one side, the blade of a knife forms a shining line across my vision. I turn to my left, and there it is: the mouth of the beast, a concrete monstrosity coming to a single massive point at the black hole of the door. A fierce yawn of machinery — am I inside? It's black; I can't tell — I see her face, pale lily white with the sweet, innocent look of terror in her eyes. Never seen that look before on her face, and it makes me love her ten times more than I ever have. But that face is snatched from me — there's a white current coming closer — her face returns and it's swirled into the tide: distorted now, hideous.

Out of the corner of my eye I see something red — a flash — gone. Outside again, running. A silhouette far ahead, nearly invisible and a reflection in the pools near the side of the lot — just the single eye, but in it so much: longing and regret and terror and muddy-brown anger. Now it's just the eye, me and the eye, and I'm running. And behind me, no, in front, I hear her. Not Karen, though, the drowned one, the one that wails like a siren, and, at last, her scream spreads thin across the night.

Waking, my sweat is hot and I feel intensely claustrophobic. I claw at my blankets, kick at them and shove them down until they're around my ankles. Gradually, the dream starts to come back. Detail by detail, I pull it out of wherever dreams come from until it stands before me, a jigsaw puzzle only half-done. Who knows if these gaps were filled in as I dreamed it, or if they disintegrated somehow as I brought them to light? Just a dream, I make myself repeat, but not a normal one. Some parts were so crisp, clean, almost artificially bright and smooth, others fragmented into a million shards and scattered across my consciousness. I hold each up to the light but get no more out of them. I try to fall back asleep, but my nerves have taken over and I'm way too jittery.

On the way downstairs, I glance at the clock.

4 a.m.

In the kitchen, I grab myself some ice water and try to sip it slowly to calm myself down, but I keep on standing up and pacing back and forth between the kitchen and the living room, back and forth, back and forth, just a dream, just a dream. But there was something off kilter about it, not in the way dreams usually are, but as if it was its own breed of nightmare.

It was her face, I think, Karen's terrified face. I've never seen her look like that, but I know that that's how she would look, that's how she would shape her face if she was in a state of extreme terror. Dreams, even nightmares, are made of what you know and fear, the images you see out of the corner of your eye that haunt you when you don't think about them. But I'm sure I've never seen Karen like that.

I feel compelled to call her, just to make sure of her, just to have somebody real ground me in the darkness. But her cell phone is always turned off after midnight, and her parents sleep next to the phone. How would I explain myself? I'm sorry, Mr. and Mrs. Gardner, but I had a nightmare and was wondering if Karen could comfort me and tuck me back into bed? I don't think so. For now I'll just sit here, and when my parents come down they'll see me and be so sweetly disapproving, and if I want I can go back upstairs and spend the day in bed.

But at five forty-five the phone rings, and Mrs. Gardner's voice is shaky on the other end.

"Can I speak with your mother, please?" she asks, not even apologizing for calling so early or asking why I, of all people, was the one to pick up. "It's urgent."

I dash up the stairs, nearly tripping on the loose thread that runs the length of the bottom step. I pound on my mom and dad's door until my mother's sleepy putty-color face swings around its edge.

"Karen's mom," I state, and I pass the phone off to her. I continue my pacing in the upstairs hall — past my parents' door, the study, the bathroom, my room, and back. Parents', study, bathroom, my room, back. I feel like stopping would cause a train wreck, might send me completely off the track. When Mom comes out, I know I was right to be tense.

"They don't know where Karen is," she said. Just like that. As if it happened all the time. "You seen her?"

I haven't actually, though we've been going out for a couple months and Saturdays are usually the nights we have actual dates. She had a babysitting job this weekend, which she was doing mostly as a favor to her godmother, because she wanted to go to the chamber orchestra at BU that night. Karen lives a block away from her godmother, who is an excellent family friend and not a woman to break her promises. She had said she would be back at around midnight to pay Karen and resume the care of her five-year-old son, Jeffrey, who according to Karen was a pure nightmare to take care of.

She was going to walk home after the job, or at least that had been the plan, a rather controversial one, because her mother didn't think even their own block was safe for a sixteen-year-old girl to walk at midnight alone. But her godmother's husband left her a year ago and she was unwilling to leave Jeffrey completely home alone for any longer than two minutes, so Karen offered to walk. It was a sweet gesture, really, the kind Karen is known for across Norbury High.

"Ms. Carlson told her that Karen was there when she got back," my mother was saying. "But apparently she got lost walking that one block home. Or at least that's what Dora claims." My mother sighed. "Dora's never been able to admit that sometimes her daughter might not walk straight home the way she's supposed to. Her daughter might want to have some fun." In a moment of almost unspeakable vulgarity, my mother winked at me.

I knew my mother was wrong. Karen — well, Karen had never been the sort of girl to do things like that. Deep down in my stomach acid churned. The glint of a knife returned to the edge of my mind, and almost seemed to press its cool blade against my thoughts. And where is she? No one knows. No one knows. It's almost as if somehow she were transposed into my dream world, her face now imprinted solely in the fabric of my fantasy. Gone.

But wherever she is, she's scared. Dreaming of her contorted face convinced me of that. I don't know how or why, but that face crossed the miles of distance between us and came to me. Was it a cry for help? Who knows? But if it is, I can't ignore it.

"You're probably right," I told my mom. "It's probably nothing."

God, how far from nothing that dream and this morning were. But doubt did not register on her face. It seemed bizarre to me that I could lie so transparently to my own mother and that she would believe me. How could she ever think that my girlfriend's disappearance was nothing? There were lines around the corners of my mother's mouth, tributaries feeding sorrow to her aches. Nothing of mine there, just her own regrets and denials. No place for me existed in my mother's mouth or eyes. I turned to go. "I'm going to try and get some sleep," I said.

"All right. I'm going downstairs to make breakfast. Too late for an old woman like me to go back to sleep."

Another lie had passed through my lips, and again she believed me. Even the implication that the phone had woken me was wrapped into my words — for whatever reason I didn't want to tell my mom that I had trouble sleeping some nights, not just last night but around three nights a week. My mother had her own problems. She didn't need the burden of mine.

Back in my room, I began my search for leads. I planned it all out carefully in my head — I would start with my old e-mails and phone messages, checking for hints of plans she'd made or reasons for her disappearance. Next, I would insist on talking to Mrs. Gardner, who knew if my mother was telling me everything she knew. A shiver ran down my spine as I contemplated just how easy it was to lie, and how possible it was that my mother had done so often in the past sixteen years.

To get to my computer I first had to wade through the stacks of old papers and dirty clothes that seemed to breed like scruffy rabbits on my rug. If you asked my mother, she would tell you that the heaps of paper were old tests and quizzes, math problems I was too lazy to throw out. But that wasn't right. It wasn't right at all. Once on my computer, it took me only a few seconds for the Web page to load. I kept glancing anxiously at the clock, terribly aware of how little time I had to do this. A few hours? A week? Who knew?

"That's weird," I muttered to myself as I skimmed my inbox. Maybe I had just read too fast and missed something, I thought. But when I read it again, slower, I realized I had been right the first time. No messages from Karen were recorded. I clicked on my contact list; she wasn't listed. But in "Sent," I finally saw something.

"Message sent to 'Karen' <sugarkookie@comcast.net> deleted," it said, the same thing repeated all the way down the list. Next to each deletion, it recorded the date I had first sent it. I recognized the first date on the list.

Last Wednesday we had had some minor fight, and I had e-mailed her to make up. The fight had been stupid and shallow — she had forgotten our anniversary, which we both found funny when we thought about it, because, after all, I was supposed to be the one forgetting and she the one who was mad. I closed the e-mail window and stood up. Grabbing my cell phone from the front pocket of the black messenger bag I took to school, I flipped it open with one hand and checked for messages. No voicemails were recorded, but one missed call. From 2 a.m. the night before, from Karen's cell.

I nearly fell backwards, I was so shocked. How was it possible that the one call in my life that mattered, the one call that might have determined someone's fate, had been placed in my hands and I had missed it? I hadn't picked up the damn phone, and now, for all I knew, she was dead, gone, forever, because of me. Frantic, I realized that it might not be too late. Maybe her phone was still on, and I could pray that she still had access to it. I hit the "Contacts" button on the left, and it seemed to take a full ten minutes before the screen came up.

I scrolled up and down through all my contacts, until I was wavering back and forth between Jim and Lawrence, J to L, and back again. No Ks were listed. I dialed her number as fast as I could, having to start over more than three times because of mistakes made in my haste. Eventually I got it right. The phone rang on the other end, rang and rang and rang until finally I heard, "Hi, I'm not available right now. Please call me back, uh … I don't know. Later?" That stupid message she had made as a first draft and kept as a joke. I didn't leave a message.

Throwing my phone across the room, I cursed myself and my luck. I know this is selfish, but I didn't give a thought to Karen for a while. I just sat there and thought about how sad it was that I was doomed to idiothood, that I'd have the emotional baggage of being responsible for Karen's fate (whatever it was) my whole life. Only when I had calmed myself down and centered myself a bit did I begin to pull apart what had happened. What did it mean that I had dreamed Karen's terror? Was it a cry for help? Maybe two people as close as we were could be linked like that, across time and space. Or was it a prophesy?

I had no proof that the fragments of my dream had happened, yet, though I felt somehow that at least some of them had. It wasn't so far-fetched that if I could dream her disappearance before it was discovered, I might have seen events that hadn't yet unfolded.

That was when it hit me. Maybe it was my duty — my destiny — to find her before it was too late. Who knew who had sent this dream to me, but I knew with certainty that I had no intention of misusing it. But what about the e-mails? The phone contact? The voicemails I knew I had saved?

It was as if someone had taken a Swifter Duster and swept the traces of Karen right out of my life. Foolishly, I had an urge to see her picture and confirm that we had had something together, that she was my real-life girlfriend. But when I opened the drawer beside my bed, the snapshot of her was gone. Instantly my thoughts leapt to my mother. No one else had access to my room, not since my brother went off to college last fall. So, either she was responsible, or she had welcomed whoever was. But why? Why take part in such selective destruction? I snapped my mind back to what mattered just then: Karen's terrified face and the aching need I had to fix it, to turn it into the smile that was her natural state of being. Because she was the last to see Karen before the disappearance, I had to talk to Mrs. Carlson. At first she didn't answer her phone, but seconds after I hung up, she called me back.

"Hi, Mrs. Carlson?"

"Yes, it's me," she said. "I'm so sorry I missed your call. I was in the shower and — "

"Have you heard from Karen?"

"What? Oh, no, not since I came home last night. She said she was fine walking home alone. I saw her start out in the right direction, but her mother tells me she never arrived. She thinks she's been abducted or something. Poor girl's going to be in a hell of a lot of trouble when she gets home and tries to explain herself. So she's not with you?"

I stopped myself from explaining that if that were the case, I wouldn't be asking Mrs. Carlson where she was. "No, she's not with me," I said patiently. "I haven't seen her since Friday."

"Huh? That's odd. Would have thought she'd be with you. Look, I know you must be worried, but I promise you she'll come home tonight at the latest. Just because she didn't want to call and wake you when some plan came up doesn't mean she's lost forever, okay?"

"Okay," I repeated. "Thanks for the help."

239

"Oh, you're welcome. Call when you track her down, all right?"

"All right," I repeated. "I'll do that. Good-bye, and thanks again."

"Bye," she said absently, her mind already moving on to something more pressing, like laundry or grocery shopping.

No luck there. I had exhausted my known eyewitness and my "records," and now it was time to devise a new method of inquiry. Mrs. Carlson had mentioned "plans" that Karen might have created last-minute, and I wondered idly who she thought Karen would make such plans with. I made a mental list.

Could Adrianna have called Karen? No, she lived too far away and neither girl had access to a car. Tessa? No, Tess had bragged for a week about how romantic her first date with Rob had been and how she was thrilled that he had asked her out again for the very next weekend. June? Maybe. Kelsey? Maybe. I checked the contacts on my phone — I didn't have June, but I did have Kelsey.

Glancing at the time, I realized it was still only seven o'clock. It was way too early to call the average seventeen-year-old girl. I resolved to sleep until ten, but within fifteen minutes I was up again. Inaction was not possible with Karen missing. But what could I do? It wasn't as if I had thousands of leads. In fact, I had none — except for the dream. Maybe sleep was my best option. Who knew what might come to me?

With that new confidence, I got back into bed and sagged into sleep almost instantly. I woke at eleven, frustrated and just as tired as I had been at seven. No dreams had come, not even idle, playful ones, and I had slept an hour longer than I had meant to. I got up from the bed, threw on some deodorant and some clean clothes, and hurtled down the stairs. Even though I already had Kelsey's phone number, I decided to pay a visit to June before I called her. June lived close, had a car, and seemed exactly the kind of girl to get messed up in midnight trouble.

The walk took only twenty minutes, but it spanned the two major halves of Norbury, defined by the highway that cut through our town, which was strange since there wasn't even an exit within fifteen miles. I have always been almost ashamed to admit to people that I come from the more affluent, higher-class North Norbury, a fact which seems to cling to me like women's perfume, with about the same effect. "You from North?" people ask me all the time, puzzled when they see me with southerners. I always want to tell people that I live right next to the highway, barely north at all, and in a worse neighborhood than many southern homes. But I know that makes no difference.

Walking across the overpass to reach June's, I was once again struck by the contrasting scale at the bridge's two ends. To one side, all the houses were like miniature mansions, with high gables and two-color trim. And to the other, houses were half or one-third that size, falling apart and seeming to blur at the edges because of badly applied siding. I always felt that I belonged to both, spending so much time with Karen's friends down in South Center, but I knew how the world really saw me. I was north of the highway, so north for the rest of my life.

A few blocks away I spotted June's house, painted a vibrant pink. Sprawling expansions extended to either side like open arms, and the broken shades in the front windows made it seem as if it had buckteeth. Though it was the largest house south of the highway, it was also the least likely to sell — Karen had been in there more than a few times and reported an excess of black toilets, crumbling walls, and what appeared to be both asbestos and flaking lead paint. The additions had been added when we were little, after June's parents' first attempt at selling. Apparently the house's condition had been just as bad then as it was now, and they got no takers. But June's mother was pregnant (again), and space was already cramped, so they decided to make a build-it-yourself addition to the back.

No building permit had been purchased (none needed in the South end) and I wondered if I would dare to set foot in it if invited. A little boy appeared on the doorstep as I repeatedly jabbed at the bell, after no one answered it the first three times. I poked it lightly and patiently waited. He was an odd little creature, almost gnome like, with a face that somehow reminded me of that of a disabled kid's. Squashed, it seemed, and a little too flat.

"Doorbell doesn't work," he said, swinging it open a little to reveal a whole collage of small faces staring up at me from the shadows behind the door. "You want Nick?" Without waiting for a response, he turned and hollered into the dinginess behind him. "Nicky! Someone at the door!" Soon a rumble issued from above us, and flakes of plaster landed on the boy's head. He didn't seem to notice. A voice traveled down from what I assumed was the landing on the stairs.

"Who is it?" the voice growled.

"Who is it?' the boy turned to me and asked impatiently.

"Actually, I'm not ... I'm here to see June."

A kid just a little younger than I was, maybe fifteen, approached the door. He was dressed all in red, head to toe, but there was nothing else about his style, nothing you could pin down as distinctively Goth or punk or Indie.

He chucked as he saw me. "Hey, I know you," he said, grinning maliciously with an air of assumed superiority emanating from his pores.

"Caleb, right?"

"Right. I'm just here to talk to June. I don't know why — "

"Don't worry about it. Gary here just likes messin' up. I think it's 'cuz he has a secret love of wedgies, ain't that right, Gar?" Unabashedly, he reached down and yanked on the poor boy's boxers, letting them go and snapping them before a true wedgie was achieved. Gary lifted his nose loftily and led the little tribe of younger kids away.

"Come down here, June. That Caleb kid's here to ask you out," Nick shouted upstairs. "That is why you're here, right?"

he murmured to me with that superior smirk still on his face. "Actually, no," I said, raising my voice as I saw June descend the stairs in the hope she would hear me, "that's not why I'm here."

"Then what do you want?" she demanded, reaching the door and pressing her face right into mine, so close I could see both the tiny blackheads that covered her nose and the makeup that was meant to conceal them. "I just came down here to tell you that I hate you for what you did to Karen. Now get out of my house!"

As she slammed the door in my face, I could hear Nick tell her playfully, "June! That wasn't *nice*."

An Excerpt from Savoring Sitto

by Stephanie Boosahda

Best Teaching Practice suggests that
teachers write while their students write;
below is such a piece.

This is an excerpt from a larger memoir about the author's
grandmother,
which was revised in conjunction with Workshop participants'
work on setting and character development.

Introduction

Everyone who knows me knows her. I often picture her on the Grafton Street porch. That's not the only place I remember her, though, but I usually go there first. It was there, on Grafton Street, at her home, that I first met her. The house is still there, peace filled in her day: a very tall, impeccably shingled sky-blue three-story home with what people now call a farmers' porch gracing the front and wrapping all the way around the left side along the driveway, almost to the back porch, where I also remember Sitto, my grandmother, sitting and telling little anecdotal stories about the "old country." Many lives, including mine, have been shaped on this extended porch. Yes, everyone who knows me knows her, or at least they know of her.

People who are getting to know her ask, "What's her niche? Why is she so special?" But, it doesn't take long for them to realize that Sitto, as it was once said about Rose Kennedy, radiates uncommon common sense. Unlike Rose, though, she did not have monetary wealth, fame, or any of those other widely known elegant graces. Sitto's rose is endangered. She does not have one specialty, or just one strength; she is a jack of all trades and a master of them, too. Her graces are fine-tuned charms of kindness and thoughtfulness, behaviors and lessons taught through joy, often without notice. But, I noticed, and intelligent people noticed too.

She is not a hot-house, cultivated rose. She's a rose with her own unique qualities that bloomed in the way she told stories, nursed, sewed, cooked, summered on Cape Cod, entertained watermelon seed-spitters, dealt with the boogie man, cleaned, went on unusual shopping sprees, had own "gym," made clocks, entertained fish, ran crab races, and pioneered all kinds adventures, and much, much more. A top-notch combination Martha Stewart, Annie Camden, Florence Nightingale, June Cleaver, and a passionate Amelia Earhart who made her family click: a family that extended beyond borders, beyond generations, and beyond her lifetime.

* * *

I remember one lively spring day, when I was about three or four years old; I remember it like it was yesterday. On this day, when Sitto finished mixing up several batches of that special dough that we used to make meat pies, she asked me, "Do you want to go out on the porch and have a pomegranate?" At that moment I noticed all her arm muscles; what I saw caused me to be stuck in sheer amazement.

Sitto usually got up about five or six in the morning, before anyone else in the house, and baked at least four or five batches of some kind of bread. She was kneading one of these batches when she asked me about sharing a pomegranate. From my vantage point, I could see Sitto, her muscles, the side and bottom of the table, and nothing else.

I stared in amazement and thought about her muscles and the pomegranate; I knew having a pomegranate meant a long, slow, fun talk with her, as she peeled the many-seeded globus fruit. I love those talks and perhaps that pomegranate-red is why, to this day, I love the color red; however, noticing her muscles somehow kept me from answering her right away, which was quite unusual.

"What are you looking at? What's the matter?" she said with her comforting yet concerned smile.

"You have muscles, big muscles," I respectfully blurted back.

"Everyone does," she pleasantly answered.

"No, only boys do, and you're not a boy," I answered, dumbfoundedly.

"Why do you think only boys have muscles?" she replied in a tender and accepting way.

"Well, because Giddo Albert and all my uncles always ask me to show them my muscles, and when I do, mine are never as big as theirs. Giddo usually says, 'It's jelly. See? It wiggles.' And then they tell me to work harder, help with more chores and it will get bigger. But it never does."

"Oh, honey, theirs are only bigger because they're older and they've been trying to make muscles for a longer time than you have. It's not because they're boys. Girls have muscles, too. You can get a lot of muscles in the kitchen and working around the house. No one can see the muscles in your head, but you're always thinking and getting those muscles stronger, too." With a larger smile and a twinkle in her eyes, she continued, "Do you feel strong enough to carry this pomegranate out to the porch?"

She laughed encouragingly and I just wondered about what she said, as it was with most of what she'd tell me. Everything she told me was highly nutritious food for thought. I know other people would go out on the porch with us and eat those slowly peeled pomegranates, but I have little or no recollection of them being there. Sitto had a way of making each of us feel particularly special; there could be ten of us there, and each one of us would feel like the *special* one.

I can't remember what story she told me that day, but it was probably one about "the old country." I know I loved and hung onto every word she said. When I got older, she'd ask me to also share a story with her, about this country, school, or myself. We became very good companions, even though she was about fifty years older than I was.

- Always remember to exercise those muscles in your head.
- A good story is better when accompanied by a special friend and a slowly peeled pomegranate on a back porch.

* * *

I could count on Sitto for many things. In fact, I could always count on Sitto, even when I was in college. One of my favorite childhood things that I could always depend on was Sitto's late-afternoon climb up the back stairs of the triple-decker to our apartment, "Hello, eddybody," she greeted us with her slightly foreign accent. "It's time for Mickey Mouse."

When I was really young, I thought she just came up to watch Mickey Mouse. I think she had a TV set, but I don't remember for sure. In those days, we were too busy having fun to watch much TV. I don't even remember where our TV was located, but I do remember Sitto coming up the stairs. Sandie, the only sister I had when I lived on Grafton Street, would run with me to greet her at the top of the stairs. We'd run so fast, it's a wonder we didn't knock her down as we stopped and squeezed her legs.

That's how I told time and the days of the week before we moved and I went to school. I knew it was 5 p.m. and a weekday if Sitto came up the stairs and announced, "It's time for Mickey Mouse."

I later learned that she used to come up to be with us and to give my mom a break so she could more easily make supper. Maybe the television was near the kitchen, because I can recall her cooking a lot with my mom, too.

When we moved to our new house, I learned to tell time the usual way, and for a while, we'd telephone her every night and remind her that it was "time for Mickey Mouse." I wondered if she still watched Mickey Mouse, or if she just watched to be with us.

- Being dependable is one of the greatest ways to show someone you care; being unsolicitously thoughtful is another one of these great ways.
- There are many ways of telling time; some are more meaningful than others.

Awards Night
Guest Speaker,
Cheryl Park,
shared how her time at the
YWW affected her life

248

Awards Night

Awards Night
Guest Speaker,
Cheryl Park,
Congratulated the
Young Writers

Poetry
Students'
Work

Golden Nuggets

A Small Sampling of the Poetry Students' Work

Joan Tavares-Avant was the 2007 poetry instructor. She noted, "This tutorial was designed for young creative poetry writers, including those who had not started but were inspired to write." In the unit "Enrichment and Understanding," participants explored the essentials of what they had written or what they felt they wanted put into poetry. Students worked at capturing a greater interpretation of their own thoughts by reflecting and sharing ideas in a classroom setting. This course provided an opportunity to focus on elements of poetic imagery and the power of words. "Respecting Mother Earth," a Native American value, was an important theme for this class. Students jotted down thoughts on their responsibilities are for caring for Mother Nature in the form of poetry, but the primary focus of the week was to learn, share, and write happily.

Portfolio Selections
by Zach Burrage-Goodwin

Fire

Fire heats people up
It gives light but still.
Fire will stay fire.
Fire cannot be water.
Fire cannot wash our hands
Like sky cannot be land
Or Pluto cannot be Earth.

Triathlon

by Zach Burrage-Goodwin

The Earth provides for us.
It provides food, entertainment, and shelter.
On Earth, we eat to survive,
Survive in shelter
And have fun in
Or out of shelter.
Mother Earth cares for us.

Different

I want to be different
Every time I feel that I am ugly
Or that my life is bad.

I want to be different
When school didn't go so well
Or I failed a test or a project.

I want to be different
When I can't play the violin very well
Or if there is a quiz the next block.

I want to be different
In a lot of ways,
But every time
I want to be different,
I put the thought out of my head,
Deal with the task at hand.
I say, "This is stupid"
And get on with my life.

Israel

by Zach Burrage-Goodwin

Many people die
Of unjust causes
Endless battles
No peace
Margaret's brother, Joe
Died in the war
All she had
Was a little star
And his belongings
Not him
You put it out
Of your mind,
But it stays.

Young Writers' Workshop Reflections — As the Week Began

Walk in the door,
No familiar faces.
Sit down,
Think of what is to come.
Listen to the teacher,
Write a poem.
Hesitant at first,
Building confidence.
Worst work first,
Best work later.
Watch writing improve
As the days pass.
Listen to guest speakers,
Take notes.
Wonder,
How to improve?
Write poems by morning,
Watch TV by afternoon,
Read books by night.
I could get used to this schedule.
Wake up at 10
Go to bed at 1
Write good poems
Read good books,
Have a good week.

Target

by Zach Burrage-Goodwin

Mother Earth is the center.
The center of life,
Center of death,
The center of peace,
Center of war,
The center of crime,
Center of justice.
The Earth flows in a continuous motion,
The start and end of everything.

Progression

The Earth is us.
We come into the Earth,
Live our lives on Earth,
Undergo changes on Earth,
Get tired of Earth,
Die a human death.
Earth creates us,
Earth nurtures us,
Earth takes us for its own.

Yin-Yang

by Zach Burrage-Goodwin

A flash of pink catches my eye
In the dying green bush.
A pink flower sitting alone
Among dead leaves.
I pick up the flower,
And dead petals fall to the ground.
The flower hates me,
Yet loves me.
It pricks my finger
With its small thorns,
Yet graces me
With its soft petals
I feel the petals,
But however hard I press,
It feels as if my fingers are numb,
and can't touch.
I see the image,
But can barely feel it.
I distinctly see every thorn,
And the perfection of the petals.
This flower, a mere inch long,
Reflects humans.
Their perfections,
Their imperfections
Their kind sides,
Their evil sides.
This small flower,
So delicate,
Is life itself.

I Am Special

by Zach Burrage-Goodwin

People say that.
"You are special," they say.
And whatever mood I'm in
Determines if I think
That is true.
When I sing a solo in chorus,
When I play a solo in orchestra,
When I can do
What nobody else can,
I believe myself
To be special.
When I write a poem,
When I can run fast,
I am special.
But in a bad mood,
I am not so special.
I am a normal fourteen-year-old boy.
I do my homework,
I go to school,
I feel boring,
Normal.
I don't go on any
Wild adventures,
Any crazy police chases,
I am not a movie star,
Rich,
Or famous,
But then I think,
I am a special,
Normal kid.
I am special to normal people,
But normal to special people.
Caught hanging in the balance,
I feel satisfied,
That,
There is almost no chance
Of being really special,
But being normally special
Is okay, too.
And I will always be
Special.

Mother Earth as I Know Her

by Zach Burrage-Goodwin

I live on the land where my grandfather lived
And where his grandfather before him lived
Where they farmed the land
And struggled with oxen and dirt
And labored to pile stones into walls

This land gives food
Clean air
The water flows through pipes
Once copper, now plastic
Into the sink for me to drink

This land is beautiful
A place to come to after school
Where I run with squirrel and chipmunk
And create my imaginary home
With rock and rotted log

This land has crabapple, oak and pine
Planted by my family
And shoots of those
Grow wildly nearby

I am surrounded by people
Who descend from farmers
Or who moved to town recently
From other parts of the world

I am lucky to be here
Comforted by the spirit of my ancestors
Energized by the land
And by my friends

At times I feel unsettled too
The roads are filled with cars
The rumble of tractor-trailer trucks
Shake the foundation of the house
A film of smog can be seen from the sky

Newcomers unhappy with small
    houses
Tear down the trees and forests
To build mansions
While deer, raccoon, fox and coyote
    are displaced

I see packs of deer on my way to
    school
Standing in the road
Wondering where their forest has
    gone

And I worry why the temperature is so warm
In December
And why the rivers and streams are so low
In summer

I see injustice in school.
Asians separate from blacks separate
    from Jews
I feel worry.
I feel sad
I feel outrage
I write it down

Thank you

by Zach Burrage-Goodwin

She does my laundry,
And makes my bed,
And cleans my room,
And loves me.
She functions for me
At 6 a.m.,
When my brain
Is a vegetable.
When I miss the bus,
She drives me to school,
She makes my food,
And loves me.
She writes her dissertation,
And researches for her degree,
She does all these things
And still loves me.
Sometimes on weekends,
She makes bacon and eggs,
And lets me stay up 'till four
To read a book.
She makes me feel good
When my dad makes me feel bad,
She would do anything
To protect me.
When I do crazy things,
And make her worried,
She hugs me
And loves me.
My mom is an awesome mom.
She is always there for me.

Two Poems

by Khalia Parish

My Trees

A twig?
A simple, boring twig?
To some, certainly.
But I have seen its siblings, its cousins, its mother, its aunts.
For me, I see
Its bark, textured and varied,
And I think of the weathered life
This twig has seen.
I remember its cousin,
Whom I felt,
Whom I used,
And I know of the link between them, two twigs.
I look at its mother,
A tree,
Short, modest, soft-spoken,
And I remember its aunts,
Whom I knew,
Whom I loved —
Innocent, diligent, beautiful, comforting —
They didn't deserve their fate.
I wonder,
Of their long life's work,
If I might find
A twig —
One twig —
By which to remember them,
My trees —
My trees.

My Jordan, #1

by Khalia Parish

Dedicated to Jordan S. Ashe

She's always herself.
My anchor, she is what preserves myself,
Keeps me from drifting away
In bits and pieces
With the flow of others,
Of the world.
Instead, together
We sail through passing time
And all it brings.
Together we face all obstacles.
She strengthens me, and I her.
Every feeling, every deep emotion
That passes between us
It's mutual.
We share
So much,
Oftentimes without a word.
Not a poem or a song
Could ever express,
Given even eternity,
How much my Jordan means to me.
Like a body without a heart,
Like Rosie without Balto,
I'd be lost without my Jordan.
For that —
For everything —
I love her first.

Poetic Triptych

by Taylor Holland

Untitled

When I am angry
I crash onto the sandy shores.
When I am calm
I lap onto the rocky beaches.
I am filled with life,
Tiny organisms too small to see,
Giant whales larger than life,
Coral pink starfish,
Five points each,
Seaweed so green,
It glows with the color of earth,
Sea cucumbers,
Not very talkative,
But a pretty sight anyways.
Mighty Great Whites,
Bulls, and hammerheads
Gentle creatures, really
Except when they're hungry.
Dolphins,
Bottlenoses, the most popular of the pack.
I can be cold;
Forgive me.
I can be warm;
Cherish me.
I am the ocean.
Worship me with love
Saved for only me.

Forever Ago

by Taylor Holland

To many days
Shared between us
To count.
The same goes
For laughs.
We stuck together,
Friends forever,
Bumper boats
Water fights,
Sharing orange soda
On the bright yellow school bus.
Racing down water slides
And taking hundreds
Of pictures
Of funny faces
And bunny ears
And milk shooting
Out of your nose.
We named our water balloons
Jimmy, Georgette.
Stuck up for each other
When things got rough.
Ditching
Was out of the question.
We were Siamese twins,
Like brother
And sister
Best friends
Camp buddies
Together forever.
When things got too boring
For us, Imagination
Was our new best friend.

Untitled

by Taylor Holland

Slinking
Stepping silently

So skilled
In his line of work
Neither seen
Nor heard
This creature that resembles
Darkness itself
Stalks his prey.
Head down,
Ears perked
For signs of anyone
In pursuit of him
His black fur matted down
With the dampness of the fog
Now encasing him
His head swivels side to side
His gaze leaving the gazelle
For a moment
As he scans the forest
Around him
His black paws
Pad silently along the ground
Covered in decaying leaves
And moist soil
Wet from the recent rain
And now the extremely thick fog.
Branches hang down
Dripping crystal clear water
A drop lands on our predator's black leathery nose
And he snorts
His almost silent snort
Is enough warning to be gazelle
That she is being trailed.
The prey bolts
Calls out a warning
To the rest of her kind
Of the imminent danger.

The predator begins to lope after
The gazelle
Taking long
Steady strides
His fur dries off in the wind
As he easily catches up with her
And enjoys dinner
The mighty jaguar.

Two Poems Exploring Nature
by Alicia Pollard

A Rainy Day

The rain comes down
A thousand liquid diamonds
Bucketfuls of tears
Leaving watery footprints on windows.

Busy people are annoyed at the rain
Delaying them in their hurry to go nowhere
Perhaps they should see how slowing down suits them
Perhaps they should be glad for an excuse to stay home.

Thirsty plants soak up the rain
Delaying them in their hurry to nowhere
Perhaps they should see how slowing down suits them
Perhaps they should be glad for an excuse to stay home.

Children see the rain and smile
Prepared for an indoor day
Books and board games and laughter awaits them
They have no fear of the rain.

Laugh at the rain, inconvenient delay
That nourishes crops, and the friend of children
Look up as it stops, and if you are quick
You might glimpse the rainbow, stretched from sky to sky.

A Little Green Leaf and the Earth

by Alicia Pollard

A small piece of the Earth,
A specimen of nature,
I am drawn to this small green leaf
Veins like spider webs cover its surface
This bit of mystery intrigues me.

Hundreds of leaves, thousands of leaves,
Millions of small green leaves are on Earth
They grow and die, decay and nourish other plants
If it was never grown, if it never dies
Each circumstance disrupts the balance of the Earth.

All benefit from this cycle, all profit from what becomes of it
Animals eat the leaves
Humans grow food in the soil from their decay
We need this cycle, and all earth cycles
To live, and to grow and to die.

Poetic Perspectives
by Nicolette Gendron

The Onlooker

inspired by a simple green bulb waiting to blossom

You are overlooked
The odd one out
Differences are often ignored
But not forever
Green and speckled
You are patiently awaiting
Your rebirth into something
Beautiful
You try to cower in the corner
Watch the world pass by
But I captured you
Holding you hostage
For everyone to see
One day
You will peel away the layers
To reveal a blossom
That steals away an onlooker's breath
But unlike the others
You will keep your woes
Safely stored beneath your petals
A hidden past
Shield of armor
That has made you stronger
You are a gift
Unaware of your potential
As you try to hide away
From dreams
Caressed by sunlight ♥

My Mother's Daughter

by Nicolette Gendron

You love
Moody summer eves
That release
To a golden dusk
The importance of
Raising your family
Long days on
The beach
And festivities
With good friends
You love
Life
Joie de vivre
You have raised me
With strong feminine values
Pride
Intelligence
Beauty
Achievement
You told me
I can do
Anything
Live by the
Rhythm of my heart beat
In grade school
I neglected to
Name you my hero
Choosing instead
My favorite writer
I have defied you
Yet
Will always love you
As I find my
Own way
In a crowded world
But as I glide
Down the stairway

Dressed as a lady
You capture the moment
Behind the camera's lens
A sparkle
Of understanding
In your
Beautiful tiger eyes
I am
My mother's daughter ♥

Why I am Special

by Nicolette Gendron

I am
The little girl in a princess dress and purple rain boots
Reassured and confidant
Laughing
Always smiling
She wears her heart on her sleeve
I am
The little girl spinning in circles
Trying to catch a raindrop on her tongue
As free as a bird in the sky
She lives only by her own rules
That little girl grows
And grows
Nurtured by independence
         equality
         kindness
But rough words
And pressure
She tests limits
Sometimes rising
Often falling
But always willing
To brush herself off
And get back UP
Band-aids are for babies
This girl
She loves too much
Thinking she's invincible
She vows to never get hurt
But people play games
With her heart
And sometimes
She plays back
Yet from the ashes
         the sunlight
         broken glass
         poems

learning
dreaming
The little girl knows who she is
She understands her capabilities
　　　　her inner beauty
And that there is only one
Of the little girls with a princess dress and purple rain boots
Twirling in the rain
Searching for bigger things ♥

Instructor's Poetry

by Joan Tavares-Avant,
YWW poetry instructor

Again, in accordance with
Best Practice protocol of
teachers writing while their students write,
some of Joan's poetry
from the Workshop
follows.

Your Untimely Death Will Not Fade

I remember when you learned to walk
Skipping across the wood floor
I remember your drawings.

Gray clouds, lines of a rainbow
You expressed heaven
The moon, the sun, the storms
Your untimely death will not fade.

When you smiled, you were happy
Your brown eyes shined,
Sending a message of tranquility to your mom
Dad, brothers, sisters,
Your children and even me
Your untimely death will not fade.

Now I know why.
You wrote and sang your rap songs
Symbolizing deep thought.
Now I know why
Your untimely death will not fade.

You sang in night clubs
Sharing your triumphs.
The love for family
The love for your friends
Your untimely death will not fade.

Titled, My City, Rotten Apple, Teary
One Night Stand, Rock with Me,
I'm Not Sober.
Then Nana did not understand
Your untimely death will not fade.

Before Thanksgiving, you sent a letter
About Crossing Over
Then, Nana did not understand
Your untimely death will not fade.

She Is a Gift

by Joan Tavares-Avant,
YWW poetry instructor

Corn is part of our Wampanoag heritage
Corn is part of our spiritual Tradition
Corn is the basic gift of our diet.
The Spirit of Corn is honored.

She is more than a kernel
She is indigenous to our land
She is personified as grandmother
In our cooking.

Yesterday she was the foundation of our
Soups and boiled bread,
She was roasted in her husks in the coals of fire,
Today she continues to nourish us
Blending into our stews, fritters.

Passed down from generation to generation
We maintain connectedness and celebration
Our tradition, our heritage.

Since creation,
Corn is like the rising sun
Like the moon at night.
She is Spirit, substance, life.

Student Bios

These are the students whose work is included in this anthology.
In order to be selected for the Young Writers' Workshop,
each applicant had to submit writing samples,
write an essay telling why (s)he wanted to attend the Workshop, and
then wait for the good news: that had been accepted into the
Forty-fifth Annual Summer Writers' Conference.

Alex Bahrawy, (Sandwich High School – afternoon prose student) Alex often goes by the pen name "Skid." He loves reading, making movies, and playing video games. Other than writing, his passion is editing movies and short clips. His inspiration comes from famous fantasy movies and books. Lately, he's been trying to convince himself that he's capable of writing more than fantasy. Of the writing conference he states, "It's a great experience; it's great I was a part of it." Classmates described him as "smart, nice, and having a good laugh, not to mention brave (he was the 'only guy' in the afternoon session) and dedicated." Alex was sixteen at this year's YWW.

Courtney Bergh (resident of the lower Cape, MA – morning prose student) One of our younger students this year, Courtney was twelve this summer. Her classmates stated, "She's full of surprises, often quiet, but when she has something to say, it's something you don't want to miss ... She's a very creative writer." Courtney explained further, "I have always wanted to become an author, and I hope to publish many novels."

Niki Bousquet (Sandwich High School; resident of Sandwich, MA – afternoon prose student) A high school sophomore whose writing focuses mainly on fictional prose, Niki also enjoys writing poetry, and memoirs are her favorite type of writing to read. She has written book reviews for the Sandwich Public Library, one of which was published in the *Sandwich Enterprise*. The aspect of writing Niki fancies most is making individual word choices, because she loves to twist them around to create different images. She also thinks a piece of writing doesn't necessarily have to make sense to be enjoyed. She's not very fond of writing in third person, because "it seems too impersonal." "The Prose Workshop helped me to think of writing as something enjoyable and to appreciate the process instead of focusing only on the finished product." Fellow students describe Niki as "creating great stories, as colorful as she is, unique, full of quiet surprises, 'volunteerive, she's not afraid of volunteering to share her work,' " and " she's exceptionally creative, quietly funny, and a creator of 'smart memories,' who 'captures character and setting really well and makes us feel like we're really there.' "

Christina Brown (Wixon Middle School; resident of Dennis, MA – afternoon prose student) Christina's interests in writing just recently sparked her imagination. "The reason I write is because I enjoy it, and you can make it up depending on what you enjoy and what you want to write. I cannot wait to go back to school this upcoming year and write." She came to the workshop to experience working with published authors and "to write with other kids who enjoy writing as much as I do." She likes to write fun, adventurous stories that will draw in readers and further clarifies, "My goals are to publish a piece of writing in a book or magazine in the near future. The YWW experience was great and I hope to come back again next year." She's known by her fellow writers as someone who jokes a lot, is a positive influence, has a great sense of humor – it sometimes shows up in her writing– friendly, helpful, has a pretty smile, memorable flip flops, and even more memorable writing.

Lydia Burrage-Goodwin (Weston High School; Weston, MA – afternoon prose student) Lydia states, "Life is boring in Weston, and I love to come down to the Cape to get away from homework and swearing businessmen on their frantic morning commute. I love to write historical fiction and about things in life like hurricanes and life in the 1800s. In my other spare time, besides writing, I love to be on the Cape, riding my bike, going to different pizza places, going to the Wellfleet Drive-In, and playing the violin. I play in the school orchestra, and I sing in the Weston chorus. I have one crazy dog named Huxley, a brother named Zach, and a sister named Miranda, and all are just about as crazy as ... well, they just might appear in one of my stories." Classmates remarked that Lydia is a great story writer, has a good use of adjectives, and one of her fellow classmates said, "because she's such an inspiration, I used her name in piece I wrote this week."

Miranda Burrage-Goodwin (Weston High School; Weston, MA – afternoon prose student) Miranda was one of the students selected by her peers to read at the Thursday evening awards ceremony. Being a sixth grader, she was also one of our youngest writers at YWW. While she shared, "I'm just beginning to have an interest in creative writing," fellow members of the workshop consistently chose her work to be read and reread. Miranda gathered a large fan club of appreciative older fellow writers. One student wrote, "Miranda's writing is very alive and has a very clear voice."

Zack Burrage-Goodwin (Weston Middle School, Weston, MA – poetry student) Zack was fourteen years old and had just graduated from the eighth grade when he attended this conference. Besides writing poetry, Zach likes technology of all kinds, enjoys his computer and his iPod, plays the cello, and sings bass in the chorus. He notes, "I feel very lucky to be in the Cape Cod writers' workshop."

Chris Chacon (Camden Hills Regional High School, Camden; resident of Lincolnville, ME – morning prose student) Born in Orlando, FL, Chris soon after moved to Cancun, Ecuador, and he became a Mainer while still a preschooler. He loves to fish, and does so every chance he gets. He began writing short stories when he was nine. Now fourteen, Chris says he has been writing for as long as he can remember. Chris's short-term goals include improving his editing skills, adding depth to his characters, and developing his scenery. His classmates say he's "awesome at creating settings" and "describes stuff well."

Megan Cronin (Sandwich High School; Sandwich, MA – afternoon prose student) Meg first got into writing at an early age and enjoyed writing fiction. Once she started high school, she got into writing poetry, too. She says, "Poetry caught my eye." In her sophomore year, she was in the Teen Poetry Slam, which gave her the confidence to continue developing her poetry. Now, a sixteen-year-old, Meg is working on a fantasy/adventure story, though, she says, "more poetry is never far behind." She stated that being in the Young Writers' Workshop was a privilege. "It helped me expand my creativity." Described as "descriptive and a powerful writer" by her fellow writers, Megan was also noted for her "great stories."

Angelica DellaMorte (home schooled: resident of Sandwich, MA – afternoon prose student) A fifteen-year-old junior, Angelica is a general fiction and fantasy writer; she is currently working on two books and hopes to get them both published. She states, "My love for writing branched off my love of reading." Angelica really enjoyed the conference this summer and hopes to be accepted again next year. She is enjoying staying in touch with fellow YWW students and is looking forward to meeting up again in a writers' group. "She has the most interesting names for her characters and a beguiling sense of humor," noted one of her fellow writers, and "her great work goes well with her great smile."

Alex Denton (Buckingham, Browne, and Nichols, Cambridge; resident of Newton, MA – morning prose student) "I write for fun, mostly," Alex explains. This twelve-year-old doesn't have any aspirations of becoming a published author; he "just enjoys writing for fun." He explains, "I always turn to writing to express myself and tell what's on my mind." He came to the YWW so he could better develop his writing skills. In his free time, he likes to ride horses and play sports. "He's wicked creative," noted one of his YWW colleagues.

Emilie Foy (Lycée Français de New York; resident of the Upper West Side, Manhattan, NY – morning prose student) "Unfortunately, my writing doesn't fit any particular category. I write for every reason, whether it's for school, for fun, because I have nothing better to do, or for this writing class, which is a combination of all those things. My main interests in writing are historic settings and horror movie settings (well, not quite, maybe Halloween-ish settings is a better description). I find writing in English much easier than writing in French for some reason ... probably because French is so much more elaborately phrased. Born in the Big Apple, Emilie used to summer in Cotuit and now goes to Osterville "just about every vacation. My dad is a writer and he introduced me to this workshop, which has been great, by the way. I can't name all my literary goals."

Maret Gable (Waldorf School, Bourne; resident of Mashpee, MA – morning prose student) Maret writes because she enjoys it and because it "comes in handy with schoolwork and things." Maret came to the YWW after hearing about it from her two older brothers and applied "because it sounded interesting." Classmates use the word "interesting" when they describe Maret. They also agree she's "an awesome writer, kind of quiet and shy 'til she reads her writing, which is dependably smart and clever." She writes about what she's interested in: fantasy, adventures, and mythical creatures.

Seth Gable (Waldorf School, Bourne; hails from Mashpee, MA – morning prose student) A fifteen-year-old while attending the conference, Seth explains why he writes: "I just happen to enjoy it. The fact that I enjoy writing is why I wanted to come to the Young Writers' Workshop. I usually write whatever I happen to feel like writing, and I don't have any specific literary goals." Among his fellow writers he's known as someone with "a lot of interesting ideas, an honest writer with a contagious laugh, and a good writer who is funny and obviously smart."

Nicolette Gendron (Milton Academy, Milton; resident of Wellesley, MA – poetry student) Nicolette loves writing poetry and has been doing so for as long as she can remember. "I gather inspiration from the ocean, nature, experiences I have had, what I value, and people I meet. Things that define me are family, friends, alternative music, starry nights, sunsets, chocolate, shopping, late nights, sports, traveling, long phone calls, smiles, and LOVE." ♥

Rebecca Harris (Shady Hill School, Cambridge; resident of Newton, MA – morning prose student) "Ever since toddler-hood," Rebecca writes, "I have loved stories, narratives, and the way a plot unfolds with such magical serendipity." Her goals include developing the ability to "create a plot that twists and turns and at the same time goes somewhere, characters who seem life - like and complete, and descriptions that are as clear on the pages as they are in my head."

Caroline Hibbert (Sturgis Charter School, Hyannis; resident of Sandwich, MA – morning prose student) Caroline reflected that three unexpected things she learned were the importance of keeping journals for observation, because they can be a lot more valuable later than you think; historical events can branch off into fictional stories, and an adult view is jaded, so journals from youth will help capture the essence of a child's view later on. Explaining why she writes, Caroline noted, "Because I enjoy it and I love to come up with a different world for myself through my writing. I write about a lot of things. I like to come up with fictitious stories, but I also enjoy history, so I also would like to write nonfiction pieces on historical events. My literary goals are to finish my works-in-progress and eventually get some published. Even if I don't become a full-time writer, I will most likely go into a profession where I can use the tools and skills that are linked to writing." And, regarding coming to this conference, "I thought it would be a great opportunity to expand my writing techniques and learn helpful strategies. Being here has really motivated and inspired me."

Taylor Holland ([School], Guilford, CT – poetry student) Taylor has been writing since she was eight years old. When Taylor isn't busy writing, she enjoys mountain biking and swimming. Taylor was twelve years old when she attended the YWW. She aspires to become an author of young adult books.

Tom Lemberg (Cranbrook High School; resident of Bloomfield Hills, MI – morning prose student) "It wouldn't be fair to call myself a novelist, because I have yet to write a novel I am content with. But I do call myself a writer." During Tom's free time in middle school and high school, he has written numerous short stories and three unedited "novels," and he hopes to someday be published. But for now, he's "just enjoying writing." His classmates remember him for "his awesome Six Word Stories, great accent, nice manners, 'broccoli-ating,' reserved, serious writing ethic, and politeness."

Rachel Liu (Dover-Sherborn High School; resident of Sherborn, MA – morning prose student) Writing was one of the things that kept Rachel from skipping kindergarten when she first moved to Massachusetts. She's loved writing in journals since she was in first grade but started writing in them more seriously when she was awarded the Emily Dickinson Award by her fourth-grade teacher. In seventh grade, she won her first international award in a science fiction/fantasy student contest. Also, she's won other contests, including the Will McDonough *Boston Globe* Sports writing contest, and she's been a finalist and semi-finalist for the science fiction/fantasy student contest in other years. Rachel has written for the *Hometown Weekly* newspaper and is the poetry and layout editor of her school's literary magazine, *RUNES*. She's been to various workshops, including sci-fi/fantasy conferences, a program at Emerson College, and the CCWC YWW. This is her third year at the Young Writers' Workshop, and she says thank-you to Rosemary Graham, Lara Zeigst, Stephanie Boosahda, and all the students, as well as everyone else who helped her develop as a writer. "It certainly was a lot of fun, and I learned a lot," she says. Classmates feel the same about Rachel, saying they "learned tons from her; she's a fantastic writer, brave, always volunteering to share and read. She's friendly and insightful, an awesome writer with a nice smile, and her piece, 'The Tea Room,' is amazing."

Rachel Maginis (Sandwich High School, East Sandwich, MA, resident – morning prose student) "Writing allows me to express my creativity," Rachel explains. A ninth-grader who especially enjoys writing short fiction, Rachel particularly likes creating new characters and events in imaginative settings. A few of her favorite authors are Ann Brashares, Jodi Picoult, and J. K. Rowling. Her fellow writers refer to her as "thoughtful, always ready to say something helpful and nice, talented, and someone who puts a lot of creative thought into her writing."

Katrina Malakhoff (Barnstable High school; resident of Barnstable, MA – afternoon prose student) Katrina notes that this year's conference taught her to think of all six senses when she writes, and to remember that setting includes time, place, and mood. Katrina enthusiastically writes, "This was my fifth year at the Young Writers' Workshop and it just keeps getting better. I love sharing my ideas and hearing the stories of other young writers. Primarily, I write fictional stories just for fun, but I'm sure writing will help me in the future as I pursue a career path in marine biology. Writing has always interested me, because there is so much freedom to express your creative potential and throw out crazy ideas just for fun. This week has been a highlight of my summer, and I really enjoyed getting to know everyone." Classmates appreciated her "perceptive feedback" and her "confidence and willing[ness] to share her work. She's a good listener with good ideas."

Sarah Martin (Barnstable High school, Hyannis; resident of South Dennis, MA – afternoon prose student) Because of "an amazing fourth-grade teacher," Sarah started writing fiction when she was nine. She also credits much of her love of writing to her teacher/ mentor at the Lighthouse Charter School, Ms. Pace. Sarah loves to read and write. "Reading and writing is like second nature; they flow naturally." Sarah has been reading since she was five. This is her first time being published and her third summer as a student at the Young Writers' Workshop. She plans to "come back every year as long as I can." Fellow YWW students describe her as "insightful, a great peer editor, nice and constructive, introspective in a creatively insightful way, and great with adjectives."

Ashleigh McEvoy (resident of central MA – afternoon prose student) A fifteen-year-old, first published in 2006 for her poetry, Ashleigh plays soccer and basketball and rows at her school. She also likes photography, "and of course, writing. I write fiction, mostly, especially what I call 'tragedies' about things like death, substance abuse, illness, suicide, and so forth. I'm not really sure why, and I know most people would find that disturbing, but I find it meaningful and realistic. This conference has helped me branch out, though, which I am happy about, and that is just one of the many things that made this week of writing so great." She also notes, "At the YWW, I learned that our lives are a 'library of knowledge,' that great ideas for settings and stories are all around us, as evidenced by the place game we played as a pre-writing activity and also by the exercise where we described everyday pictures. I learned so many random things at the conference that will help my writing. The people were also friendlier than I imagined." Fellow YWW writers note that Ashleigh is "humble, helpful, amazing with words, and clearly writes interesting stories." Ashleigh reflects on writing with this statement: "You begin with a piece of blank paper, and yet, by the end, you have created a whole other world full of new and complicated people with depth and lives of their own."

Kaitlin Meiss (Sandwich High School; Sandwich, MA – afternoon prose student) Fourteen-year-old Kaitlin enjoys writing "like some of my peers enjoy basketball or soccer." She has always enjoyed reading and writing, which she finds closely intertwined. As a freshman, this was Kaitlin's first Young Writers' Workshop. "Because I was so impressed by the guest authors and our teacher," she says, "I plan on writing even more and applying again next year. I hope to be back next summer and have a few more writing pieces completed." She added that some things she learned that she wasn't expecting to learn include: to remember, when writing description, that we have six senses; that story ideas are everywhere; and that writing can show the experience through a different lens or camera, depending on the writer's point of view. She also notes, "I thought this workshop was going to be stressful and full of pressure, but I was going to learn something, so it would be worth it. But now that I'm here, I realize writing, especially at this conference, is a lot of fun, it's a supportive environment full of great people with similar interests. This has been a great experience. The setting ice-breaker was great; it really caused me to stretch, and I learned to think beyond colors and the obvious." Described as a "hard worker, polite, quiet, but dynamic with words," Kaitlin is "an eclectic writer."

Tosh Mihesuah (Baldwin Junior High School; resident of Baldwin City, KS – morning prose student) Called "patient, contemplative, quiet, hard-working, and a thoughtful writer with interesting ideas" and "a good sense of humor" by his writing workshop peers, Tosh traveled the farthest to attend the YYW. In his introductory letter, he wrote, "I want to learn to like to write well. I have so many stories to tell; I don't want to forget them." Thirteen while at conference, Tosh further explained that he "writes because it's fun and it's a retreat from the real world. I came because I wanted to learn to edit my stories better, and I learned even more. It was a lot of fun, too."

Amelia Mumford (Cape Cod Academy, Osterville; resident of Marstons Mills, MA – afternoon prose student) Amelia explains why she came to the YWW: "I wanted to learn to fine-tune my skills and really make a powerful impact on my readers." Amelia is known by some of her classmates as "a wicked awesome writer, nice, funny, and creative, ... an honest and caring editor, poetic, and having a big way with words." Others remarked that she is "talkative – in a good way, smart, insightful, creative, articulate with words, and obviously really passionate about her writing."

Khalia Parish (poetry student) was born in Manhattan and raised in St. Joseph, Missouri, and Worcester, Massachusetts. She was fifteen years old during the conference and looking forward to her junior year of high school, when she would most likely continue to participate in school plays and gymnastics. Outside of school, she enjoys reading, writing, and kissing bubbles.

Alicia Pollard (poetry student) has three sisters: Carrie, Caitie, and Julia, her twin. Since she was little, Alicia can remember thinking deeply and writing down stories and poems. In addition to writing, she enjoys reading and swimming.

Wisima Samantha "Sam" Nipatnantaporn (Cyrus Pierce Middle School; Nantucket, MA – afternoon prose student) Nicknamed Sam, her writing peers think of her as "insightful, original, a huge Red Sox fan, quiet but funny, and one student noted, 'it's definitely worth waiting to hear what she has to say'." This was Sam's first year at the CCWC's YWW. "I really enjoyed it. I am hoping to be accepted back again next year." In the fourth and fifth grade, Sam wrote for her school newspaper. In sixth grade, she was chosen to be a contributing writer for the Nantucket High School newspaper, *Veritas*. In seventh grade, Sam started a newspaper for her Middle School, *CPS Voice*, and is the editor. Sam was born in the United States, but she shares that she lived in Thailand. She explains why she writes: "It is fun and a good way to express myself. I would actually really like working as a journalist." She adds, "The CCWC's YWW has been a great experience for me this summer. I really learned a lot, and I had a ton of fun, too."

Liam O'Connor (Red Hook High, resident of Red Hook, NY – morning prose student) As a sixteen-year-old, Liam has been writing fantasy for a few years, and his goal is to publish a novel before graduating from college. He has been published once before, in the *Poughkeepsie Journal*, for winning first place in a scary story contest. Classmates say he'll be "remembered for his scary stories, his great, quiet sense of humor, and his smile. Liam's friendly, great at imagery, comical, able to create vivid settings, and has a flare for crumpling paper!"

Andrew Herschel Roiter (Old Rochester Regional High School; Mattapoisett, MA – morning prose student) Entering his senior year of high school, Andrew writes because it is the creative medium in which he excels. "It is an outlet for my creativity," he says. He came to the YWW to disrupt the long writer's block he had been facing. "I like to write about sci-fi, but I am not committed to any one genre [as readers will see by his screen play, prose, and poetry entries]. I do write almost entirely fiction, though." His current literary goal is to finish his book, *The Twalker Chronicles* (working title) and try to get it published. "This conference totally did away with my writer's block." Andrew was complimented by his classmates for his seriousness and focus, especially when listening to and giving feedback to others.

Jessica Schiffman (Ashland Middle School; Ashland, MA – afternoon prose student) Jess shares, "I write because it helps me express myself. When I'm angry, I write. I write about someone having a rough life. If I'm happy, I might write a poem about a bird, springtime, or anything that comes to mind. Writing also helps me let others know how I feel. When my brother surprised me and cleaned my room, I wrote him a story about a girl who shows her brother twenty ways to say thank-you. I love to write. I write because that's who I am, a writer. The Writers' Workshop helped me a lot. It taught me a lot that I didn't know about writing, and I loved hearing my fellow writers share their work and the guest authors speak to us. It was really interesting and exciting to hear published authors speak firsthand." Her classmates described her as really creative and an appreciative critic. One noted, "She told me she liked my story and why, which I really appreciated."

Hannah Van Sciver (Cape Cod Academy, Osterville; resident of Marstons Mills, MA – morning prose student). Her classmates call her "a natural leader, kind, funny, smart, hard working, confident, funny, outgoing, imaginative, introspective, a good speaker, and a clearly expressive writer." They've also granted her an "honorable mention in the paper crumpling category."

Rebecca Van Sciver (Cape Cod Academy, Osterville; resident of Marstons Mills, MA – morning prose student) Why Rebecca writes: "I love to imagine things that make me happy." It makes sense that her fellow writers note "she is funny, nice, a fantastic reader with an impressively powerful reading voice, clever and effective at purposeful ambiguous writing, insightfully creative, smart, and quiet, too!"

Sarah Van Sciver (Cape Cod Academy, Osterville; resident of Marstons Mills, MA – morning prose student) Sarah explains that she likes writing because "it's a fun outlet for expression." She was described by her classmates as "smart, insightfully imaginative, excellent at giving feedback, funny, a good speaker, introspective in a creatively insightful way. She has a fun writing style, and is great at giving helpful comments."

Faculty Bios

Stephanie E. Boosahda, M.Ed., LPN, and the 2007 Young Writers' Workshop prose teacher, is a teacher, pediatric nurse, and photojournalist whose work has been published in numerous newspapers, magazines, and journals. She was graduated from Lesley University with a Masters' Degree in Curriculum and Instruction and received her Bachelors' Degree in English and education from Springfield College. Most recently one of her articles appeared in  *Midlines*, the New England League of Middle Schools quarterly educational publication. The piece, "Kids Love a Mystery Program Fosters Love of Reading," was a four-page feature story. Stephanie was first published in the *Worcester Telegram and Gazette* when she was fifteen, and she wrote her way through college working for two Worcester, Massachusetts, newspapers. Since then, she has written for numerous newspapers and magazines. Currently she has several other books in the works, one of which is currently seeking publication; Stephanie is also a member of the National League of American Pen Women.

She was chosen by the faculty and student council of her school as Teacher of the Year "for Outstanding Instruction, Dedication, and service to the Students and to the entire Keith Middle School family." Stephanie was also selected as a 2008 South Coast Teacher of the Year finalist by the *Standard Times* in New Bedford, Massachusetts, where she taught English at Keith Middle School. Additionally, Stephanie was presented with the 2008 Master in the Middle award for teaching excellence by the New England League of Middle Schools. She is not only a traditional classroom teacher; she was also a teacher-leader for several educational travel abroad programs. In this latter capacity, she has co-led numerous student delegations abroad.

Stephanie is the mother of three grown children and the grandmother of two preschool boys. In addition to working and traveling with upper elementary, middle school, and high school students, she enjoys kayaking, biking, skiing, reading, writing, traveling, and photography, especially when she's doing these activities with her family.

Students have commented on Stephanie's teaching:

- "I just wanted to thank-you for running such an awesome class. That was probably my favorite of all three summers! I'm working on getting my anthology stuff to you, but I just keep writing and rewriting and not minding it."
- "I'm so psyched for [the anthology] to come out, however long it may take! You got everyone to do such great work."
- "Thanks for everything you did for us in the YWW. You taught us tons in just one week!"

A parent also weighed in: "I can't believe you got our son reading and writing non-stop in just three days. Thank-you."

Stephanie, in turn, thanks her students for their enthusiasm and further explained that the Young Writers' Workshop provided her with the very special opportunity to combine her love of working with young adult students and her love of writing. "The opportunity to work with such enthusiastic, dedicated, hardworking, talented, and well-mannered teenagers is something I will treasure for many years." She adds, "These budding young writers showed self-motivation, a growing potential for writing, and a love of writing that inspired this anthology. Their eclectic mix of writing, sharing, editing, responding, and enjoying each others' work was a joy for all involved, and we hope that this anthology will provide its readers with a glimpse of that exciting enthusiasm."

Ms. Boosahda is a professional tutor at Cape Cod Community College and a pediatric nurse employed by Pediatric Services of America. She runs workshops, Professional Development seminars, and is available as a private tutor and consultant.

Joan Tavares-Avant (Owamaskqua), instructor of the 2007 Young Writers' Poetry Workshop, is a champion for the rights of the Wampanoag people, a Mashpee Wampanoag elder, as well as the mother of four children, six grandchildren, and three great - grandchildren.

For twenty-six years, Joan served as director of Indian education in the Mashpee Public Schools. Under this umbrella she developed Native American curricula for grades K-12. Joan has taught and lectured in public schools, in social agencies, and in higher education at Cape Cod Community College, Tufts University, Wheelock College, and at the University of Massachusetts, Amherst.

Joan's literary contributions include authoring *Issues in Mashpee Wampanoag History and Culture: A Study Guide for Teachers,* for use in the school curriculum, and *Wampanoag Cooking.* She has served as the Mashpee Wampanoag Tribal Historian and was elected for three terms as president of the Mashpee Wampanoag Tribal Council. She is a member of the National League of American Pen Women.

Joan holds a bachelor's degree from the University of Massachusetts, Boston, a master's degree in Education from Cambridge College, and is presently a doctorial candidate in the School of Education at the University Massachusetts, Amherst.

Our Guest Authors

The students thoroughly enjoyed the visits from published authors on the adult Conference's faculty, and learned a great deal from them. Here's a collection of the students' reflections of their visits. In summary, a great big **thank-you** to all of you.

Tuesday

Devon Mihesuah, author of *The Roads of My Relations* and numerous other books

Students commented, "It was a great that you came to speak to our class. I enjoyed what you had to say Sunday at the Tabernacle, so I was extremely excited to hear that you were coming to speak to our class ... Funny how you shared the importance of journal writing, because I was cleaning my room just last week and found some old journals — they really were surprisingly very interesting to read, and they did give me writing ideas, just as you predicted ... The journals were from when I was seven! ... I'm going to start journaling again ... I loved how you explained creating realistic fiction from nonfiction; it was freeing knowing I don't have to remember everything. I can "develop" a non-fiction story ... It is so great that you cleared up our misconceptions about indigenous American people and shared your story about your great ... great grandfather and the light horsemen. I can't wait to read your book *Roads of My Relations*. I found your writing tool and techniques very helpful ... You gave me some great ideas about journal writing that make it exciting and less tedious, thank-you. I can't wait to start journal writing, again ... Thank-you for sharing the importance of recording our observations, particularly because even we wouldn't see those same observations the same way in the future ... Journaling and perspectives never went so well together before ... I really enjoyed how you demonstrated to us the importance of branching off and creating both fiction and nonfiction stories from historical events and family histories ... The skills and strategies that you shared with us and how to develop them were really helpful. I'm looking forward to using them to expand my writing style and create new stories ... I am grateful for the writing tips you gave us ... I think you were a great speaker ... If your books are as great as your talk, I'll take a dozen of each ... Appreciate your devotion to writing and dedicating your time to us Young Writers ... Especially enjoyed your tales about indigenous people ... recounts of the light horsemen, Wilson ... I can't wait to read your books ... I think I'm going to enjoy every one of them, even the nonfiction ... You gave us a new, more respectful perspective on indigenous life in the 1800s and of how the media not only informs, but also misinforms — WOW! ... Your writing tips were great ... now I realize the importance of keeping a journal ... Thank-you for illustrating that to us, and not just telling us ... I now understanding how my ideas can be even more useful to me and others in the future ... It's cool to see how much you love what you do ... Thank-you, TONS!"

Jean Stone, a.k.a. Abby Drake, author of over fourteen books including *Dare to Dream* (co-authored with Tim Daggett), and *Good Little Wives, Four Steps to the Altar,* and *Three Times a Charm,* just to mention a few

"Thank-you for sharing all your writing and publishing trials and triumphs," one student wrote. Others commented, "Your stories of what you've been through were very interesting and inspiring ... I love how you clearly love your work and everything involved with it ... It was really brave how you decided to become a full-time writer, left your job, changed your whole lifestyle, and then did it, become a successful full-time writer, I mean ... Thank-you for sharing how you focus on your writing and let publishers, editors, and so forth deal with "their part," and you don't get caught up in that — that was very eye-opening to me in a lot of ways ... I can't believe your lipstick story and I love the idea that it evolved into not just a story idea, but also maybe a book series ... and when is your TV movie going to be on Lifetime? ... Sharing how you get your ideas was inspiring for me, thanks for doing that ...Thank-you for explaining the roles of agents, publishers, and editors — I get it now ... I really enjoyed our time with you ... Publishing is so important to being a writer — I understand that now — but no one's ever discussed it with me before. Thank-you ... It was wonderful for someone to demystify where you get ideas from, the commercial writing process, and all the variations ... I never heard of commercial writing before ... Your stories and your perspectives were so refreshing and exciting ... You made me want to even more than I already do ... WOW! Cool to know there's such a thing as women's literature (you can bet we don't get to that genre in school) ... Thank-you for sharing all the name-calling and name-creating (wink, wink) stories; interesting doesn't begin to describe that ... Even before you told us, it was obvious you were a motivational speaker; you definitely motivated us ... Have you ever considered writing young adult literature? Please do. Unbelievable how much you squeezed into a half hour; I thought only Stephanie could fit so much in and have us enjoy it so much *and* get so much out of it. Thank-you ... So women's literature and romance are different — how cool is that? You got so much into your time and managed to teach us all something new — how did you do that? In fact, we each probably learned more than a thing or two ... If your writing is like your speaking, I don't care if it's women's literature, I'm in ... You really gave us all a new, uniquely interesting perspective on what it is like to be a writer, and we thank-you for that ... It is great to know writers don't just have to pick one professional genre ... Your explanation of women's fiction was very helpful, clear, and totally new to me. Thank-you ... I never heard of commercial writing before, but when you explained it, it made a lot of sense ... good to know some people can actually earn a living writing if that is your focus. You may be the reason I stay focused. Many thank-yous to you ... and thank-you for your entertaining but real anecdotes. They'd made a good book. Have you done non-fiction after your first book? ... I actually found *Dare to Dream* at a used book store on Cape, on our way home that day, and it's excellent ... It was really interesting to learn how covers and titles come about ... It was so important to learn how flexible a writer has to be and to see how you still love writing ... Yikes, I never realized how much research goes into writing believable FICTION ... I love your Website ...Thank-you so much."

Wednesday

Judith Moffat, author-illustrator of numerous articles and more than two dozen young children's books, among them *Too Many*

Rabbits: And Other Finger Plays about Animals; Nature, Weather, and the Universe; and *I Am a Star (Hello Reader, Science)*

In appreciation, students noted, "Thank-you for speaking to our writing workshop about your writing and illustrations and particularly how much you love your work; I especially liked the slideshow that so clearly showed us about cut-paper illustrating. I thought that was very unique and your drawings were beautiful. I learned a lot about illustrating that I knew nothing about ... Thank-you for speaking to us about your exciting career — you got us pretty excited, too ... It was great to see and hear how much you enjoy your work ... You got me excited when I learned I don't have to choose between writing and drawing or photography ... Your drawings are beautiful! I really enjoyed your informative slideshow ... It was exciting to see how you incorporated your dog and cat into each book like a secret signature; what a fun idea ... We all really appreciate your carefully prepared slideshow presentation and all the stories about what you learned on the way to becoming famous ... The way you and your husband collaborate on your artistic work and writing skills with his computer expertise was amazing ... You taught us about way too many things to mention, but thank-you ... Your books should cost more; they're great ... I love your Website — thanks for telling us about it ... Thank-you, also, for giving us your insights into the publishing world ... Your enthusiasm was contagious and made me not only want to write more but also want to try illustrating (and coming up with some characters to hide in there) ... Even though the slideshow showed us, I can't imagine how you do those cut paper illustrations, never mind how your husband does that stuff on the computer — beyond amazing, literally ... It was so cool to see you enjoying Bonnie Neuberger's presentation with us, too. Thank you so much."

Mel Donaldson, director of the 1998 film *A Room without Doors,* and the author of several screenplays

Several students wrote, "It was very interesting to hear about all the things you wrote and about how you needed to shorten some of your scripts..." While others wrote, "Thank you for coming to our class. ... It was fun to learn how pop culture, writing screen plays, and how your love of history all tie into your writing ... Awesome how you explained the reading and writing connections ... The hip hop introduction was a great ice breaker (can you believe some of us were a little nervous about you coming knowing we were going to be talking with a real playwright?) ... It was great when you opened it up to questions and really wanted to hear about us and our writing ... interesting and good to know some published writers write to keep sane, too. I thought I was the only one ... It's so cool that you teach pop culture. I think that is so important. Boy, there is so much to learn ... Your stories sound exciting ... I can't imagine writing screenplays ... I love the connection you portrayed between film, poetry, music, academic essays, and creative writing: fiction, non-fiction, or otherwise ... Interesting when you shared how your work evolved ... I was intrigued when you shared the adaptations and publishing/writing rules of thumb ... I agree with you so much when you said that in our world today, writing is the best way to keep sane ... Love that you teach Pop Culture; I'll have to put that on my college "must have" list ... Liked how you explained that with all the logos and advertising on clothes nowadays, we actually become a billboard helping to sell products — that was a huge eye-opener ... you taught us so much more than what we expected, well, not that we knew what to expect, but more than "simple" writing lessons."

Thursday

Bonnie Neubauer, author of *The Write-Brain Workbook: 366 Exercises to Liberate Your Writing_*

I, we, "... really appreciate what you said about the rules ..." several students noted and further commented, "Thank you so much for coming in. It's amazing to know all the professional areas of writing that you've worked in. They sound so interesting and I'm glad to know I may still be able to be a writer, even if I don't write a book ... Like you did, I could write catalogue descriptions! How cool! Thank you for showing us that even though we may 'not get rich writing,' you obviously enjoy doing it, anyway ... Your idea for getting rid of writer's block really worked well, and it's great to have other techniques, in addition to the ones Stephanie taught us, to get rid of it. Thank you ... I can't wait to do more exercises with your writing Spinner — GLAD I WAS THE ONE WHO WON IT! It was good to hear your advice on not comparing our work and appreciating it for what it is — I need to hear that ... Your advice really helped me, and I could really relate to what you said ... I really benefited from your handouts and I loved your talk. Thank you ... You were so engaging, I really felt like a part of your presentation. It was so cool that you did stuff with us and actually had us do the things you were talking about. Thank you ... Some of your exercises were so amazing; thank you for staying long enough not just to do some of them but also to share them so we could get your feedback as well ... Your Story Spinner is ingenious — I love using it ... I can't wait to check your Website and get the *Write Brain Workbook* ... Thank you for making your exercises, Spinner, and workbook available online — that's awesome. I love how you share your ideas and techniques. It was great to hear someone else say, "Just write and quit editing until later." Thank you ... You got my mind working in a whole other direction. Thank YOU, again!"

Friday at our Picnic Luncheon with the Authors

Áine Greaney, author of *The Sheep Breeders Dance, Im Honiglicht,* and *The Big House*

Many students wanted to thank Áine "for explaining how you discipline yourself and create time to write. It's hard to remember that writing is work, even if it isn't assigned. ... And, it was good to hear that real writers have to really work at it, too." Others reflected on Áine's presentation and specified, "I like how you explained the importance of journal writing; it's cool how almost all the guest authors see journal writing as important, even though most of you explain different reasons why. It was funny, but it made good sense that people keep notes, even if they're written on napkins and stuff. I do that a lot, but then, I don't keep them. Now I realize that those are the purest kinds of notes, the ones that come when I am observing or otherwise 'writing life.' 'Great analogy to writing and working out: if you work out once a week, you won't get very far, and if you only write on Saturdays, well, you won't get very far that way, either.' You talk like a writer; that was wicked inspiring. Even when you speak, your words are insightful and poetic. You had me at the Sunday evening opening when you said, 'Welcome all you weird people who like to write,' and everyone laughed. It was kind of amazing, and it will stick in my head for a long time — that's for sure — that there were so many people, hundreds, kids included, all gathered in the Tabernacle because they love to write. It was like a huge Super Bowl pep rally for writers. Had you not given that welcome, I wouldn't have realized that. You cracked me up when you reminded us to be creative, to have fun with our writing and to be wild with it if we want to, to be inventive. You're right: taking risks with writing is fun, and when I relax and do that, I create good stuff ... Wish I could remember that story you told us about writing outdoors. I can still see that bird you described, right off the top of your head. How do you choose words so well? You sure were right when you told us how lucky we are to have a program like this; I cannot believe we got to hear real authors like you tell us about their writing and coming over here from Ireland and all ... Thank YOU, so much."

G. F. Michelsen has published twelve novels. His latest, *Mettle*, was published in August 2007

Students had very focused thank-yous for Mr. Michelsen, "It was great how you shared your writing schedule and how you make time to write ... It's good to know that writers have other related jobs, too ... I like how you get your ideas. You have such unusual titles and topics ... Thank you for explaining your journaling techniques and how they help you with your work. I'm glad we had some male authors speak, too. Thank-you. I can tell you really enjoy writing."

Betty Anne Lauria, former columnist for the *Cape Cod Times*, an eighth grade English-language arts teacher, and a published poet

How Betty Anne began her newspaper career was foremost in what wowed students about this professional writer; one student noted, "It was cool how you said to write letters to the editors and that maybe, if we write enough and they like what we write, we may get to have a column. I never thought of that, and I have a lot of things I could write in about ... I like how you reminded us that when we're the writer, we get to create it whatever way we want to. Hope I can remember what you said about not comparing myself to other writers and appreciating what I do well, not being afraid to take risks and create, and that when I write I get to be anyone, anything. I love how your face lights up when you talk about your writing; hope mine will do that more often. It was so good to have someone come talk about writing something besides a book; that made becoming published not seem so overwhelming. It was exciting how you talked about free writing and not censoring yourself, but to just write, write, write, and then edit ... Like Bonnie and Stephanie, you had different strategies; trying them all will surely help me, a lot. I like how you get your ideas ... Wish you taught at my school; it must be great to have a real writer teach writing. Thank you for sharing all your great ideas and enthusiasm. I hope you're a YWW teacher soon, so I can take your workshop."

Elizabeth Moisan, author of *Master of the Sweet Trade* and illustrator of *The Beautiful Duckling*

"Thank you very much for speaking to our class ... I'm sorry you got lost, but it turned out you were really worth waiting for; we really enjoyed you sharing your manuscript ... It was mind boggling and good to know how your manuscript-filled edits motivate you, not discouraging you. I have to remember that when I get an edit-filled paper back from a teacher ... It was great how you read us excerpts and asked for our feedback; I have never really been involved in advising an author about her young adult novel. I love historical fiction, but I have never heard of one dealing with the Whydah or pirates ... I can't wait to read your whole book ... I think including the glossary is a great idea, but do it alphabetically, not by chapters — your son was right; thanks for asking for our opinion, too. It's cool that you valued what we had to say; that really impressed all of us ... I forgot to ask, are you going to illustrate this book, too? That'd be great. You may want a map for kids that don't know Cape Cod; everyone likes pirates. Thank you for sharing all your research and it's so important to writing believable historical fiction. I guess I should've realized that, but I didn't. When you read it, you don't always look at how the writer decided to include things. I am going to start reading more like a writer. Thank you. Some of your drawings, I think, would really add to your unique, very believable, and authentic voice. It was cool to hear an author — you, actually — read sections ... I want to find out if I'm predicting it right ... I got so into your book, I kept thinking about it days later ... Your manuscript is the first I have ever seen — all I can say is, WOW, I'll never see a book as just a book again. Thanks for thinking to bring it. I loved that you asked us for feedback and explained how you have to work to get into each of your character's head, so you can actually "be" them when you write and that getting into a guy's head way back then was really a challenge ... Good thing the guys stayed for the luncheon to give their input (j/k) ... Your descriptions of the settings and the surroundings in your book were great; you painted a very clear picture for me, and I think everyone else as well ... No doubt, your storyline is really well done, and it seems impossible to separate fact from fiction — that's so cool ... I wish you all the best and please get in touch with Stephanie so she can alert us when the book gets done at the publisher's and printed. Thank you tons."

Editor's Note to Teachers

Inklings from Cape Cod can simply be enjoyed as a celebration of student writing or it can be savored as a resource for teachers and other writing enthusiasts. The lessons provide an endless variety of creative writing endeavors, all aligned with state frameworks and other academic standards applicable to students at the elementary through college level.

Pursuing any of the given *Inklings* lessons, just as they are, provide several initial opportunities to use this anthology as a teaching tool. The lessons can be preceded by a discussion of the samples in this book. The pre-writing use of *Inklings* dialogue will teach and inspire tentative writers; or, the samples can be shared afterwards. In the latter case, students can critique the writing in *Inklings*, perhaps as a lesson on how to analyze a composition. Then, after developing this critiquing skill via the *Inklings* samples, students can then be instructed to revise their own writing and / or peer-edit and critique a classmate's work. Since the focus of this book is student writing, the connections students make and see are much more real, and relevant than when trying to teach critiquing using a piece of adult writing. Also, because the anthology students are not your students' classmates, your writers will feel more comfortable suggesting revisions and/or editing. Many additional creative spin-off lessons will develop once these lessons are explored; you'll find that often the lesson ideas come from the students. What an exciting start to lifelong writing. As you can see, the writing possibilities *Inklings* inspires are endless.

The lessons described at the front of each section give enough guidance to teach entire writing units. For example, using *Inspired by Others* as a model, a teacher can excerpt a setting from an appropriate piece of literature and read the passage aloud. Then, the students would create a character or characters and some action to take place in that given setting. This simple, activity synthesizing the elements of setting, characters, and plot can be completed with or without students previewing the corresponding section in *Inklings*. Discussions following the students' shared writing would be a powerful segué into a conversation about how setting affects plot and could further extend to a discussion of how prior knowledge and personal experiences influence an author's writing. This exercise can also be repeated with different settings, as a history or social studies assessment where students write to reflect on knowledge of a place or time period or research the setting and write to learn and experience the setting. In the spirit of differentiated instruction, the scope of this lesson can be widened further into students writing short stories. Students will be amazed at the variety of pieces that can be created from the reading of one scene or small section of another literary composition.

Inklings facilitates many lessons that satisfy state frameworks. Some of these include developing and creating the persuasive essay, summarizing or analyzing written work, organizing and composing a compare and contrast, crafting and describing an expository piece, as well as exploring and discussing narration. For example, as a persuasive essay, students could choose a favorite *Inklings* composition or section and convince their readers of its value and special qualities. Their responses could be oral or written, composed individually, in pairs, or in small groups. Likewise, the scope of this endeavor would lend itself equally well from journal entries through to finished publishable pieces.

Further, *Inklings* provides opportunities for comparison and contrast essays: students could pick two pieces and discuss the similarities, the differences, or the use of a specific writing strategy. The impact of the setting is vital to both, "Letters Home," and "The Hunting Adventures of Tosh Mihesuah," but each with a uniquely different effect. A summarizing description of one of the longer *Inklings* texts and comparison to another selection will also give students a chance to focus on the writing styles and authors' inclusion of specific supporting details. Analyzing student creations and making suggestions, or actually revising them, are all exciting options for making this anthology a resource-filled teaching tool as well as a "a joy to read, and an awesome voyage into the creative minds of young, imaginative writers..." - John Prophet, author of the Casey Miller Mystery Series.

Inklings can also be used for cross-curricular lessons and interdisciplinary connections. "Letters Home" could be the springboard for research or a skit creation related to the 1960's, the Woodstock era, or the specifics events of 1969. "Brian" is a realistic invite into a discussion or research exploration of family issues, divorce, intergenerational relationships and other health class, psych class, or sociology curricula. The "Rowing" section lends itself to exploration and interpretation of word meanings, both literally and figuratively, denotatively and connotatively. In all of these activities, students will climb various "rungs" of Bloom's ladder as they skim and read through *Inklings* classifying selections in effort to locate an *Inklings* entry to which they relate and, in this particular case, recognize as having the potential for cross-curricular interpreting, questioning, analyzing, composing, evaluating, acting out, researching, and pursuing in other higher order critical thinking endeavors.

Using the *Young Writers' Workshop Overview* or *The History of the Cape Cod Writers' Center and the Young Writers' Workshop* sections of *Inklings*, students have the opportunity to analyze a modeled summary of an organization's history. Then, after discussion and instruction, they can then go on to research and create their own overview of an organization's history. The writing of these compositions involves some summarizing which students can find challenging. Talking through the significant details included will make students' composing of their own work less daunting. Your students' drafting of a "History of ..." a local organization or one mentioned in a history text, health class, science activity, or even a (local) sport's organization related to a Physical Education unit will be facilitated through viewing, discussing, and modeling of these two *Inklings* anthology sections. Co-writing their organizations' histories will naturally lend itself to ongoing revising, productively collaborative composing, and some natural peer or reciprocal teaching. The more areas in which students write, the more relevant and fluid their writing will become and the more they will see writing as a valuable tool for them to learn and express themselves. Likewise, the more varied the approaches students learn to take with their writing, the more confident and creative they will become.

In addition, this anthology provides a garden of revision instruction opportunities. Each piece is a ready subject for focused revision. One topic of revision would to analyze the use of dialogue. Your students can then compare two or more different styles of dialogue or discuss which are the most realistic. That would lead to which piece might benefit from more or less dialect or from more or less formal language. Exploring different points of view can also provide a medium for revision. For example, Tosh's Hunting Adventures could be retold or re-written from the dad's or the deer's perspective. Again, this activity may be done in pairs or in small groups followed by sharing and discussion.

Re-writing is sometimes an overlooked possibility. Using the *Inspired by Others* prompt, the teacher can choose one of the anthology selections to inspire another writing. For example, (s)he might use the first sentence from the one of the *Inklings* prompts or an exceptional opening line from one of the *Inklings* student compositions to read to the class, and have the students write from that inspiring opener. Doing this activity before reading the *Inklings* offerings and then comparing the two – theirs and *Inklings* – is another unique higher level thinking opportunity *Inklings from Cape Cod* provides its (student) readers. More inspired by *Inklings* prompts include:

- list several of the *Inklings* titles, choose one, and use it to prompt a writing
- choose an *Inklings* title or character and a technical goal (sentence variety detailed descriptions, realistic setting, vivid dialogue, etc.) and then writing for ten or fifteen minutes with the technical goal as the focus. The writing can be done as a review of techniques previously taught: anthology titles and / or characters can be placed in one hat with technical goals in another; students literally pick their prompt. After students write, give them a chance to read he anthology offering of their title. This is another good opportunity for discussion, either in small groups or as a class.
- instead of "Rowing," try other single words like swimming, balance or balance, reflections (or reflecting), run (or running), the phrase "all set" ... toss out a single word and see where it takes the writer in you(r students).

There are still more ideas at the author's website:
http://www.authorsden.com/stephanieeboosahda

Remember, teaching Best Practices notes that teachers should write and share along *with* their students. This opens the window for student writers to see and experience how writing is a process, even for the most experienced teachers. It also allows teachers the opportunity to experience exactly what they're asking of their students. When teachers write with their students, it also forces students to become more independent writers. Since the teacher is also engaged in writing, the students are therefore required to trust themselves and work independently. Writing when your students are writing – whether it's a lab report, a history skit, a biography of a germ, a creative writing piece, what ever the assignment – allows teachers an opportunity for modeling the assignment, sharing the challenge, and trusting others to critique and revise the writing. When students critique the instructor's writing it also empowers both the students and the teacher. Students find they have constructive feedback for their teacher, and teachers get unexpected encouragement and constructive commentary. Also, students discover that they can do the requested writing more autonomously than they realized, a great segue into creating independent, confident, lifelong writers.

Reading and talking about writing is much of what writing teachers do. Isaac B. Singer said, "The wastebasket is the writer's best friend" before the age of computers, but his sentiment is still valid; good writers are only good because they know and exercise their revision routine." Find, or have students find, other observations of the writing process either within this anthology's pieces or in the quotes that follow and discuss them with reference to your students' writing. Or, have students discuss how the quotes speak to them and connection to their writing. After discussion, students can process what they heard, sorted out, and realized about writing through sharing in a journal entry. This writing process, quote-related activity is very versatile. In addition to, or as an alternative to writing a paragraph explaining the quote, or an essay discussing author's intended meaning, a well-crafted paragraph elucidating who is author is, or an essay discussing how the author's statement on writing is autobiographical and what it reveals about his or her life, culture, etc. are also a possible related activity. This latter assignment can conveniently bring writing into the content areas. After using the _Inklings_ quotes as class models, students can search for a quote related to a topic in another class and create a similarly a well-written explanatory paragraph.

The connection between visual expression and the written word is also vital here in _Inklings_. The included photographs and illustrations are groundwork for an endless assortment of characters, settings, plots, literary devices, dialogue, and more. For example, using the _Inklings_ drawings, have students brainstorm similes and metaphors describing person rendered, or create a dialogue between a class mates and the character pictured. If the writing doesn't give your students an inspiring notion, or an encouraging idea, the pictures and illustrations will definitely guide students - especially those needing a little extra motivation - to delve into their sensory tool boxes and create. Andrew notes in his student bio, with this Workshop -and therefore with *Inklings*- there are endless incidences that" disrupt ... long writer's block."

The student bios included in this anthology invite interaction between the authors of *Inklings* and your students. They model yet another genre and are another great resource for guiding students to write short bios. In doing so, it would be noteworthy to discuss, either with the class or as a small group exercise, the different choices each student made when sharing who (s)he is. Such a discussion could be followed by students writing their own bios, a bio about a literary character, a bio about an historic figure, a bio about a personified object – say a rhombus or a scientific notation, or – in a science class - a biography of a genus of protozoa, perhaps an Amoeba (also spelled ameba); even here, the possibilities are endless.

Simple sharing and revising guidelines can be adopted from the highly effective National Writing Project's *Bless, Address* , or *Press* technique. Notice, these are sharing and revising guidelines; for this type of revising the author reads the piece aloud to one or more editors who jot down notes related to the level of feedback requested. Before a critiquing session, either the teacher or the student author states what level of feedback (*Bless, Address* , or *Press*) is desired; the reviewers or listeners respond in kind. *Bless,* is just that; listeners or readers pick out the parts they like and tell why they are so effectively striking: "I like how you created such a clear picture of what Brandon was going through sitting at that restaurant with Brandon's grandmother. Saying the conversation exploded really got to me; you created such a clear picture, my stomach was getting upset just picturing him at the table with his grandmother," or "Your opening line really grabbed me; I hate it when I wake up and I can just sense something is 'not quite right'."

Of course, the critiquers can't write all that down, they just write enough notes to reference for the author the specific part or parts (s)he is going to praise. *Blessing It* is helpful to writers in all stages of composition. The *Bless* technique, the first of the three techniques, needs modeling. An instructive show and tell or "Watch, here's how you do it ..." are good starting points. The pieces in

Inklings provide excellent samples for picking out specific examples of great writing and giving a reason why a word phrase, sentence, or section really works. The *Bless* technique only praises, but peer editors do so in specific terms, "On page 233, I like the mysterious airy-ness Rebecca creates when she opens with 'A sign hovers in page the darkness ...' " or "Lydia's beginning of *The Storm* on page 155, 'Are you afraid?' really grabbed my interest. She gets right to the point without a lot of words, and then gives the setting, so the reader can get into the story right from the start."

When *Addressing It*, the peer editors focus on a specific aspect of the writing, one that either the instructor or the author specifies; for example, "Do the last three lines of my poem add to the picture I am trying to create; or, should I just omit them and end three lines earlier?" or "Are my verbs strong enough? Can you feel the character's anxiety?" The "*It*" the editor is addressing can be even more exacting, "Do you think 'reverberate' is the right word to use in this paragraph?" or "Help me figure out a better name for main character, one that really fits him." As you can see, *Addressing It* means to focus on a specifically noted element of the writing.

The most analytically comprehensive of these critiquing techniques is *Pressing It*. Copies of the work being shared and discussed definitely need to be given to each reviewer. An overhead projection or a SmartBoard presentation of the composition is especially helpful when modeling the technique or when doing a class-share and edit. This is also a great way to review a teacher's draft and to have students proofread and suggest revisions. In this type of sharing and feedback, the reviewers constructively comment on anything they notice that needs revising, any part of the writing can be mentioned, and suggestions are welcomed and discussed.

As seen with the first two levels of sharing and revising, modeling is essential to successfully *Pressing It*. Students definitely need a lot of modeling, before doing any *Pressing*. Practicing *Pressing It* with selections from *Inklings* will guide students in making constructive suggestions; learning how to phrase a comment in a constructive manner is crucial. For example, rather than saying, "Your dialogue is too formal for the action of the story," feedback could go like this, "Wow! You really know how to write and punctuate (if a written copy is also available) dialogue, but what kind of people are your characters? I don't picture a teenager saying, 'I cannot assist you right now.' Perhaps his lines could be a little more informal." The *Pressing It* level is a highly skilled mode of giving feedback, and should only be used after careful instruction and practice in supervised groups. Only one of these techniques should be used at a time. Focus on one level - *Bless*, *Address* , or *Press* - at a time. Do it in such a manner that the author eventually feels equipped to improve his or her own paper.

Other resources for expanding these lessons and more information on revising, sharing writing, and peer editing can be found at:

- http://www.discover-writing.com/,

- http://www.maryledbetter.com/books.htm,

- http://www.slideshare.net/aszardini/tutorial-peer-editing-113187 - a peer editing tutorial site with a series of student centered PowerPoints suitable for class viewing

- http://www.nwp.org/cs/public/print/nwp_docs/ea/guidelines.csp - the National Writing Project site with a variety of resources related to teachers teaching writing

- http://www.authorsden.com/stephanieeboosahda - this editor's website with an ever-growing series of writing exercises, articles, resources including - Writing Across the Curriculum – and related links

Quantity book order discounts can be purchased directly from www. iUniverse.com

Other Inklings on Writing

"Words are timeless. You should utter them or write them with a knowledge of their timelessness."
- Kahlil Gibran, Lebanese born American
philosophical essayist, novelist & poet

"The role is the writer is not to say what we all can say, but what we are unable to say."
– Anais Nin, author, <u>Little Birds</u>

"The wastebasket is the writer's best friend."
– Isaac B. Singer, storyteller

"Writing is easy. All you do is sit staring at a blank sheet o f paper Until the drops of blood form on your forehead."
– Gene Fowler, screenwriter, <u>Billy the Kid</u>

"The difference between the right word and the almost writer word is the difference between lightning and the lightning bug."
- Mark Twain, author, <u>The Adventures of Huck Finn</u>

"The pages are still blank, but there is a miraculous feeling of the words being there, written in an invisible ink, and clamoring to become visible."
- Vladimir Nabakov, <u>Lolita</u>

"I don't know much about creative writing programs. But they're not telling the truth if they don't teach, one, that writing is hard work, and, two, that you have to give up a great deal of life, your personal life, to be a writer."
- Doris Lessing, Persian born British Novelist
and short-story writer

"The beautiful part of writing is that you don't have to get it right

the first time, unlike say, a brain surgeon.
> *- Robert Cormier, author, I am the Cheese*

"Writing is a struggle against silence."
> *- Carlos Fuentes, novelist and political activist*

"The worst enemy to creativity is self doubt."
> *- Sylvia Plath, poet and novelist, author of The Bell Jar*

"Every writer I know has trouble writing."
> *- Joseph Heller, author, Catch 22*

"You can't wait for inspiration; you have to go after it ..."
> *- Jack London, author, Call f the Wild*

"Yes, there is Nirvana; it is in ... putting your child to sleep, and in writing the last line of your poem."
> *- Kahlil Gibran, author of The Prophet*

Young Writers' Workshop Overview

The **Y**oung **W**riters' **W**orkshop is held during the week of the Cape Cod Writers' Center's annual summer conference. The YWW is for twelve- to sixteen-year-old students. These workshops are held in three sessions — in the morning, midday, and in the afternoon, Monday through Friday. There are two prose writing sessions and one poetry session; students are enrolled in only one session during the summer. Traditionally, applications are available starting in January with an April deadline. Students are selected on the merit of their application letter and their juried application manuscript.

On Thursdays, a Young Writers' Recognition Ceremony is held in the Lodge at the Craigville Conference Center and parents and friends are invited to celebrate the literary and creative accomplishments of these talented writers. The 2007 guest speaker was Cheryl Park, from the morning show on radio station WQRC; she was one of the original YWW students.

It is a great honor to be one of the forty-five students selected for the Young Writers' Workshop. There is no tuition fee. The program is made possible through grants and donations. Please see the thank you section for a complete listing of the Young Writers' Workshop and Cape Cod Writers' Center sponsors. More information is available at the Website www.capecodwriterscenter.org.

The 2007 Prose Workshop classes were led by instructor Stephanie Boosahda. This prose writing program, aimed at expanding students' creative writing and editing strategies, was designed for young writers who love to write and those who believe they can't but really wanted to. Students dabbled in fiction and non-fiction. Experienced, agile writers were guided and inspired to stretch their vocabulary, more articulately depict their characters, sharpen their settings, and broaden their perspectives.

Frustrated and enthusiastic writers alike were given the opportunity to experience a variety of techniques, practice them, work at perfecting new strategies, and experience fun exercises and editing activities with their writing. The goal for all participants was to develop further confidence in their writing and to create a greater ease with which to approach it. Developing beneficial sharing skills and increased students' satisfaction with their writing were also primary objectives of this workshop group.

Various genres were explored: bare-bones, objective reporting, creative exposition, structured and free verse poetry, and narrative storytelling, just to name a few. Along the way, senses were tweaked, focus and perspectives were fine-tuned, increased reading-writing connections were made, more than a few laughs were shared, and daily guest writers and speakers were welcomed. The prose student writers are featured in this book; they created diverse portfolios including publishable pieces and many, many works in progress. This weeklong workshop facilitated young writers in improving the level of their composition and critiquing skills, whetted their writing palettes, and sharpened their skills in a venue of enthusiastic creativity and intellectual camaraderie. This creatively structured, student-centered overview course guided students in pushing their writing potential and provided new approaches for students to carry out their inklings of creativity. There was a morning and afternoon session of the prose workshop.

The works contained in this anthology were either created or revised at the workshop.

The Poetry Workshop was held between the two prose workshops. In 2007, it was taught by Joan Tavares-Avant. This tutorial was designed for young poets, also showcased in this collection, including those who had not yet started but were inspired to write. Through enrichment and guided discussions, students explored what they had written. or what they felt they wanted to put into their poetry. Students learned to glean meaning from their writing and understand their thoughts by reflecting and sharing ideas in a classroom setting.

The poetry workshop provided an opportunity for students to focus on elements of poetic imagery and the power of words. "Respecting Mother Earth," a Native American value, was an important theme during the class sessions. The primary focus of the week was to learn, share, and be happy.

Selections from the Young Writers' Poetry Workshop can be found in the "Golden Nuggets" section of this anthology.

The History of the Cape Cod Writers' Center and the Young Writers' Workshop

by Jacqueline M. Loring,
CCWC executive director, 2001–2007

The Cape Cod Writers' Center was founded more than forty-five years ago by Cape writers who called their group the Twelve O'clock Scholars. Among the original committee members were authors Kurt Vonnegut, Marion Vuilleumier, Marion Logan, and editor Abe Burack.

The Cape Cod Writers' Conference was incorporated in 1973 as the Cape Cod Writers' Center, Inc., and the foresight of the original founders to build a sustainable foundation continues to be demonstrated in ongoing programs and services and author events, which include Books and the World, one of the longest running author-interview cable access television program in the country; Breakfast with the Authors, a monthly series that features three authors who discuss their books with a large audience of readers; and Pathways to Publication, an all-day instructional workshop.

In August of 1963, approximately thirty-five conferees gathered for the first annual summer writers' conference in the Tabernacle at the Craigville Conference Center in Centerville on Cape Cod. Here they received instruction, inspiration, education, and the opportunity to network with writers, publishers, agents, and editors.

The energy and enthusiasm from that small gathering became a yearly event, held during the third week of August, which has since gained national recognition. In August 2007, the Cape Cod Writers' Center (CCWC) sponsored its forty-fifth annual conference, A Place in the Sun for Writers. In recent years, faculty and participants have come from all across the United States and as far away as Canada, Germany, England, Ireland, and Vietnam.

The 2007 conference hosted a faculty of more than twenty, with 180 participants attending courses that included fiction, non-fiction, and poetry as well as courses in screenwriting, publishing, writing book proposals, writing for the young reader, and writing for comic books. An agent and an editor are in residence each year, and select faculty members conduct individual manuscript evaluations and personal conferences.

For almost thirty years, the CCWC has presented a Young Writers' Workshop concurrent with the weeklong conference. In its early years, up to fifteen prose writers and poets between the ages of twelve and sixteen attended a morning session for two hours, taught by published authors. In early 2000, the number of applications had grown, and an afternoon session was added. In 2005, the board of the CCWC added a third session, devoted especially to young poets. These courses for the young writers run Monday through Friday and, due to the generosity of grantors and benefactors, are tuition-free. In 2007, forty-five prose writers and poets attended the Young Writers' Workshop, which was taught by Stephanie Boosahda (prose) and Joan Tavares-Avant (poetry).

Past attendees of the Young Writers' Workshop keep in touch and tell us how valuable their week at Craigville was. Many have gone on in their professional lives to become writers, journalists, and playwrights, and some come back in the summer to share their accomplishments with the newest sessions of students.

Many thank-yous to CCWC member, writer, and teacher Stephanie Boosahda for the many hours she devoted to the students and to editing this anthology and getting it ready for publication.

Our Sponsors

The Cape Cod Writers' Center would like to acknowledge the following individuals and organizations for the support of their programs, events, and services.

Anne Harmon Memorial
Barbara J. Hosmer, Inside Cape Cod Magazine
Ben & Sara Muse and Parnassus Book Service
Bob Sproul
C. H. Newton Builders, Inc
Cape Cod Potato Chip Company, Inc.
Craigville Conference Center
Creative Baking Company
Greg Greenway
Isabel Golden Memorial Fund
Janice Glover Memorial Fund
Kathleen Lundberg Memorial Scholarship Fund
Lynn Titus Memorial Fund
Mary Littleford
National League of American Pen Women, Cape Cod Branch
Ocean Spray Cranberries, Inc.
Pierre Vuilleumier Memorial Program Fund
Professional Writers & Editors
Rose Gotsis Memorial Scholarship Fund
Shaw's, Hyannis
Stop and Shop, Hyannis
Trader Joe's, Hyannis

A very special note of appreciation to the Marion Jordan Charitable Foundation and the Cape Cod Five Charitable Foundation, whose support of the CCWC made the Young Writers' Workshop possible.

The Cape Cod Writers' Center is supported, in part, by the Arts Foundation of Cape Cod, the Massachusetts Cultural Council, a state agency, and the Mid-Cape Regional Cultural Council.

Index

LaVergne, TN USA
04 May 2010
181471LV00007B/19/P